"YOU'RE A WORTHY OPPONENT, MADDIE."

His lips were close to hers now, and Maddie had the unnerving sensation that she was poised on the brink of a precipice, eager to leap into the unknown, even if it meant her own destruction.

"I thought men liked women to be sweet and helpless."

"Generally, they do. However, since meeting you, I've begun to re-evaluate my youthful preferences."

His hands tightened around her waist and his mouth descended and met hers. She found herself leaning into him to support herself. Her legs threatened to buckle and she feared she might collapse at his feet. But he held her up and then lifted her so their bodies fit together perfectly.

"Chase!" she gasped.

He stopped kissing her. She wanted him to stop. At the same time, she wanted him to go on kissing her forever. Most of all, she wanted to see where all this delicious anticipation led . . .

* * *

PRAISE FOR KATHARINE KINCAID'S *WILDWOOD:*

"In her usual rich, unique style, Ms. Kincaid has written a powerful, sensual romance about forbidden love and its triumph."

—*Romantic Times*

ROMANCE FROM HANNAH HOWELL

Race The Dawn

Katharine Kincaid

Zebra Books
Kensington Publishing Corp.
http://www.zebrabooks.com

ZEBRA BOOKS are published by

Kensington Publishing Corp.
850 Third Avenue
New York, NY 10022

First Printing: December, 1997
10 9 8 7 6 5 4 3 2 1

Printed in the United States of America

In Memory of
John K. Wakelin Sr.

July 20, 1919 January 21, 1996

This one's for you, Daddy
With All My Love

One

Hopewell, Kansas—1877

"Maddie, there he is! It's him. Chase Cumberland. The man who's been tellin' everybody how his mare is gonna beat our stallion."

Head held high, face expressionless, Maddie McCrory ignored the sudden racing of her heart and marched straight down the boardwalk on the east side of Main Street. She never so much as glanced in the direction where her sister was gawking.

"Ignore him, Carrie. Pretend you don't see him and haven't heard what he's been saying. Above all, don't act nervous or afraid. Pa always says it's a big mistake to let your opponent sense any weakness."

"But Maddie! He's comin' this way. He's sure seen us. Don't you even wanna know what he looks like?"

Maddie clamped a hand on her thirteen-year-old sister's shoulder and maneuvered her around several barrels of flour lined up in front of Grover's Mercantile and Fashion Emporium. "For all I care, he could be stark naked and riding a buffalo down the middle of Main Street. Keep walking. Zoe and Little Mike are waiting for us. We don't have time to talk to Mr. Chase Flap-Jaw Cumberland. *After* the race will be time enough to take the man's measure—and then I'll only be interested in claiming the prize money he'll owe us. The man himself can go back to wherever he came from—with his tail tucked between his legs and a lesson learned about bragging."

"Maddie, he'll hear you. . . . Oh, my! Maddie, he's gaining on us . . ."

"Miss McCrory!" boomed a deep male voice. "Wait a moment. I'd like to speak with you."

Maddie spun around so fast she almost fell off the boardwalk. "Mr. Cumberland?" she inquired in her frostiest tone. "Whatever do you want, sir? The race is only an hour away, and we have preparations. We must get ready."

Maddie told herself he was nothing special—a mere man, after all, but her first view of the gentleman she'd been hearing about for days severely rattled her composure. For starters, he was tall and broad-shouldered. She had to tilt her head back to look up into his sun-bronzed features. Next, he was all lean muscle, gleaming white teeth, and hard, predatory eyes.

Something about him reminded her of a prairie wolf. Beneath his black Stetson, and a spill of dark hair, his eyes were the color of a coyote's—glowing amber, and they were just as ruthless. She could easily imagine him ripping people apart and gulping down their livers for breakfast, then smacking his lips with relish and wondering what he'd have for supper.

The wolfish gaze swept over her—starting with her fly-away red hair that had partially escaped her single long braid hours ago. It traveled down the none-too-clean, one-piece, brown calico day dress she always wore when she came to town, then flicked over her decidedly *un*-feminine mud and manure encrusted leather boots.

Maddie suddenly realized she didn't look much like the lady her mother had raised her to be, but then few women in Hopewell—a dust-laden, would-be Kansas cow town—could have met those strict Boston standards. Maddie herself had all but given up trying years ago.

"Why, Miss McCrory, since we haven't met, I want to make your acquaintance and ask whether or not you've changed your mind about match racing your stallion against my mare this afternoon," he drawled in a deep voice that had the unaccountable effect of setting her nerve endings aquiver.

Determined to maintain her dignity despite her absurdly thundering heart, Maddie lifted her chin another notch higher. "No, Mr. Cumberland, I haven't changed my mind about racing you this afternoon. Not only do I have the better horse, but according to the rules, if either of us withdraws, the race is forfeit to the other, and that person gets to collect *half* the stakes money. Half of two thousand dollars is a lot of money to lose, and I, sir, have no intention of losing it."

He grinned, and the change in his face was downright startling. His eyes lit up as if candles flared inside his skull. Wry humor flashed like lightning across his flint-edged features, leaving her to grapple with the disturbing notion that the man was handsome. *Dangerously* handsome. The type to make some goosey female lose her head—and her heart—over him. Fortunately, she was nobody's goose and long past the age of silly schoolgirl infatuations. Today was her twenty-second birthday, not that anyone had bothered to remember.

"You may count on it, sir. I don't intend to lose this race," she repeated, locking gazes with him.

"This may come as a surprise to you, Miss McCrory, but neither do I. I'm ready, and so is my mare. However, I couldn't help hoping I could persuade you to withdraw and spare yourself the shame of defeat in your own home territory. You can claim your horse is lame or colicky, and no one will be the wiser. The McCrory reputation will remain intact."

"Today's race will only *enhance* our reputation, Mr. Cumberland, so you might as well cease these transparent efforts to destroy my confidence. Obviously, you're hoping to make me nervous, so that my anxiety will transfer to our stallion and his rider, who just happens to be my brother, and they'll do badly. However, I'm privy to such petty endeavors, and in any case, we McCrorys don't scare easily. If anyone should be worried, it's *you,* sir, not us. Gold Deck has won his last ten races. He's only lost twice in his entire life, when the paths were muddy. Today," she nodded toward the azure sky and fiercely shining sun, ". . . Hopewell Paths will be hard and dry—precisely the way he likes them."

The arrogant grin flashed again. "I've still got an hour to pray for rain. . . . Of course, if you're that confident, why not raise the stakes to three thousand?"

Three thousand.

Gulping hard, Maddie managed to conceal her reaction. She didn't have three thousand dollars. Actually, she didn't have two thousand, the sum they had agreed upon. She didn't even have *half* that amount. But she wasn't worried. This was the first time she had met her newly come-to-town opponent, but she *had* seen his mare shortly after his arrival ten days ago. He had stabled her at the local livery, and she had sneaked in to have a peek at the competition before she ever agreed to the deal.

The mare had been filthy and exhausted after her long journey from God-knows-where. She didn't look thrifty. Wormy and underfed she was, "easy pickin's," as Pa would say. It had been too dark in the livery stable to really study how she was built, but the best conformation in the world couldn't compensate for a lack of corn and being ridden to death on the trail. Maddie had accepted the challenge in a minute, and Jake Bussel, the town blacksmith, had set it up for this afternoon.

Jake handled all the responses to the handbills she had posted all over town; they must have been what had caught Chase Cumberland's eye. Gold Deck had already beaten every contender in the nearest five counties, and now, no one but strangers ever answered her advertisements. *Match Race A Kansas Champion. Distances to 600 hundred yards. Catch weights acceptable. Name your stakes and owner will oblige. Cash preferred.*

But *three thousand!* Most of Gold Deck's races involved only a thousand or so—and last fall, he had raced for a wagonload of corn. She had put up all the chickens in the hen house because she couldn't afford to feed them anyway, and the corn had kept them all alive last winter. . . . Even if she were willing to go that high, Chase Cumberland didn't look prosperous enough to have such a fortune in his skin-tight britches.

"It's too late to change the stakes now, Mr. Cumberland. We agreed to two thousand, and I insist we stick to the original bargain. If you're greedy, you can always place a few side bets.

Wagers can be had all over town. That's what folks do around here for entertainment—bet on match races."

Chase Cumberland rocked back on his booted heels. He crossed his arms over his indecently wide chest—clad in faded blue flannel. The garment was missing the proper number of fasteners, and she could practically see down to his navel. Black curly hair blanketed his chest, and it embarrassed her to be caught looking at it—at *him*—though she could scarcely pretend she hadn't noticed. Dragging her eyes to his face, she saw that his strangely devastating grin still played about his mouth, and a rather sensuous mouth it was, too, putting her in mind of kissing, an activity to which she was sadly unaccustomed. . . . Drat it all! The rogue seemed to be thoroughly enjoying himself.

"I've already made a few wagers," he informed her with a rakish tilt of his head. "Most folks are betting on *you,* Miss McCrory. Rather, I should say, on your horse. Wasn't any trouble at all to arrange for a nice stake. If I decide to remain in the area after I win this race, I'll have all the tools I need, plus a wagon and a new set of harness."

Arrogant moose! Who did he think he was? He deserved to lose just for being so conceited. She certainly wasn't mistaken in thinking him a puffed-up flap-jaw, or "flannel mouth," as Pa would call him.

"I thought I'd made myself clear a moment ago, Mr. Cumberland. You aren't going to win this contest. Do you honestly believe your mare can whip my stallion? I've seen her. She's been ridden hard and lacks condition. Six weeks rest is the minimum I'd advise to restore her vigor—yet you agreed to race her almost immediately upon your arrival."

Maddie herself wasn't above undermining an opponent's confidence. Not as good as Pa yet, she was learning fast. As Mr. Cumberland had yet to find out, match racing involved far more than just having the fastest horse; sometimes a horse won before it ever set foot on a racing path—and sometimes, it lost simply because its owner doubted its abilities, the weather turned bad, or the rider had indigestion. Positive thoughts practically guaranteed success, Pa always claimed.

"Now, Miss McCrory," came that infuriating drawl. "How can a horse be ridden hard and still lack condition? It's *because* she's been ridden hard that she's in perfect shape to beat your stallion. You haven't raced your horse even once this season, and you had a late, rainy spring. It was so wet you probably haven't been able to work him much and get him fit after a long, hard winter. My mare, on the other hand, never had time to go soft. She worked all winter long."

The first tentacles of fear wrapped themselves around Maddie's heart. What he said was true. Gold Deck hadn't raced since the corn episode, and the bad weather had delayed any serious training until almost mid-May. This was early June. The only real exercise the stallion had gotten was mounting a few mares, and Maddie always worried that breeding sapped his strength rather than increased it. Whenever possible in years past, Pa had always scheduled Gold Deck's races after the breeding season had ended—in July, or better yet, August.

But of course, she couldn't afford the luxury of doing that anymore. With the farm's mortgage payments already three months behind, and the taxes coming due in July, she had to accept any challenges that came along—which was why she had accepted this one.

"Exactly where are you from, Mr. Cumberland?" she blurted, changing the subject.

"A long way south of Kansas—where we don't get your bad winters."

Texas, she thought. He's got a Texas drawl and a Texas look about him—and he's *still* trying to undermine my confidence.

"This wasn't such a bad winter or spring," she lied. "Our stallion received all the exercise he needed. Fortunately, he didn't wear himself out—not like your poor mare. She shouldn't be challenging a stallion anyway. Some folks don't think it's a fair contest to race a stud against a filly."

"Really? How about you, Miss McCrory? What do *you* think? Somehow, I didn't take you for the sort who concedes that males are superior to females." One dark brow lifted sardonically, daring her to deny it.

"They certainly are *not*—except when it comes to horse racing," she retorted. "In most everything else, women are capable of holding their own quite nicely, thank you."

He burst out laughing, and chagrin simmered in Maddie's soul. She hated to be laughed at—especially by tall, handsome, conceited Texans. In that moment, she began to hate Chase Cumberland. She wanted Gold Deck to win for no other reason than to wipe the smirk off this man's arrogant face.

"If you'll excuse me, Mr. Cumberland, I really must be on my way." Dragging Carrie by the hand, Maddie moved to step around him, but he planted himself on the boardwalk in front of her, blocking a graceful departure.

"Listen, Miss High and Mighty. I'm planning to win this race. But if you want to back out now, I won't enforce the rule that you'll have to forfeit half the stakes money. I hear your family's had a run of bad luck lately. If your father had made this deal, I'd hold him to it, but considering your inexperience, I'm prepared to . . ."

"Go to hell! I mean perdition—sir. You just hope I'll quit because you're afraid *you* might lose. You've reconsidered your hasty challenge. Well, I'm not letting you out of the deal. Our horses are racing at two o'clock, and if your mare doesn't show up, you owe me one thousand dollars. Is that clear, Mr. Cumberland?"

"Perfectly, Miss McCrory." A narrow-eyed glare replaced his smile. Stepping aside, he tipped his hat to her. "I'll see you at two. And may the best horse win."

"I'm sure *he* will." With a curt nod, she proceeded brusquely down the boardwalk. Her departure would have delighted her genteel, dignified mother whose perfect manners had been capable of reducing the most blustery of men to tongue-tied embarrassment. But just then Carrie tripped over her own skirt, caught herself on a porch railing, and turned to Maddie with shining eyes.

"Ohhh, Maddie! He's so handsome!" she babbled in a voice that carried for three miles in every direction. "Wait 'til I tell Zoe. She'll be green with envy that I saw him first. . . . Do you think he's married? Do you think he noticed me? How old do you reckon he thinks I am?"

"Two. You're behaving like a two-year-old," Maddie snapped and kept going, propelling her man-crazy sister down the boardwalk in front of her.

Behind them, more laughter erupted. Maddie didn't have to turn around to identify the source. Mercifully, the mocking sound shut Carrie's mouth and—Maddie hoped—taught her to be more careful about articulating her every foolish thought. Both Carrie and Zoe were far too forward these days. The twins fantasized that every male they met was smitten by their great beauty and must be assessed as potential husbands. Ever since the wedding of the sixteen-year-old daughter of an acquaintance, the twins had been plotting their futures. They didn't want to wind up like Maddie, a dried-up "also-ran" no red-blooded man could possibly want.

In Hopewell, Kansas, if a girl didn't marry before the ripe old age of twenty, she was deemed a hopeless case, a lost cause, an object of ridicule, a filly who got left at the starting post. In short, she was a dismal failure known far and wide as an "also-ran." But Maddie couldn't help it that during her prime courting years—from thirteen to nineteen—she had been too burdened with family responsibilities, too tired and overworked, to pay much attention to the young bucks who had shown interest in her.

Now, the young bucks were all taken, either married or gone off to seek their fortunes elsewhere. Some had already fathered children. She had apparently lost her chance at matrimony and motherhood, but she would *not,* by God, lose the family farm. The McCrorys must win this race and go on to win *more* races, so that everyone in Kansas would want to breed their mares to Gold Deck, and the family would prosper as they had always done before that terrible day when Maddie's ailing mother had finally died and Pa had given up on living.

"Hurry up, Carrie," she exhorted. "Oh, I knew I shouldn't have taken the time to slip into town for more of Mrs. Watson's elixir. But I figured if I didn't, Little Mike would get another stomachache just before he rides and then we'd be in real trouble. . . . Have you got that bottle? You didn't set it down anywhere, did you?"

"No, I've got it, Maddie. . . . Should I have worn my hair up, today, do you think? I look older when I do. I just wish our family didn't all have red hair; it's so crass and common. Mine and Zoe's does have some gold in it, but I wish it were pure blond; men always notice blond women. And I'd like my eyes to be greener. Lucky for me they aren't blue like yours. Blue eyes and red hair are *sooo* predictable. That's your problem, Maddie. Your coloring and your freckles. You're so *vivid,* and men don't like vivid, outspoken women. You can't do anything about your eyes, but you could wear powder to cover your freckles, and rinse your hair with buttermilk to tone down the color. As for being outspoken, even Pa says you should . . ."

Maddie closed her ears to the litany. She was outspoken because she *had* to be, or she'd never get a word in edgewise. Not with the twins chattering incessantly about clothes, hair, beauty recipes, and the latest issue of *Godey's Lady's Book,* which they pored over until it fell apart. Maddie herself preferred rousing conversations about the bloodlines of legendary Quarter Running horses. At Carrie's age, she had sometimes stayed up all night arguing with Pa over which lines were best. Now, she could talk horses with no one but Little Mike, and her fourteen-year-old brother didn't usually have much to say.

But then he had always been the quiet one of the family. After Ma's death, he had become downright broody and given to stomach ailments. Maddie hoped he wasn't sick from nervousness. He always got scared before a race. She was just glad Mr. Cumberland hadn't had a chance to match wits with him beforehand. The main reason they shunned town before a race was to avoid the kind of disturbing confrontation she had just had with their opponent.

"Never run a race with your mouth," Pa had always counseled. "Spend time with your horse. Think about winnin'. Success is an attitude as much as anything, an' if you ain't got it, your mount sure as hell won't."

Small and wiry, shrewd and unflappable, the elder Mike McCrory knew everything there was to know about winning races, but he hadn't had time to pass it all down to Little Mike before the boy had to take over for him. Maddie was doing the best she could to train her brother. She had ridden horses all her life, inhaled every bit of advice her father had ever offered, but hadn't actually *ridden* any races, since match racing was a man's sport—and her mother had been adamant about barring her from the saddle when money was involved.

Still, she knew enough to keep bad influences away from Little Mike before a race. Pa and Zoe were at the wagon on the outskirts of town with Little Mike and Gold Deck. Not that Pa would be aware of the race today, but Zoe had her instructions. She was to keep *everyone* away from Gold Deck and Little Mike until Maddie got there, and then they would all go together to the Hopewell Paths, the quarter-mile track laid out near the town, not far from the Saline River.

Nearly every small town had its own quarter-mile track, a set of double paths running side by side between two sets of markers. Gold Deck had raced on paths all over Kansas, Oklahoma, Nebraska, Arkansas, and parts of Texas and Colorado. During the peak years of his career, while Ma was still healthy, the stallion had been the king of "short horse racing"—as it was often called.

Now he was getting old, and Maddie didn't know what she would do when his racing days ended. Hopefully, by then the twins would be married and Little Mike able to take over the farm. As for Pa . . . well, she didn't know what would become of Pa. She had spent the last five years of her life caring for her mother and her siblings, and she imagined she'd be spending the next five caring for Pa. By then, *no* man would be interested in her. She'd be facing a lonely old age . . . but fretting over problems never seemed to help much—and her brother needed her to be bursting with confidence if he was to muster enough enthusiasm and determination to win this race.

By the time Maddie arrived at the wagon with Carrie, she had worked herself up to a full-blown state of competitive zeal. "Little Mike! Zoe!" she hollered. "Where are you? Is Gold Deck saddled yet? Did you fetch water for him or feed him his corn while I was gone?"

Shovel and Hoe, the team horses, were tied on one side of the wagon, and Gold Deck on the other. Shovel and Hoe—big, homely, draft-type animals who never raced—still wore their harnesses, and Gold Deck wasn't yet saddled. He whinnied when he saw her, letting her know he was hungry and thirsty after his long journey into town.

Maddie erupted into a fury. "Zoe! Little Mike! Can't I trust you two to do as I say even on race day? Get out here, you lazy layabouts." She didn't see them around the wagon and surmised they must be inside it.

Pa had designed the special, tall, wooden-sided wagon to carry everything he needed when he traveled from race to race. A cabin on wheels, it contained cupboards for storage, narrow bunks for sleeping, and a tiny table and benches for eating inside during bad weather. Both sides had wooden awnings that could be lifted up and fastened to provide the horses with shade from the sun and shelter from the rain.

He had thought of everything when he designed it, and the wagon was a conversation piece wherever it went. Maddie had never seen another like it, though she had viewed a number of poor imitations.

No sooner did she yank open the small back door of the wagon when Zoe spilled out, red-gold hair flying and skirts aflutter.

"Maddie! You're back. What time is it? I didn't think it was that late."

"Where's Pa . . . ? And what's that gray slime all over your face?"

Something that looked and smelled like the innards of a long-dead fish smeared Zoe's pretty face—normally the mirror image of Carrie's. The noxious mixture had splattered the apron covering her good town dress and soiled her sleeve.

"Freckle remover. I've been waiting till I had a few minutes alone to try it out, but so far, it isn't working."

"Oh, you look awful!" Carrie chortled from behind Maddie.

"If Nathan Wheeler could see you now, he wouldn't say your skin is as soft and pink as a calf's nose."

"Don't you *dare* tell Nathan about this, Carrie—or I swear I'll claw out your eyes. Nathan is *my* beau. You stay away from him. And don't be tellin' everybody things I told you in confidence either."

"Moooooo," Carrie taunted, then negligently shrugged her shoulders. "I don't care a fig about your crane-legged Nathan. I met a man who's much older and better-looking today, someone *far* more mature and interesting . . ."

"Girls, stop it!" Maddie intervened. "We have a race to run in less than an hour, and Gold Deck isn't even ready. Zoe, where's Little Mike? Didn't I tell you to keep an eye on him?"

"How should I know, Maddie?" Zoe's eyes were exceptionally green as they peered out of the clumps of gray slime dotting her face. "He went off with a couple of his nasty old friends. I told him he'd better stay here, but he wouldn't listen."

Maddie peered into the depths of the wagon. "And Pa. I asked you where Pa is, and you still haven't answered."

"Pa took his jug and went down by the river. I begged him to stay in the wagon, but he wouldn't listen either. Nobody in this family minds me or Carrie. Anyway, you know how Pa is; he especially wouldn't pay attention to me."

Yes, she knew. Oh, God, did she know. By now, Pa was probably skunk drunk and sleeping it off in the rushes.

"Well, there's no time to look for him now," she sighed. "First, we've got to find Little Mike. I don't know how many times I've told him; he can't climb on Gold Deck and win a race without warming him up first. . . . Are you sure he wasn't sick when he left here? Zoe, rinse your face and help me get Gold Deck saddled. Carrie, go look for your brother."

Maddie had the stallion saddled and bridled by the time Carrie returned with Little Mike. She took one look at her brother, and her heart plummeted. "Mike! What happened to you?"

Her brother's nose was bleeding, one eye rapidly swelling shut, and he was holding his left arm and wincing. Clearly, Little Mike had been fighting—and on race day, too!

He shuffled up to her, barely able to remain on his feet. They were the same exact height, but he suddenly seemed much smaller. He wouldn't raise his eyes to meet hers. Instead, he stared at the ground and mumbled.

"Sorry, Maddie, but Amos Graft called Pa a drunken sot and you a bloody hellion. He said it ain't natural the way you ride horses astride and boss all of us around like we were weanlings and you're the head mare. He said I shouldn't do what you say any more, 'cause I'm a man, and you're just a woman. Well, actually, he called you a sour old maid."

Oh, Ma would be spinning in her grave to hear her only son using hurtful, cruel expressions like "bloody hellion" and "sour old maid."

"He called me and Pa nasty names, did he? Well, he's probably right—at least, about me. I'm getting older and more sour by the minute. Are you hurt bad? Can you still ride?"

" 'Course I can ride. Just let me wipe my face and . . . Ow!" He held up his hand and gazed at it with amazement. He tried to move his thumb and grimaced. "I think he broke my thumb. It sure hurts like he broke it."

"A broken thumb is all we need," Maddie muttered. "If it's actually broken, there's no way you can ride Gold Deck. Here, let me see."

She reached for Little Mike's shoulder to draw him closer, but he flinched and stepped away. "Don't! My shoulder hurts, too. It burns like fire whenever I move it."

"Oh, why did you have to fight today of all days? Couldn't it have waited until *after* the race? Don't you have any idea what this contest means to us?"

Gazing into her brother's hazel eyes, Maddie saw that he didn't know how important a victory was today. She hadn't told her siblings how bad things had finally become. Little Mike was only fourteen, yet already doing everything Pa no longer did around the farm. The boy didn't need a man's worries on top of a man's work. The twins must be shielded, too. They all deserved to grow up with a measure of security. Maddie had determined long ago to protect them from life's harsh realities for as long as possible. It was bad enough *she* lay awake nights wondering how they were going to survive.

"Hell, Maddie, I'm sorry." Little Mike looked on the verge of tears.

"Never mind. It's all right. No need to cuss as if you weren't raised any better. Get in the wagon and strip off your clothes. Give me everything but your boots."

"What're you gonna do? What do you want with my clothes?"

"I'm going to ride in your place, of course. I'll stuff my hair up under a hat, and nobody'll know the difference."

"Girls—*ladies*—don't ride in match races."

"Neither do young men with injuries. Do as I say, Mike. We've *got* to win this race. If we don't, we may lose the farm."

"But Maddie, you haven't ridden Gold Deck in . . . in . . . well, I can't remember the last time."

"I used to ride him all the time. I can do it. Hurry up, Mike. Gold Deck and I both need to warm up our creaky old bones."

"Pa won't like this. And Ma would have had a fit."

"Ma isn't here to have a fit, and Pa doesn't know what day it is, much less that we're about to lose the farm." Maddie couldn't quite conceal her bitterness. All her father seemed to care about anymore was drowning his sorrow in rotgut.

"But you'll be racing against a *man,* Maddie," Carrie pointed out as if Maddie herself hadn't thought of it. "Mr. Cumberland's riding his own horse. And *he* might recognize you."

"I'll smear dirt on my face and hope for the best. If he does recognize me, it won't make any difference. It won't change anything. There's nothing in our agreement that says *I* can't ride Gold Deck. . . . Don't just stand there, Mike—get moving."

Her brother gave her one last doubtful look, then climbed gingerly into the wagon, leaving Maddie to cope with the horde of grasshoppers careening around in her stomach. She had no business doing this, but no way to avoid it either. She had to win that two thousand dollars.

Would Gold Deck take exception to running a race with a different rider on his back? Though usually well-behaved, the stallion *could* be temperamental. . . . Lord in heaven! What if

Chase Cumberland's mare was in season? Gold Deck would think he was supposed to breed her, not race her. He'd want to stick his nose—or worse—in her tail and follow her all the way to the finish line. That was another reason why Pa never wanted to race him during breeding season.

These are bad thoughts to be thinking, Maddie McCrory. Instead of imagining possible tragedies, plan how you're going to spend your winnings. First, you make up the mortgage payments, second, you pay the taxes, and if there's any left after that, you buy Little Mike some new trousers and the twins a couple of hair ribbons . . . oh, and pay Pawnee Mary what you owe her . . .

Pawnee Mary was the handsome Indian woman who sometimes helped out with the laundry and cooking. Mary always insisted that her meals and the companionship of the family were payment enough, but Maddie felt guilty about taking advantage of the woman's generosity, especially since the rest of their neighbors wouldn't dream of allowing a lowly squaw to set foot in their houses.

Yes, Maddie decided. If she won this race, she'd insist that Mary accept payment for some of her services in the lean, difficult months since Ma's death. Without Mary's help—the woman always seemed to know just when to appear—life would be ten times as hard. Thus resolved, Maddie managed to paste a confident smile on her face and prepare for her moment of destiny.

Two

Chase Cumberland stood in the shade of a scraggly cottonwood tree near the Hopewell Paths and whispered in his mare's ear, a technique that always seemed to calm her before a race. He knew she was listening because her long golden ears flicked back in his direction, and her breathing sounded like a long low whuffle of agreement.

"We're gonna win this race, Lass," he informed her, ignoring the noise from the spectators taking up positions near the track. "This is our big chance. Then we'll finally have enough money to buy a farm, Buck and I can quit running, and you can settle down and raise pretty golden-coated babies instead of galloping your feet off every other week all spring, summer, and fall. I'll set you up with a big handsome stallion, and your progeny can do all the racing from here on out. All you'll have to do is loll around a wide, green pasture and get fat on corn and prairie grass. Sound good to you, girl?"

Bonnie Lass whuffled into his shirt front, and Chase scratched along her neck beneath her mane, which she particularly liked. He cast a fond glance down the length of her gleaming body. Like her sire, the renowned Bonnie Scotland, Bonnie Lass was a blond bay with black points and a white star on her forehead. She stood sixteen hands high at the withers and had the long shoulders, deep heart girth, short back, loaded forearms, and powerful hindquarters of the born sprinter.

She had grown thin, he had to admit, her ribs visible through the glossy golden-brown of her coat, but she didn't look tired or out of condition to Chase. Ten days' rest after months on the trail had done her good, and she stamped impatiently, eager for the race to begin.

Chase couldn't help smiling to himself. Miss Maddie McCrory was dead wrong; Bonnie Lass had never been fitter or more ready to whip the stallion whose reputation had spread through Texas all the way down to the Rio Grande.

Chase thought of all he'd heard in town about the McCrory family and abruptly stopped grinning. He desperately wanted—*needed*—to win this race, but the idea of taking money from the family of a man grieving so hard for his dead wife that he'd taken to the jug and all but abandoned his children didn't sit well with him. Chase didn't harbor any great sympathy for Big Mike McCrory, whom everyone said was a shrewd horse dealer and formidable opponent in a match race—but he did feel guilty about robbing the man's offspring, including the prickly, red-headed creature who looked like she needed lessons on being female.

According to the town gossips, the four young McCrorys, under the leadership of the eldest daughter, had been living a hand-to-mouth existence since the death of their mother a little over a year ago. Stiff-necked Maddie McCrory had refused help from her neighbors and was struggling to manage the family business alone, while her father drank up whatever meager profits she managed to obtain.

It was a scandal, folks said, the way Big Mike McCrory had let himself go—but then his wife had always been the rock of the family, the one folks could count on, until a mysterious debilitating disease forced her to bed. There, she had valiantly fought a losing battle for several years before claiming her eternal reward.

Chase had heard the story from several sources, but only *after* he'd made his challenge. He had known some hard times himself, so he'd been ready to give Miss McCrory a chance to back out of the bargain. Instead of sensibly doing so, she had ground his compassion to dust beneath her manure-caked heel.

That was her choice. At least, he had tried—and now he intended to win this race and take the prize money, plus whatever else he could gain from the town. He and Buck had been on the trail too long. After three and a half years, they were entitled to start over. By now, the Madisons *must* have quit looking for his brother, and the law in Dallas County had to have found better things to do than pursue a man they knew wasn't guilty anyway. Clint Madison's death had been an accident. Buck had never meant to kill Clint when he broke that barrel of whiskey over his head; he had just been driven to violence by Clint's constant bullying. If the Madisons weren't the richest family in Dallas County, things would never have gone this far. A month after it happened, the incident would have been forgotten.

After crisscrossing several states, Chase believed he had successfully evaded marshall's deputies and bounty hunters alike. He and Buck had left no trail. No other living person over the last year had even *seen* Buck, who at this moment, was camped far out on the prairie, waiting for Chase to come get him and the horses as soon as he'd found a place for them.

This was going to be the place—Hopewell, Kansas, as remote a backwater as Chase could hope to find and still keep match racing, breeding, and selling the horses for which he and his brother had once been famous in Texas. If—*when*—he won this race, he'd finally have enough money to buy a farm where he and Buck could do what they did best—raise horses. No one in Hopewell would have to know about Buck; they'd keep his existence a secret. Considering Buck's startling appearance and peculiar disability, it was better no one knew about him. All Buck had to do was walk into a saloon—or a store or a livery stable or even a church, for that matter—and people started whispering behind their hands. Sooner or later, some bully would say the wrong thing or pick a fight, and Chase's butt would be back in the saddle.

"Win this race for Buck," Chase whispered in Bonnie Lass's ear. "I hate to take money from the McCrorys, but I gave Miss McCrory a chance to change her mind, and the mule-headed little spitfire elected to stick to the original agreement. So now we race. Can't let Buck down, can we, girl? He's counting on us. Besides, I got a feeling it's our lucky day. Show that stallion your heels. I don't care if he does trace back to Cold Deck and Steel Dust; you can beat him. Your blood is as good as his. And he's smaller than you—and uglier. Short and chunky, with a big square jaw and little pig eyes. I know. I saw him once in town and looked him over good. I'll bet he can't run any faster than a three-legged dog."

Chase rubbed Bonnie Lass's soft nose—continuing his insults while watching for his opponent's arrival. A murmur in the crowd told him Gold Deck had come. Turning his head, he saw the horse approaching with its small, diminutive rider. The size of the rider worried him; Chase weighed twice as much. No wonder Miss McCrory approved of "catch-weights," which meant each contestant could decide for himself—or herself—the weight his horse would carry. However, the extra fat on the stallion's big-boned frame more than made up for Chase's additional pounds.

With an eye sharpened by years of experience, Chase studied his rival. He liked what he saw—the unmistakable stamp of Steel Dust, who had sired the great racer, Cold Deck. Steel Dust had been bred in Kentucky but died in Lancaster, Texas, so Chase knew the look of his get: Fifteen hands or more of solid, chunky muscle, that big jaw, and those powerful hindquarters that enabled a horse to sprint like a mountain lion for short distances and turn on his haunches like a cat chasing its tail.

Gold Deck was a sorrel like the great Cold Deck, but with more yellow in his coat—and he didn't really have pig eyes. Chase had merely said that to discourage Bonnie Lass from taking a carnal interest in the handsome fellow. Fortunately, his mare wouldn't be in the mood for flirting this afternoon; it wasn't her time. But she'd be coming into season soon, and when she did, Chase wouldn't mind breeding her to Gold Deck. The stallion wasn't going to win this race, but he still had plenty to offer.

"Competition's here, girl. Time to mount up."

As Chase swung into the saddle, Bonnie Lass pranced and fidgeted. He spun her around a couple of times to settle her, then turned her nose toward the new arrival. The stallion snorted an inquisitive greeting, but the boy on his back hunched his shoulders and looked away, his face hidden beneath a slouch hat. The crowd surged around them, and comments flew like a rain of arrows.

"Little Mike, you bring that horse home now, y' hear? I got a lot ridin' on this race."

Chase recognized Silas Grover, who had bet a winter's supply of beans, coffee, and flour against Chase's beautifully tooled Mexican saddle that Gold Deck would beat Bonnie Lass.

"You sure that mare of yours kin outrun a stallion?" a man in a red wool shirt demanded. "I backed you, Cumberland, and it'll cost me a hunert dollars if you prove me a liar."

"She can do it," Chase answered. "Where's the blacksmith? I thought he was supposed to manage this race."

"Hold yer hosses. I'm right here." A huge, barrel-chested man with biceps like mountains pushed through the crowd of men, women, and children assembled to watch the race.

All of Hopewell had apparently shown up, including the fellow who had put up his wagon and a bunch of farm tools against Chase's intricately engraved spurs that the McCrorys' stallion would beat Chase's mare.

"Y'all know the rules," Jake Bussel announced in his gruff, unlettered manner. "The start'll be turn-ask-an'-answer. Soon as you break, I'll fire the pistol, an' the fust one t' cross the finish line wins the race."

Chase glanced at the boy astride Gold Deck; the young man's hands were trembling as they clutched the horse's reins in a near death grip. Chase had a notion to say something to ease his nervousness, but stopped himself just in time. Too much was at stake, and he ought to be hoping the boy *was* nervous and would make mistakes. He scanned the crowd for Maddie McCrory, but her scruffy red braid and earnest freckled face were nowhere in sight.

She had a cute turned-up nose, he remembered, one of the few feminine things about her—that and the little dimple in her chin—and he wondered if her brother had inherited the same features. He recalled that Miss McCrory's little sister had shown promise of becoming a real beauty, with her reddish-gold hair and nearly flawless skin, but Maddie herself had been so prickly and sourpussed that Chase couldn't remember much about her except for her cold, forbidding manner. She walked around as if she had a rake handle up her spine. His inability to conjure more details was unusual since he always took note of women. He got to spend so little time with them that he rarely forgot the shape of a woman's body, the sweetness of her smile, or her scent, especially if it was unusual. Maddie McCrory, he now remembered, had smelled faintly of horse manure.

To hell with protecting his own interests; the lad was so nervous he was shaking like an old dog thrown out in a hailstorm. Taking pity on him, Chase leaned over and tapped the boy on the shoulder. The small body jerked, the head swung around, and two blue eyes stared out of a dirt-smudged face. . . . Now, where had he seen those eyes—so vivid a blue and full of outrage? Then it came to him. The boy had his sister's eyes—and her nose. And her dimpled chin. And her scrappy spirit.

"Whaddya want?" came the surly response.

"Relax. It's only a race," Chase counseled. "Win or lose, the sun will come up tomorrow morning same as ever."

"Keep yer hands to yerself, mister," the boy muttered, no friendlier than his sister. He tugged his hat further down over his eyes so that nothing showed but his compressed mouth.

Chase had to admire his spunk, if not his hospitality. "With your hat pulled down like that, you won't be able to see the finish line. Not unless your eyesight can bore through felt."

"I don't need t' see it. I know where it is."

"You two ready?" Jake Bussel waved his pistol impatiently. "Let's git this over with. I got two hosses waitin' to be shod this afternoon, so turn yer mounts around and face away from the startin' posts."

Chase eyed the two wooden stakes marking the starting line and the pounded-down paths running side by side. A quarter mile away, the distance to which he and his opponent's sister had agreed, a second set of stakes marked the finish. Satisfied he knew where he was headed, Chase spun Lass on her haunches and could feel her muscles bunch in anticipation. Bonnie Lass liked this method of starting a race, and so did he, because his mare's ability to spin and break away fast usually gave her the advantage. He had been the one to suggest it. Miss McCrory could have insisted on any one of several alternatives, but she hadn't, and Chase now wondered if the boy would make a clean start the first time or keep demanding restarts, as often happened in match races. He mentally prepared himself for a period of "jockeying" for the best position.

"Ready!" he heard the boy croak.

"Go!" he responded, sitting deep as Bonnie Lass whirled and hurled herself down the track.

The gun went off a split second later, confirming the official start of the race. Leaning over Lass's neck, Chase urged his mare onward. She flattened her ears, listening, and he reminded her of all this race meant to him and Buck. Her mane whipped back in his face, and her long, powerful body felt supple and fluid between his thighs. She flew like a bird, and it came to him why he loved match racing so much. Very few thrills in life could match this one: the sensation of flight. The certainty of winning. The joy of conquering and beating a worthy opponent. Only making love to a beautiful woman could possibly compare, and it had been so long since he'd done *that,* he could scarcely recall the experience. *This* was what he lived for—what defined who he was and the pride he took in himself and his horses.

He had bred Bonnie Lass, attended her birth, guided the wobbly-legged foal to her Mama's milk, trained, and taught her to race. This was his reward for a job well done. As she found her rhythm, her stride lengthened, and if he didn't know better, he would have sworn her feet never touched the ground. Then it was over. She crossed the finish line, and he straightened in the saddle to slow her forward momentum. No horse ran ahead of him, which meant he had won.

Snatching his hat from his head, he tossed it high in the air and let out a whoop of triumph that echoed the roar of the crowd. "Yahoooo! You done it, old girl."

Before the words left his mouth, Gold Deck galloped past, fighting his rider's efforts to slow him down. The boy's hat had come off, and red hair streamed out behind him. A long disheveled braid bounced on his shoulders, and the truth cut Chase like a whip: This was no *boy.* The rider was Maddie McCrory.

She spun the stallion on his haunches—as nice a spin as he'd ever seen. Blue eyes glittering with fury, her mouth a grim slash, she came riding back to him. Her little boyish bottom—a very nice bottom, he duly noted—seemed molded to the saddle as if glued to the leather, and she no longer looked afraid. Actually, she looked mad as a rattler stepped on by a horse.

"You won!" Her voice sliced through the general clamor around them. "You won. But I don't think much of your tactics, you miserable, low-down, two-faced, lying skunk."

Her hostility totally baffled him. "What do you mean? All I did was ride my own race. I won fair and square, Miss McCrory. Maybe you should let your brother do the riding from now on. Match racing is no sport for a woman. Makes 'em too emotional. Hell, scared as you were at the start, you could have broken your neck this afternoon."

"I'm not talking about *now!"* she screeched. "Why, the horse you're ridin' today doesn't look at all like the same one I saw in the stable when you first came to town."

"Are you accusing me of switching horses?" Chase mustered a look of wounded innocence. He wasn't about to admit he had done what he always did when he rode into a strange town in search of a race. He had rubbed sand and ashes into Bonnie Lass's coat and cued her to limp when anyone was watching. But Maddie McCrory couldn't have seen her limping if she'd only glimpsed her in the stable.

"I thought she'd be no competition—skinny as she was and poor as she looked in her stall. Now that you've cleaned her up and poured feed into her, I can see what I missed before—what you *intended* I should miss. This horse has the lines of a champion. I bet you've raced her all over the Continent. Raced and won. Do you deny it?"

Chase was dimly aware of people moving closer, craning their necks to see better, and straining to hear every word. He allowed a slow, lazy grin to slide across his face. "I admit we've won a few races."

"There! You see?" Maddie McCrory shrieked at the crowd. "But did you or did you not tell Jake Bussel you'd *lost* your last race?"

"Well, hell, I did—because we did lose. But I also told you she was fit 'cause I rode her all winter. Do you deny that?"

Chase wouldn't have believed a person's face could get as red as Miss Maddie McCrory's. Her beet-dark cheeks outshone her hair, and her blue eyes fairly crackled with anger.

"You sucked me into a high-stakes race by making it appear your horse is a loser. That's dishonest, and I won't forget it, Mr. Cumberland—and neither will anyone else around here."

"Whoa," he said, his own anger rising. "Didn't I offer you a chance to back out of this race?"

"Yes, and a chance to raise the stakes, too. You're the best I've seen at talking out of both sides of your mouth. You played my gullibility like a man sawing away on a fiddle, only I didn't recognize the tune until just now."

"I never played a tune you haven't heard before—or maybe even played yourself. I've been told a few tales since I came to town. Seems your pa used to ride up to farms claiming he was just a cowhand with a plain old range horse. And your champion stallion would be lookin' all rough and dirty, so no one would guess he had a single ounce of speed. Then, when the right moment came along, he'd . . ."

"You leave my pa out of this! When it comes to false impressions, he can't hold a candle to you. Why, you . . ."

She seemed to be searching for an insult bad enough to express her feelings.

"Miss McCrory . . ." Chase leaned over his mare's withers and lowered his voice. "If I were you, I'd let the matter drop now, before folks accuse you of whining just because you lost."

"I'm not whining!"

"You're not?" Chase raised his eyebrows. "You coulda fooled me."

"Ohhhh!" Spinning the stallion around again, almost trampling the onlookers, she sped away.

"Miss McCrory!" he hollered after her. "Don't forget you're supposed to meet me in town in an hour with my prize money."

He doubted she'd heard him, but she knew the rules. They had agreed beforehand that one hour after the race, the loser must hand over the money at the foot of the big bur oak growing in the center of town. Normally, it was the stakeholder's job to take care of this important detail, but Jake Bussel had informed him that in Hopewell, things were done a little differently, according to a tradition involving the town's only tree.

Chase looked down to see Maddie McCrory's little sister standing nearby watching him—good Lord, there were *two* of her! No, they were twins. He remembered that now. There was Maddie, Little Mike, and twin girls—Carrie and . . . He couldn't recall the name of the other one.

"Tell your sister I'll be waiting at the bur oak in an hour," he told them.

He thought their eyes would bug out of their heads. They nodded in unison. "Yes, sir, Mr. Cumberland," they chorused.

"Maddie will bring the money," Carrie—or was it the other one?—assured him.

"Good. See that she does." Having settled that matter—he hoped—Chase rode among the crowd to collect the rest of his winnings before the losers disappeared.

Maddie returned to the wagon, slid down from Gold Deck, removed his bridle, pulled on his halter, tied him up, and called out to her brother. "Little Mike, I'm back! Can you walk Gold Deck and cool him down? I've got to find Pa."

Her brother stuck his head out of the back door of the wagon. "Did we win, Maddie?"

His one good eye looked hopeful; the other resembled a large purple grape. When he saw her face, he grimaced. "Damn! We didn't, did we?"

She shook her head. "Put *my* clothes on if you have to. I'm going after Pa. We owe Chase Cumberland two thousand dollars. I need Pa to help me figure out what to do."

"Pa won't be any help. Might as well forget about asking *him*."

The scorn in her brother's voice echoed the despair lodged like a stone in Maddie's breast. "He wasn't always like this," she defended, as she always did when one of her siblings pointed out the obvious. "Just remember that, Mike. There was a time Pa could handle anything. He can't help the way he's become."

"Maybe not, but Amos Graft is right, Maddie. Pa's a drunken sot. He won't know how to get two thousand dollars."

"Don't say that! Maybe he will. Anyway, I've got to find him. Take care of Gold Deck. I'll be back as soon as I can."

Maddie headed for the river to search in the rushes and a quarter of an hour later, stumbled over her father's left foot. Propped against a big rock, the jug unstoppered beside him, Pa was lying on the bank overlooking the water. Eyes closed, he was loudly snoring, his exhalations sounding like a blacksmith's bellows. His hands lay crossed upon his chest in a dead man's pose, and Maddie could see none of the charming, charismatic man she had known as a child and young woman.

This man was a stranger; he didn't even look like himself. His red hair had gone gray seemingly overnight, his nose and cheeks reminded her of over-ripe apples, and he sported a three-days' growth of beard. Unless Maddie nagged him, he no longer bathed or shaved, though he'd never worn so much as a mustache while Ma was still alive and wouldn't have dreamed of coming unwashed to the supper table.

Dropping to her knees beside him, Maddie picked up the jug and turned it upside down. A single drop plopped onto the buffalo grass. He had finished off the jug, which had been more than half full yesterday afternoon when Maddie had last checked it. That meant she would have to watch him like a hawk again to prevent him from taking something valuable to town to barter for a new one. One day she'd caught him riding Gold Deck into Hopewell to sell!

As it was, he had practically stripped the house of every item of worth it contained—all of Ma's little treasures from back East, as well as the small luxuries they had acquired over the years of their marriage. Little remained to recall the prosperity the family had enjoyed during their "good years," as Maddie now thought of them.

She had managed to hide away a few things Pa had forgotten about, but the sum total of the items still hidden up in the barn loft wouldn't amount to two thousand dollars. Wouldn't amount to much more than two hundred—enough to provide a modest wedding supper and give each girl a small stake when she married, by Maddie's reckoning. Despite all this, she had to discuss this problem with Pa—or at least, *try* to discuss it; she had simply never planned on Gold Deck losing this race to a mare who had appeared to be on her last legs. Surely, when he realized how serious their situation was, her father would attempt to pull himself together and assist her in this crisis.

"Pa!" She shook his shoulder. "Pa, wake up."

He didn't stir, and she shook him harder. "Please, Pa. I've got to talk to you."

He opened one bloodshot blue eye and mumbled: "Lee me alone."

Maddie's desperation swelled. "Listen to me, Pa. You've got to wake up and get sober. I lost a race with Gold Deck this afternoon, and I don't know what to do. I owe the winner a huge sum of money. . . . Pa, this could be the end for us—we could lose the farm! I can't make the mortgage payments, the taxes are due next month, and this hard-eyed stranger is waiting for me to bring him the prize money."

"Clara?" Suddenly coming to life, Pa pushed himself up on one elbow. "Clara Ann, honey, is that you?"

Clara Ann had been her mother's name.

Maddie swallowed back a sob. "Oh, Pa. How can you do this to us? We lost her, too, you know. It isn't just you who misses Ma. . . . Pa, we *need* you. Carrie and Zoe and Little Mike and me. Have you forgotten us? Don't you care what happens to your own family anymore?"

Her father gave no indication of comprehension. With a shaky hand, he fumbled in the grass. "Where's my jug? Help me find my jug. I'm thirsty."

Maddie scrambled to her feet, picked up the jug, and hurled it as far as she could into the brownish-green waters lapping at the brush-strewn bank. It landed with a splash, but didn't immediately sink. In the middle of the river, it bobbed forlornly, the water slowly rising up its sides to overwhelm it, exactly the way Maddie's problems were now overwhelming her.

"It's gone, Pa. Gone. And I don't know where you'll get money to buy another. It won't be from me. No matter how much you plead, beg, and threaten, you can't have any more money, because the money's all gone, too."

Her father slumped against the stone and closed his eyes. "Lee me alone. Jus' lee me be. I doan wanna go home yet. Not if Clara ain't there."

It was what he always said when Maddie came to take him home. At least, at this time of year, it wouldn't hurt to leave him here to sleep for a while and make his own way home when he was good and ready. She wouldn't have to worry about him freezing to death, as she did in winter. If he didn't show up at the wagon in a couple of hours, she'd send Little Mike back to get him before they started for the farm. . . . But, oh, she was angry! And disappointed. And scared.

Now, when she needed him most, Pa had let her down. How could a man sink so low in such a short space of time? It wasn't fair. First, she had lost her mother, and then, her father, too. She had lost him to grief and whiskey. Ma's death had been a double blow, only at the time, she hadn't realized it.

Plodding back toward the wagon, Maddie racked her brain for a solution: What to do? She had less than half an hour before she had to face Chase Cumberland. She needed more time! Lifting her gaze to the sky, she studied the angle of the sun, and the answer came to her. Even if she had the money sitting in the town's one and only bank, the Hopewell Savings and Trust, it was too late in the day to get it out. The bank closed at noon on Saturday—two hours before the race had even begun. She had the perfect excuse for delaying the payment until Monday, when it would reopen. That gave her another full day and two nights to figure out a way to come up with two thousand dollars.

She laughed softly to herself. Why hadn't she thought of this sooner? The reprieve could have tasted no sweeter had she been facing a gallows tree instead of Chase Cumberland. She'd meet him at the bur oak and simply tell him he had to wait until Monday for his money. No doubt he'd holler and fuss, but what could he do? Did he actually expect her to produce two thousand dollars in cash this very afternoon?

She *had* agreed to the method of payment, of course, for it was a long-standing tradition in Hopewell—one that benefitted her since she couldn't have given the money to Jake Bussel ahead of time anyway. Surely, Mr. Cumberland would understand . . . and if he didn't, that was too bad. Her explanation would have to suffice. By Monday, she'd think of something; maybe the bank would lend her some money!

She shuddered at the thought of approaching Horace Brownley, the bank president and also the Mayor of Hopewell. She'd have to explain—yet again—why she couldn't make this month's mortgage payment and now needed to *borrow* money. Fortunately, the racing season was only just beginning, and another defeat like today's was highly unlikely.

Next time, she'd win . . . because next time, she wouldn't rely on a single visit to a darkened stable to evaluate a potential rival. Next time, she'd make certain she saw the horse in broad daylight first—and she wouldn't be fooled by any of the old horsemen's tricks or "endeavors," as they were called, that her own Pa had once employed to gull the unsuspecting. She herself would be better prepared to ride in Little Mike's place, if necessary, and Gold Deck would be better conditioned. As of today, she was cutting his corn ration in half and doubling his exercise.

She could blame no one but herself for the loss of today's race, but it wouldn't happen again. She wouldn't allow it. Now all she had to do was convince Horace Brownley of that fact—and persuade Chase Cumberland to be patient.

Three

"What do you mean—wait until Monday? You're the one who insisted the loser hand over the prize money exactly one hour after the race."

Arms folded across his broad chest, amber eyes slitted, Chase Cumberland stood scowling in the shade of the bur oak. More than ever, he reminded Maddie of a hungry, furious wolf radiating danger and possessing a disquieting fascination. Fortunately, Maddie had changed back into her brown calico, and he couldn't see how badly her knees were knocking together beneath her skirt. She brushed a strand of unruly hair from her eyes and attempted to appear undaunted.

"I've already apologized for the inconvenience, Mr. Cumberland, and explained how I got so caught up in the preparations for the race that I quite forgot to withdraw the money before the bank closed at noon. What more do you want? Must I get down on my knees and beg your pardon?"

She glanced at the faces of the little circle of onlookers who had gathered to witness the exchange of the prize money. In years gone by, her father had treated these men to a free round of drinks at the Ruby Garter after previous victories. Obviously, they were hoping Mr. Cumberland intended to celebrate in like manner, though she could have told them differently; there wasn't a kind, generous bone in Chase Cumberland's entire body.

"I don't want your apologies; I want my money, Miss McCrory. This is a man's game, and if you intend to play it, you'd better play like a man—or risk getting shot. When a loser tries to weasel out of a deal, he—or she—can expect swift retaliation."

Hands on hips, Maddie forced herself to stare straight into his cruel yellow eyes. "So shoot me. It was a simple mistake. I'm certainly not trying to weasel out of a deal. I simply never expected to have to produce the money this afternoon; I was sure we would win. We always do—don't we, gentlemen?"

She smiled encouragingly at the assembled men, but not a single one looked supportive—the traitors! Without his money, Mr. Cumberland couldn't possibly treat them all to a victory celebration.

"Beggin' your pardon, Miss McCrory, but your pa would have had the prize money ready and waitin'," said old Amos Pardy, who washed glasses and swept floors at the Ruby Garter to make a living. "He rarely lost, but when he did, he wasn't too proud to meet his obligations."

"Well, as you probably already know, Pa's been too ill to look after our business of late, Mr. Pardy, and Little Mike's too young yet, so it's fallen upon me to do so. I'm truly sorry I forgot to visit the bank this morning, but I will do so immediately on Monday, and then Mr. Cumberland can be on his way again, off to fleece the next unsuspecting sheep he encounters on his travels through Kansas."

"It's none of your business, ma'am, but my intentions are to *remain* in the area—so I imagine I can wait until Monday to get my money."

The last thing Maddie had expected was an easy capitulation—especially after his initial reaction. Chase Cumberland's dark features held an expression she couldn't begin to fathom . . . and didn't trust one bit.

"Thank you, sir. I appreciate your forbearance. Shall we meet here at eleven o'clock on the day after tomorrow? Would that be satisfactory?"

"Well, now, I did have other plans for Monday at eleven. I had intended to ride out to take a look at a farm that's for sale in the area. But I guess if I want my two thousand dollars, I'll have to readjust my schedule, won't I?"

He wasn't going to make it *too* easy, she saw. "Name the day and time," she snapped. "I will endeavor to be there."

"What farm you talkin' about, son?" drawled Hiram Garret, another frequenter of the Ruby Garter. His own farm had fallen upon hard times due to his penchant for visiting the saloon too often, but he kept close track of everybody else's agricultural and ranching affairs.

"The old Hanaway place," Mr. Cumberland informed him. "I heard it was for sale, and I plan on riding out to see it, Monday."

"Won't do you no good—place sold four days ago. Feller who bought it told me so yestidy."

"Damn!" Chase Cumberland exploded, then, with a glance at Maddie, "Excuse me, Miss McCrory, but I had intended to use my winnings to help buy the place if I liked it."

"If it's land yer wantin', why doncha look at the old Parker place—out there next t' the McCrory's?" Jefferson Potts directed a stream of tobacco juice at the stump of the bur oak. A large, untidy man with a big belly and fists the size of anvils, he, like Hiram Garret, made it his business to know everybody else's business. Maddie heartily wished he would swallow his tongue.

Pa had been eyeing the Parker place for years, and Maddie herself had decided that if she ever managed to get ahead, she would buy it to add to the McCrory holdings. They needed more pasture, and the parcel abutted their own land. It had stood vacant ever since old Mr. Parker died, three years before Ma's death, but they had never gotten around to buying it and now could not afford it.

"Mr. Cumberland wouldn't be interested in the Parker place," she interjected. "Water's bad."

"Water's bad?" Hiram questioned. "I never heard that."

"That's cuz you don't know nothin'," scoffed Jefferson Potts. "I always did hear water was bad out that way. Probably alkaline, like the Saline River."

"It may only need a new well," Chase Cumberland coolly observed. "I believe I'll take a look at it anyway—bad water or not. Since it's near your place, Miss McCrory, I can stop by Monday afternoon to pick up my money. That should give you more than enough time to make whatever arrangements you need with the bank."

"Whatever gave you the idea I needed to make *arrangements?* Actually, I'd *prefer* meeting you in town, Mr. Cumberland. It isn't at all convenient for you to stop by on Monday afternoon."

The last thing Maddie wanted was for Chase Cumberland to set foot anywhere near her home. She didn't want him to see how they really lived—with fences falling down and house and barn roofs that had sprung leaks over the winter and caused water damage to both structures. With a garden badly in need of weeding. With broken porch steps and a shed door ready to fall off. Built primarily of limestone blocks, the McCrory farm had once been the best built and maintained farm in the county—but no longer. Neglect was fast taking its toll.

"It isn't at all convenient for me to *wait* until Monday, Miss McCrory. So the least you can do is be ready with the money when I get there. I'll see you Monday at four o'clock."

"But . . . but . . ." Maddie sputtered, but Chase Cumberland was already walking away, every movement graceful and predatory, as if he owned the town or intended to buy it one day real soon.

With supper over, Pa tucked into bed and snoring, and dishes washed and dried, Maddie sat down in her mother's rocker to plan what she was going to say to Horace Brownley, the bank president, on Monday. Try as she might, she couldn't think of a good explanation for why she needed a loan, other than to tell the truth. The man had been surprisingly lenient about the overdue mortgage payments, but she didn't know how long his compassion would last, especially in view of the fact that she now had to beg him for two thousand dollars. If he refused, she didn't know what she would do. Gold Deck had another race scheduled for next week in Salina, but it was only for a thousand dollars, enough to cover this month's mortgage payment and a portion of the taxes, but not to pay off their other debts. In addition to their past-due payments, they owed money all over town—to Jake Bussel, for trimming the horses' feet all winter, to Mr. Grover for items bought on credit from the mercantile, and—to Maddie's great mortification—the Ruby Garter for credit extended to Pa, which, until this afternoon, Maddie had known nothing about.

Lily Tolliver, the buxom, black-haired, scarlet-gowned proprietress of the Ruby Garter, had waylaid Maddie after her confrontation with Chase Cumberland and demanded immediate payment of no less than three hundred and forty-eight dollars for "entertainment" Pa had supposedly enjoyed over the winter and spring at the saloon.

"I took pity on him in his grief and downheartedness," Miss Tolliver had huffed to Maddie, thrusting out a bosom already in danger of exploding. "But now that your horse is losin' races, Big Mike's gettin' no more credit, and you better pay up what he owes me, or I'll have him hauled off to the county jail where he can rot 'til he produces the money."

Maddie hadn't been aware her father was carousing at the Ruby Garter, but she supposed she ought to have guessed before now. Pa had bedeviled them all with his mysterious disappearances. Whenever he rode into town on Black Jack, she had assumed he was passing time with some of his old friends, not running up bills at the saloon in the company of a notorious "calico queen," otherwise known as a "soiled dove."

Maddie's humiliating encounter with Lily Tolliver had been the final blow on a day already ruined by the tragic loss of the race. She couldn't imagine how a day could get much worse; it was a relief to have it nearly over. The twins had disappeared upstairs over an hour ago, and Little Mike had gone to bed in his little room under the eaves to nurse his injuries right after supper.

Yawning, Maddie wondered if she ought to postpone worrying until tomorrow. In her present state of exhaustion, she couldn't think clearly anyhow—certainly not clearly enough to reason a way out of this dilemma. Their problems had been brewing for over a year now and weren't likely to disappear all at once. Even if Horace Brownley offered to loan her ten thousand dollars on Monday, and Chase Cumberland never showed up demanding his prize money, Pa would still be a worry and a heartache.

A peculiar burning sensation stung Maddie's eyes, and tears threatened to spill down her cheeks. If only she had someone with whom she could share these trials and tribulations! Someone who would listen, make suggestions, and ease her feeling of abandonment. She longed for her mother, though it had always been her father with whom she'd had the most in common. Still, as long as Ma had been alive, things had been right in Maddie's world. She had never had to worry where the family's next meal was coming from, when the next race would be run, or how they would pay their debts. Now she had to worry about everything and couldn't depend upon anyone but herself to fix things.

A low, suppressed giggle came from the stairwell, and Maddie hurriedly blinked away the moisture in her eyes and sat up straighter in the rocker. Cob, the corn-colored cat whose job was to keep the house free of mice, suddenly leapt into Maddie's lap, and she idly stroked its thick yellow fur as the twins crept into the front room and stood giggling and fidgeting just outside the circle of lamplight.

"I thought you two had gone to bed. It's late, and I was thinking of going upstairs myself in a few minutes."

"We have something for you, Maddie." Zoe looked girlish and innocent in her old-fashioned, longcloth nightdress with her braided red-gold hair hanging down her back.

A bit of pink ribbon trimmed Zoe's nightdress, while a bit of blue adorned Carrie's. Maddie noticed that each twin had one hand behind her back; what could they be up to now?

"Happy birthday, Maddie!" the girls chorused, jointly extracting something from the darkness and thrusting it under Maddie's nose.

"My goodness! I thought you had all forgotten my birthday; I did—until just this minute."

"Pa and Little Mike forgot, but *we* didn't," Carrie boasted.

"We knew exactly what we wanted to get for you, but first we had to trim it properly. We've only just finished, and here it is. Go on. open it."

Nudging Cob off her lap, Maddie gingerly accepted the odd-shaped, bulky parcel. It was draped and tied in a length of muslin that looked like Zoe's oldest shirtwaist. Eyes shining and laughter brimming, the twins eagerly waited for Maddie to unwrap it.

"I can't imagine what it could be," Maddie mused. "We can't afford anyth- . . ."

The words caught in her throat as she saw what the twins had given her: It was a new bonnet. A blue-checked slat sunbonnet made of heavy calico and trimmed with an edging of white rick-rack and a whisper of expensive lace.

"It's to keep the sun and wind off your face, so you don't get so many freckles," Carrie informed her. "Assuming a patch of shade and a windbreak will help."

"And it's blue to bring out the color of your eyes," Zoe proudly added. "We wanted to get you a matching apron, but we couldn't afford it. Anyway, this should go with your white shirtwaist, and that dark blue skirt you sometimes wear for special occasions."

Maddie decided not to mention that her dark blue skirt had shredded at the seams and resisted her inexpert attempts at mending. "I hate to ask, but is this . . . paid for?" she dared to inquire. "It wasn't purchased on credit, was it?"

She ran her fingers lovingly over the bonnet's wide brim. Any article of apparel that hadn't been fashioned at home didn't come cheaply, and neither did white rickrack and lace. "Girls, you'd better tell me the truth. You didn't talk Mr. Grover into extending credit on this purchase, did you? If so, the bonnet will have to go back. We already owe him too much for necessities; in our present condition, fripperies are out of the question. Besides, he lost a great deal today betting on Gold Deck; I doubt we'll be welcome in the mercantile for a good long time."

Carrie slammed her hands down on top of the bonnet. "This bonnet isn't going back, Maddie. No matter what you say. You haven't had anything new since I can't remember when—but it was way before Ma died."

"You haven't had anything new either," Maddie started to protest, but Zoe quickly interrupted.

"It's *almost* paid for. Every time me and Carrie took fresh eggs to town to sell in the mercantile . . ."

"Carrie and I," Maddie automatically corrected.

"Carrie and *I,* we set a wee bit of money aside to buy this bonnet for your birthday."

"And here I thought eggs were going so cheaply these days!"

"They are!" Carrie hastened to agree. "Just not *that* cheaply." She exchanged a look of gleeful complicity with her twin. "And we only have a few more pennies to go before the bonnet is completely paid for!"

"Only a few more pennies," Maddie sighed. "That's still more than we can afford right now, so maybe we should . . ."

"No!" the girls shouted in unison. Two identical pairs of hazel eyes lit with determination.

"It's too late, Maddie," Zoe assured her. "Now that we've put the rickrack and lace on it, the bonnet isn't the same one we originally bought. Mr. Grover won't take it back once it's been tampered with."

"You have *improved* it, not ruined it. I'm sure Mr. Grover will agree."

"No, he won't." Carrie crossed her arms over her budding bosom. "If anything, he'll be angry. Our agreement calls for three more deliveries of our eggs at the lower price. Do you want us to be known all over town as folks who don't hold to their bargains?"

Carrie was right, Maddie had to concede, but the trouble was that after Monday, the McCrory family *would* be known all over the county for that very reason—indeed, they'd be known all over Kansas and even beyond, as cheats and liars, if Maddie couldn't come up with two thousand dollars.

Chase Cumberland hadn't been wrong when he warned that men were shot for lesser sums. Shot, hanged, or run out of town. . . . Over the years, Maddie had heard many stories of retaliation and revenge. Pa himself had gone after losers with a horse whip if they didn't fork over his winnings fast enough.

Shivering, Maddie resolutely reminded herself that Mr. Grover *would* be livid if she took the bonnet back to the mercantile—and it was so pretty and feminine. Such a perfect color for her! The twins had outdone themselves. She pictured them drooling over all the temptations in the store, but setting aside their own desires to buy something special for her birthday, and tears threatened once more.

"You aren't going to cry, are you?" Zoe demanded in disgust. "We wanted to make you smile again, Maddie, the way you used to do when Ma was still alive."

Maddie mustered her biggest smile, and it did feel foreign on her lips. "You two are really quite wonderful, do you know that? So I guess I'll have to keep the bonnet, after all. But wait! Maybe I should try it on first. What if it doesn't suit me? Then none of us would mind so much taking it back and having Mr. Grover subtract its value from the large sum we owe him."

"Zoe, fetch Ma's hand mirror," Carrie commanded. "Here, put it on, Maddie, and let's see how you look."

In a few breathless moments, while Maddie closed her eyes in anticipation, Carrie set the bonnet on Maddie's head, adjusted it, then tied the two bonnet strings together beneath her chin.

"All right, you can look now!" Zoe sang out.

Maddie opened her eyes and gazed enraptured into the small mirror her sister held. She hardly recognized herself. Her carrot-colored hair no longer flamed around her face like a fire burning out of control. Indeed, she couldn't see her hair at all. It was completely hidden in the depths of the large bonnet, and her eyes had grown larger and more brilliant, their sky blue color heightened by the solid blue lining of the bonnet.

"Ohhh," she breathed, glimpsing her own mother's delicate features in the pert lines of her nose and the dimple in her chin.

Her mother's skin had been very white and soft, with nary a freckle, while Maddie's was already richly tanned from going bareheaded in the sun—and of course, she still had her freckles. Even so, she appeared undeniably feminine, even mysterious, gazing out from the depths of the eight-inch brim. The bavolet, a generous ten inches of chambray hanging down to protect her neck from sunburn, was also trimmed with lace, adding to the bonnet's charm.

She was sure she wouldn't mind wearing this one as she always minded wearing the plain, black, hand-me-down that had once belonged to her mother. Not only was it falling apart, but it did nothing for her coloring, except to make her appear sallow and consumptive.

"Thank you, girls," she whispered past the lump in her throat. "I really do love it. It's a beautiful sunbonnet, and I promise to wear it whenever a special occasion arises."

"No, no . . ." The twins shook their heads.

"Every day," Carrie insisted. "You must promise to wear it whenever you go outside."

"Just to feed the chickens? Or milk the cow? Or—heaven forbid—when I help Little Mike exercise the horses or muck out the barn? Not likely, my dears. I don't intend to ruin it. And I won't wear it in situations where it will obstruct my vision, so I can't see what I'm doing."

"Maddie, you are impossible!" Zoe squealed. "That's why we bought it—so you wouldn't have to go outdoors in that ugly old black bonnet that makes you look like a scarecrow."

"That's why I don't like to wear it; it's so ugly. Plus, I can't see."

"You're a lady. You're not supposed to see—or be seen, except when you're indoors. A bonnet protects your skin and hides your hair," Carrie chided. "And in the case of *your* hair, that's a definite advantage."

"You don't always wear one," Maddie pointed out. "You didn't wear one in town today.

"I forgot to put mine on before we left home, but you can be sure I won't forget the next time. My nose got burnt today."

"That's too bad," Maddie commiserated, aware that her own nose felt tender. "Well, I am delighted with your thoughtfulness. It means so much to me—especially after a day like today."

As if the same thought had occurred to each twin at the exact same time—a phenomenon with which Maddie was already well acquainted—Carrie and Zoe simultaneously reached out to lay a consoling hand on Maddie's shoulder.

"Everything's going to be all right, isn't it, Maddie?" Zoe looked worried.

"We'll find the money somehow, won't we?" Carrie echoed.

Maddie summoned another stiff-cheeked smile. "Of course! You mustn't doubt it. First thing Monday morning, I'll visit Mr. Brownley at the bank—and I'll wear my new bonnet. I'm sure he'll be so charmed by my dazzling beauty that he'll hand over the money without a single objection. Why, he'll probably insist that we borrow even more than we need."

The very idea of the pompous, balding, potbellied bachelor, Horace Brownley, being overcome with admiration for Maddie prompted Zoe and Carrie to burst into giggles. "Oh, Maddie, you ought to try my new freckle-remover remedy tomorrow! Then he'll be struck dumb as a doorpost and *eager* to assist us."

If only that were possible, Maddie thought in a new surge of despondency. People said Horace Brownley was so stiff-necked and uncompromising no woman would have him as a husband—and he a prosperous bank president and the mayor of the town! She had already stretched his patience uncommonly far; it would be a miracle if he had any more to spare. He might view Gold Deck's loss with the same greedy cynicism as Lily Tolliver.

Oh, Lord, please let him be in a good mood on Monday!

"Run along to bed now, you two. I'll be upstairs shortly. I want to look in on Pa first."

It had been necessary to send the girls after Pa to bring him back to the wagon, but by the time they'd gotten him home and fixed supper, Pa had refused to eat it. Surly and bad-tempered, he had headed for the barn and come in a bit later, weaving and grinning. The jug Maddie had thought was his last apparently wasn't; he had another hidden away somewhere. Without having a bite to eat since breakfast, he had collapsed into bed, where Maddie had had to remove his boots and get him settled for the night.

How long could a body live, filling his gut with corn liquor instead of food? It was another question to which Maddie didn't have the answer, but she was terribly afraid she would eventually find out.

" 'Night, Maddie."

Carrie and Zoe gave her quick kisses and hugs, and Maddie watched them disappear into the stairwell. Then she carefully removed her new sunbonnet and rose to check on her father.

He was snoring when she looked in on him, but the light from her lamp spilled across his grizzled features and seemed to rouse him. "Who's there?" he demanded, blinking and bringing up his arm to shade his eyes.

"It's me, Pa—Maddie. I wanted to make certain you're all right." Maddie set down the lamp on the bedside stand and leaned over him, inhaling the sharp-sweet odor of stale whiskey and the equally unpleasant aroma of unwashed old man. Tomorrow, she must get him bathed, shaved, and into clean clothes, for he was beginning to smell like a pig and his room like a pigsty.

"You didn't eat any supper, Pa. Can't I get you something? A little warm milk and a bite of bread, perhaps . . ."

"No, darlin'. I couldn't eat a morsel. Not even bread . . . not unless it was fresh and hot right from the oven. I always did relish fresh-baked bread."

The bread Maddie had to offer was at least three days old and *needed* warm milk to go down easy. She felt a pang of guilt, as though his lack of appetite was somehow *her* fault.

"Tomorrow or the next day I'll bake bread," she promised, wondering how she'd fit it all in to a schedule that already had her rising before dawn and seeking her bed long after sunset.

"You're so good to me, Maddie." He lifted his arm and peered at her with bloodshot eyes. "You've always been such a good girl—so responsible and kind. My sweet little Maddie, my wee, red-headed, horse-lovin' darlin' . . ."

His lucidity fueled a small spark of hope, and Maddie rushed to take advantage of the rare occasion. "I do my best, Pa, but sometimes my best isn't good enough. Sometimes, I make mistakes, and then I don't know what to do. Just recently, for example, I . . ."

"Don't worry about it," he interrupted, waving a hand to brush off her concern. "If you've got troubles, you'll think of a way out of 'em, Maddie. You always do."

"But Pa, this time I . . ."

"So tired," he groaned. "So damn tired."

Closing his eyes, he turned his face away from the light, and Maddie realized he wasn't listening anymore. He had retreated to wherever it was he went when he didn't want to hear what she was saying—what any of them were saying.

"Pa!" she whispered, stricken, wishing she could draw him back again. Wishing he would be the man he had always been—the laughing, charming figure of her youth who could solve any problem, answer any challenge, and win any argument. He'd always had time for her then and never shut her out, as he did so often lately.

"Love you, Maddie," he responded so softly she could barely hear him. "Love you, girl . . ."

Then he was gone again, breathing in the slow cadences of sleep, completely unaware that she still stood there, her throat choked with tears and her heart breaking.

"Oh, Pa," she sighed, reaching for the lamp.

Slowly, battling worry, fatigue, and sorrow, she took the lamp and departed the room.

Four

"My dear Miss McCrory! Do come in. . . . Why, you look so charming this morning. Is that a new bonnet? I don't believe I've seen you wear it before."

As Horace Brownley took Maddie's hand and ushered her into his private office in the Hopewell Savings and Trust, she couldn't help wondering if he was mentally figuring the cost of her new acquisition and wondering how she could afford it. Perhaps it had been a mistake, after all, to wear it.

He led her over to the straight-backed wooden chair in front of his large desk. The desk shone with a rich patina rarely seen in Hopewell's motley collection of clapboard buildings or in its surrounding farms and ranches. Other than the huge desk adorned with a scattering of documents, and a brass-trimmed wall clock hanging on the wall behind it, the office held few furnishings, but what it contained was of the highest quality. A shiny brass spittoon stood in one corner near the window that overlooked a small side street, and a thick red and blue rug graced the floor.

Otherwise, the room was empty—save for the imposing, black-clad figure of Horace Brownley who more than filled it. Maddie cast a quick glance at his impeccable clothing. In a town where even at funerals, men rarely appeared in suits, vests, and shiny shoes, Horace Brownley looked out of place. Maddie imagined that he dressed so ostentatiously because it proclaimed a position of importance to anyone who saw him.

A bit in awe of him, she struggled to remember that he wasn't nearly as important as he wanted to be. Like many others, he had come to Hopewell hoping to get rich when the town became a thriving cattle center, but the railroad—and the trade—had gone to Abilene instead. In Abilene, Dodge City, or Ellworth, Horace Brownley would have been a king-maker and empire builder; in Hopewell, he was merely the town banker and the mayor, the latter because no one else wanted the non-paying position.

"To what do I owe the pleasure of this visit?" he inquired when Maddie had seated herself in front of the desk. He took his own seat behind the gleaming wood expanse and peered at her through the wire spectacles perched on the bridge of his broad nose. "Dare I hope you have come to town to settle the matter of your overdue mortgage payments?"

"Well, no, um . . . actually, I came on another matter, Mr. Brownley."

"Horace. Do call me Horace, my dear Miss McCrory . . . Maddie. Come now, why do you look so unhappy? Didn't you have a match race scheduled for last Saturday? I regret I wasn't here to witness your victory. I had business in Abilene and only just returned to town late last evening."

He hadn't heard that Gold Deck had lost. She *was going to have to tell him.*

"We didn't win the race, Mr. Brownley. However, we have another race set up in Salina next weekend. I have no doubt we'll win that one. And others. The racing season is just beginning, and I'm certain I'll be able to pay you everything we owe you—with interest—by the time it ends. That's not the problem. The problem is . . ."

She paused, unable to say it.

"Yes?" Horace Brownley leaned forward, the welcoming smile gone from his face. "Do spit it out, my dear. I'm waiting with bated breath."

"I need two thousand dollars immediately—today—to cover my losses from last Saturday."

A long moment of silence, punctuated only by the ominous ticking of the clock, followed Maddie's announcement.

"You put up money you didn't—don't—have on last Saturday's race?"

Loath to admit it, Maddie slowly nodded. "I was sure we would win, Mr. Brownley—Horace. Nearly everyone else expected us to win also. You know our stallion's reputation; had you been in town, you yourself might have bet on him."

"Undoubtedly, I would have. What a relief I missed the opportunity. But surely, you know it's the height of recklessness and fiscal irresponsibility to bet money you don't have on the outcome of a horse race."

"Of course, I know it. . . . But what was I to do? Match racing is our main source of income. It's our family business, and we've always done exceedingly well in it. Nothing else—not the breeding or trading of horses, not our modest efforts at ranching—have ever yielded the same profits. I'm not telling you anything of which you aren't already aware . . . Horace. So of course I *had* to accept the challenge, whether or not I had the money in hand at the moment, which unfortunately, I did not."

"You bet two thousand dollars you don't have." He seemed dumbfounded by the mere notion. "What did your father do all winter? Didn't he follow his usual custom of hunting ducks and geese and shipping them in barrels out of Abilene to the Eastern markets? He always made a tidy little sum on that venture, did he not?"

In years past, Big Mike had often taken Little Mike and gone hunting in the Cheyenne Bottoms during the winter, augmenting the family's income during the time of year when no money came in from match racing. Prior to Ma's death, all of his pursuits had been successful, but this year . . .

"Pa wasn't well enough to hunt this past winter, and I refused to let Little Mike go by himself. That's one of the reasons why we've fallen behind in our mortgage payments, and I don't have the money to pay the winner of Saturday's race."

"Your sire—I mean your father, not your stallion—is a good-for-nothing, self-indulgent, old rascal, Miss McCrory. It's high time he stops grieving for your mother and faces up to his responsibilities."

Maddie longed to punch Horace Brownley in the nose, as Little Mike had punched Amos Graft for saying almost the exact same thing. But she knew it wouldn't help her case; she *had* to convince the banker to aid her. Besides, much as she resented him for saying it, she agreed that her father's grief *had* passed the point of being reasonable.

"Be that as it may, Mr. Brownley, I do not have the funds to pay my debt to Mr. Chase Cumberland, and he is coming to my house this very afternoon to collect his winnings."

"Nor do you have the funds to make your overdue mortgage payments!"

Or pay my taxes, Maddie defiantly added—but silently, so he couldn't hear her.

Mr. Brownley ponderously rose to his feet, came around the side of the desk, and began to pace up and down in front of the closed window. Grasping hands behind his back, he paced first one way, then the other, precisely four steps in each direction. Maddie sat frozen and numb, fearing the worst, until he finally stopped and turned to her, betraying in every aspect his extreme agitation. His cheeks were as red as Lily Tolliver's gown, sweat beaded on his forehead, and patches of dampness had spread beneath the armpits of his very proper coat. Feeling half-suffocated herself, Maddie wished he would open the window to admit the fresh air of the sweet June morning.

"Miss McCrory, there is only one way out of this abominable situation," he pompously intoned.

"And what might that be?" Maddie hoped he meant to loan her the money without making her beg for it.

"You must marry someone of means—a man who also has the discipline and will power you sorely lack. Someone able to take your irresponsible family in hand and resolve these thorny problems."

"Marry!" In her astonishment, Maddie tilted back her chair and would have gone crashing to the floor had Mr. Brownley not caught it and righted her.

A feverish glint appeared in his little blue eyes. "I've been meaning to say something to you for quite some time. I have not done so out of respect for your family's loss and the role you have had to assume since your mother's untimely passing."

"What role do you mean?" Maddie had a sinking feeling she knew where this conversation was heading, and she desperately hoped to forestall their arrival at that dreaded destination.

"Since your mother's death, you have had to take everything on yourself, dear girl, while your reprobate father sinks deeper and deeper into the pit of his own making. The only way out of your present predicament is for you to begin living your own life and forcing your father and his other children to live theirs, whatever that life might be."

Maddie half rose from her chair. "If you are suggesting I run out on my family, abandon them in their hour of need . . ."

His large, pudgy hands—soft and white as cabbage slugs—gently pushed her down again. "No, no . . . not quite. I am putting this badly, I suspect, but what I am suggesting is that you marry me and . . ."

"Marry *you!*" Maddie squeaked. "Mr. Brownley, I don't even know you, much less entertain any inclination to marry you!"

"Yes, but all that can change, my dear. I am, as you know, a bachelor. In my efforts to achieve power and success, I have had no time to waste—I mean, expend—on women or marriage. Lately, however, I find myself earnestly contemplating taking a wife and producing heirs to my modest kingdom. In that regard, Hopewell has little to offer—with the sole exception of *you,* Miss McCrory."

"Me?" Maddie could hardly push the word past the huge lump in her throat. Even her chest felt constricted, as if someone had pulled her stays too tight, only she wasn't wearing a corset.

"Yes, you. Considering the lack of unmarried females in this part of the country, I've had my eye on you for at least several months, if not years, and I have discovered a great deal about you. To begin with, you are sober, sane, and industrious. You rarely smile, which might deter some men, but not me, since I abhor frivolity in a female. You are intensely loyal, a quality that does you as much harm as good, and also too kindhearted and indulgent by far. I am, however, willing to overlook these small defects, for you are of an age when domestic pursuits should appeal to you, and if you are provided the right setting, I am certain you will blossom like a flower in the sun with all the necessary feminine virtues I require in a wife."

Maddie didn't know whether to laugh or cry. She chewed her lower lip to keep from doing either. She wondered what Horace Brownley would think when he heard about the race *she* had ridden. He certainly knew little or nothing of her day-to-day activities, which centered around horses not housekeeping. His assumption that she possessed no sense of humor stung, for in happier years, she had laughed as much as—if not more—than most people. It was only in the last year that she had found little to encourage levity.

"You are not unattractive," he continued after a moment. "Especially in that pretty blue bonnet that conceals the rather garish shade of your hair."

"Garish?" Maddie's hackles rose. She was offended that he should mention the color of her hair with as little tact as one of her sisters. "Shall I also wear a bonnet in the bedchamber—or would you prefer I place a burlap bag over my head every night before I approach the bed?"

"What?" Mr. Brownley blinked like a startled owl.

"Nothing, sir. I was making a small joke, that's all."

A frown beetled his bushy brows again. "Do not make light of my proposal, my dear. Might I remind you that you have come here to voice a need for funds, and instead, I have offered a great deal more—security, respect, and status in the community, as well as freedom from financial worries. If you agree to marry me, I will of course assist your kinfolk in this present crisis, though I don't promise to spend the rest of my life—*our* lives—rescuing your family from every misfortune they bring down upon their own heads."

Maddie sought to curb her flaring temper. "Forgive me, Mr. Brownley," she said in a brittle, controlled voice. "I am indeed flattered by your interest, but a proposal isn't at all what I expected. Besides, you make it sound so . . . so devoid of emotion. Like a business proposition rather than a union of two loving hearts. I am stunned, sir. Actually, stunned is too mild a word for what I am feeling at this moment."

"I see I have caught you by surprise. And in truth, I never meant to approach you in this crude fashion. It merely seemed to me we might possibly suit each other. I am a great deal older than you, of course, but . . ."

"I have just turned twenty-two."

Mr. Brownley's frown deepened. "Twenty-two already? Why, I mistook you for being much younger—but age doesn't really matter, does it? Let us say we are both at that stage in life when we must take care to look after our own best interests, before all hope for the future is gone. *I* represent your best interests, Maddie. Marry me, and I'll release you from the fetters that bind you now."

"Mr. Brownley, I don't regard my family in the same light as fetters that bind me. We have our difficulties, yes, but I am quite fond of my brother and my sisters—and my father, too, no matter how irresponsible he may seem to outsiders. At present, we may be destitute or close to it, but I anticipate our condition to be temporary, and . . ."

"Miss McCrory, you *need* me," Horace Brownley rudely interrupted. "Why else did you come here if not to presume upon my good will toward you? Why did you wear that new bonnet, if not to draw attention to your femininity?"

"I came in the hopes of borrowing money, sir, not to ensnare a husband!"

About to launch into a blistering tirade, Maddie hesitated long enough to weigh the consequences. She had no intention of ever marrying Horace Brownley, but neither did she wish to alienate the man. He didn't seem the type to take a woman's rejection lightly, and she could not afford to have him as an enemy. Keeping a firm grip on her emotions, she clutched her hands together in her lap and carefully cleared her throat.

"It's kind of you to make the . . . the offer of marriage, Mr. Brownley, but I . . . I need more time to consider the matter. We should both get to know one another better. And in the meantime,

I must still meet my financial obligations. Please, Mr. Brownley—Horace, can't we separate the two issues?"

"Separate them? You are saying you wish to enjoy a period of courtship before setting the date for our nuptials?"

"Yes, that's a good way of putting it."

"And you want the money in any case."

Maddie nodded, but nearly choked on her humiliation. "I . . . I should be able to pay you back by the end of the season. I'm not asking you to *give* me the money, you understand. I *will* repay you."

"All right, my dear, the Hopewell Savings and Trust will loan you two thousand dollars at the going rate of interest. Furthermore, it will grant you until the end of the racing season to raise the money to repay your loan *and* resume your mortgage payments."

"I won't have to make my regular payments during that time period?" Maddie croaked. Now, all she would have to worry about was paying her taxes!

"No, my dear. However, the interest will continue to accrue on the ones already overdue. Whatever my compassionate inclinations, I must uphold the integrity of my position."

"Oh, Mr. Brownley—Horace!" Swept with exuberant relief, Maddie bolted from the chair and hugged the man, knocking his spectacles off his nose in the process. "Thank you, thank you, kind sir!"

Before she could reach down to retrieve them, Horace Brownley wrapped his arms around her waist, pulled her to him like a grizzly about to maul a lamb, and planted a big wet kiss on her open mouth. Maddie was too startled to resist. By the time she came to her senses, he had backed off—red-faced and puffing, but also looking inordinately pleased with himself.

"Well, my dear!" he exclaimed. "This is quite a day—quite a day, if I do say so myself."

Maddie wanted nothing so much as to wipe her mouth and rid herself of the taste of his unwelcome kiss, but she suddenly realized she had asked for it. "Yes, it is," she weakly agreed, wondering if he thought she had actually consented to marry him. But no, she hadn't said a word to that effect, nor would she. All she had done was thank him for his generosity and consent to a period of courtship, at the end of which, when the time was right, she would extricate herself from this mess as gently as possible.

"Now, about next Saturday . . ." he said, beaming down at her.

"Next Saturday?" Gold Deck's race was scheduled for Sunday afternoon, and she needed Saturday to prepare for it. Actually, they should journey to Salina on Saturday so that the stallion would be well rested for the race on the following day.

"Have you forgotten? It's the town social. And I expect you to accompany me, Maddie. It will be the perfect opportunity to let everyone know of our intentions."

"Our intentions." The words fell on her ears like heavy blows, knocking her half silly. She should object right now—set him straight regarding her own intentions, which did *not* parallel his.

"Do wear your pretty new hat. It makes your eyes look so very blue."

"Does it?" Maddie stepped back from him, lowering her head so that the brim of her bonnet hid her expression.

Oh, Lord! She would have to endure this pretense of courting or risk rousing his anger. She must do nothing to cause him to reconsider making the loan to which he had just agreed. They'd have to leave home in the middle of night and travel in darkness to Salina, but she couldn't say no to his plans for Saturday.

He reached out and tilted up her chin, forcing her to look at him. "You have rendered me a happy man, today, my dear. Thus, it pleases me to see *you* happy. Tell Mr. Chase Cumberland to stop by the bank at his convenience, and I shall see that he gets his winnings."

"I would prefer taking the money with me. I assured him I would have it by this afternoon."

"You did? . . . Then I am not so far wrong in thinking you have plotted and planned the outcome of today's little visit, am I?" He looked disgustingly smug.

I never plotted and planned to become your betrothed, Maddie screamed from the depths of her being.

"I . . . I had simply hoped to persuade you to come to my aid."

"And so I shall, in my own particular manner, my sweet little prairie flower."

Prairie flower? Now, he was becoming maudlin!

Fearing she might be sick to her stomach, Maddie ducked her head to avoid another kiss. "All right, I will do as you suggest and send him to the bank to collect his winnings. Thank you again, Mr. Brownley. Now, I really must be on my way."

"Horace . . . Especially now, you must remember to call me Horace." Grabbing her hand, he pressed it to his full, wet lips. "Until Saturday, dearest. I'll come fetch you in my buggy. Does half past the hour of three suit you? It's a goodly distance from your place to town, and the social begins promptly at six. I must be there at the appointed hour to commence the activities with a welcoming speech—part of my duties as mayor, you understand."

"I understand. That . . . that will be fine." Maddie snatched back her fingers, stuck them behind her back, and wiped them on a fold of her skirt, where he couldn't see what she was doing.

"Excellent." He saw her to the door, and she fled through it.

"Miss McCrory!" a familiar voice summoned from the front yard.

In the house, where she was up to her elbows in flour, Maddie froze. It couldn't be time for her meeting with Chase Cumberland; it was only three o'clock. What was he doing here a full hour ahead of time? She hadn't yet decided what to say to him—how to explain that he must return to town and go to the bank to get his money. He'd be angry about that, she suspected. Might even accuse her of trying to avoid paying him.

She brushed a strand of hair from her eyes, realized she was smudging her cheek with flour, and began scrubbing her hands on her apron. She had intended to clean up before he came, and now there was no time. He had caught her in the middle of baking bread, a chore she had undertaken in hopes of tempting her father's nonexistent appetite. Drat it all! She was totally unprepared for another confrontation with the disturbing Mr. Cumberland.

Well, I suppose I'll have to talk to him, ready or not, she thought rebelliously and marched out onto the porch.

"You're early, sir!" She blinked against the glare of sunlight that bathed him in radiant splendor.

He looked twice as dark, handsome, and wicked this afternoon as he had when she first met him. Dressed all in black—shirt, vest, fringed leather chaps, Stetson, and boots—he sat on his sleek, golden mare with a casual grace that made her furious about the race all over again. Had she seen him ride beforehand, she would never have consented to accept his challenge. He and the mare had developed that fluid harmony that made them seem like one being, rather than two separate entities. She had first noticed it on the day of the race itself, but had hoped that his greater weight would prove to her advantage. It hadn't, and the fact still nettled her.

"I said you're early," she repeated, thinking perhaps he was deliberately ignoring her greeting.

"I heard you," he calmly disputed. "But I was too stunned by your appearance to answer you immediately."

She straightened her shoulders and glared at him, wishing she had a frying pan she could throw at his head if he dared make another insulting comment. Horace Brownley had already insulted her enough for one day with his remark about her "garish" hair.

"What's wrong with my appearance?" She swiped self-consciously at her flour-smudged cheek. "I'm baking bread at the moment. I don't have time to worry about how I look."

He grinned—one of his dazzling, unexpectedly charming grins that caught at her heart and twisted it painfully. "I'm just surprised to see you in a nice white apron, like a normal female, instead of decked out in your brother's britches. As for the flour on your face, I rather like it—makes you more human. I can talk to you better when you're not being so prim and proper. Or so full of venom."

"Aren't you going to mention my hair?" she retorted. "Haven't you some outrageously brilliant comment to make about the color of my curls?"

Squinting at her hair, he eased down from the saddle. "No, Miss McCrory. Your hair looks fine—red as a bonfire. Hasn't changed any since the last time I saw it. And neither has your attitude."

"My attitude?" She moved closer to the steps. Now that he had dismounted, and she stood on the porch above him, they were at eye level, and he wasn't quite so intimidating.

"I see you're still on the prod, Miss McCrory. You haven't got much use for me or anybody else, have you?"

"I haven't much use for *you.* But we've already been over that. Now, about your money . . ."

"Yes, about my money . . ." Dropping his mare's reins on the ground, he came halfway up the steps toward her, his fancy spurs jingling. "I've a proposition to make to you."

Suspicion flowered in her breast. "What sort of proposition?"

"You know that field of yours that abuts the Parker place?"

Maddie nodded. The field was a broad sweep of grassland where she and Little Mike often exercised the horses. A creek ran through a corner of it, and it had but one tree—a huge old gnarled thing, one of the few trees around, where a body could enjoy a slice of shade on a hot summer's day.

"Of course, I know it," she added churlishly. "Did you think I wouldn't?"

His grin flashed again. "Oh, I suspect you know all there is to know about most everything," he taunted. "Or if you don't know, you make it a point to find out."

"What about that field?"

"I want to buy it. In fact, I'd be willing to settle for the land instead of the money I won last Saturday—especially if you throw in a free breeding or two to your stallion. That would sweeten the deal considerably."

"I'm sure it would! But that field isn't for sale, Mr. Cumberland. We cut hay off it to see our stock through the winter, so there's no way we'd sell it to you or anyone else. Why would you even want it?"

He was almost nose to nose with her now—so close she could see the gold and brown flecks in his eyes that gave them their peculiar amber color, smell the heady aroma of leather and man, and sense the heat of his lithe, masculine body. In response, her own body quickened, as if a part of her that she had never before acknowledged was suddenly awakening.

"Because—as of first thing this morning—I'm your new neighbor. I bought the old Parker place sight unseen, and now that I've ridden out to see it, I realize it isn't quite big enough for what I have in mind. I want the field to go along with it."

Unable to hide her surprise and dismay, Maddie staggered back from him. "Well, you can't have it! It belongs to us, and we plan to keep it. Maybe you should have thoroughly examined the Parker place before you made up your mind to purchase it. Buying a farm without seeing it is a very risky thing to do."

"I didn't need to see it to buy it; I spoke to enough people in town to determine it was fit for my needs. However, when I saw the field, I knew I wanted it, too. Two thousand dollars is more than a fair price for it. I doubt you could get that much from anybody else around here. I'm only willing to go that high so long as you understand that I'm a man who values his privacy. I won't tolerate any trespassing on the land once it belongs to me. Neighbors or not, you'll have to mind the boundaries and not come snooping around my place where you're not welcome."

"Why, you . . . you . . ." Once again, words failed Maddie. She couldn't think of anything vile enough to call him and greatly regretted not having the two thousand dollars in hand so she could fling it in his face in a grand gesture of contempt.

"Your money is safe in the bank in Hopewell," she managed to get out. "The bank president, Mr. Horace Brownley, wouldn't allow me to travel about the countryside with that much cash on my person, so you'll have to go there to get it. Just pretend it's another match race, and you'll be halfway to town before you know it. In any case, I'd like you to clear off *my* land, Mr. Cumberland. I've had about all of your high-handedness I can endure, and . . ."

A shrill scream rent the golden air, causing the mare to throw up her head and sidestep, swiveling her body so she could see in the direction of the sudden commotion.

"What the . . . ?" Chase Cumberland jumped off the steps and grabbed the mare's reins before she could bolt—a good thing, for shouts and another scream told Maddie that something awful was happening behind the house by the barn.

The excited whinny of a horse mingled with the sound of human voices, and from the guttural noises that followed Maddie knew that Gold Deck must be involved. She half expected the stallion to come charging around the side of the house, tail and mane flying, nostrils dilated as they did when he scented a mare in season.

"It's Gold Deck," she breathed. "Something's wrong. Little Mike better not be trying to breed that stallion without me. If I've told him once, I've told him a thousand times: He's to wait until I can assist before he allows that stallion within ten feet of a mare."

Rushing down the steps, praying she wasn't too late and that no one had gotten hurt, she picked up her skirts and flew in the direction of the barn.

Five

Chase wrapped Bonnie Lass's reins once around the porch railing and sprinted after Maddie McCrory. The farm's outbuildings, built of sturdy limestone block like the house, stood in a slight hollow a quarter mile or more downwind of the main structure. Chase couldn't see what was happening until he rounded the chicken house and poultry yard. The screaming and whinnying were coming from the open area in front of the stable, and the first thing Chase spotted was one of Maddie's sisters down on the ground doing her best to dodge the flying hooves of a madly bucking mare. Amazingly, the girl wouldn't let go of the animal's lead rope. Instead, she clung to it for dear life, putting herself in grave danger of being trampled to death.

Before Chase could do anything to rectify the situation, Maddie shouted precisely what he was thinking. "Let go of her! For God's sake, let go, Carrie, so she can get away!"

A youth—probably Maddie's brother—stood off to one side, grimly gripping the lead rope of a rearing and highly aroused Gold Deck. Determined to mount his elusive quarry despite the distinct possibility of getting kicked in the teeth for his efforts, the stallion seemed oblivious to anything or anyone but the bucking mare. He stood on his hind legs, pawed the air, and emitted a piercing scream. Gone was the well-mannered horse of race day; this was a fourteen-hundred-pound breeding machine responding to the call of nature.

Leaving Maddie to deal with the obstinate girl, Chase dove for the stallion, grabbed the lead line out of the young man's hands, and dragged the frustrated stud in the direction of the open stable doors.

The stallion fought him, flinging him about like a piece of kindling wood, but Chase hung on and managed to loop the rope around the animal's sensitive nose. Fashioning a slip knot that tightened every time the stallion pulled against him, Chase further demonstrated his authority by twisting the nearest ear he could grab. Gold Deck squealed in indignation, but, distracted from his main goal, finally allowed himself to be hustled down the barn aisle and into a large, sturdy stall.

As soon as he was inside it, Chase shut the heavy wooden gate and secured it, leaving the stallion to whinny his fury and batter the sides of the stall in aggravation. By the time Chase returned to the front yard, the mare had stopped bucking and was standing perfectly still, her sides heaving, looking for all the world like a trembling virgin rescued from brutal rape. The girl had regained her feet and was loudly weeping, while Maddie frantically checked her over for broken bones. The boy—who already appeared to have come out the worst in a fistfight—glowered at all of them.

Thinking how close they had all come to disaster, Chase laced into the two young people with a fury. "Just what in hell did you two think you were doing? Don't you have any better sense than to get between a stud and a mare he's trying to breed?"

"That's what we were trying to do—breed her. It's Carrie's fault we had all this trouble. She didn't keep the mare in the proper position." The young man squinted at Chase out of a partially swollen blue, black, and yellow eye.

"She shouldn't have been holding the mare at all!" Chase thundered. "That mare could have kicked her in the head. She wasn't ready to breed—or else she wouldn't have been bucking."

"Gold Deck thought she was ready—and he's usually right," the boy retorted. "If me or Maddie had been holding her, this never would have happened."

"I didn't want to hold the dumb old mare anyway," Carrie wailed. "You said it would be easy. You said she'd just spread her legs and stand there, and you'd keep control of Gold Deck.

It's not *my* fault—it's yours. You should have taken him away when you saw she didn't want it."

"Neither one of you should have *attempted* this without me," Maddie McCrory erupted. "Little Mike, I've told you time and again; I don't want Carrie or Zoe involved in the breeding end of the business. You should have waited until *I* could help you, and considering your recent injuries I wouldn't have attempted it today regardless of how ready the mare was. Don't tell me you're not still hurting; I can see by your eyes that you are."

"Are all of you completely witless?" Chase hollered to get everyone's attention. "Breeding horses is no business for women or children. *None* of you should have attempted this today or any other day. It's far too dangerous."

"I ain't no kid," the boy resentfully informed him. "I hold mares all the time when we breed 'em. And Maddie usually holds Gold Deck. Sometimes, like t'day, both Gold Deck and the mare act up, but what else are we supposed to do? We gotta get the job done. Only this time, Maddie was busy in the house, so I asked Carrie t' come out and help. I gave her the easy job. How was I supposed to know she'd get all nervous and do everything wrong?"

"You do this all the time?" Chase was incredulous. "You're lucky one of you hasn't gotten killed long before this. Why don't you just put the mare and the stallion together in a corral and let them mate the way God intended?"

"Because we can't risk Gold Deck getting kicked or hurt by a reluctant mare like this one. . . . Look, Mr. Cumberland. We know what we're doing," Maddie argued in a tone cold as ice. "Little Mike and I take care of everything. Usually the mares cooperate, and Gold Deck is exceedingly polite and well mannered. Only occasionally does . . ."

"Polite! He didn't look polite to me. And what about this crazy mare? What have you got to say about her? She wasn't even hobbled."

"Poor baby." Maddie McCrory stroked the mare's sweaty side. "It was her first time. She was just scared."

"So was I," Carrie sniffled. "It was my first time, too. I know

I was supposed to keep her hind end toward Gold Deck, but I couldn't make her stand still, and then Little Mike started hollering at me, and . . . and . . ." She sighed dramatically. "That's when the mare started bucking. I was afraid she was going to hurt Gold Deck; that's why I hung on so long."

"She might have hurt *you,"* Chase grimly pointed out. "Maiden mares will often buck or kick, even when they're ready to be bred. They aren't sure what it's all about yet, and they get too excited when the stallion comes near them. Did you even bother to test her readiness *before* you brought the two of them together?"

"Sure, I did," the boy protested. "I led Gold Deck down the barn aisle past her. That's how we usually tease mares. We can tell when they're ready by how they . . ."

"I said we *know* what we're doing, Mr. Cumberland," Maddie McCrory haughtily interrupted. "We're grateful for your help getting Gold Deck into his stall, but please don't trouble yourself any further on our behalf. Carrie will not be holding any more mares in the near future. She and Little Mike have seen the error of their ways, I'm sure."

"The *last* thing you know is what you're doing," Chase countered. "But it's hard to teach fools a blessed thing when they think they know it all."

He was so angry and appalled by what he had just witnessed that he wanted to take the two young people over his knee and wallop some sense into them. As for Maddie McCrory . . . well, she was worse than the other two put together. He couldn't imagine her holding a stallion during the dangerous breeding process. Hell, she was so prim and proper she probably closed her eyes in the middle of it! What could she be thinking to take such chances with her own life and that of her siblings?

He himself had discovered there were better, more enlightened ways of managing horse breeding, but it wasn't up to him to share his expertise or build them a chute like the one he had specially designed back in Texas, so that humans didn't *have* to hold the mare and stallion when they brought them together for breeding. She and her damn family weren't *his* problem; he had problems enough of his own. Besides, as little as she apparently thought of him, Maddie McCrory wouldn't listen to him anyway.

"Where did you say my money was?" he snarled.

"In town at the bank," Maddie responded, her blue eyes snapping. Apparently, she didn't like the change of subject any more than the argument they had been having. "But you'll have to wait until tomorrow to get it. By the time you ride back to town, the bank will be closed for today."

"You do about as poor a job of paying your debts as you do breeding horses," Chase snorted, hitching up his pants. "I sure hope you're better at baking bread than you are at pretending to be a man."

"I don't pretend to be a m-man!" she sputtered indignantly. "Nor would I want to be one. From what I've seen, men are the most stupid, stubborn, ornery creatures God ever put on the face of this earth, you included, Mr. Cumberland." Then, with a sideways glance at Little Mike, she amended: "Except for you, Mike—though sometimes I wonder even about you."

"Thanks for your impartial, unbiased, fair-minded assessment," Chase drawled in a deliberately insulting manner. "Having met me only a day or two ago, you sure form opinions in a hurry."

"I am an excellent judge of character, and yours, sir, is sorely lacking!" Miss McCrory tossed her outrageously red hair, which today was drawn back from her temples, loosely pinned in place, and spilling down her back in a fiery waterfall.

"Maddie!" Carrie hissed, looking scandalized.

Chase had a sudden irrational desire to plunge his fingers into Miss McCrory's red hair, pull out all the precariously placed pins, and see for himself what the damn stuff felt like in his hands. Would it be soft, feminine, and silky—or springy, untameable, and full of life, like Miss McCrory herself? . . . Lord, but she had a way of distracting him with her odd, prickly, haphazard femininity!

"I see no need to mince words, Carrie," the object of his sudden lusty thoughts continued. "Mr. Cumberland has already proven what sort of man he is. He needn't claim any false concern over our well-being when all he really wants is to obtain a portion of our land at a mere fraction of its worth and breed his mare to Gold Deck for nothing."

All thoughts of exploring Miss McCrory's hair evaporated like mist on a sunny morning. "As I've already pointed out, I offered you a fair deal, Miss McCrory. In fact, it was more than fair. From what I've seen of *your* character, I should have known you'd refuse. You're the most contrary female I've ever run across. Does logic ever enter your mind—or do you rely purely on female instinct and an excess of emotion, however foolish and illogical?"

"I am not emotional! I live and breathe logically. I assess what needs to be done and then I do it." Two spots of hectic color blossomed in Maddie McCrory's cheeks. Her blue eyes shot sparks.

Chase sucked in his breath. When she was angry, Maddie McCrory seemed the most vibrant, thoroughly alive woman he had ever met. She gave off energy like heat radiating from a stove, and he wondered—for the briefest instant—what it would be like to bed such a hellion. If she displayed only half the fierce, pent-up emotion she exuded now, bedding her would be like mating with a wildcat, and his blood boiled just to think of it.

"Meaning you set up match races, ride them yourself if your brother isn't around to do it, risk your neck breeding horses, and scoff at anyone who comes along and offers to help. Is that it? I make you a perfectly reasonable business offer, and you take it as an insult. . . . Oh, that's *logical,* Miss McCrory. How could I think otherwise?"

"I think we have nothing more to say to each other, Mr. Cumberland. Please take your sarcasm elsewhere—and your greedy interest in our land, too. I wouldn't sell that field to you if you offered us *ten* thousand dollars for it."

"But Maddie" said her sister. "If it would mean we wouldn't have to pay Mr. Cumberland two thousand dollars we don't have, maybe we should . . ."

"Absolutely not!" Maddie yelped in the tone of voice of a woman who had gone from mere dislike to outright hatred.

Two thousand dollars they didn't have?

"You said my money's in the bank in Hopewell, Miss McCrory." Chase leveled a look at her that had made men quail in their boots and/or run for their guns. "If it isn't, I'm coming back here with the sheriff, and we'll see about that land you won't sell. Refuse me then, and you'll be on your way to jail."

"You ain't taken my sister t' jail!" Balling his fists, wincing as he did so, Little Mike stepped in front of Maddie.

"Listen, you scrappy young pup." Chase poked Little Mike in the chest. "Your sister owes me money. Hell, all of you owe me money. If you haven't got it, you'd better be prepared to offer something else I want instead. The next man you aim t' cheat might not be as understanding as I am; he'll pull a gun on you if you can't produce the money the same day as the race."

"We *do* have the money!" Maddie McCrory pushed her brother aside. "It's right where I said—in the bank in town. All you have to do is go get it."

"Tomorrow," Chase snorted derisively. "Since you've owed it to me since Saturday, maybe I should charge you three days' interest."

"One of those days was a Sunday, sir. Only a godless heathen would think of charging interest for Sundays."

"So now I'm a godless heathen. Are there any other conclusions you'd care to jump to, or have you had enough exercise for one day?"

"If I think of any more, I'll let you know," the tart-tongued little minx replied.

"Sorry, but I'm leaving." Chase pivoted on his heel and stalked back toward the house. "Be careful you don't choke on your own venom, Miss McCrory."

"What?" she cried, hot on his heels. "What did you say?"

He turned, swept off his hat, and bowed to her. "I said, have a pleasant afternoon, Miss McCrory."

"Good afternoon to you, too, sir." Narrowing her remarkable eyes, she regarded him suspiciously. "Do be careful someone doesn't shoot you in the back on your return trip to town."

"If I do get shot, at least I'll know where to place the blame, won't I?" Grinning to himself, glad she wasn't entirely immune to his barbs, Chase spun around and resumed walking.

It was nearly dark by the time Chase arrived at his newly-bought ranch with his brother, Buck, and their string of horses in tow. In no time at all, they got the small herd of mares and foals settled in their new corral and forked them some dusty but still palatable hay they had found stored in the barn. Chase worked silently alongside his brother, filling the water trough with water he had already determined wasn't the least bit alkaline, unsaddling his tired mount, and rubbing her down before turning her in with the others.

The stars had come out by the time he and Buck finished the outside chores and Buck had examined all the outbuildings, concealing his reaction beneath the brim of his hat. At last, they trudged into the darkened house, and Chase easily located the lamp and matchbox he had set out earlier.

Lighting the lamp, he set it on the round wooden table in the front room of the simple, clapboard house. Due to the scarcity of lumber in the region, the dwelling was modest in size, but it had come almost completely equipped, containing everything old Mr. Parker had owned before he died. The man's needs had been simple, but all the basics were there: furnishings, cupboards, dishes, household utensils, and so forth. Best of all, there were two bedrooms off the main room, allowing for each of them to have their own sleeping quarters. And there were beds in the rooms. One held a large four-poster big enough for two people, while the other contained a smaller, less comfortable bed more suitable for a child than a grown man.

"That's your room over there, Buck." Chase nodded toward the larger room that boasted the bigger bed, a wardrobe, and even a wash stand with a basin and pitcher.

It was probably the room Mr. Parker had occupied until the day he died; the bed still had linens on it—goose down pillows and a patterned quilt that must have been Mrs. Parker's pride and joy. The house held other feminine touches as well—calico curtains at the small windows, a square of yellowed lace in the center of the round table, and some pretty blue and white dishes stacked neatly on the shelves of an open cupboard.

A thick layer of dust lay over everything, but Chase was pleased at what he'd found—a degree of neatness and orderliness that bespoke years of pride in the humble dwelling. He especially liked the large old fireplace, in front of which stood two sturdy rocking chairs, one for each of them. The barn, outbuildings, corral, and adjacent pasture land were why he had bought the place, but he was glad the house suited them as well, and he waited patiently for his brother to express some sign of approval.

Across the room from him, Buck had his back turned. He had bent down to examine an old cradle in the corner. Had the Parkers had children? None had been mentioned, but perhaps they had long since moved away or died. Chase had been told that there were no living relatives; the farm was being sold to cover the taxes which had accumulated over the years since old man Parker's death.

Buck straightened, took off his battered brown Stetson, and unexpectedly flung it at the row of wooden pegs on the wall beside the front door. The hat caught and hung there, and the gesture brought a lump to Chase's throat. Buck had perfected his hat-throwing trick years ago, when the two brothers still had the family ranch in Texas. Chase hadn't seen him toss his hat since, for no place had ever felt enough like home for either one of them to want to hang their hats there.

In that single gesture, Chase read his brother's approval.

"So you think it'll do, huh?" He concealed his glee beneath a knowing smirk.

Buck grinned and nodded, and Chase grinned back to cover how dismayed he still felt at Buck's unusual appearance, even after all these years. In his late thirties, Buck was only four years older than Chase, but looked old enough to be his grandfather.

Snow white hair hung to Buck's shoulders, matching his silvery beard, lashes, and eyebrows. Chase had their father's brownish-gold eyes, but Buck's were a stark gray-blue, the color of their mother's. The unusual hue gave him a wild-eyed look heightened by his white lashes and brows.

In his youth, Buck's hair had been as dark as Chase's, but one day Buck had ridden out in a thunderstorm to help Chase bring in a herd of cattle. Chase had peered through a downpour to see his brother riding toward him across the open range . . . and then a jagged bolt of lightning had ripped open the sky, and the earth itself had nearly split in two.

The horses and cattle had spooked and run. Chase himself had nearly been thrown from the saddle. As soon as he regained his seat, he went looking for Buck and found his older brother lying unconscious on the ground. Buck was barely breathing, and every hair on his body had turned silvery white. Indeed, he had looked like a dead man. Afterward, he'd been unconscious for almost a week. When he awoke, he could see and hear, but couldn't speak. Worse, he was prone to fits of violent trembling and sometimes rolled on the ground and foamed at the mouth. The fits eventually passed, but Buck was no longer the blustery, good-natured, teasing, hard-working, always-laughing companion and friend Chase had looked up to and admired.

He had become a brooding stranger with an unpredictable temper—and no wonder. People thought his wits were addled and treated him as if he had become a simpleton overnight. He hadn't. He just wasn't good with people anymore. Oddly enough, his ability to communicate with animals seemed enhanced, to the point where he appeared to know what a horse or cow was thinking before the animal itself figured it out.

In the course of the past several years, Chase had discovered it was best to keep Buck away from people. This little, abandoned ranch tucked into the folds of one of the few relatively hilly places in all of flat Kansas seemed like the perfect place to do that. It had everything they needed to survive and prosper. Even the landscape around Hopewell reminded Chase of parts of Texas—especially the part where he and Buck had grown to manhood on the family ranch. Following the deaths of their parents, they had been well on their way to becoming rich before fate dealt them that tragic blow. Chase was just damn glad that

Buck liked it, too. They were done running; this was it. From now on, this would be home.

"How about a hot meal to celebrate?" Chase went to a cupboard, opened it, and gestured toward the supplies he had put away earlier that afternoon. "I'm afraid it'll have to be tinned beans tonight, but breakfast should be better, soon as you figure out how to work that stove, big brother."

He took down a bottle of whiskey. "Guess we can have a drink first. Now that the horses are safely bedded down, and we've got a roof over our heads, I see no harm in bending our elbows in a toast or two."

Buck's eyes gleamed at the suggestion, reminding Chase to take care how much liquor he brought into the house. Given half a chance, Buck liked to drown his loneliness in cheap whiskey, but Chase had put a stop to such behavior long before it had gotten out of hand. A celebratory drink was another matter; tonight, Chase felt the need to celebrate.

Grabbing two tin mugs, he set the bottle on the table and pulled out a chair. "Place needs a broom and a mop taken to it, but tomorrow will be time enough for that."

Accustomed to carrying on a conversation for two, Chase did so without awkwardness. He had learned to behave normally rather than allow Buck's disability to turn both of them into a couple of silent, taciturn old bulls. While they sat and made themselves comfortable, he continued a running commentary.

"The Madisons won't find us here. Haven't seen a sign of them or any bounty hunters on our trail for more than a year. I think they've given up by now—don't you? It must appear to 'em as if you've dropped off the face of the earth."

Buck nodded in agreement and lifted his mug in a silent salute before downing its contents. Chase took his time and sipped the fine whiskey. As the liquor burned a pleasant path to his stomach, he thought about Clint Madison and his brother, Luke—who had once been Chase's closest friend. Clint had been a fine-looking man, but a confirmed bully and a braggart to boot. As the oldest son, he had been shamelessly indulged by his wealthy parents and thought he could do whatever he damned well pleased.

That included harassing Buck every chance he got—calling him names, mocking him in public, and just generally amusing himself at Buck's expense. Luke had been a different story; a quiet, thoughtful man, he possessed none of his brother's cruelty or instinct for hurting others. The same age as Chase, Luke had been like a second brother, and when Luke decided to marry, he had invited Chase and Buck to attend the wedding. Chase had worried about taking Buck, but he and Buck had gone, the whiskey had flowed like water, and Clint hadn't been able to resist such a prime opportunity for once again making a fool out of Buck.

Chase couldn't remember how it had all started, but a fight had broken out between Buck and Clint—a fight which had ended tragically when Buck broke a keg of whiskey over Clint's head, rendering him unconscious. At first, no one had been that upset with Buck over the incident. Half of Dallas county had witnessed it, and they all knew how Clint had bullied Buck. Most of the onlookers thought Clint deserved his comeuppance. But three days passed, and without ever waking up, Clint died. Enraged, the grieving Madisons sent a lynch party after Buck—and Luke rode at the head of it. The man who had been Chase's dearest friend was now his worst enemy, a vigilante sworn to kill Chase's brother.

Taking only their horses—a string of fine mares descended from the legendary race horses, Bonnie Scotland and Kentucky Whip—Chase and Buck had fled Texas and the swarm of bounty hunters eager to claim the reward the Madisons had offered for Buck's capture.

During the first couple of years, the brothers had attempted to settle down in various, far-flung places. Running was hard on the horses and made breeding them almost impossible. But each time they thought they had found a new home, something happened to spoil their plans. Buck couldn't seem to stay out of trouble. No matter where he went, he became a target for bullies who found his unusual coloring and inability to speak a good reason for ridicule. They had had to flee more than one town in the dead of night, and if Buck didn't get into trouble on his own, trouble soon found him—in the form of wanted posters that made their way to godforsaken places and into the hands of men only too anxious to make a buck gunning down a man branded as a killer.

"Yep," Chase said, recalling all this. "The best decision we ever made was to keep your existence a secret. It might be lonely, but it's gonna be a good life, Buck. Now, we can breed our mares the way we want to, I can do enough match racing to pay our way, and no one will be the wiser. Buck Courtland has vanished, and nobody's ever heard of the name Cumberland, so as long as we're careful, we can live the life we've always wanted."

Buck set down his mug and made a few hand gestures. *What about women?* he asked in the special sign language that was a combination of Indian lore and the unique mode of communication they had managed to develop over the years.

Chase shook his head emphatically. "No women. We can't risk it, Buck—not even an occasional visit to a whorehouse or saloon, unless it's a long, long way from here."

Buck grimaced, reached for the bottle, and poured more whiskey into his mug. Before his accident, Buck had been a lady-charmer, so he keenly felt the loss of female companionship and sex. At the time of his accident, he had been seriously courting a comely young woman named Ella Mae Cass. Ella Mae had decided that the changes in Buck were too great to be borne and had run off and married another man without even telling him. That experience had embittered not only Buck, but also Chase, who had long ago decided that women, decent or not, couldn't be trusted to remain loyal to a man through thick and thin. . . . Now, Chase himself wanted nothing to do with them.

An occasional tumble with a soiled dove provided all he needed or wanted from the opposite sex, but he was willing to sacrifice even that for the sake of safety and anonymity. If he and Buck got truly desperate, they would have to pick a town far enough away from Hopewell so no one would recognize

Chase or discover that he had spent a night carousing in the company of a mute, silver-haired giant.

"If you get too sick of my face, big brother, we'll go up to Abilene, where a man can buy anything he wants for the right price. First though, we've got to fence the pasture so we can leave the horses—and I want to buy that field I told you about that has a creek cutting through it. With water and good grass, we could leave the place for several days and not have to worry."

Buck signed that Chase should just go buy it, if he wanted it that bad, and Chase saw that he'd have to explain about their neighbors—a topic he had been avoiding.

"I've already tried, but the McCrorys, the folks who own the land, aren't interested in selling. I offered to take the field instead of the money I won last Saturday, but Maddie McCrory wouldn't hear of it. Now I've got to think of some way to soften her up. We really need that field, especially if we plan to start running cattle in the future, as well as breeding horses. . . . Speaking of breeding, I'd like to cross Bonnie Lass with that stallion of hers, too. If he's really the get of old Cold Deck, then joining his line to the Bonnie Scotland line should produce a truly spectacular animal. But I haven't had much luck there either. Miss McCrory seems to hate the sight of me."

How much does she want for a breeding? Buck signed.

"Fifty dollars per mount. That's what I heard in town. For Bonnie Lass, she'll probably demand more. She's real hostile because our mare beat her stallion. Guess she isn't accustomed to losing."

Chase leaned back in his chair, the whiskey warm in his belly, making him mellow and loosening his tongue. "She ought to be a hell of a lot nicer to me, considering how badly she needs money. Her pa's a hopeless drunk who's run up bills all over town. Gossip has it he's dropped a bundle at the local saloon, and Maddie and her siblings are struggling to make ends meet."

Maddie? Buck mouthed, his blue eyes lit with mocking inquiry.

"Miss McCrory," Chase corrected himself, surprised at his own slip of the tongue. "She and her brother and her two young sisters have to do everything—even breed the horses. The old man apparently doesn't lift a finger anymore. The only assistance they can afford is the occasional help of some old half-breed Indian squaw by the name of Pawnee Mary. The squaw's the town whore, I hear, and no other decent family will give her work. Aside from that, bein' an 'Injun' an' all, she's already considered the dregs of local society."

Buck's shoulders shook in a bitter laugh. *You mean she's on a lower level than I am?*

Chase joined in Buck's laughter. "Brother, she's even lower. Folks around here don't have many fond memories of Indians. Most of the tribes have already been run off or shut up on reservations. I don't know how this one escaped the roundup, but the McCrorys are the only ones dumb enough or desperate enough to let her inside their house. Could be she's not a thief, whore, or for that matter, a murderer, but you know how folks think when it comes to Indians."

Or men who look like me.

"Or men who look like you," Chase agreed. "At least an old Injun squaw is still good for something, even if it's just whoring—but an outcast man is truly outcast."

No more, Buck said, shaking his head. *No more. This is our new home, and here we're gonna stay.*

"You got that right, brother." Chase poured more whiskey for himself and Buck, lifted his mug, and clinked it to his brother's. "Here's to our new home—to doing whatever we must to stay here and succeed."

They drank deeply. In the warm haze that followed, anything seemed possible, and Chase resolved to find a way to overcome Maddie McCrory's initial dislike and elicit her cooperation in his future plans.

"If I have to get down on my knees and lick the boots of that feisty little redhead in order to convince her to sell me that field and breed Bonnie Lass to her stallion, I guess I'll do it—with a smile. I'll show her that the Cumberlands aren't the sort of men to take no for an answer."

Is she pretty? A wistful expression crossed Buck's face. *What does she look like?*

"Plain as a snubbin' post," Chase scoffed. "Hair like a prairie fire, freckles too numerous to count, and built like a boy. Old, too. Past her prime they told me in town."

Oughta be just right for you then, Buck signed with a grin.

Chase threw up his hands in protest. "Don't wish her on me, brother. You know how I feel about females; I can ride a good mare all day and all night and think of her as my best friend—but a *woman?* Women are different. They're only necessary when a man's got an irresistible urge; if he wants loyalty, he should stick with his horse."

Buck slapped his knee in silent laughter, and Chase leaned back in his chair and let his thoughts drift. The truth was, Maddie McCrory wasn't his type. Nor did he have a place in his life for a woman. With Buck for a brother, what would he do with a wife? Where would he put one if he had one? . . . Where would he put Buck?

He could just imagine asking a woman to marry him, then bringing her home to meet his brother—and explaining that Buck would always live with them, and folks must never know about him. That would be some wedding present for a new bride!

Abruptly, he sobered, and an image of Maddie McCrory came to mind: blue eyes flashing, red hair flying, cheeks and lips stained a becoming shade of crimson.

She could scarcely be called "plain as a snubbin' post," but he preferred sultry brunettes or milk-white blondes to redheads. Still, she was a compelling sort of female—one he enjoyed watching if for no other reason than to see what she would do or say next . . . and he did like her hair. And her snapping blue eyes. And her pert little bottom. And the way she challenged him every time he saw her.

Her feisty spirit made him want to conquer and tame her, much as a sassy filly intrigued and drew him. Fillies required great sensitivity in their handling; if a man took the time to train them with patience and rewards, rather than trying to bully them, they gave their best in return. But if he made unreasonable demands and used harsh methods, they often as not turned sly and sour, and were likely to kick, bite, buck, or bolt when a fellow least expected it.

Maybe he should handle Maddie McCrory the same way he handled Bonnie Lass—with respect and kindness. It would be interesting to see if she responded like a temperamental horse. He'd never know until he tried. In a week or so, after he got things under control here, perhaps he should ride over and give her more advice about breeding—or better still, show Little Mike how to build a breeding chute.

He had noticed other things that needed doing at the McCrorys, too, but most were tasks that required more than one pair of hands to accomplish. If he made a show of being neighborly and offered to help Little Mike with some of the heavier chores, perhaps Maddie McCrory would reconsider selling him the field and allow him to breed Bonnie Lass and a couple of his other mares to Gold Deck for half the going rate.

It was something to think about. He wouldn't mind seeing Maddie McCrory again either. He wondered if he could get her to smile at him, instead of scowling. During their short acquaintance, he had yet to see her actually curve her lips into a genuine smile. Somehow he knew it would be a rewarding experience—like a ray of sunshine appearing after a week of rain.

Yes, he'd pay the McCrorys another visit in a week or so, and this time, he'd charm Miss Maddie McCrory right down to her little pink toes. Before he left, she'd be begging him to buy her field and cross his mare with her stallion.

He smiled to himself just thinking about it.

Six

"We won, Maddie! This time, we won!" Carrie and Zoe flung their arms around Maddie's neck and almost bumped heads giving her a victory hug.

"Yes, yes, I know! I saw the whole thing, remember? Oh my, I'm so relieved. We do need that thousand dollars in the worst way."

Maddie disentangled herself from her sisters' embrace, leaving them to join hands and dance a wild jig right on the dusty main thoroughfare of Salina, while she hurried to meet Little Mike and congratulate him on a job well done. Like his sisters, her brother was grinning so widely his face was in danger of splitting. Even Gold Deck looked pleased with himself; he pranced up to her, arching his neck and blowing hard through his nostrils as if to say: "See? I've redeemed myself. I'm still the fastest horse in Kansas."

"Good job, Mike—and you, too, my friend." Maddie planted a kiss on the stallion's velvety nose before turning to accept the adulation of the still-excited crowd.

"Guess he knows who's ridin' him today, don't he?" one man called out to her.

Maddie nodded, too pleased to take offense at the notion that Gold Deck did better for Little Mike than he ever would have done for her. It might be true, but she doubted it. She was just thrilled he had lived up to his reputation here in Salina. His easy victory over today's contender made up for his loss against Mr. Cumberland's mare—not financially, of course, but it restored

Maddie's confidence in his speed and ability. He was still at the top of his form, not fading fast as she had feared. His victory also helped to banish the cloud of frustration and despair that had hung over her head all during last night's disastrous outing with Horace Brownley.

Maddie had hated every minute of the banker's company; she had been bored, irritated, annoyed, and embarrassed by turns, particularly disliking the way Horace behaved as though she already belonged solely to him and ought therefore to be admiring his every utterance—silly or otherwise, and abandoning her own opinions on every subject in favor of his.

She had worried the whole time that they wouldn't be ready for the race today in Salina and had begged Horace to take her home early. Citing his duties as mayor, he had refused, then reminded her that from now on, *her* time was *his* time, and she needed to rearrange her priorities. She was thoroughly exhausted from lack of sleep, her stomach still clenched in knots. Only now she could relax and enjoy the soothing effect of triumph. *Gold Deck had won, and her family was a thousand dollars richer.*

"Miss McCrory, ma'am?" a voice said at her elbow. "Kin I speak with you a minute?"

A tall, thin rancher with beady black eyes and a prominent Adam's apple waved one of her own handbills under her nose. "If'n you could give me a moment of yore time, I'd like t' talk t' you about racin' my stallion against yore horse, the one that just won this here race."

"Of course," Maddie said. "But now isn't the best time to talk. I've got to . . ."

"Five thousand dollars, ma'am. I'm willin' t' put up five thousand that my stud can beat yore stud on the paths in Abilene one month from today."

"Five thousand?" Maddie echoed in disbelief. "You want to challenge my horse for five thousand dollars?"

"You hard of hearin', gal? That's what I jus' said."

Maddie recognized a prime opportunity when she heard it. However, she hesitated over the dollar amount, just as she had when Chase Cumberland had mentioned a large stake. However, this man was a far cry from Mr. Cumberland; maybe his horse was a far cry from Bonnie Lass. The offer was certainly worth investigating.

"Just a minute," she said. "Give me a minute, and we'll go someplace and talk. . . . Carrie! Zoe!"

She motioned for her sisters to join her. "I have some business to attend to with this gentleman. Look after Little Mike and Gold Deck, will you? And Pa. Don't let Pa go off celebrating by himself. Keep him at the wagon. I won't be gone long. Now then, Mr. . . . um . . . I don't believe you mentioned your name, sir."

"Gratiot. Lazarus Gratiot. I'm new in these here parts. Just bought me a place near Abilene, and I'm lookin' to campaign my stud 'round here."

"Well, come along, Mr. Gratiot. You couldn't do better to establish your reputation than to race our stallion, who's well known throughout Kansas and the surrounding states. Even if you lose, people will give you credit for challenging us. If they like the looks of your horse and he performs well, they'll think about bringing you their mares."

"I ain't gonna just match him; I'm gonna beat him. That's the main reason I come here—t' make a name fer my horse by beatin' the great Gold Deck. An' I want all Abilene t' see it."

Another boastful braggart, Maddie thought. *Just the kind she loved to beat.*

Less than an hour later, Maddie had cut the biggest deal she or her father had ever made. In one month's time, Gold Deck would race Mr. Gratiot's stallion, One-Eyed Jack, in Salina for five thousand dollars. Heedless of what Horace Brownley would say—or perhaps because she knew very well what the banker would say—Maddie had again bet money she didn't have.

But she had gotten a good look at the horse first, and this one was definitely a loser. His long legs, narrow girth, and modest-sized hindquarters suggested he was incapable of short, powerful bursts of speed and could never win at the quarter-mile distance she had insisted upon. He was also blind in one eye—hence his name, and she intended to have Little Mike race on his bad side, thereby giving Gold Deck the advantage of being able to see his opponent without his opponent seeing him. Some horses only ran well in an effort to keep other horses from passing them, and Mr. Gratiot's stallion might be one of them.

By the time Maddie joined her sisters and brother at the wagon, she was feeling euphoric about the deal. Her only worry concerned Mr. Gratiot's desire to leave the race open for additional entries. He had been most emphatic that if someone else offered to hazard the same money, that person should have the right to enter the race. Maddie had finally agreed to allow for one other contestant, but she hoped no one else would appear. At such high stakes and considering the competition, it wasn't likely. Abilene was more than a day's ride away from home; still, she dreaded the thought of Chase Cumberland somehow getting wind of the race. If he were to enter Bonnie Lass, she'd have reason to worry.

Since Mr. Cumberland hadn't attended *this* race, she suspected that match racing might not be as important to him at the moment as establishing his ranch. If she carefully avoided him over the next month, chances were good he wouldn't hear of the race until it was over. Or if he did hear of it, he wouldn't think about entering it; he would just assume it was a typical, one-on-one match race in which no other contenders were allowed.

The trip home from Salina was a joyous one, with Carrie. Zoe, and Little Mike all laughing and babbling over the victory and making plans for the next race, while Pa slept inside the wagon and Gold Deck trailed it, tied to the back end. As they pulled into the stable yard in the long golden light of early evening, the sound of hammering smote Maddie's ears. As Little Mike drove the team around to the back of the house, she saw that the man wielding the hammer was none other than Chase Cumberland!

In her leap down from the wagon seat, Maddie entangled her skirts in her legs and fell on one knee. Picking herself up and yanking down her skirt, she hollered at the tall, bare-chested man busily engaged in building something next to the barn.

"What do you think you're doing, Mr. Cumberland? How dare you come on our property unannounced and make yourself at home in our backyard constructing Lord-only-knows-what! You made such a big fuss over the possibility of one of us trespassing on *your* land, but you seem to think it's perfectly fine for you to trespass on *our* land. Well, it isn't. I'll thank you to set down that hammer right this minute and go back to wherever you came from."

Hammer still in hand, Chase Cumberland pushed his Stetson back on his head and slowly turned to face her. Maddie gaped at the sight of the wide expanse of hairy, masculine chest, rippling with muscles, that he so carelessly displayed. She had seen a portion of his chest once before, and of course, Little Mike and Pa had often doffed their shirts to chop wood in the heat of summer, but this all-over view of Chase Cumberland's chest affected her in an entirely different manner.

Moreover, the way he looked her over with his hooded, amber eyes that seemed somehow to be *smoldering,* let her know that *he* knew she was greedily looking her fill at him and had noticed him *as a man.*

"I'm not trespassing, Miss McCrory. I've got permission to do what I'm doing."

"I didn't give you permission. And I can't think who else might have done so without telling me."

Maddie glared at each of her sisters and her brother in turn, but they all shrugged, looking as perplexed and confused as she felt.

"When I got here this morning, I encountered a woman—a tall, handsome female by the name of Mary. I explained why I had come, and she told me to go ahead and . . ."

"Where is Mary now?" Maddie demanded, not allowing him to finish. The night before they had left for Salina, Pawnee Mary had come to stay and look after the house and the stock while they were gone. But it wasn't like Mary to invite a stranger onto the premises, and it was also highly unusual that she had not yet come out of the house to greet them and ask about the outcome of the race.

"Damned if I know where she is, Miss McCrory." Still holding his hammer, Chase Cumberland strolled toward her with that limber grace that so reminded her of a wolf. "She doesn't seem to be the sort of wide-eyed female to hang over a man's shoulder, spying on him while he works."

His tone implied that Maddie herself was that sort of woman, and an icy-hot blush spread from the region of her collarbone up to her cheeks and into the roots of her hair. Chase Cumberland would be all too easy to watch; even at this embarrassing moment, Maddie could hardly ignore the splendor of his partial nudity. Rivulets of sweat ran down the sculpted muscles of his bare chest, but instead of being revolted, she was fascinated. The terrain of his torso was so alien to her own—and so intriguing, positively inviting exploration.

As Maddie realized what she was thinking, her face flamed even more, and her reply came out with more asperity than she intended. "I shall tell Mary when she returns that she is remiss in her duties. I never dreamed she would allow a drifter onto our property in our absence."

"I'm not a drifter. I'm your neighbor—whether you like it or not, Maddie."

"*Miss McCrory* to you, *Mister* Cumberland," Maddie bit out.

At that moment, a loud thump came from the back of the wagon. Gold Deck snorted in alarm, and Maddie instinctively whirled to see what dire thing could be happening now. With Chase Cumberland right behind her, she hurried to the rear of the vehicle and—merciful heavens!—saw her father sprawled half in and half out of the back end of the wagon. His foot had caught on the doorjamb, so that he lay with his leg hooked over it, and his hat had rolled beneath Gold Deck's feet.

Fortunately, the stallion had pulled back as far as his lead rope would allow and was doing his best not to step on either the hat or the man.

Grinning stupidly, Pa squinted up at her. "We home yet, Maddie, darlin'? Why's everything upside down and spinnin'?

Damn, but I got me a headache. Sounds like Injun war drums beatin' in my temples."

"Oh, Pa, you've been drinking all the way home, haven't you? And here I thought you were sleeping." Maddie quickly untied Gold Deck and handed his rope to Little Mike who had come around the other side of the wagon.

"Go put Gold Deck in his stall, Mike, while I get Pa into the house." Maddie dropped to her knees beside her father. "Get up, Pa. Come on, I'll help you."

She slid an arm under his armpit, but her father gave a long sigh, closed his eyes, and seemed content to lie right where he was, half in and half out of the wagon.

"Girls, come here! I need your help. Carrie, you lift one leg, Zoe, you get the other, and I'll take his hands . . ."

"Out of the way, all of you."

In a single, swift, fluid motion, Chase Cumberland dropped down on one knee, gathered the older man in his arms, and lifted him—cradling him effortlessly as if he weighed no more than a sack of grain.

"Where do you want him? Lead the way," he said to Maddie.

"Girls, see to the team." Maddie hurried to walk in front of Chase toward the house. "Make sure all the horses are fed, watered, and rubbed down, and put everything away while you're at it. Oh, and don't forget the rest of the barn chores either—remind Little Mike."

The girls groaned behind her, but Maddie didn't look at either of them as she marched toward the house with Chase Cumberland in tow. Having her drunken father tumble out of the back end of the wagon utterly mortified her. Her only recourse was to keep her head high and pretend nothing embarrassing was happening—but, oh, she was embarrassed!

She led Mr. Cumberland inside the shadowy interior and into the downstairs bedroom her parents had shared for so many years. Chase deposited her father on the creaking bed, then straightened and looked at her closely in the semi-gloom. "You're damn good at giving orders to your sisters and brother," he commented. "So how come you let your pa get away with *this?"*

He jerked his head in the direction of her snoring, intoxicated father. "Such behavior is a disgrace to all of you. I can't think why you put up with it."

His upper lip curled in a gesture of contempt that released all of Maddie's defensive feelings in one huge outburst. "Do you think I *allow* or encourage this?" she screamed at him. "Do you actually believe he was *always* this way?"

"Was he?" Chase Cumberland's tone held no pity. "He ought to be ashamed of himself—and you should be ashamed for permitting it."

"What do you expect me to do?" Maddie choked out in an agonized whisper. "He never drank like this before my mother died. Oh, he always enjoyed his 'wee nips,' as he called them, but it was only after her death that the wee nips got bigger and bigger until he was consuming half a jug at one sitting. . . . I've pleaded with him and begged him to stop or at least moderate his drinking, but nothing I say has any effect on him anymore. Oh God, I don't know what to do . . ."

"Take the jugs away," Chase snapped. "Pour them out or destroy them. Lock him out of the house when he's drunk. Make him face up to what he's doing not only to himself but to you and your brother and sisters. You're allowing him to wallow in self-pity, and as long as you let him get away with it, there's no consequence for his actions and no incentive for him to change."

"You think it's so simple—so easy. Just remove the temptation, and he'll instantly reform, is that it? Just let him suffer the consequences. Well, he doesn't care about consequences anymore and certainly doesn't mind what people think either. Besides, he's my father. Until this past year or so, he's been as perfect a father and husband as a man could possibly be. He doted on my mother and loved all of us dearly. Is that how I should repay him—by locking him out of his own home? By smashing his jugs of liquor, which are the only things that matter to him anymore?"

"At least, tell him how you feel—preferably when he's sober."

"Oh, yes," Maddie muttered under her breath, fighting back tears. She felt as if she might explode; her emotions defied containment, but she *wasn't* going to let herself scream again.

"Oh, I'll certainly tell him how he's tearing me up inside," she responded in a wooden voice. "And how sometimes I hate him for what he's doing to me and to himself. I'll tell him how I lay awake at night worrying, and how I wonder what will become of him and of us without him. . . . I'll tell him how I sometimes watch him sleep at night in a mindless stupor and I almost hope he'll never wake up . . . and how guilty I feel afterwards. I'll tell him how afraid I am for the future and how lonely for the man I once knew. Oh, yes, I'm sure I can tell him all that, Mr. Cumberland—right after I tell him I'm no longer going to go after him when I know he's been drinking, and the weather's turning bad, and if I don't find him, he'll freeze to death all alone in the night or catch his death of cold . . ."

Maddie's shoulders began to heave as sobs welled in her throat. She fought desperately to subdue them, but it was no use. With a little gurgle, she hid her face in her hands and began to weep in earnest.

"Maddie, I'm sorry . . ." Condemnation gave way to sympathy in a dizzying instant, and Chase Cumberland reached out and pulled her into the circle of his arms.

Maddie was so undone she let him embrace her—and even wrapped her arms around his neck and sobbed into the crook of his shoulder. All the feelings she had been holding at bay for so many long weeks and months refused to be submerged any longer. They poured forth like the waters of a rain-swollen river breaching its boundaries. But even as she wept and made embarrassing little mewling sounds, she was conscious of the strength, warmth, and hardness of Chase Cumberland's bare chest with its pelt of crinkly, soft hair.

Her breasts were pressed against him in a most intimate fashion that would have made her blush had she not been so devastated by her fit of weeping.

"It's all right," he crooned, stroking her back and entangling his fingers in her disheveled hair. "Cry it all out, Maddie. I didn't mean to imply that it's all your fault that your father has become a worthless drunk. It isn't. But trust me when I tell you that unless you get tough with him, you'll break in two, and your father won't get any better. When whiskey becomes a man's master, only toughness helps. If he senses any weakness in you—any weakness at all—he'll try to manipulate and control you, just as his desire for whiskey is manipulating and controlling him. The weak can't survive. I've been through this; I know."

"But he used to be so wonderful!" Maddie wailed. "You should have seen how tenderly he cared for my mother during her final illness. There was nothing he wouldn't do for her, no task he considered too low or demeaning. And before that, he was such a strong man. Always laughing and finding joy in life. He built this farm from nothing, stone upon stone. But no matter how busy he was, he always took time for me and made me feel special . . ."

"All the more reason why you can't let him continue like this, Maddie. . . . Hell, we're making enough noise in here to wake the dead, and he doesn't even know we're in the same room with him."

"I doubt I can do it," Maddie sobbed. "A daughter can't turn her back on her father and put him out of his home just because he's . . . he's old, sick, and weak and no longer meets her expectations."

"This isn't sickness or old age you're dealing with—it's a terrible craving for whiskey. A craving that's killing him. And destroying you and your family right along with him. It's already gone too far, Maddie; you mustn't let it go any further."

"Oh, you're right! I know you're right. But I'm not sure I can bear to do what you're suggesting." She clung to Chase Cumberland and let the sobs wrack her. It was a perfect measure of just how low her father had sunk that he never stirred on the bed or showed any awareness, either of her misery or of the presence of a stranger holding his eldest daughter.

Chase Cumberland said nothing more; instead, he just soothed and comforted her. When she had finished sobbing and drew back slightly, he took her face between his warm, callused hands and gazed down at her, his amber-colored eyes warmly glowing.

"Maddie McCrory, you're one of the strongest, feistiest females I've met in a long time. You'll think of the best way to handle this, and when you do, you'll find the courage to do what must be done."

She believed him. It was impossible to doubt a man who looked at her the way Chase was doing. Suddenly, she didn't feel so devastated, overwhelmed, and alone. Mutely, she nodded, unable to deny the compelling intensity of his gaze. He smiled, and she couldn't detect even a hint of sarcasm or wolfishness. But as they stood closely together, his hands clasping her face, his body touching hers all down the front, something shifted and changed between them.

She grew aware of him as a man again. Her breasts ached where they grazed his naked chest. Her body trembled, and a yearning uncoiled itself deep inside her like a leaf unfolding in the spring. Something similar seemed to be happening to him. She could see it in his face. Sense it in the slight stiffening of his torso. His eyes darkened, and his gaze dropped to her mouth. His breathing quickened, matching her own erratically drawn breaths.

She had the unnerving sensation that her lips were swollen, and she quickly moistened them with a stroke of her tongue. Avidly, he watched the tiny movement, and his thumbs traced delicate burning circles on her cheeks. He swayed toward her, or perhaps she did the swaying; she couldn't be certain. She only knew that his breath caressed her forehead, both warming and cooling her feverish skin. He tilted her head upward, and his hands moved to the back of her neck. His fingers threaded through her hair.

"Maddie . . ." he said, and her name sounded like a growl. Never had she heard it spoken with so much . . . feeling.

Ever so slowly, his mouth descended toward hers.

The moment before their lips met, she heard the unmistakable *thump!* of the front door banging open. With a startled cry, she jumped backward.

Disappointment flickered in Chase Cumberland's eyes, then his smile turned mocking, and he gestured toward the door. "Better go see who's here, Miss McCrory, before you fall prey to the fact that I've been a long time without a woman."

Without a woman. He meant it as a blatant sexual challenge, an acknowledgment of his needs and appetites as a man. He wanted—*had* wanted, anyway—to kiss her. And that was not all he wanted. She knew with terrifying certainty that he also wanted to couple with her. To mate. To breed. He wanted her with the same stunning immediacy and instant readiness as the stallion wants the mare. What astounded her even more was that she responded to him on the same level, desiring him with the same fervor as the mare desires the stallion. Such an instantaneous physical reaction had never happened to her before, and it forever changed the way she felt about herself—and Chase Cumberland.

All at once, she couldn't meet his eyes. Couldn't deal with the mockery she found there or the intimate knowledge he had gained of her. *He knew she had wanted him to kiss her.* He had guessed exactly how she felt. Her shocking vulnerability and the way she had exposed her raw emotions deeply shamed her. How could she have wept in his arms like that? And gone so quickly from weeping to lusting?

"You'd better leave now," she countered. "Thank you for helping me with my father, but I can manage the rest."

"I'm sure you can," he murmured, reminding her of his earlier pronouncement that she would think of a way to handle this problem with her father and find the courage to do what needed to be done.

She was less certain of it now. Without the security of his arms around her, she was once more the dutiful daughter trapped in the behaviors of the past, dreading what lay ahead, and feeling powerless to change it. Nothing she had said or done recently had stopped her father's withdrawal from life or kept him from retreating into drunkenness; there was absolutely no reason to believe that anything she said or did in the future—short of totally abandoning him and putting him out of the house—would turn him back into the man he had been. Even resorting to abandonment wouldn't work.

Scurrying from the bedroom, she nearly collided with Little Mike. "Where's Pawnee Mary?" her brother asked. "Did she make any supper? Everything's done outside, and I'm starving."

"I don't know. She's not here, but she probably did make something to eat. She usually does. Go check the stove. You know Mary; she comes and goes when she pleases. Come to think of it, I did tell her we were coming back tonight, so I'm not surprised she's left already."

While she was having this conversation with Mike, Chase Cumberland stepped quietly around both of them and departed the house without another word. Maddie let him go. She could think of nothing more to say to him. It was only after he was gone that she recovered her wits enough to wonder why he had come and what on earth he had been building out back by the barn.

The next morning, after a nearly sleepless night, Maddie arose, went to start breakfast, and found Mary stirring a large pot of corn mush on the stove. The handsome Indian woman stood tall and silent in her fringed buckskin dress, her back straight, her face serene and inscrutable. Ignoring Maddie's presence, she stirred and stirred, looking almost as exactly as she had when Maddie had first met her—silently stirring mush on the stove the day after Ma had died.

Then as now, she gave no explanation for who she was, where she had come from, or why she was there. She simply stepped in to fill a need, her manner proclaiming that she believed no other explanation was necessary.

"Good morning, Mary," Maddie said, heading for the cupboard to fetch some bowls. "Thank you for the wonderful rabbit stew you left last night. It was the best I ever tasted, and everyone else thought so, too."

The corners of Mary's mouth lifted ever so slightly. Maddie

had never seen the woman truly smile or indeed display any overt emotion. Mary's face seemed carved of smooth golden oak, possessing a rare beauty, but incapable of showing either sorrow or delight. Only her dark brown eyes ever betrayed her feelings; they were wide, serious eyes, shadowed with a sadness too deep to articulate and a dignity that Maddie thought must be apparent to anyone who looked closely—yet she knew that few white people ever cared enough to look closely. When they saw Mary, they saw only *hated Indian,* and never bothered to probe the depths of this handsome, mysterious woman.

Maddie refused to believe all that was said about her; Mary's actions spoke louder than all the gossips in Hopewell. Mary had cared for the McCrory family in their grief, and she still came and went silently whenever she sensed they had a need. Her sudden appearances were uncanny, and her disappearances equally so—but since she condescended to accept the small gifts of food, clothing, and money that Maddie surreptitiously slipped into the rush basket she always carried with her, Maddie never asked questions or refused the woman's help.

She was deeply grateful for Mary's assistance and would never insult her by making an issue out of her unexpected comings and goings.

As she set the table for breakfast, Maddie pondered how to broach the subject of Chase Cumberland and why Mary had allowed him on the property yesterday. She was curious about the project Mr. Cumberland had started—and anxious to hear about the exchange that must have ensued between Chase and Mary. Mary so closely guarded her thoughts that conversation with her was usually minimal, even when it concerned neutral topics such as the weather or the best way to skin a rabbit.

While Maddie was fussing with the silverware, Mary suddenly stopped stirring and turned to her. "Son of Wolf come yesterday while you gone to race," she said in her blunt, clipped fashion.

"Son of Wolf?" Maddie's heart began to pound. "Do you mean the man with the amber-colored eyes?"

How amazing that Mary had had the same first impression of Chase Cumberland!

Mary nodded. "Eyes like wolf. Moves like wolf. Maybe even thinks like wolf. He say he make something you need to breed horses. I say fine, go ahead."

"But you don't even know Mr. Cumberland!"

Mary gave her a long, soul-searching look. "I know him. I look in eyes. See soul. See wolf spirit. My spirit comes from earth. I am mother and sister to wolf. I know his heart good. So I say yes."

"But . . . but . . ."

Maddie was astonished. She couldn't recall hearing Mary utter so many consecutive sentences. And she couldn't begin to comprehend all this nonsense about spirits. Such talk made the hairs prickle on the back of her neck.

"You need chute," Mary calmly continued. "Put mare in. Bring stallion up. Mare no can kick or run away. Nobody get hurt."

"A chute? You mean a . . . a chute especially for breeding?"

Mary's head bobbed in assent. "That what he call it—breeding chute. Good idea. Wonder why no one think of it before. Make good sense."

"He was building this . . . this breeding chute for us, and instead of thanking him, I ordered him off our property. Oh, Mary! I behaved like a perfect shrew!"

Maddie dropped the rest of the silverware on the tabletop. "I'm going over there right now and apologize. Here he was, trying to be neighborly, and I wouldn't even listen. How can I make amends? Do you think he'll come back and finish it if I ask him nicely? Will he show us how to use the thing? Yesterday in Salina, after we won the race, I lined up a half dozen more breedings for Gold Deck. The mares will all be here soon, and if there's any way I can make the whole process safer . . ."

"Ask him for supper," Mary said, stone-faced, but Maddie could have sworn she had a twinkle in her eye. "Tomorrow night. I make good supper. You brush hair and wear pretty dress. Then he finish chute for certain."

"Mary!" Maddie was shocked to her soul. "You make it sound like we're trying to trap him into something."

"No trap. Lure. Lure him into finishing chute. Besides, inviting to supper is neighborly thing to do."

"You're right!"

Only after she was half way out to the barn to saddle a horse did Maddie remember that she had vowed to have nothing more to do with Chase Cumberland. She didn't want to sell him any land or give him any free breedings—which was probably why he had been there in the first place, building them a chute. He had already tricked her out of two thousand dollars. Just because he had held her while she wept and almost kissed her last night was no reason for her to ignore her initial dislike and mistrust of the man and go running over to invite him for supper.

Why, she hadn't even had breakfast yet! And he had said he wanted no trespassers. She could get along fine without a breeding chute; they'd been getting along without one for years.

Yet, as her steps slowed, and she debated the merits of her hasty decision, she also realized that she wanted very much to see Chase Cumberland again. Apologizing and inviting him to supper was just an excuse; she really wanted to see him for herself alone. All night long, she had agonized over the feelings he had aroused in her when he held her. They were magical feelings—feminine feelings, feelings she had never allowed herself to feel before. . . . Or no man had aroused in her before.

By morning, she was convinced she must have imagined the whole thing. Perhaps he never had meant to kiss her; she had only been foolishly wanting it. Had he really made her go weak in the knees? Had the sight of his naked chest actually prompted lascivious thoughts? Alone in her own bed, she hadn't been able to believe it of herself. She was the same person she had always been—practical, down-to-earth Maddie McCrory, so dedicated to her family that she wanted nothing to do with *any* man, let alone a mysterious, arrogant stranger with a horse who could beat Gold Deck.

Fanciful romantic notions were the providence of her younger sisters. Undoubtedly, when next she laid eyes on Chase Cumberland, she'd feel nothing at all—no shortness of breath, no trembling of her lower limbs, no rush of heady excitement.

Yes, that's why she was going over to his place: to prove to herself that he had no effect on her whatsoever. She didn't even like him! He had no business making a shambles of her life, telling her how to handle her father, showing her "so-called" better ways of doing things . . .

Her list of his shortcomings multiplied as she saddled a trusty old mare whose breeding days were nearly over. She intended to be civil, but if Mr. Cumberland said one wrong word, or gave her one of those mocking looks again, or slanted her another wolfish, hungry-eyed, disrespectful glance, then she . . . well, she *wouldn't* invite him for dinner, after all.

She'd spit in his eye and ride away, and she would *not,* under any circumstances, permit herself to think about him ever again.

Seven

"See you later, Buck. I'm going line riding today to see what problems we're likely to encounter when we start putting up fencing. I should be back before supper." Chase tightened the reins on a fidgeting Bonnie Lass who was eager to be off and crow-hopping sideways in her enthusiasm.

Buck's attention never strayed from the young filly he was leading toward the small corral, where he intended to start breaking her this sunny, hot morning. When Buck worked with the horses, he seemed to enter another world altogether. Perhaps that was the secret to his success. While Chase was sometimes distracted by the thought of what needed doing on a particular day, Buck closed his mind to everything and concentrated on the animal in hand.

Shaking his head in bemusement at his brother, Chase headed Bonnie Lass toward the furthest corner of the ranch. He had meant to ride the boundaries yesterday, but had changed his mind in favor of visiting the McCrorys. Now, he was sorry he had gone over there. When it came to Maddie McCrory, he could do nothing right. He had set out hoping to win her over by helping her brother build a breeding chute. When they weren't home, he had decided to go ahead and start the thing anyway—with the permission of Pawnee Mary. The Indian woman had said he might use some old lumber piled out behind the stable.

And what had happened? Maddie and her family had come home in the middle of the project, and before he knew it, he'd been drawn into an embarrassing situation he had managed to handle with all the delicacy of a skunk showing up at a wedding. To top it all off, he had almost wound up kissing the difficult, perplexing, contrary woman!

Last night, he'd lost sleep over the incident—wondering what had possessed him to say and do the things he had—and wishing, at the same time, that he *had* managed to steal a kiss. Whenever he thought of Maddie McCrory's sweet bosom crushed to his naked chest, recalled the clean, earthy scent of her sun-warmed hair and body, and relived the sensation of holding her while she wept, he couldn't subdue his body's responses. In plain terms, he lusted after her.

He wasn't one bit more civilized than a randy stallion scenting a mare in season. It bothered him mightily to discover he had so little self-control. Maddie McCrory hadn't said a kind word to him from the first day he'd met her and never given him a single smile, yet here he was sniffing after her skirts like some totally besotted fool. All she had done was bawl on his chest, and he wanted to take her to bed and make her forget all her troubles in some delirious whirlwind of passion. What in hell was wrong with him?

Thoroughly disgusted with himself, he urged Bonnie Lass into a trot. Had he really grown that desperate for a woman—any woman—that he would stoop to deflowering a spinster with a passel of needy kinfolk?

One thing he wouldn't do was go back and finish that damn chute. Let her wonder forever what he had been building, if indeed, she was wondering. She hadn't been curious enough to ask, even after she'd broken down in front of him and watered his chest like a teapot. No more being nice to her! He should have stuck to his original plan: minding his own business and insisting that the McCrorys mind their's.

Chase rode for more than an hour, so lost in thought he barely noticed the broad sweep of the gently undulating land he could now call his own, or appreciated the endless stretches of flat prairie visible in the distance when he chanced to arrive at the top of a rise. He ignored the ever-present Kansas wind that blew hotly at this time of year and never once raised his eyes to the cloudless, blue sky overhead.

As he reached the top of a modest ridge, he suddenly stopped, looked around, and realized he had no idea where he was or even if he was still on his own land. He had forgotten to watch for boundary markings and couldn't even remember where the house and outbuildings stood.

Slowly, he turned Bonnie Lass around so he could more fully view the terrain and hopefully spot a familiar landmark. He was surprised to discover he could still see the house from this vantage point, which was probably the highest spot in the entire area. Buck was still working the filly in the small corral, and the rest of the horses were bunched in a corner around the water trough of the larger corral.

"You daydreaming jackass." Bonnie Lass flicked back her ears as if she thought he might be talking to her. "You've wasted half the morning thinking about Maddie McCrory's red hair lying tumbled across your bare chest."

No sooner had the words left his mouth when he saw a distant figure on horseback riding in a bee line toward the house. He narrowed his eyes, studying the intruder, and had no difficulty identifying her. She was wearing a man's cowboy hat, but a red waterfall spilled down her back, and the way she sat her mount was exactly the way she had sat Gold Deck that day she had raced against him.

Chase spat an oath. In five or ten minutes, she'd reach the ranch, and Buck might not notice her until she had ridden right up to the corral. . . . Oh, why hadn't he stayed at the house this morning! He might have known she would take it into her head to come calling, riding all alone across the countryside, and doing what he had specifically ordered her *not* to do—trespassing on his property.

Chase took off his Stetson, swatted Bonnie Lass on the hind quarters, and dug his spurs into her sides. As if propelled from the mouth of a canon, the startled mare shot forward down the hillside. With complete disregard for prairie-dog holes, hidden boulders, or tangles of berry vines, they barreled down the side of the rise.

In a distant corner of his mind, Chase knew he was risking the life of his most prized horse—not to mention his own life. But his desperate need to save his brother from discovery outweighed all other considerations. He knew it was futile; Maddie would arrive at the ranch far ahead of him. Still, he couldn't stop himself from trying to get there first—or at least, as soon as possible.

The idea of Maddie coming face to face with Buck horrified him. He didn't want her to know he had a mad-looking brother with snow white hair whose face still adorned wanted posters proclaiming him a murderer down in Texas. She might have seen one somewhere. How would he ever explain? What would she think? And what would Buck think—or do—when a strange, solitary female suddenly appeared out of nowhere?

Buck hadn't been near a woman in months, and his carnal appetites far surpassed Chase's. He hadn't seen a *decent* woman in years; he'd probably forgotten how to behave around one. Chase couldn't precisely imagine his brother taking advantage of Maddie, but he still had a feeling of terrible foreboding when he thought of Maddie and Buck unexpectedly meeting.

So he rode like the devil from hell, and Bonnie Lass responded with all the speed she had to give. But even as he galloped across the rough terrain, Chase knew he would be too late.

As Maddie rode toward the old Parker place—now Chase Cumberland's place—she told herself it was ridiculous to feel nervous and afraid. She was only going there to apologize for her rudeness of the day before and to invite Chase to supper to make amends. Still, it was so unlike her; she had almost turned back a dozen times already.

Chase had told her to stay away, so maybe he wouldn't appreciate her gesture of reconciliation. To make matters worse, she was dressed in an old shabby skirt and shirtwaist, and riding astride, which meant that her skirt and petticoat were bunched up in front of her, and half her legs—limbs—were showing. She had grabbed one of Little Mike's battered hats to shade her face from the fierce sunshine, but she should have worn her pretty new bonnet; the back of her neck was going to get burnt, unless her hair hid it well enough.

That was another thing—her hair. She had tugged a brush through it this morning, shoved in a couple of pins, and the pins had all fallen out on the way over. By the time she arrived, she'd be hot, sweaty, and grimy—looking her worst—when pride demanded that she look her very best in front of Chase Cumberland.

In the entire time she'd known him, she hadn't once looked her best. She couldn't fathom why a man would even want to kiss a woman who looked as untidy as she usually did. If he failed to give her the barest glance of appreciation this morning, it would only be what she deserved. But someday—maybe tomorrow night, if he consented to come to supper—she would contrive to look pretty, or as pretty as she was capable of looking, and he would realize that she was someone to treat with respect, a woman worthy of his romantic interest. If he were very nice, she might even *allow* him to kiss her.

The thought of kissing Chase Cumberland gave her a fluttery feeling in her lower abdomen. Oh, she was indeed a wanton! No better than a calico queen. Since she'd met the man, she hardly knew herself anymore. He provoked her into saying things she never meant to say and feeling things she'd never dreamed she could feel. Because of her family responsibilities, there could never be anything serious between them, but just once, before she got too old, she'd like to know what it felt like to be well and truly kissed, and to be admired by a man she found extremely attractive.

She only hoped he wouldn't bring up the topic of her father again. With Pa the way he was these days, it was crazy to consider having a dinner guest. On the other hand, since Chase already knew about her father, it wasn't the same thing as inviting someone to dinner for whom her father's behavior would come as a big surprise. Besides, if Chase Cumberland did agree to come, she would enlist her brother and both her sisters in a campaign to keep Pa sober for the evening. Whatever it took, she'd do it—even if it meant locking Pa in his room.

As she drew closer to the house, she spotted a man out in a corral working a horse. She couldn't see him clearly because the horse stood between them, but she assumed it must be the man she had come to see.

"Chase! I mean, Mr. Cumberland!" Removing her hat, she waved it to catch his attention.

To her astonishment, he grabbed the horse's halter, led it quickly through the corral gate, and headed for the barn. He never so much as waved back or acknowledged her in any way.

Maddie slowed the old mare to a walk and pondered what to say to him. Obviously, he was angry. She recalled that she hadn't spoken a word to him before his abrupt departure last evening, hadn't even said goodbye. Perhaps he was upset because she had failed to mention the chute he was building—or because their near-kiss had been interrupted, or because she had rudely asked him to leave.

Well, today she was going to be humble, beg his pardon, and make it all up to him by asking him to supper—and then she was darned well going to enjoy his company when he came! A hitching rail stood in front of the house, and Maddie rode up to it, dismounted, and looped her horse's reins over it. Summoning her courage, she started for the barn.

After the bright sunlight outside, the barn's interior was cool and dark. She needed a moment for her eyes to adjust to the gloom. She walked down a narrow aisle heaped high with various tools and implements. A single horse, the filly Chase had been working, stood tied to a ring in the wall, but there was no sign of Chase himself.

"Mr. Cumberland? Where are you? Please don't be angry for the way I treated you yesterday. When I realized how rude I'd been, I decided to ride over to apologize. I . . . I think you might be right about how to handle my father. I'm still undecided as to whether or not I can do it, and whether or not it'll work. Do you honestly think it will?"

She paused in the center of the barn and peered down a smaller side aisle. Again, she saw no one, but had the oddest sensation that someone was there, watching her every move. She grew increasingly uneasy. She couldn't believe he meant to avoid her—or worse yet, to frighten her. Surely, she hadn't angered him that much!

An old wagon stood in the center of the side aisle, and behind it was a huge mound of hay completely blocking the closed door at the far end. Dust motes danced in the air, as if the hay had been recently stirred.

Holding her breath, Maddie walked step by step down the aisle toward the wagon. "Is someone here?"

Straining to hear any sound, she thought she detected the intake of a deep breath. If Chase was hiding from her, she meant to give him a good scolding for trying to scare her and almost succeeding. Tiptoeing around the wagon, she came face to face with a tall, silent man.

Gasping like a fish out of water, Maddie stood there quivering, rendered momentarily speechless. He was about the same height as Chase but had a slightly heavier build. His features reminded her of Mr. Cumberland's, but he most definitely *wasn't* the man she had expected to find. This man had snow white hair hanging down to his shoulders, long white lashes, and bushy white eyebrows. His coloring was startling enough, but his eyes were even worse. They were a strange gray-blue color, and his odd, wild appearance struck fear in her heart.

Remaining perfectly motionless, he stared at her in a hostile, resentful manner, but didn't say a single word—and that scared her more than anything.

"Ex-Excuse me," she stammered through chattering teeth. "I didn't mean to disturb you. Forgive me for intruding; I'm l-leaving now."

She slowly backed away, fully expecting the man to come after her, or at least to make some comment. But he didn't open his mouth or move a muscle, and she was able to retreat to the center of the barn. When she reached that point, and he still hadn't done anything, she turned and ran.

Picking up her skirts, she raced down the barn aisle as fast as she could go, burst from the barn, and kept running until she reached her mare. Within seconds, she clambered into the saddle, spun the mare around, and galloped away from Chase Cumberland's ranch as if all the devils in hell hotly pursued her.

She drove the mare hard, little caring that the poor animal was unused to such strenuous activity. She didn't slow down until she reached McCrory land—the large field Chase Cumberland wanted to buy from her family. By then, the mare was stumbling and blowing; Maddie herself feared she might faint.

She pulled her mount down to a walk, resolving to go slow the remainder of the way home in hopes of cooling the mare before they arrived. Then she heard hoofbeats pounding behind her. Alarm clanged through her as she whirled to see who was following.

She recognized the horse before she did the rider; it was Bonnie Lass, and astride her, looking worried, came Chase Cumberland.

"Are you all right?" His gaze raked her from head to toe, as if he were taking inventory of her body parts and wanted to assure himself they were all there.

"I'm a little hot and tired," she admitted. "And so is my horse."

"But you're all right?" he persisted. "You look all right."

She supposed she looked a fright, but nodded to ease his concern. "I haven't any injuries, if that's what you mean."

She didn't mention her fear. She thought it best to let him do the talking first.

"I'm sorry I wasn't at the ranch when you rode up," he said. "I had gone out line riding, but then I saw you coming for a visit."

She waited for him to explain about the stranger in his barn, and when he didn't volunteer, she realized she'd have to introduce the topic. "I looked for you in the barn. You weren't there. But I encountered someone who . . . who . . ."

"Who what?" he demanded sharply. "What did he do? Tell me. I warned you not to come snooping around my place. As you've just discovered, I had a good reason."

"He didn't do anything," she said, surprised at his vehemence. "All he did was stand there and look at me. I don't know why, but I got frightened. *Would* he have done something if I'd stayed?"

"I don't think so . . . I can't say for certain. My brother doesn't take to strangers. And people don't usually take to him. That's why he hid in the barn when you got there, and why I didn't want you on the premises in the first place."

"What happened to him? Why does he look like that? And why wouldn't he speak to me—introduce himself at least?"

"He was struck by lightning. Happened a long time ago. As a result, his hair turned white, and he hasn't been able to speak since."

"I'm so sorry," Maddie murmured. "The poor man."

"Don't pity him. He would hate that. Besides, he's not some kind of a freak or monster."

"I didn't mean to imply that he is. I only meant that . . . that it must be hard to be different. People aren't always understanding of differences in behavior or appearance that set others apart from them."

"He gets by without other people's approval. He's wonderful with animals, and he just avoids contact with people, except for me. . . . Look." Chase leaned forward and briefly touched her hand, which sent a tremor up her arm. Maddie sat stock-still and attempted to conceal her reaction.

"Promise me you won't mention him to anybody," he continued in a low, urgent voice. "You mustn't let another living soul know he exists. That's the way he wants it, and I do, too."

"You mean to keep him a secret?" Maddie was shocked. She couldn't imagine anyone living like that—hidden away on a farm and never seeing or speaking to other people.

"It's for the best, Maddie." Chase eyed her closely, and a defensive note crept into his tone. "He's tried mixing with folks, and it plain doesn't work. Sooner or later, someone picks a fight with him. We had to leave the last place we lived, because the woman who lived next door became fearful for her children. One day, they saw my brother out riding his horse, and his appearance scared them. If he could have spoken to them . . . put them at ease . . . but he couldn't, and their father rode over the next day and deliberately picked a fight."

"What happened then?"

"Buck broke his nose, and we knew it was time to leave again. When we found this place, I was hoping we'd finally discovered a ranch that was isolated enough from town and neighbors that he could avoid chance encounters. Seems I was wrong. Apparently, he isn't safe even in his own front yard, working his horses. . . . That's why I'm asking you to forget you ever saw him. Please, Maddie. For Buck's sake, so he can live in peace, don't tell anyone about him."

Maddie had to glance away from the earnest entreaty in Chase's golden-brown eyes. It didn't sit well with her to keep secrets from her family. Little Mike or one of the girls might spot Chase's brother, and if they did, it would be better if they knew about him ahead of time. She considered the problem a moment, and an idea came to her.

"Chase!" she exclaimed, turning back to him. "I rode over here with the intention of inviting you to supper tomorrow night as a way of thanking you for coming by to build that breeding chute for us. Pawnee Mary explained why you were there, and I felt so terrible about being rude to you. Instead of hiding Buck away on this ranch, why don't you bring him with you? That way, my family could all get to . . ."

"No!" Chase was adamant. His handsome features settled into grim, determined lines. "First, he wouldn't come. Second, it's a lousy idea. Once your family knows about him, it'll only be a matter of time before all of Hopewell knows."

"They won't tell anyone! The McCrorys can keep a secret. But at least this way, Buck won't come as a surprise to them if they happen to meet him unexpectedly. And Buck himself will feel more comfortable riding around your ranch if he knows we know about him. No one else is likely to encounter him; are you afraid we might make fun of him or treat him badly?"

"Folks usually do—even the church-going ones. They're often the worst kind. They take one look at him and think he's the devil's spawn or some other such superstitious claptrap."

"*We* wouldn't. You aren't being fair to us. We treat Pawnee Mary like one of the family, though most everyone else refuses to have anything to do with her because she's Indian. They say bad things about her, too, but it's all just gossip. The McCrorys aren't about to judge people on the basis of vicious gossip. If we're going to be neighbors, you should know that about us. Pa always taught us to make up our own minds about folks."

A wicked gleam appeared in Chase Cumberland's eyes. "They say in town that Mary's a 'fallen woman,' a soiled dove, if you will. You don't believe that, I take it."

"I most certainly do not. Nor do I believe she's likely to scalp us all in the middle of the night or steal us blind or harm us in any way. She's a kind, gentle woman with a loving, generous heart. If folks can't see that for themselves, it's too darn bad, but I regard it as their problem, not mine. They're only denying themselves a unique opportunity."

Chase Cumberland laughed. "I wish I had someone like you defending me when I'm accused of wrongdoing."

Maddie, too, broke into a smile. "Then you'll come to supper tomorrow night and bring your brother with you, so we can all meet him and make him feel welcome."

Chase's grin disappeared. "I've already told you; he won't come. And he won't be pleased we had this conversation. It's easier for him to live as a recluse, then to try to fit into society and risk being rejected again. He's had enough rejection to make him wary and determined to avoid more of the same."

"But you'll ask him! Surely, you'll try."

Chase shook his head. "I'll try, but don't be disappointed if he doesn't show up."

The fact that he was agreeing to make the effort filled Maddie with happiness. She couldn't keep from smiling, and Chase smiled back at her. They sat on their horses, grinning foolishly at each other, and Maddie wondered at the sheer joy bubbling in her heart. To see this normally taciturn, scowling man turn up the corners of his mouth and flash his white teeth in an honest-to-God smile, with no mockery in it, unleashed all sorts of bubbly, warm feelings.

"Do you know," he said, again leaning over his saddle horn. "This is the first time I've seen you really smile at me?"

Maddie flushed. How odd that he should be thinking the same thing about her that she had been thinking about him! "Maybe neither one of us smiles as much as we should."

"Maybe you're right," he agreed. "I'll promise to smile more often if you will. When you curve your lips like that, I almost forget you're such a little spitfire. I start thinking: 'Where did this pretty, sweet thing come from, and how come I never noticed her before?' "

The compliment caused a wild tumult in Maddie's breast—a disturbance she was sure he could detect on her features. To cover her embarrassment, she cocked her head, studying him. "Are you flirting with me, Mr. Cumberland?"

"Haven't we progressed to Chase by now? I thought after yesterday, we surely had."

Thinking of their near-kiss fueled another rush of excitement. Maddie self-consciously lowered her lashes. "In view of yesterday—and especially in view of all the bad things I've thought about you, and you've probably thought about me—I think we should start fresh and renew our . . . acquaintance. I'd be pleased to call you Chase, and you in turn, may call me Maddie."

"Well, I'm glad we've gotten that out of the way. What in hell—excuse me, heck—does Maddie stand for anyhow?"

She raised her lashes to look into his glowing eyes. They were beautiful eyes, she suddenly realized, their unique color mirroring the golden sunlight. "Madeline. I was named for my Aunt Madeline on my mother's side of the family. But I've always been called Maddie. Madeline is too formal to suit me, Pa always said."

Chase squinted and peered down his nose at her. "He could be right. Do you have a middle name?"

"Elizabeth. Madeline Elizabeth McCrory is my full name. What's yours?"

"Chase Ezekiel Cumberland . . . at your service, ma'am." He swept off his Stetson and bowed to her, almost impaling himself on the saddle horn. That and his name prompted her to giggle.

"Ezekiel?" She tried not to laugh outright, but it was impossible. He didn't look in the least like an Ezekiel.

"You find my name humorous? It spawns an unseemly levity?"

His use of five-dollar words, as Pa would call them, struck her as funny also, and Maddie succumbed to impulse and guffawed. The eruption gave way to a loud hiccup. As the awkward sound emerged from her mouth, her cheeks burned with embarrassment. Oh, why did she always have to make a fool of herself in front of this stunningly attractive man?

"Careful you don't fall off your horse, Madeline Elizabeth," he gravely counseled, his eyes twinkling. "If you were a man, I'd have to call you out for laughing at my name."

That sobered her immediately. "Forgive me. I didn't mean to insult you."

His brows rose. "You didn't? You could have fooled me."

"I'm sorry, but you just don't strike me as an Ezekiel, that's all."

"You don't strike me as a Madeline Elizabeth."

"What do I strike you as?"

He thought a moment, then grinned. "If I had to name you, I'd call you . . . Sassy."

"Sassy! What kind of name is that?"

"One that fits. You've got sassy hair, a sassy mouth, and a sassy little bottom."

"Mr. Cumberland!"

He was completely unrepentant. "Chase . . . or Ezekiel, if you must."

"No . . . Wolf. If I had a choice, I'd call you Wolf."

He looked quizzical. "Wolf?"

"Or Son of Wolf. That's what Mary calls you. You've got eyes like a wolf, and you move like a wolf. I thought of a prairie wolf the first time I saw you."

He leaned over, wrapped his hand around the nape of her neck, and pulled her closer—so close she was in danger of toppling from her horse. "You know what can happen when you get too near a wolf, don't you?"

"What?" she asked breathlessly, wishing—hoping—he would kiss her.

"You might get eaten. I have this sudden, irresistible urge to devour you. But instead, I think I'll just . . ."

Bonnie Lass chose that moment to flatten her ears and take a bite out of Maddie's horse. Maddie's mare squealed and jumped away from the unexpected attack, and Maddie fell forward and had to grab the mane to stay aboard.

Chase's grin stretched from ear to ear. "Before one of us gets hurt, I think I'd better say good-bye for now, but I'll come join you tomorrow night for supper. Good day, Miss Madeline Elizabeth McCrory."

He tugged on the brim of his Stetson, wheeled his mare around, and galloped back in the direction of his ranch—leaving Maddie to stare after him in a state of spiraling agitation and excitement.

Chase Cumberland was coming to supper tomorrow night; what—oh, what—should she serve? Even more important, what should she *wear?*

Eight

"Now, remember everyone. If Mr. Cumberland's brother appears, please don't remark upon his strangeness. He *will* appear strange to you, but try not to single him out or do anything to embarrass him. Have you all got that? . . . Carrie? Zoe? Little Mike?"

Hands on hips, Maddie stood in the middle of the scrubbed and shining main room of the house and glared at each of her siblings in turn. In answer, she received only frowns and sighs of exasperation.

"Honestly, Maddie. Do you think we grew up on a farm in the middle of nowhere? Maybe we did, but Ma was the most genteel lady in all of Kansas." Zoe tossed her glistening red-gold hair, and her fingers flew to the high lacy collar of her best white shirtwaist, worn over a dark green patterned skirt.

Fluttering her lashes outrageously, she purred: "How nice to meet you, Mr. Cumberland's brother. Whatever happened to your eyebrows, sir? . . . What? You can't answer? Mercy me, you must be possessed by the devil, sir!"

With a mischievous glance at her sister, Zoe collapsed into gales of laughter, and Carrie heartily joined her. Even Little Mike cracked a grin—and Pawnee Mary, busy peeling potatoes at the worktable in the corner, couldn't hide a smile.

"Stop that this instant," Maddie scolded, trying not to join them. "I'm warning both of you—actually, all three of you. Please be on your best behavior. It's bad enough I have to worry about Pa; I'll be very upset if I must live in terror that one of you will say or do something inappropriate."

"We won't, Maddie. Quit fussing at us like an old broody hen and go get dressed," Carrie told her. "Our guests should be here any minute, and you aren't even ready."

"I am too ready. This is what I'm wearing." Maddie smoothed down the crisp, white, frilly apron covering the sprigged black calico wrapper that boasted a Watteau pleat in back. She plucked at the puffy sleeves of the gown and frowned at her sisters, who were making faces at each other and rolling their eyes at the ceiling.

"Is something wrong? This was one of Mama's favorite dresses when we had company. It's still stylish, so I thought I'd wear it."

"But . . . it's mostly black, Maddie. It does nothing for your coloring . . . Well, maybe it does tone it down a little," Carrie observed, studying her. "Still, it's so somber and emphasizes your age. Makes you look ancient, doesn't it, Zoe?"

"Oh, the dress is all right, I suppose. I'm more concerned about her skin. Did you use that paste I told you about, Maddie?"

"Which one? You told me about several disgusting concoctions you thought I should put on my face."

"The one of buttermilk and oatmeal, of course. Then you were supposed to rinse with glycerine water."

"I *did* try it," Maddie admitted, half-ashamed of her sudden desire to improve upon God's handiwork. "Can't you tell? My face feels as if it will crumble if I so much as smile this evening."

"You put some of Zoe's awful glop on your face?" Little Mike reached for a slice of fresh bread, then quickly withdrew his hand when Pawnee Mary slapped it. "Come on, Mary. I'm hungry. The smell of that frying chicken is making my mouth water. I can't last until supper. Just let me test it to make sure it won't poison us or something."

"No touch food before guests arrive," Pawnee Mary stonily warned him. "You touch, you lose a finger. Maybe two."

"Aw, Mary. Just one little old piece of bread—or better yet, a chicken wing. Nobody'll miss a chicken wing."

Mary eyed him menacingly. "No, but you miss fingers."

"What about my hair?" Maddie asked her sisters. "Does my hair meet with your approval? I tried my best to make it a little less . . . noticeable."

"Too restrained," Carrie said.

"Not restrained enough," argued Zoe.

"No matter what she does with it, it's still too red," Carrie insisted. "You'd better wear a bonnet."

"Not during supper or while I'm in the house," Maddie protested. "I hate wearing bonnets—except for the new one you girls gave me," she quickly added. "But I didn't think the blue would go well with black, and I couldn't find one I liked that matched the dress."

"You don't look like yourself with your hair all smoothed down like that," offered Little Mike. "If you want to look natural, you should let your hair stand straight out from your head, like you just were caught in a windstorm."

Maddie laughed. Coming from Little Mike, the teasing didn't make her angry; she rejoiced that he was taking part, instead of withdrawing and brooding, as he so often did these days.

"Thank you all for your comments and suggestions." She drew back her skirts and dropped into a deep curtsey. "And thank you also for cleaning, polishing, and cooking all afternoon. I am forever in your debt."

"Oh, we didn't mind," Carrie announced. "We haven't had guests for so long I can't recall when the last one came. Do you remember, Zoe?"

Zoe shrugged. "Mama's burial. That's the last time anyone came to visit, wasn't it?"

"Guess I'll check the barn and make certain everything's done out there," Little Mike muttered, frowning. He left the house a moment later, letting the door slam shut behind him.

"Oh, Zoe. . . . I wish you hadn't mentioned Mama's burial," Maddie sighed. "Just when Little Mike was starting to act normal again, too."

"He *never* acts normal," Zoe responded. "No more than Pa

does—except he doesn't drink. He just stays by himself most of the time and scowls whenever anyone bothers him."

"That reminds me. I'd better see if Pa has changed into the clean clothes I laid out for him." Maddie headed for the closed bedroom door. "Carrie and Zoe, see if there are any flowers blooming in my garden, will you? I wanted to gather some to put in a pitcher on top of the table, but I'm running out of time."

"Why didn't you ask before we got dressed?" Carrie wailed. "I spent half the morning picking peas. I could just as well have picked flowers while I was out there."

"Go around back and check Mama's rosebushes. I bet they're blooming now; they had buds all over them a couple of days ago, but I haven't looked lately to see if the buds have opened. You won't get dirty picking a few roses." Maddie lifted her hand to knock on her father's door. "Pa, are you dressed yet?"

"I'll get all scratched picking roses," Carrie grumbled. "Come on, Zoe. If I have to do it, you do too."

The twins departed, slamming the door behind them just as their brother had done. Shaking her head, Maddie knocked hard on her father's door. "Pa?"

She opened the door and peered into the room. Her father was still sitting on the side of the bed, right where she'd left him. He hadn't touched the clean clothes lying beside him.

"Pa, you aren't dressed, and our guests will be here shortly. Please change your shirt, at least. The one you're wearing needs laundering."

Actually, it reeked of whiskey. Apparently, her father had spilled some down the front of it. Maddie stood in front of him and started to unfasten his shirt, but before she could finish, he grasped her hands and held them away from him.

"Leave me alone, Maddie. I don't feel well. If you wanna do something, fetch me a jug. I know you've hidden 'em, but I should have one around here someplace, and I need a wee nip. Just a wee one, Maddie, darlin,' t' make me feel better."

Maddie had all she could do not to wrinkle her nose at her father's stale breath and the whiskey fumes emanating from him. Yet he sounded sober, and his eyes had lost the befuddled look that usually accompanied his drinking. She had risen early that morning to search for his stash and was fairly certain she had located all he had—three, to be exact, hidden in various places in the house and barn. She wished she knew how he was getting his hands on so much liquor; every time she thought his supply had run out, he managed to produce another jug from somewhere.

This time, she had found all of them—she hoped!—and put them in the hen house, where her father was unlikely to look. Later, when she got up enough nerve, she intended to empty them and give the jugs to Little Mike to use for target practice when he worked on improving his aim with Pa's Winchester.

"Pa, you don't need a wee nip tonight. We've company coming, remember? I told you all about it this morning, and you agreed to eat supper with us, and be your old charming self again. . . . The twins, Little Mike, and I are really looking forward to this evening. Please, won't you change your clothes and join us?"

"Not if you won't fetch me my jug, Maddie," her father stubbornly replied. "I don't feel well enough to join you, girl. That's the only reason why I nip from the jug, t' help my rheumatism. And also to make me forget . . . you know . . . about losin' yer Ma. Seems the rest of you have already forgotten."

Maddie bit back a denial. Now wasn't the time to argue with her father—not with company coming. She wanted to protest everything he was saying and point out to him the error of his ways, but she knew him too well. If she said a single word, they'd soon be fighting, and the last thing she wanted was to arouse one of his combative moods only minutes before Chase Cumberland's arrival.

"We're having fried chicken—your favorite," she cajoled instead. "And mashed potatoes and new peas, and Pawnee Mary's corn pudding, which you've always loved, and some of her wonderful biscuits, too. All that good food can't help but make you feel better; I myself baked two dried apple pies just the way Mama taught me. Please, Pa . . . join us. It will be so much fun."

Pa released her hands, almost shoving them back at her, and

lay down on the bed, right on top of the clean clothes she'd left there. "I ain't hungry, Maddie."

"Not," she corrected. "You're not hungry. Ma wouldn't want us to forget proper speech, now would she? I have to remind the girls and Little Mike all the time. It would help if you supported my efforts."

"I ain't supportin' nothin'. If you ain't gonna fetch my jug, get outa here and let me sleep. I'm so tired I can hardly lift my head off the pillow, and all your yammerin' is makin' me dizzy."

Maddie's ire rose like a fountain. "You've no reason to be tired Pa. You didn't do a damn—darn—thing all day but sleep. What you need is a good, hot meal with your family."

"What I need is to be left alone. Only friend I got anymore is my jug."

His whining, self-pitying tone grated on Maddie's nerves. Still, she strove to be reasonable. Losing her temper never helped; all it did was drive her father further away from her. This helpless, complaining old man was a stranger, and somewhere inside him, she strove to remember, was the strong, loving, laughing father she had always known. Somehow, some way, if it was the last thing she ever did, she would get him back again.

"Your jug is hardly your friend, Pa. Or ours. To us, it's an enemy who's taking you away from us. That's why I don't want to give it back to you."

Tears gathered in her father's eyes. Maddie spotted them the instant before he lifted his hand to shield his face from her gaze. "You don't understand, Maddie. You're a good girl, and you try hard, but you jus' don't understand. . . . I don't know myself why I feel as I do. I jus' wanna go where your Ma is. I can't believe I'm still here, and she's gone. It wasn't supposed to happen this way. With me bein' the older one, we always thought I'd go first—but she beat me to it. Now I don't know what to do with myself. The jug eases my pain. . . . It's the *only* thing that eases my pain. And anyway, if this is a social occasion, there ain't a thing wrong with a man imbibin' a wee bit. I've worked like a dog all my life, an' I'm entitled to this one small pleasure."

In the midst of her anger and aggravation, especially at his latter comments, Maddie suddenly wanted to weep with sorrow and give her father anything he desired. Guilt threatened to strangle her. If only she could make everything right for him! She was his oldest daughter; wasn't it her duty to make things right for him, especially now when he was old and weary and life had beaten him down?

"Ma wouldn't want you to suffer like this, Pa. She surely wouldn't want you to drink yourself to death. Think of how upset she'd be if she knew you were still so miserable, more than a year after her death. Even if you don't feel like it, you have to get on with your life. Think about Little Mike, Carrie, Zoe, and me, too. So many things need doing on the farm . . . and . . . and we've had some financial problems . . . and racing season has started, and you always loved racing season . . ."

"I can't think about none of that, Maddie. I can't think about nothin' anymore, and I've lost all my strength. Hell, most of the time, I can't even remember what day it is."

"It's Tuesday, the eighteenth of June, and if you rose from that bed and joined us more often at the supper table, you might feel stronger . . ."

"Godawmighty. Do you have to bully me so, girl? Let me sleep a bit, and maybe I will come join you in a while."

"Oh, Pa! Would you? That would be wonderful. I'll have Mary fix a plate for you, and we'll keep it warm on the stove until you're . . ."

"Miss Maddie?" Pawnee Mary stuck her head inside the door. "Son of Wolf coming. I see him riding toward house."

Maddie whirled around, her heart suddenly slamming against her rib cage. Crossing the room in three strides, she lowered her voice to inquire: "Is anybody with him?"

"No. He come alone. Ride beautiful golden-brown horse."

"That's his mare—the one who beat Gold Deck. Goodness, where are the twins? Have they come in with the flowers for the table? Is Little Mike still out at the barn?"

Mary's dark eyes lit with amusement. She raised her hand as if to ward off Maddie's enthusiasm. "He is only a man, my friend. Do not let him see that he stirs your heart."

"Stirs my heart?" Maddie repeated, stunned. "Why, of course, I know he's only a man. And he doesn't stir me in the least," she hotly denied.

Pawnee Mary's brow lifted in disbelief, and a smile hovered around her mouth. "If you say so, I believe it. Or maybe not. Your eyes speak differently."

"My eyes aren't saying a single word. I'm just excited because we have a dinner guest—not because I harbor any personal feelings for him. Cease this nonsense, Mary, and let's go greet him."

Maddie swept past the tall Indian woman without saying another word. Goodness, if her emotions were so transparent everyone knew of them before she herself had come to grips with them, she would have to work extra hard this evening to make certain Mr. Cumberland—Chase—never guessed how disturbing—and exciting—she found his presence!

As it happened, the evening went far better than Maddie had dared hope. Everyone was on their best behavior, and Chase proved to be a charming, entertaining guest—regaling them all with hilarious stories of races he had witnessed or taken part in. He looked wonderfully handsome in a dark green shirt that somehow emphasized the whiskey-color of his eyes. The twins promptly fell in love with him, Little Mike joined in the questions and conversation, and Pawnee Mary even volunteered a few comments.

Best of all, Pa joined them for a short while, ate a bit of dinner, and actually chuckled at Chase's jokes before deciding that he had exhausted himself beyond his meager endurance and must return to his bedchamber.

Over pie and coffee, they debated the merits of several lines of Quarter Running horses, and Maddie learned that one of Chase's mares had been sired by a well-known thoroughbred named Frank James, whose get she had always admired. She also discovered that Chase had been taught to ride by being thrown atop a horse's bare back, having a surcingle drawn around the horses's middle and fastened down over his knees, so he couldn't fall off, and then let loose to discover how to fend for himself.

The only instruction he'd been given was to hold onto a throat collar, rather than the reins, and to use his legs to steer, as well as to make the horse go faster.

"Wasn't your father worried you might get into trouble?" Zoe gazed at him, awestruck, her sweet face alight with admiration.

"If he was, he never let on," Chase informed her with a chuckle. "His method must have worked, because by the age of five, I was chasing wild range cattle with him."

"Where's your pa now?" Little Mike asked.

"Died of snake bite when I was eleven. And my ma got kicked in the head by her mare three years after and followed him to the grave. It was my brother who finished raising me."

His sudden flush told Maddie he hadn't meant to mention his brother at all this evening.

Carrie immediately took advantage of the slip. "Why didn't you bring your brother with you tonight, Mr. Cumberland? We'd like to meet him. Maddie told us all about him, and we'd make sure he felt welcome in our home."

"She told you all about him, did she?" The amber eyes sought Maddie's face, and she could have sworn they glinted yellow with a spark of anger.

"I thought it best," she hastened to explain. "My family's bound to see him riding about sooner or later, and in case you *did* decide to bring him with you tonight, I wanted them to know about . . . about . . ."

"His strangeness," he finished for her.

Chase glanced around the table at the eager, interested, young faces. Three pairs of blue-green eyes were all watching him. Even Pawnee Mary seemed fascinated, Maddie thought, and she wished anew that Buck Cumberland had accompanied his brother tonight.

"I'm asking all of you the same thing I asked your sister yesterday morning. Please keep my brother's existence a secret. Buck is extremely shy and needs his privacy. That's why we moved here, so we could start over without anyone knowing about him. He doesn't intend to ever leave our ranch. He's perfectly content there and just wants to be left alone. It's not that he's disfigured, but his appearance always provokes comment. Then my brother gets angry and frustrated—all the more so because he can't speak up and let folks know that he's just like they are underneath. Can I count on you not to bother him or tell anyone else about him?"

Wide-eyed, the twins solemnly nodded. Little Mike shrugged his shoulders. "Ain't nobody's business who's living on your place," he said, sounding like Pa.

"It isn't," Maddie corrected, but it sounded more like she was simply agreeing instead of taking exception to Little Mike's grammar.

"I keep secret, too," Pawnee Mary suddenly spoke up from the end of the table where Maddie had insisted she join them for the meal. "But I not agree with why you want this. Living hidden life only make your brother miserable. I know; I live with scorn and prejudice my whole life. Better to face it. Stand proud. Look enemies in eye."

"We've tried that, and it hasn't worked," Chase curtly responded. "Enough about my brother. This is the last I'll speak of him. He doesn't exist—remember?"

There was a long moment of silence, and then Carrie said brightly: "Why don't we retire to the front porch where it's cooler and . . . and visit some more? I know my sister's just dying to tell you about the bloodlines of *our* mares . . ."

"Carrie!" Maddie remonstrated, but the twinkle had returned to Chase's eyes.

"Have you any mares worth mentioning, Miss McCrory? Somehow I was under the impression that the only horse of value you owned was that lazy old stallion."

Glad of a change of topic, Maddie nonetheless refused to rise to the bait. "We do have a few old nags in the barn whose bloodlines might be of interest you. Then again, they might not. You may not have heard of their sires."

"Short horses?" His tone vibrated with curiosity.

Maddie rose with a feminine swish of her full skirts. "Come out onto the front porch, and maybe I'll tell you about them. Girls, you'd better help Mary clear the table . . ."

"Aw, Maddie!" both girls chorused. "We can clean up after Mr. Cumberland's gone home. Or maybe Mike can help for once . . ."

"Not me." Little Mike pushed back his chair. "Washin' dishes ain't my job. Besides, I'm tired. If y'all excuse me, I'm goin' to bed."

"Nice meeting you, Mike." Chase Cumberland stood and extended his hand to the young man. "If you can find the time, I'd like to come by in a day or two and finish that breeding chute. Show you how to use it, too. But I'll need your help. Between the two of us, we can have it done in no time. Then you can tell *all* your sisters to keep their noses out of your business."

"Sure. All right. . . . Thanks."

Maddie tried to keep from beaming. Chase had handled her brother just right—appealing to him in a grown-up, masculine fashion that implied he was capable of handling the entire breeding operation on his own. She had worried that Little Mike might resent Chase's interference and take it as an insult that he thought they *needed* a breeding chute. But Chase had neatly sidestepped those potential problems and kept Little Mike's pride intact.

Happier than she could remember being in a long, long, time, Maddie rose from the table and led the way to the front porch.

With Maddie and Chase Cumberland out of the house, Pawnee Mary swiftly cleared the table with Carrie and Zoe. When that was done, she excused the girls from helping with the dishes and told them they were free to rejoin their sister and her guest. Both Carrie and Zoe gave her a quick hug.

"You sure you don't mind cleaning up all this mess by yourself, Mary?" Zoe asked, while her sister hurried toward the front door without a backward glance.

"Not mind. What not finished tonight can wait 'til morning. I put away food and stack dirty dishes. Then I leave. Today long day. Feet want rest. You tell Maddie I think we do enough for one day."

"You're such a dear, Mary! I'll tell her. Coming from you, she's bound to listen and let things go for one night. I don't want to miss a minute of Mr. Cumberland's company. He's sooo handsome, don't you think?"

Mary nodded, smiling at the girl's obvious infatuation. "You stay only short while, then yawn and drag sister away. Leave Maddie alone in moonlight with Son of Wolf."

"Leave them alone! But . . ." Zoe sucked in her lower lip and sighed. "Oh, I guess you're right. Mr. Cumberland—Son of Wolf—is a much better choice for Maddie than that horrible Horace Brownley. Only I like him, too, Mary—and so does Carrie."

"Too old for you and Carrie. Better you have him for brother-in-law. Must make it happen. Help love to blossom. Tell Carrie."

"Carrie won't like it; she's planning on marrying Mr. Cumberland herself. She told me so last night."

"What wrong with her? Oldest daughter must marry first. Then little sisters. You tell her I take switch to bottom if she not leave Maddie and handsome neighbor alone."

"You'd do that? Take a switch to her bottom? Goodness, she wouldn't like that!"

Mary nodded, carefully concealing her amusement at Zoe's gullibility. "Tell her Pawnee Mary remember savage ways of her people. Not afraid to use them in good cause. Miss Maddie need one, true mate. Not ugly banker with little pig eyes. Son of Wolf much better. Sisters help or won't be able to sit down for one week. I see to it."

Zoe's eyes widened at the threat. "I'll make her leave, Mary. I'll drag her away if I have to. We'll both go to bed, just like Little Mike and Pa."

"Your brother have good sense. You and Carrie do this, and I promise make blackberry cobbler tomorrow. Blackberries ripening down by river, where I live."

"Blackberry cobbler! That's my favorite—Carrie's, too."

Mary nodded, sure she had achieved her objective now. "You go visit now—little while. I leave soon. See you tomorrow."

She watched as Zoe sprinted toward the front porch. Then

Mary began to gather up the remnants of their meal and pack them into a basket. The talk about Mr. Cumberland's mysterious brother had greatly intrigued her. If the man had indeed been struck by lightning and survived the experience, his medicine must be very powerful.

This was yet another example of how stupid and blind whites could be; it was just like them to be cruel and heartless to a man blessed by the spirits! Indians recognized and revered men who were different and set apart from others, while whites only feared and despised them.

Mary thought of men who behaved and dressed like women; whites were likely to shoot them or run them out of their towns, but the Indians of most tribes treated them with respect and accorded them special ceremonial duties. Buck Cumberland could be no different; the fact that he looked unusual and couldn't speak meant he possessed a special connection to the world beyond the knowledge of men.

Yet he must hunger as men did, and she—who understood these things—would take him food and let him know that she revered and honored him, as others did not. All her life, she had walked a lonely path, for the most part despised and feared by those around her; already she felt a deep kinship for this man she had not yet met. Tonight, she would meet this silver-haired man—and let him know he was not alone.

Nine

Perched on the slat-back chair on the porch, Maddie watched her sisters giggle and flirt with Chase Cumberland. Chase sat on the porch railing, one booted foot lifted to steady himself on the railing and the other resting on the floor. Little lamplight spilled from the house to illuminate the setting, but the stars were bright enough to silver his profile, revealing just how handsome and masculine he really was. . . . Looking at him, Maddie felt an aching tightness in the region of her heart.

Now that she knew him better, she realized that Chase was exactly the sort of man a woman could imagine for a husband, a lover, a friend . . . someone who prompted her to laugh and turned her insides to calf's foot jelly every time he looked at her. Someone to share her dreams, run the ranch, and assume some of the financial burdens that now weighed so heavily on her shoulders.

Yes, she could one day turn most of her responsibilities over to Little Mike, but it wouldn't be the same as having her own man to stand between her and the oftentimes harsh, cruel world. Maddie had never met anyone who made her think of all these things; certainly, Horace Brownley didn't come to mind when she thought of having children—either breeding them or raising them! Until now, she hadn't minded her loneliness, hadn't even admitted to herself that she was lonely. Until now.

For his part, Chase seemed totally charmed and fascinated by Carrie and Zoe, yet every once in a while, his gaze sought hers, and he gave her a slow, languorous grin that was surely meant for her alone. She suddenly realized he was just being nice to her sisters for *her* sake; his expression said he was patiently waiting for the girls to say good-night so he could spend time alone with her . . . at least, she hoped that's what his look meant.

"Girls, it's getting late, and Mr. Cumberland will have to leave soon. You ought to be saying your good-byes now," she prompted, and Chase's grin widened.

"It's not that late," Carrie objected, but surprisingly, Zoe agreed.

"Come on, Carrie. You promised to brush out my hair tonight and help me tie it up with rags and witch hazel so it will be curly tomorrow."

"Oh, I forgot. Your *beau* is coming by to bring a mare for breeding, isn't he?" Carrie's ploy to inform Chase that Zoe already had a special male friend was transparent to everyone, including Zoe. Zoe, amazingly, did not take offense.

"He said he *might* come by; I can't be certain. But I do want to try a new hair style, and you promised to help me with it, Carrie."

"Oh, all right," Carrie ungraciously conceded after Zoe elbowed her in the side for good measure. "You don't have to break my ribs. I can take a hint I'm not wanted."

"Goodnight, girls. Thanks for a fine evening," Chase said to both of them as they uttered their final pleasantries.

"Do come back now," Carrie gushed, boldly touching his arm. "We'd love to have you any time you'd care for a nice home-cooked meal. Wouldn't we, Maddie?"

Her effusiveness embarrassed Maddie; she made a mental note to scold her sister once again for being too forward. "I'm sure Mr. Cumberland is going to be much too busy at his ranch this time of year to come visiting very often."

"It's not that far away," Carrie doggedly pointed out. "Oh, and you *must* come to Abilene the next time we race Gold Deck!"

"The next time?" Chase's brows lifted at the same time as Maddie's heart sank. "When will that be? Do you do much racing in Abilene?"

Don't you say a word, Carrie McCrory. Maddie sent a furious, unspoken message to her sister, but Carrie was intent on nailing down the next time she might get to see Chase Cumberland again.

"We just won a race in Salina the day you came over to start building that breeding chute, and we have another set up in Abilene for the fourteenth of July. This one's for five thousand dollars—can you believe it? When we win, we're going to be rich!"

And if we lose, we're going to have to hand over the farm, lock, stock, and barrel. You foolish, foolish girl! How could you have mentioned this to Chase—the last person in the world I wanted to know about it?

"Five thousand dollars," Chase repeated, looking both thoughtful and impressed. "You must be real confident to agree to such high stakes. I assume it will be one-on-one, like your stallion's race against my mare."

"Sure, I guess so," Carrie blathered on, blissfully unaware that she had committed a grave error. In her usual feather-headed way, she couldn't have been paying close attention when Maddie told her the specifics of the race, because she failed to mention that the race was still open to one other entry—thank God!

Maddie leapt to her feet. "Time for bed, girls. You've lingered long enough, and we've lots to do tomorrow. I don't want to hear another word from you—off to bed with you now."

"Honestly, Maddie," Carrie sniffed. "You treat us like babies. Whether you like it or not, we are grown women."

"That is a debatable subject, Carrie, but we'll not go into it at the moment. Don't wake Pa or Little Mike when you go in—and send Pawnee Mary out for a moment, will you? I need to ask her if she can help me with laundry sometime this week. If she can't, you girls will have to do it on your own, because I'm going to be busy with the horses all week."

"Pawnee Mary already left," Zoe murmured over her shoulder. "But she did say she'd be back in the morning to finish cleaning up the dishes."

"Humph! No need for her to do it when I've got two *grown* women in the house besides myself."

Both Carrie and Zoe shot her a look of disgust. "Good-night again, Mr. Cumberland!" they sang out and quickly departed before Maddie could think of other jobs for them to undertake tomorrow.

Chase chuckled and removed his boot from the railing. "Hard on your sisters at times, aren't you, Maddie? From the way they were looking at you, they must think you're a regular tyrant."

"I have to be," Maddie answered, giving him her full attention. "Or else nothing would ever get done around here unless I did it."

Please, dear God, don't let him ask me anything more about the race! If he does ask, I'll have to lie to him. I can't *tell him the race is still open. He'd be perfectly within his rights to enter Bonnie Lass, and then we'd lose for certain! Well, maybe not for certain, but it's a risk I don't want to take.*

She hoped her face and eyes didn't reveal her thoughts, and they must not have, because Chase didn't reintroduce the topic of the race. Instead, he stepped closer to her and simply stood there, smiling down at her, and making her pulse pound wildly as a result of his physical proximity. She didn't know whether or not to step backward from him or remain where she was—and she didn't know where to look to escape his perceptive gaze. As the moments ticked by, and he didn't say anything, all thoughts of the race fled from her mind; the only thing she could think about were the waves of heat radiating from Chase's looming body and the certainty that something was about to happen. She half expected a twister to appear off the prairie and sweep them both up in a whirling maelstrom.

Chase reached out and lightly encircled her waist with his hands. "That was a great supper, Maddie," he said quietly.

"Oh, you should thank Pawnee Mary." Maddie strove not to appear flustered. "All I did was make the pie."

"I liked the pie best of all." He drew her to him, and her breasts brushed his chest. She suddenly felt as if she were burning up with fever. If he held her any longer—or touched her anywhere else—she might go up in smoke or burst into flame.

"I also want to tell you how charming you looked—look—this evening, and what a good time I had. It's been much too long since I last ate a civilized meal in a family setting. I thoroughly enjoyed myself."

She struggled to keep things light, though an undercurrent of something heavy, dark, richly enticing—and highly inflammatory—still simmered between them. "Not everyone would consider a meal eaten with the McCrory family as a civilized encounter. Sometimes, our meals more closely resemble what happens when a pack of coyotes bring down a fresh kill."

He laughed softly. "You shouldn't worry so much that someone might see your family members when they aren't on their best behavior. Scrapping and fighting are as much a part of family life as being sweet and polite to one another."

She couldn't help smiling. "Have you been spying on us, perhaps? If you have, you've undoubtedly noticed that we spend far more time scrapping than we do being sweet and polite."

"So?" He shrugged. "I discovered long ago that provoking my older brother was a lot more fun than getting along with him. . . . Maybe that's why I feel so drawn to you, Maddie. You're a worthy opponent—tart and spicy, not like most females, who make a man want to run and hide from all that cloying sweetness."

His lips were close to hers now, and Maddie had the unnerving sensation that she was poised on the brink of a precipice, eager to leap into the unknown, even if it meant her own destruction. "I thought men *liked* women to be sweet and helpless."

She drank in his breath, which hinted of cinnamon from the pie. Inhaling the same air as he did was a heady experience—like sniffing the wind just before a storm off the prairie.

"Generally they do. However, since meeting you, I've begun to re-evaluate my youthful preferences."

His hands tightened around her waist, and his mouth descended and grazed hers—gently, as if he were experimenting with kissing her. She brought her hands up to rest on his shoulders. Beneath her fingertips, those shoulders were very wide, broad, solid, and strong, exactly the way a man's should be. The feather-light touch of his lips was nothing like being kissed by Horace Brownley or the one or two young men who had dared to kiss her years ago. All her earlier kisses had been fumbling, awkward affairs, occurring when she was about the same age as Carrie and Zoe and had attended a few socials with her parents. Now, with Chase, she discovered there was nothing either awkward or disgusting about the way his lips slanted lightly across hers—as if he were teasing her. Tempting her. Savoring the kiss and inviting her to kiss him back.

She found herself leaning into him to support herself. Her legs had become dangerously wobbly, like a newborn foal's. He slowly deepened the kiss, pressing his mouth more firmly against hers, then opening his lips and withdrawing slightly to whisper into her mouth.

"Open for me, Maddie. Don't be afraid. I won't hurt you."

She realized she had been holding her lips stiffly closed—resisting the feelings his kiss engendered and trying to keep from abandoning all caution and allowing delirium to overtake her. She parted her lips, licked them nervously, and before she realized what he was about, he pulled her tightly to him and kissed her in earnest. Open-mouthed. Tongue to tongue. Their breath intermingled and their bodies forged together. The proof of his arousal bulged against her lower abdomen, and she feared she might collapse at his feet.

Her legs threatened to buckle and slide out from beneath her, leaving a quivering puddle on the floor. But he held her up and then lifted her off her feet so that their bodies fit together perfectly, reminding her of a key being inserted in a lock. Only his *key* was enormous and pulsing with life. Through her skirt and petticoat she could feel it—*him,* probing between her thighs, invading her most private place. It was all suddenly too much too soon. His masculinity seemed overpowering—almost frightening. For the first time in her life, she understood why maiden mares kicked and squealed and danced away from the stallion.

Was it fear of the unknown—or just plain excitement and ignorance of what to do next?

"Chase!" she gasped into his ravenous mouth as he all but sucked the word from the depths of her being.

He stopped kissing her, and their jointly ragged breathing thundered in her ears. She wanted him to stop. At the same time, she wanted him to go on kissing her forever. Most of all, she wanted to see where all this kissing and delicious anticipation led. She was still clinging to him, her feet off the floor, and he was still holding her clasped against him, with every ridge of muscle and manifestation of his gender glaringly evident against her quaking flesh.

"H-hadn't you better p-put me down?" Her voice came out in a mortifying squeak.

Slowly, reluctantly, he let her slide down the front of him. The fascinating journey only served to tease and torture her already bedazzled senses. Her feet reconnected to the floor, but she lacked the strength to push away from him. He nuzzled her hair.

"Sorry, Maddie. I didn't mean to frighten you. I . . . I had almost forgotten what it felt like to hold a woman."

Disappointment flooded her. There it was again—another reference to his need for female companionship. What had he said the night she had wept in his arms? *". . . before you fall prey to the fact that I've been a long time without a woman."*

Any woman might have done this to him; it wasn't because he was holding *her,* Maddie McCrory, the "also-ran."

Abruptly, she found the strength to step back from him. "This wasn't all your fault. I'd almost forgotten what it feels like to hold a man."

His grin flashed in the darkness. "You do this often?"

His tone told her he didn't believe it for a minute—damn him! He made her feel shy, awkward, and woefully inexperienced, when she desperately needed to regain confidence and reassert control over her riotous feelings.

"You are hardly the first man I've ever kissed," she haughtily informed him. "And I doubt you'll be the last."

She hoped she had put him in his place. Did he think she

ought to be grateful for his attentions—poor discarded spinster that she was? What was wrong with her anyway—allowing an opponent to get this close to her and to undermine all her defenses?

"You're trying not to like me, aren't you?" he chided. "That's probably a good idea, what with my responsibilities to my brother and all."

"And mine to my family. Frankly, I have neither the time nor the inclination to pursue these intimacies, Chase—Mr. Cumberland."

"So we're back to Mr. Cumberland." He heaved a great sigh. "Maybe it's for the best . . . Miss McCrory. After all, we might find ourselves facing each other in a race again—and that would be awkward in the extreme, wouldn't it?"

She went still and cold inside—afraid to breathe lest he discover her secret. "Oh, I think we can manage to avoid that situation if we try hard enough. Why don't we simply agree not to?"

"Not to *what?*"

He was being deliberately obtuse.

"Race against each other," she snapped. "Since we're neighbors and have to get along, we should promise here and now not to challenge each other in the future. I'm preparing some of our younger horses to race, and I'm sure you will be, too—but it's pure foolishness—and financially unwise—to be constantly competing. There are plenty of other horses in the region, so why should we jeopardize our friendship by trying to outdo each other?"

He rocked forward and peered at her suspiciously. "Is that your real reason for inviting me over here tonight? You don't want to have to face me or my horses in a race ever again, so you thought you ought to make it clear right up front?"

"That's *not* why I invited you, but I do think we should agree to . . . to avoid competition, in the interests of neighborliness, of course."

"You mean in the interests of protecting *your* interests. I doubt you'd be suggesting this if Gold Deck had beaten Bonnie Lass, instead of the other way around."

He was right. She wouldn't. If anything, she'd be challenging him to another race. "Then you won't agree?"

"No, Miss McCrory, I won't. Buck and I came here to improve our fortunes. I intend to do that any way I can. I'll gladly race any of my horses against any of your horses any time, anywhere, for any amount of money. That's how much I believe in my horses. If you don't believe in yours that much, you shouldn't be racing them at all, much less for five thousand dollars. As I recall, you wouldn't go anywhere near that high with me."

"No, I wouldn't. But what I do with others has nothing to do with you. In any case, I *do* believe in my—our—horses. You just got lucky the first time we raced, Mr. Cumberland."

"Oh, then you're ready to race again? How much do you want to put up this time? How about that field I want and a dozen free breedings to Gold Deck against—say—oh, you name the figure, but five grand sounds good to me if you've got that much to wager against someone else."

"I am *not* accepting any challenges from you. Gold Deck's racing season is already scheduled," she lied, having no races except the next big one, about which they were arguing. "But even if I still had openings in his schedule, I wouldn't accept another race with you."

"Because you know he'd lose."

"Because it's *always* been our policy not to race our next-door neighbors."

"Old man Parker raced horses?"

"I didn't exactly say that."

"No, you didn't—but you aren't very good at dissembling, Miss McCrory. Dark as it is out here, I can see in your eyes that you aren't being completely honest with me."

"I don't owe you complete honesty! I *owe* you nothing. . . . Except perhaps supper for being so kind as to build us a breeding chute. Come to think of it, in exchange for that, I *might* consider allowing *one* free breeding to Gold Deck. That would be a fair exchange . . ."

"I didn't come over here to build that breeding chute so I could coerce you into giving me a free breeding for one of my mares." Chase's jaw clenched in anger; dark as it was—a cloud must have covered the sky overhead—she had no difficulty seeing *that.*

"Then why *did* you decide to build the chute? I don't recall asking for your help. We McCrorys are a proud lot who need nothing from no one—especially not from our competitors."

"Because I felt sympathy for you, damn it! You do need help before one or more of you gets seriously hurt."

"You mean you felt pity for us. Well, we don't need your pity! We're perfectly capable of solving our own problems, thank you very much."

"My brother doesn't need *your* pity either. All we ask is that you leave us alone and stay off our property. You mind your business, and we'll mind ours."

"Fine. Excellent. Good *night,* Mr. Cumberland!"

"Good *night,* Miss McCrory!"

As Chase stomped off the porch, Maddie marched back into the house and slammed the door behind her. Her temples throbbed with the need to throw something, and red spots danced before her eyes. She couldn't remember ever being so angry; neither, unfortunately, could she recall exactly what they had been fighting about. The issues weren't as clear to her now—just moments after the argument—as they'd been when she'd been trading barbs and attempting to get the best of Chase Cumberland.

Now, she remembered—oh, yes. He had all but insulted her, implying that *any* woman was capable of . . . of . . . arousing him. And he *had* been aroused when he was holding and kissing her. She knew all about aroused stallions and was thus perfectly capable of recognizing an aroused *man* when she rubbed up against one.

That had started it. Then he had *laughed* at her, knowing full well how she had been feeling and mocking her for it. Oh, and he had also accused her of lying to him, when she had gone out of her way to *avoid* telling him falsehoods, and to top it all off, he had admitted *pitying* her family. How dare he!

He and his brother were the ones to pity; they were downright pitiful. One was hiding out like a criminal, and the other permitting it, allowing his only brother to become a recluse, cut off from the entire world. Why, Chase Cumberland ought to be ashamed of himself!

Incensed anew, Maddie paced up and down the front room and only stopped when Zoe's white-gowned figure suddenly appeared at the bottom of the stairwell. Her sister looked like a wraith that had just crawled out of a grave. Her hair was divided into small hunks and inexpertly rolled up and tied with bits of rag, and she had plastered more slimy, gunky stuff across her cheekbones and the bridge of her nose.

"What happened, Maddie? Where's Mr. Cumberland? Did you two disagree over something?"

"I don't wish to discuss it."

"But . . . what happened? You were getting along so well."

"I'm sorry, but it's not possible to get along with Chase Cumberland. I don't wish to hear his name mentioned ever again in my hearing. Go to bed, Zoe. Go to bed this instant, or I swear I'll begin screaming and throwing things."

"Honestly, Maddie. If you don't learn to be nicer to eligible men, when there are so few of them around, especially ones who look like Mr. Cumberland, you are *never* going to get married."

Turning on her heel, Zoe flounced back upstairs, leaving Maddie to face the bitter truth: She probably never was going to get married. At least, not to Chase Cumberland. And not to anyone else either. In the relatively short space of time she had known him—and the even shorter time she had spent kissing him—he had completely spoiled her for any other man on God's green earth.

Pawnee Mary stood clutching her basket in the moonlight in front of the darkened house belonging to Son of Wolf and his brother, Buck, the silver-haired one. It was too early yet for sleep, but not a light shone in the small, modest dwelling. Perhaps, he had gone to bed already . . . and perhaps not. A prickling sensation swept across her shoulder blades, the same reaction she had whenever she approached the site of a grave. She sensed the presence of a spirit—only this was not a departed one, but the strong medicine of a vitally alive man.

Slowly, listening intently, Mary pivoted in a circle, but she saw nothing out of the ordinary. Her straining senses registered the presence of horses in the corral nearest the house. She could see, smell, and hear them, but nothing revealed the presence of a man. Still, she knew he was there, hiding himself in some dark patch of shadow, hardly daring to breathe lest he betray himself.

She considered speaking to him, but immediately discarded the idea. First, he must make himself known—must indicate that he desired contact. All her experience with wild, untamed creatures indicated that she must exercise patience, or the wild one would flee before she had a chance to gaze upon it. With this strange, wounded man, she knew she must be especially careful. From all accounts, he had been hurt by previous contact with his fellow humans, so he would be doubly wary about permitting present or future meetings.

Shifting the basket of food to one hip, Mary carried it to the porch step and set it down. This was her first offering; it might require several before Silver Hair consented to show himself. She did not live so far away that she could not stop regularly to leave him things. Her shack was down by the river, closer to the Cumberland property than it was to the McCrory farm. Most people thought the shack abandoned, and indeed, it had been deserted by whites several years ago, after a plague of grasshoppers had eaten everything in sight. Actually, it was an old soddy house, built of earth rather than wood or limestone, but she knew how to make it comfortable, and few people were aware she now inhabited it.

She was glad it stood so near; she relished living in the same area as a man blessed by Tirawa, the Sky-Dweller, who had created the world and everything in it. Son of Wolf's brother might not realize his own powers, but if he gave her the smallest chance, she would teach him how special he was . . . how beloved of the gods, of whom Tirawa was the greatest. Silver Hair might even be a *wakan,* what the whites referred to as a medicine man or shaman.

Mary couldn't be certain until she met him. Even then, she might not be certain. Her memory of the ways of her people had dimmed over the years; the Pawnee had lived in Kansas long ago, and very few of her bloodline were left in the region. She herself had been raised among the Kiowa. When the Kiowa were forced onto reservations, she had been taken in by white missionaries. But she had run away from them, for she did not want to forget who she was or where she had come from—the ancient tribe of the Skidi Pawnee.

Her people had once practiced human sacrifice to the god of the Morning Star, but she honored them still and strove to keep herself worthy of her heritage—which was why she had come here this night. Son of Wolf's brother was a man marked by Tirawa, and she would accord him the proper homage, as best she knew how.

Leaving the basket of food on the step, she slipped back into the wan splash of light from the rising new moon and again studied her surroundings. Perhaps Silver Hair would refuse to reveal himself tonight, and she would have to be satisfied with sensing his presence, though she longed to see him in the flesh.

"Come see what I have brought you," she whispered in her own language, then smiled at her foolishness.

Blessed or not, Silver Hair would not understand a word she was saying. Her invitation would fall on deaf ears—but over time, her actions might serve to convince him that he could trust her. She thought of a special gift she might make him: a soft, comfortable pair of moccasins—so much kinder to the feet than the stiff, heavy boots white men liked to wear!

Thinking of how she would decorate them, wondering if he had the same size feet as his brother, she turned to leave. She was halfway across the yard in front of the house when a shot suddenly rang out, and something zinged past her left ear. Mary stood still and waited, but no one spoke to her. No one appeared.

Slowly, so as not to give alarm, she faced the barn, from which she thought the attack had come. The moonlight made her an easy target for a man with a gun, but if Silver Hair meant to kill her, he would already have done so. She had lingered a long time leaving her basket on the porch step.

Raising her head, she called out to him, giving him his first gift: his new name. "Silver Hair! Fear not. I mean you no harm. I only bring food."

She waited, but the only sound was the whisper of the breeze and the thud of hooves as the horses paced restlessly, startled by the unexpected gunfire.

"Silver Hair . . . I, too, know loneliness and hurt. I am Pawnee—alone and outcast. Give me a chance, Silver Hair. Come to me. Show yourself."

Something moved in the shadows. A figure detached itself from the blackness of the barn door and slowly walked toward her. As the man drew near, Mary saw that he was tall, with hair that was indeed silver and shimmered in the moonlight. His eyes shone like twin moons in a dark, unfriendly face.

He came abreast of her, and they regarded each other silently for a moment. Knowing he would never do so, she initiated the first move. Lifting her hand, she gently laid it alongside the rough skin of his jaw. He suffered her touch, his fierce, wild eyes probing her face, as if he didn't trust her motives—or believe she had actually come to him. She dared a smile.

"I am here, Silver Hair," she whispered. "Never again you be alone."

The rifle remained in one hand, but after a long pause, Silver Hair raised the other and with a trembling finger, stroked along the curve of her cheekbone. She closed her eyes and leaned into the tentative caress. Turning her head, she brushed his palm with her lips in welcome.

The small gesture proved to be all he needed. He threw the gun to the ground and pulled her to him. She could feel him shaking—or perhaps it was she who quaked like a leaf blowing in the sweet night wind. They stood together, their arms wrapped around each other. Mary chanced to glance up at the sliver of new moon and there saw the profile of Tirawa, who had brought them to this time and place. Older than time, possessing a wisdom beyond every other living creature, Tirawa smiled down at them. It was a good omen—one that sealed her surrender.

From this moment on, she belonged to Silver Hair and he to her.

Ten

Damn woman. Maddie McCrory was getting to be as irritating as a swarm of mosquitoes after a heavy rain. Or a pack of flies around a fresh wound. Or a horse that refused to be caught. Or a muddy dog jumping up on clean clothing.

As Chase rode home in the moonlight, he made a mental list of all the ways she bedeviled him. What had he said to raise her hackles tonight and make her so unreasonable? One minute, she was melting in his arms like butter on a hot biscuit, and the next, she was pursing her lips and glaring, as if he had done the unspeakable.

He doubted he would ever be able to figure her out. About the only thing he could be sure of was that she didn't like him finding out about that race she had scheduled in Abilene. When Carrie had so casually mentioned it, the expression of dismay on Maddie's face had told him more than mere words ever could. When she had all but refused to discuss the matter—and suggested that he not challenge her to race ever again—he had known that the race in Abilene was probably open to another entry.

Most horse races in the region were match races, plain and simple, two horses and two riders going head to head in a contest to prove which was the fastest. In the East, blue-blooded Thoroughbreds now raced on oval tracks built to accommodate numerous horses for distances up to a mile or longer. But the further west a man went, the more likely he was to encounter the short-horse style of racing, where two or occasionally three horses of mixed pedigree raced for roughly a quarter mile between two well-defined points.

This style was more practical for primitive conditions, and it had led to the development of a stockier, hardier, more sensible type of animal, one that could cut cattle, pull a wagon, plow, or buggy, and still run a hard, fast race on a moment's notice. Chase himself—and the McCrorys—were attempting to refine this new breed, the short horse or Quarter horse, as some people called it, and make it more efficient, while not sacrificing the versatility that accounted for the breed's popularity.

Gold Deck and Bonnie Lass were prime examples of the new breed, and they *should* be racing other horses as well as each other, testing their mettle time and again, as often as possible and in all kinds of conditions. Only then could good breeding decisions be made about the bloodlines these horses—and others like them—should be crossed with in order to compensate for any weaknesses that surfaced over time.

For Maddie to try and dominate the local racing scene and attempt to keep him from competing with her or anyone else was downright unconscionable. He had as much right as she to enter any race available, thereby demonstrating the worth of his horses and his own particular breeding program. He certainly couldn't go home and tell Buck that from now on he was going to leave all the local races to the McCrorys. Hell, he was just getting started building the Cumberland reputation, and he'd be shooting himself in the foot if he didn't race Bonnie Lass every chance he got.

When he finally retired his prized mare from racing, he wanted people standing in line to purchase her foals in the hope that her offspring had inherited her speed and adaptability. She was the best of his string, but he had other nice mares at home capable of producing promising young stock, too. It was time to think about preparing them to enter the racing world along with Bonnie Lass.

Maddie McCrory had no one but herself to blame that she had waded into waters over her head. She had no business accepting such high stakes if she didn't have five thousand dollars to lose. It was the same as betting the family farm or her entire herd of horses, including Gold Deck, on the outcome of a race; anyone who had played the racing game for very long could tell her she was making a huge mistake.

Did her father know what she was doing? Or was Big Mike McCrory too far gone in drink to even be aware of the problems facing his family?

Chase suspected that Maddie's pa either didn't know or no longer cared that his family was headed toward disaster. Whatever the situation, Chase had to put Buck's and his own interests first; tomorrow he would ride over to Salina and send a wire to Abilene to investigate that race. If, as he suspected, it was still open to another entry, he himself would enter Bonnie Lass. He had been looking around for another race, one where he could win some big money. Every day he discovered the need for more improvements on his ranch. If he did happen to win, which he was sure he would, he'd have Maddie McCrory right where he wanted her—owing him a huge sum of money.

Then she'd have to sell him that field and allow as many breedings as he could ever want. She might even be forced to hand over Gold Deck, or—God forbid—the farm itself. He didn't want the whole damn farm or even the stallion, but he'd take the field and unlimited breedings.

Of course, she would hate him for it, and so would the twins and Little Mike. Big Mike, too, if he were sober enough to understand what was happening. And the Indian woman, Pawnee Mary, might come looking for his scalp. . . . But what did he care what they all thought of him? He couldn't save them from their own mistakes. He wasn't responsible for their current state of affairs. Better he should profit from their failings than someone else. He, at least, would make an attempt to spare their pride and preserve their livelihood; if someone else won the race, the McCrorys wouldn't be so lucky. They'd lose the farm for certain.

He sternly reminded himself that he didn't want to get personally involved with them anyway. He owed his loyalty solely to his brother. He couldn't let his growing feelings for a prickly, snappish, uppity, little spinster color his thinking and alter his business decisions. Maddie McCrory came with too much excess baggage anyway: two troublemaking sisters, a brooding brother, a drunken father, and an outcast Indian for a best friend. A man would have to be moonstruck to look twice at her.

He had enjoyed himself immensely tonight—at least, until Maddie picked a fight with him and turned from cuddly kitten into spitting cat—but an evening's pleasure couldn't be allowed to spoil all his plans for the future. He would go back in a few days to finish building the breeding chute he had promised, and that would be the end of it. He'd be done owing them anything. He had to live his own life, and the McCrorys had to live theirs. He'd race them, beat them, and take their last dollar if they were foolish enough to wager it. It was the *least* he owed his brother.

Wondering why Bonnie Lass had come to a standstill, Chase saw that she had carried him into his own front yard and was now standing there patiently, waiting for him to dismount. Once again, he had been so lost in thought about Maddie McCrory that he had forgotten where he was and what he was doing. No more, he vowed. He didn't like what was happening to him, and he wasn't going to allow it to continue. He especially wouldn't permit himself to dwell on what it had been like to kiss her and hold her slender but sweetly rounded body close to his. The mere memory of that exciting moment gave him an erection as big as Gold Deck's.

Disgustedly swinging down from his horse, Chase noticed that no lights illuminated the house. Buck must have gone to bed already. Hurriedly, he stripped off Bonnie Lass's gear, hung it over the porch railing, turned her out with the other horses, and went into the house.

On impulse, he headed for his brother's room—intending to wake him and tell him about the possibility of winning five thousand dollars. He wanted Buck's encouragement—needed to see his brother's face, his wild eyes and silver hair—to remind him of what was really important and convince him he was doing the right thing. If it came to a choice between Maddie and Buck, it was no choice at all; he had to choose Buck.

"Buck, wake up, ole buddy." Chase kicked in the partially closed door to Buck's room and peered inside.

The light from a new moon streamed across the empty bed. Neither the quilt nor the pillows were rumpled, and nothing in the room was disturbed. It looked as it usually did during the daytime—as if a very neat, organized person lived there and relished keeping things orderly.

"Buck! Where in hell are you?" In less than a minute, Chase discovered that the house was empty. In a panic, he headed for the barn, satisfied himself that his brother wasn't there either, and returned to the house. Wherever Buck was, Chase would have to wait until he showed up. In the dark—or even in the daylight—he hadn't the slightest idea where to search for him.

"I knew I shouldn't have gone over there tonight," he muttered as he lit a lamp. "I should have stayed right here where I belong."

He pictured his brother eating supper alone and feeling lonely and bitter because Chase wasn't there to share it with him. Chase knew how *he* would react if the situation were reversed; he would resent his brother going out and having a good time without him.

Buck had probably disappeared just to teach him a lesson. He must have gone for a solitary walk in the moonlight to work out his frustrations. Chase hoped that Buck wasn't getting into trouble or doing something foolish. He realized he ought to have checked the horses to make sure they were all there, and he dashed out back to the corral and did exactly that.

None of the horses were missing, which meant that Buck had to be on foot. Blaming himself for his brother's disappearance, Chase glumly returned to the house. He could hardly believe the evening had ended so badly, when it had started out so promising. Despite a twinge of guilt at leaving Buck, he had been filled with anticipation when he rode out. Now, his anticipation had turned to ashes, and apparently, it was going to be a long, difficult, blame-ridden night.

* * *

At breakfast the morning after Chase had come to supper, Maddie roundly scolded Carrie for mentioning the race.

"Don't you ever think before you open your mouth, Carrie? What if Mr. Cumberland rides over to Abilene and signs up Bonnie Lass to race against us? If no one else enters the race, it should be an easy victory, but if we're facing that mare of his again . . . well, we don't have five thousand dollars to lose, no more than we had two thousand. This could finish us completely. I should think that would have occurred to you before you prattled on like some foolish prairie chicken tempting a coyote."

Carrie's lower lip quivered, and her eyes widened in distress. "Oh, Maddie, I'm sorry, I didn't realize . . ."

"I know you didn't. That's why I'm telling you now. It's not all your fault, however. I regret inviting Mr. Cumberland to supper. I tried to persuade him to agree not to race against us, but he refused. That makes him our main competitor in the region. There's not another horse for miles around that we need to fear as much as his mare. I had hoped we could just ignore her, but now I'm afraid we'll be facing her every time we turn around. From now on, I'll have to refuse to accept a challenge unless it's limited to only two horses—ours and whoever challenges us. We can't risk agreeing to any more races open to a third entry."

Little Mike swallowed a last bite of bread and pushed back from the table around which he, Maddie, Carrie, and Zoe were seated. Pa hadn't yet shown his face, and Pawnee Mary was late arriving. Usually, if she was coming—and she had said she was—she would have been there by this hour of the morning.

"I hope Mr. Cumberland *does* go over to Abilene and enters that race, Maddie," her brother said with a trace of belligerence. "That way, we'll get to beat him and prove to everybody that we do have the better horse, after all."

"What makes you think Gold Deck can beat Bonnie Lass this time when he didn't the last? That mare of his is fast and fit. I'm still surprised—and angered—at how easily she won. Of course, as you may remember, Mr. Cumberland deliberately misrepresented her. She looked terrible when I saw her before the race, and he behaved as if her appearance was perfectly normal."

"That's no more than Pa used to do," Little Mike argued. "Only you don't have to worry about *this* race, Maddie. If Mr. Cumberland enters Bonnie Lass, we won't lose our money or the farm either. This time, *I* will be riding Gold Deck, and . . ."

Maddie jumped to her feet. "You think we lost to Bonnie Lass because of *me?* I may not have ridden him much lately, but I was the first rider Pa ever put on that horse's back. Have you forgotten? Gold Deck will do anything for me. I was nervous, yes, but I still did a good job. We just couldn't match her; that's all. If I had gotten a better look at her before the race and if Mr. Cumberland had been less devious, we never would have accepted his challenge in the first place. I wouldn't have risked it."

Little Mike set his jaw in a stubborn manner that reminded Maddie of Pa in his younger days—or even their mother when she took a strong notion. "All I'm sayin' is that if I hadn't gotten hurt that day, we would have won, Maddie. And I think we can win if we ever race Bonnie Lass again. Gold Deck wasn't expectin' you to be ridin' him. He got caught by surprise, so he didn't give his best like he usually does."

"I don't know about that, but one thing I do know: Gold Deck still isn't as fit as Bonnie Lass. That problem we can certainly fix, and we *will* fix it, won't we?"

Maddie glared at her cheeky brother. "Just in case Mr. Cumberland *does* decide to hurry on over to Abilene, you'd better start riding Gold Deck a bit harder every single day in preparation. This time, that stallion has got to be at the peak of his form. Do I have your word you won't miss a single day of training between now and the race next month?"

"You want me to ride him even on the days he's breedin'?" Little Mike returned her glare with a strength of character she had never before noticed, and Maddie suddenly realized that the day was coming when he would defy her totally and do what *he* thought best.

The idea both pleased and terrified her.

"Well . . . if you're afraid we're being too harsh on him and his strength will give out, you might cut back on those days only. I'll leave that decision to you. . . . I just don't want you disappearing like you sometimes do for a whole day and forgetting all your responsibilities, including exercising the horses and mucking out the barn."

She knew she had said the wrong thing as soon as the words left her mouth. Little Mike rose from the table and stalked out of the house, slamming the front door behind him. Maddie wondered how the door still remained on its hinges with all the abuse it had taken lately.

Resuming her seat, she damned herself for having goaded her brother. She understood why he sometimes had to leave; the pressure got to be too much for him. When it did, he went fishing or rode into town—and when he returned, he attacked his work with twice the vigor and enthusiasm he normally brought to it. It was his way of letting her know he was sorry for having run out on her.

Would she ever learn to be tactful? Her mother had been able to achieve so much with a simple lift of an eyebrow, but whenever Maddie tried it, it never seemed to work. When she lectured, that didn't work either. She only succeeded in arousing resentment. . . . Yet she needed Little Mike's cooperation so much! Without him, she could never keep the farm going.

Without waiting to be asked, Carrie and Zoe got up and began to clear the breakfast dishes. Their faces, too, showed the strain of the morning, and Maddie devoutly wished she hadn't said a word to anybody. All she had accomplished was to make both Carrie and Little Mike feel badly about things they couldn't fix.

Oh, where was Mary this morning? The older woman's presence always had a calming effect. When Maddie thought of all Mary had to deal with—the rejection and ostracism of the townsfolk, their cruel and malicious gossip, the loss of her Indian heritage—Maddie was better able to put her own trials into perspective.

Mary never dwelt on life's injustices. Instead, she took pleasure in small things—picking blackberries, trapping small game for the stew pot, digging up prairie potatoes, cleaning and tanning hides and making beautiful things out of them, tending her garden and taking inordinate pride in the huge sunflowers she coaxed from the prairie soil.

Today, I shall be more like Mary, Maddie resolved. I will let my troubles slide off me like rain from a gentle shower, and peace will possess my soul.

First on her list of unpleasant chores for the day was to empty out Pa's whiskey jugs—the ones she had hidden yesterday in the hen house. With that goal in mind, Maddie rose from the table and marched out of the house.

The morning was fresh and clear, absolving her from guilt and worry, and she inhaled deeply before heading for the hen house. She planned to carry the jugs behind the stable to the manure pile and there dispose of the noxious contents before Pa discovered what she was doing. If he then made a fuss or insisted on going into town, she'd insist on accompanying him, so he couldn't replenish his supply. She had tried sending one of the twins or Little Mike along with him, but despite her precautions, Pa always managed to outwit the younger McCrorys and achieve his objective of buying more whiskey.

This time, Maddie would make certain he didn't. She was adamant. No more whiskey. No more arguments. No more fights. No more of Pa taking matters into his own hands and finding a way around her.

When she arrived at the hen house, she discovered the chickens already in turmoil—squawking and scolding and scurrying about as if a fox had taken up residence in the poultry yard. The rooster—a big, cocky fellow with crimson head and tail feathers—flew at her skirts, as he always did when she came to gather eggs instead of whiskey jugs.

"Get away!" Maddie wished she had remembered to bring the broom to threaten him. The only thing the rooster respected was the broom—and a couple of the bigger hens. Neither rooster nor broom could intimidate the hen the twins called Big Mama. Big Mama was the terror of the poultry yard.

Chickens scattered in every direction as Maddie shooed them

away from the hen house and stepped inside. There, in a pile of feathers and droppings on the floor sat her father—grinning at her and cradling a jug to his chest.

"Ha! Thought you could hide 'em from me, dincha, girl? Well, I put my old thinker t' work, an' I says t' myself; now, where would Maddie put my jugs where she wouldn't think I'd figure t' look? An' sometime this mornin,' b'fore it got light, the answer come t' me—in the hen house!"

Oh, Lord! Had he been sitting here drinking whiskey since before dawn? Apparently so. Whiskey fumes filled the narrow enclosure, and her father's eyes had "that look." He grinned crookedly, like a little boy caught stealing apples from an orchard or a fresh pie cooling on a windowsill.

"What was you comin' t' do, Maddie? Pour 'em out? Deprive me of what little comfort I can still find in this life? Well, I beat you to it. I emptied 'em myself—right down my gullet."

"All of them, Pa? You finished off all three jugs?" Maddie sank to her knees beside him. Droppings smeared his clothing, his hands, and the whiskey jug he held. . . . He stank to high heaven, but that was the least of his problems. If he had indeed finished off all three jugs, he was surely headed for his coffin.

"Three of 'em? There's three?" Her father blinked and peered around the hen house. "I thought there was only two . . . or maybe four. You know I can't see so good no more. Sometimes, things multiply right while I'm lookin' at 'em. Must be a trick of the light or somethin'."

Maddie took the jug from his arms; it was light enough to be empty. In Hopewell, as in many other small Kansas towns, folks had begun to talk about a statewide ban on the sale of whiskey and closing down all the saloons. Dodge City and Abilene, the big cow towns, had become so wild and lawless that prohibition seemed the only way to enforce order in the cow towns. It couldn't come fast enough to suit Maddie. She hoped that the new president, Rutherford B. Hayes, would help speed things up a bit. His wife, Lucy, reportedly abhorred the consumption of alcoholic beverages and had vowed to serve only lemonade or water at parties during her husband's administration. If that were true, Lucy Hayes was a kindred spirit. . . . What would Lemonade Lucy do in a situation like this?

Setting down the jug, Maddie grasped her father's shoulder. "Can you get up, Pa? You've got to go into the house now and get cleaned up."

"Cleaned up? What fer? Have we got company comin' t'day, too?"

"No, Pa, but you're a mess. This . . ." She waved her hand to encompass everything. ". . . is disgusting. The lowest you've ever sunk. I can't believe you would sit out here in the hen house of all places and drink yourself into oblivion."

He grabbed her hand with surprising strength and focused his bloodshot blue eyes on her. "Don't tell your Ma, Maddie! You keep this between you and me—all right? Don't tell your brother or sisters neither. I don't want 'em t' see me like this. I'm their pa, and they gotta have respect fer me."

How can they have respect for you if you don't have any for yourself? If Ma were still here, she'd put a stop to this behavior.

Maddie's head spun with accusations, but she managed not to utter a word of recrimination. Pa wouldn't remember it if she did say something while he was in this state.

"Lean on me, Pa, and I'll help you into the house. We'll get you cleaned up, and I'll make you some breakfast. You need hot coffee; it will help clear your head."

"Don't want no breakfast. No coffee neither. Jus' wanna set here an' rest a spell."

Pa resisted Maddie's attempts to get him to his feet. He lay back with his head pillowed against a low shelf where a pile of straw held a perfect brown egg. If the hen came back to defend it, she could easily peck out his eyes while he lay in a stupor—especially if the hen were Big Mama.

Maddie considered her options. She would have to fetch Little Mike and the girls to assist her. This time, there was no Chase Cumberland to carry her father to bed. She knew what Chase would tell her to do, but she couldn't leave Pa lying passed out in the hen house, even though he deserved it. As usual, she blamed herself for the incident; she should have dumped the whiskey in the manure pile last night—though there was no guarantee she wouldn't have found him sitting buried to his neck in horse apples this morning, just so he could get close to his beloved liquor.

What she wouldn't give to walk out of this hen house and find another life someplace else! Somewhere in the arms of a man who would love and cherish her and never drink a drop of whiskey in his life. Somewhere she wouldn't have to watch what she said all the time and struggle with her own bossy nature and need to set things right. Somewhere she wouldn't *have* to worry about setting things right all the time.

She supposed there was no place like that in the whole wide world, and she'd be bored if she didn't have a few challenges to entertain her—but at least, she'd be free of all *this*. Having to witness her father's deterioration was a burden she had never expected; all she could do, apparently, was stand by and watch it happen.

She hated most of all having to witness the withering of her own natural optimism. She still viewed each day as a gift—the opening of some precious present, but each day, it was getting harder. She heard herself growing ever more shrewish and despised the way she sounded. Yet no sooner did she resolve to maintain a cheerful disposition when she was faced with finding her drunken father sprawled in the hen house!

Blinking back tears, Maddie started to laugh. Laughter was the only thing left to her. When the day came that she could no longer see the humor in a situation, she'd have to sit down beside Pa and take up a jug herself.

Hearing her laughter, Pa opened one eye and peered up at her. "Wha's so funny, Maddie, girl?"

"You are, Pa," she answered. "If you could only see yourself . . ."

You'd be so ashamed.

He nodded, looking pleased with himself. "So good t' hear you laugh, Maddie. Bes' sound I heard in a long time."

Her laughter gave way to a sob. Chase Cumberland had made her laugh last night—before provoking her anger. That had been *true* laughter, true merriment; this wasn't. This was a desperate attempt to salvage something good out of something so terrible she hated to be a part of it and longed for escape.

Get up and do something, Maddie. Do something before you go mad.

Feeling as old as her father, she got up off the floor and went to fetch her brother and her sisters to help carry Pa into the house.

A week passed before Chase found the courage to think about returning to the McCrorys to finish building the breeding chute. He had procrastinated because he didn't want to be the one to have to tell them he had entered the big race in Abilene. When a wire came back to Salina, confirming that the race was still open, Chase had ridden all the way to Abilene without stopping. There, Lazarus Gratiot had been only too happy to finalize the deal with a handshake, pitting Bonnie Lass against Gold Deck and Gratiot's stallion, One-Eyed Jack.

Of course, Chase had closely examined the stallion beforehand and concluded that Gratiot was one of those sorry, boastful braggarts who thought he could whip any horse to go fast enough to win a race. Obviously, he had won a few races that way and now thought he was invincible. Chase wasn't worried; he relished the idea of leaving Gratiot in the dust. To sweeten the pot, he had made it a claiming race—where the winner had the right to buy the loser's horse if he wished. He didn't make Maddie part of that agreement; this was a private matter between himself and Gratiot.

Chase intended to acquire the poor, abused stallion when Bonnie Lass won. He didn't actually want the horse, but he'd do it to keep the animal from being further abused. He couldn't stand to see horses mistreated. Gratiot had attempted to conceal the stallion's scars with a tarlike substance, but Chase had still detected them buried in the horse's unkempt black coat. Some were fairly fresh. He was surprised Maddie hadn't discovered Gratiot's sly cosmetic work. Maybe she hadn't gotten that close to the horse or just didn't want to mention it to Chase.

Whatever the case, Chase dreaded telling her that they were pitted against each other again. He figured that a week should be long enough for her to have heard it from someone else. Besides, he didn't want to leave Buck alone again so soon.

Buck had been behaving strangely since the night Chase had gone to supper at Maddie's. He had come home at dawn the next morning, nodded serenely at Chase, and gone to bed for a couple of hours. He hadn't bothered to explain where he'd been, hadn't apologized for keeping Chase awake all night worrying, and had refused to answer any questions regarding the incident. And just the other morning, Chase had discovered his brother once again sneaking in the house at dawn.

Buck was clearly up to something. However, the McCrorys were the nearest neighbors, and Hopewell was too far away for a man to walk there and back in one night. . . . So where was Buck going? And why was he suddenly looking so happy and content with his lot in life? Yesterday, Chase had caught him *whistling*. That wasn't like Buck at all; Chase hadn't been aware that his brother *could* whistle.

Buck had stopped when he saw Chase, but his step was still lighter, his grin more frequent, and his mood less somber than Chase could remember in recent years. All this could be attributed to the fact that they finally had a new home, but Chase suspected it was more than that. If he didn't know better, he'd think Buck had found a lady friend.

The only lady in the vicinity was Maddie herself, and Chase couldn't picture Maddie and his brother together. He couldn't picture Maddie with *any* man—or to be more precise, he didn't *want* to picture such a thing. The thought of Maddie laughing and talking with another man or worse yet, *kissing* and being kissed by him, made his insides churn as if he had eaten something that had set out in the sun for three days.

He didn't like the feeling, so he tried not to think of Maddie with another man. Just because *he* didn't want her didn't mean he was willing to hand her over to someone else—particularly not to his brother. Buck wasn't the right man for Maddie, though Chase was hard pressed to imagine what sort of man *would* be right for her.

He had spent the better part of the week trying to convince himself that *he* didn't find her all that appealing; she was nothing more than TROUBLE, spelled in capital letters, but he was still anxious to see her again—and he couldn't put off finishing that breeding chute forever. He had promised Little Mike he'd be over soon to complete it, and he never broke his promises.

Immediately following breakfast one hot, sunny morning, Chase reluctantly saddled Bonnie Lass and rode out to visit the McCrorys. It was a fine morning, with a fresh breeze ruffling the bluestem grasses. Chase skirted patches of prairie phlox, verbena, and ragwort. He was happy to see that despite the lack of rain in recent weeks, none of the vegetation had shriveled and died. Grasshoppers whirred away from Bonnie Lass's hooves, and he was reminded of the plague several years earlier. He could scarcely imagine the sky raining grasshoppers, but he knew it had happened, because people in Hopewell still spoke of it. It had been dry that year, too, the summer of '74, and the grasshoppers had come in early August.

If such a thing were to happen again, it would ruin all his plans. Without grass to support his horses and the cattle he hoped to buy, he and Buck might as well give up and move someplace else. What with grasshoppers, twisters, winter blizzards, and the increasing use of barbed wire to divide the range, Kansas had its challenges—but he hoped to survive and conquer the worst the state could offer, because he was beginning to love it, too.

On a day like today, Kansas was beautiful. The ceaseless wind and the vast vista of the sky beguiled him in a way few places ever had—even Texas. Here, so long as Buck remained hidden, Chase believed he could be his own man, pitting his brawn and his wits against the elements.

He rode along a limestone ridge and wondered if Maddie's father had taken the limestone blocks from here to build his homestead. If he had, it must have been backbreaking labor. In those days, Big Mike had to have been a strong, determined man to have built his house and outbuildings entirely from limestone. Thinking of that determination, Chase was able to muster some respect for the senior McCrory. The man had known his horses, too. Chase liked the look of most of the animals he had seen thus far at the McCrory farm; it was a damn shame Big Mike had succumbed to alcohol.

Feeling sorry for the man, Chase deliberately hardened his heart. He reminded himself that he couldn't allow pity, sympathy, respect, or just the fact that he liked the McCrory family to get in the way of business. Today, his goal was to finish the breeding chute, show Little Mike how to use it, and hightail it back to his own ranch as soon as possible. Whatever his reception, he would maintain his distance and refuse to be drawn into the hopes, dreams, and tragedies of the McCrory family.

Little Mike was the first to spot him when he rode up to the house. "Chase! I mean, Mr. Cumberland. Did you come to finish the breeding chute?"

The young man looked absurdly pleased to see him. He didn't exactly smile but his greenish-blue eyes lit up beneath his broad-brimmed old hat.

"It's Chase to you, Mike. Regardless of what your sisters call me. And yes, I came to finish the chute." Chase dismounted and cast a quick glance toward the front porch.

"I'm afraid you've missed Maddie and the twins. They took the buckboard into town early this morning to pick up supplies. You didn't see them on the way, did you?"

"I didn't take that route. I cut across the prairie." Chase quelled his disappointment; he should be glad Maddie was absent. It would be better for all concerned if he never saw her again. "Good thing your sisters are gone today. That means we can work without interruption."

Little Mike nodded enthusiastically. "Somehow I had a feeling you'd come by today. I got up early and finished most of my chores just in case."

"You had a feeling, did you? That's odd because I didn't decide to come until halfway through breakfast. I had planned to work with some of my young stock today—but then I got to thinking about how you must be needing that chute, and I felt guilty I hadn't made an effort to get over here and finish it sooner."

"We do need it. I got four mares right now waiting to be bred—soon as their time comes. I didn't think it would be today for any of them, so I told Maddie to go ahead into town and get her shopping done. As for Gold Deck, I already rode him this morning, so I'm free for the rest of the day."

Little Mike failed to mention Chase's entry into the Abilene race, and he didn't look upset about it. Therefore, *Maddie must not know about it yet.*

Chase was simultaneously relieved and annoyed. He hoped he could get the damned chute finished and be gone before she arrived home.

"Well, let's get to work on that chute," he urged.

"We'll surprise 'em by having it all done by the time they get here," Little Mike jovially responded.

Chase didn't ask where Big Mike was, and Little Mike didn't volunteer the information. Chase wasn't sure he wanted to know. He especially didn't want to know if Big Mike was off somewhere hitting the jug again. It wasn't his problem, he sternly reminded himself. He was *not* going to worry about it.

But despite all his resolutions, Chase worried the entire time he was there—and Big Mike's drinking habits were only part of the reason. The biggest reason was Maddie herself. Would he—or would he *not*—see her today? And if he did, should he mention that he had entered that damn race?

Eleven

Maddie hustled her sisters out of Grover's Mercantile and into the buckboard far sooner than she had intended. She had been loading a heavy sack of beans when she spotted Horace Brownley leaving the bank. Someone on the street stopped him, and while the two men were talking, Maddie sprang into action.

She loaded both her sisters and their supplies into the buckboard so fast that Zoe complained. "Maddie, stop rushing me. My head's spinning in this heat."

"Hush! Put on your bonnet. Don't look at Mr. Brownley. If he spots you, pretend you don't recognize him. We're getting out of here before he sees us."

"I think you're too late, Maddie," Carrie whispered. "He's already seen us—you, anyway. He's coming this way."

"Maddie! Miss McCrory. Wait, my dear!" Horace called out.

But Maddie was already snapping the whip over Shovel's broad back and clucking like a broody hen. Shovel responded by surging forward at a lumbering trot and snorting in protest at Maddie's eagerness to be gone.

"Get moving or I'll crack you a good one," Maddie threatened for good measure.

Shovel's ears flattened at her tone of voice. He broke into a lope that made the ground shake beneath his big feet and the buckboard creak and groan as if it might split in two. But he was putting distance between Maddie and Horace Brownley; that was all Maddie cared about.

"Don't you dare look back, Zoe!" she warned as her sister

started to turn around. "If you do, he'll know for certain that we're running away from him."

"I'm sure he knows it anyway. You aren't being very subtle—or ladylike, Maddie."

"I don't care. I was hoping to avoid Horace today. I wouldn't have come to town at all if we hadn't run out of flour. The last time I saw Horace I told him I was going to be busy for weeks and wouldn't be able to see him. Now, he'll be angry I didn't stop by the bank while I was here."

"Well, of course he'll be angry. He's been trying so hard to court you, and you're treating him like an old hound dog with fleas."

Carrie sounded cross and agitated. "Slow down, will you, before we hit a bump and go flying off this buckboard to land on our heads."

Maddie decided they were far enough out of town to risk slowing down. Horace could only waddle so far before he got winded; by now, he must have reached his limits. She resisted the impulse to glance over her shoulder to check on his progress. Better he should think she hadn't seen—or heard—him.

She hauled back on the lines, but Shovel, invigorated by all the excitement, ignored her. His legs pumped at twice their normal speed, and he continued moving as if a fire had been lit under his tail.

"Goodness!" Maddie exclaimed. "I believe Shovel wants to race. He thinks he's turned into a Quarter horse and he's trying to stay ahead of the competition, which he obviously thinks is his shadow."

Zoe giggled. "You've been backing the wrong horse, Maddie. You should have bet five thousand on old Shovel instead of Gold Deck. Even Gold Deck couldn't get us home any faster than this."

"Hang on, girls, and let's see how long it takes Shovel to wear himself out."

She arrived home in record time—about midafternoon, instead of late in the day, as usual. By then, well-lathered and blowing, Shovel was eager to drop down to a walk. Maddie let the girls out at the house. Their arms full of supplies, they trudged up the porch steps, while she drove around back to the stable.

Maddie arrived at the very moment Little Mike was leading one of the visiting brood mares over to the wooden structure Chase had started building a week ago in one corner of the small corral. The chute was finished now, and Chase himself stood beside it.

"Take her in and tie her up," he instructed Little Mike. "Then fetch Gold Deck, and I'll show you how this thing works."

At the sound of the approaching buckboard, he glanced up. The sunlight struck sparks in his amber-colored eyes, and Maddie drew a deep breath. Every time she saw Chase, she had the same disturbing reaction. Excitement flared in the pit of her stomach, the palms of her hands grew damp, and her breathing accelerated. His casual pose—he was leaning against the chute with his arms folded across his bare chest—shouted for attention. Lord, but he was handsome! Too handsome for his own good. And hers.

Once again, he had removed his shirt, though today, he wore a red calico kerchief carelessly tied around his neck, sturdy black chaps, and his usual black Stetson. The hat was tilted back on his head, as if he had pushed it there to wipe the sweat from his forehead. As she watched, he straightened, removed the hat, brushed dust from the brim, then set it back on his head—this time at a lower, jauntier angle.

"Afternoon, Maddie. Your timing is perfect. We're about to test your new breeding chute."

To force Chase to call her Miss McCrory seemed ungracious, considering that he had obviously spent the day with Little Mike, finishing this project. Still, Maddie wasn't inclined to be overly friendly.

"Good afternoon, sir," she coolly responded.

Gazing at the chute, where Little Mike was now tying up the mare, she found it difficult to avoid staring at Chase's bare chest and arms, rippling with muscles. All too well, she remembered how it had felt to be crushed against that muscular torso. Did he, too, recall the incident?

Daring another glance at his face, she found him watching her intently. Her skin prickled with sudden heat, his gaze searing her skin wherever it touched. Their eyes locked for a moment, and she was sure he knew she was remembering his kiss, his embrace, and the feel of his body against her. Even now, at this very moment, her own body reacted with predictable awareness, as if it might suddenly ignite.

Get hold of yourself, Maddie! You are behaving like a perfect ninny.

Struggling to retain her poise, Maddie focused her attention on the chute. It was a narrow affair of thick wooden slats that encased its occupant on three sides. Once inside, the mare couldn't swing her hindquarters around to escape the stallion when he came up behind her. The structure was long enough to keep the stallion from moving around as well—but she could see nothing to stop the mare from kicking the stallion as he mounted her.

As Little Mike climbed out of the front end of the chute, Chase bent down, picked up a sturdy log, and fitted it into place behind the mare's tail, totally confining her. The log lay snugly in the curve just above her hocks, so she would feel its resistance if she decided to lift a leg—or legs—and lash out with her hooves. Yet it was low enough that the stallion could still achieve his objective.

Not accustomed to such confinement, the mare moved restlessly and swung her head around to look at them.

"Make sure she's tied short enough that she can't get the leverage to pull back," Chase instructed, and Little Mike hurried to take up the slack in her lead rope.

Maddie set the brake on the buckboard, dropped the lines on the seat, and climbed down. "I don't blame her for not liking it. She can hardly move at all inside there."

Chase gave her a slow, lazy grin that managed to be amazingly sensual. "That's the general idea. Oh, if she got fussed up enough, she could demolish the whole thing, but we did try and build it to be sturdy and horseproof. The point is: she can't do much harm to the stallion when he's brought to her. If she protests too much, we'll know she isn't ready, and Little Mike can just take her out and wait another day or two. Another advantage to the chute is that once the stallion gets used to it, he'll go straight in and get the job done without a lot of jumping around and climbing on the mare at the wrong angle. That sometimes frightens mares, especially if it's their first time."

"Best of all, it's a one-man operation," Little Mike added, beaming. "I can put a mare in the chute and bring Gold Deck up to tease her without the danger of either one of them—or me—getting hurt!"

"Never forget that you can *always* get hurt if you aren't careful," Chase gently admonished. "Once, when I was first trying to perfect the design of the chute, I had a mare and a stallion completely destroy it and nearly kill themselves and me doing it. You've still got to take your time and determine that the mare is really ready before you let the stallion into the chute. Never rush things."

Maddie noticed how he avoided identifying exactly where this had occurred. Perhaps because of his brother, Chase always seemed reluctant to mention his past. Yet he showed no reluctance—or embarrassment—when it came to discussing the intimate details of breeding. Disregarding Maddie's presence, he proceeded to remind Little Mike of the signs indicating a mare's readiness: her willingness to squat and urinate in front of the stallion, the raising of her tail, and the contraction of her female parts, which he called "winking."

"Why, I've even seen them back up to the stallion, requesting to be mounted," he said, with a sideways glance at Maddie.

Maddie pretended not to be listening. She was heartily glad that the signs were much more subtle in humans; she would hate to think that Chase might discover how attractive she found him as a result of blatant physical responses akin to a mare's. She never wanted him to know how he really made her feel inside.

"What do you think of the chute, Maddie?" Chase questioned as Little Mike disappeared inside the stable to fetch the stallion.

Caught off guard, Maddie blurted the truth. "It's an ingenious invention, but I'm glad I'm not a mare who has so little choice where mating and childbearing are concerned."

"You object to her restriction? I know of folks who use hobbles to keep a mare from kicking, but I think the chute achieves the same purpose and works better as a one-man operation. Also prevents the mare from getting rope burns if she fights the hobbles, which she'll often do."

The mare chose that moment to issue her own complaint: a loud, anxious whinny.

"No, I . . . I just think it's unfair that she can hardly see the stallion, much less decide if she wants to mate with him."

"But that's the beauty of the chute. The two can have a chance to get acquainted first, and the chute allows them to do it safely."

"You said Little Mike should be careful to ascertain her readiness, what we usually define as teasing. You didn't say anything about allowing them to get acquainted first. Do you regard the two as one and the same thing?"

Chase heaved an exaggerated sigh. "Well, now, horses aren't people, Maddie. Don't make them out to be more than they are. You think the stud should court the mare perhaps—bring her flowers and whisper a few compliments in her ear? I suppose he could offer her carrots or a nice shiny apple. He could tell her that her mane feels like silk, and he loves the way her tail tickles his nose when the breeze blows it in his face."

He was teasing again; mischief danced in his eyes, and his mouth softened in the little half-smile that was fast becoming familiar.

"He could," she agreed. "But she still might say 'neigh,' when it comes down to . . . to actually doing it."

"Doing it?" he drawled.

"You know what I mean," she retorted, flustered.

"I imagine I do," he said in a low voice that flowed over her like a caress. "But I'd enjoy hearing you describe the act in detail. *Explicit* detail, the more explicit, the better."

His seductive tone evoked images that brought a hot flush to Maddie's cheeks. When he saw it, Chase's grin widened. Oh, but he was disgustingly pleased with himself! He cocked his head, waiting for her answer. Thankfully, Little Mike emerged from the barn with Gold Deck, and the demonstration of the chute's safety features continued.

"Now, bring Gold Deck up to the mare and let them sniff each other's noses. Your sister thinks they should be allowed a period of courtship before they make a serious commitment."

The mare squealed, wrung her tail, and tried to retreat when Gold Deck got close to her. Despite her negative reaction, the stallion promptly became aroused. Normally, Maddie found nothing shameful or awkward about the teasing procedure, an important prelude to the actual breeding, but this time, aware of Chase's amused scrutiny, she wished she were somewhere else.

"He's definitely ready," Chase calmly pointed out.

Little Mike grinned and nodded. "Yep," he agreed. "But I don't think she is. If she could, she'd kick him to Kingdom Come."

Maddie feared her knees might buckle if the mare changed her mind and decided to "wink." She could just imagine what Chase would find to say about that. Fortunately, the mare failed to display a single tendency that indicated a willingness to proceed.

"Might as well put him back, Mike. Nothing's going to happen today."

"Sure would if Gold Desk had anything to say about it. He's rarin' t' go." Little Mike had to drag the stallion away. Gold Deck didn't want to leave a potential new conquest and whinnied a forlorn protest.

"Always a woman's decision, isn't it?" Chase said as he went to untie the mare. "Doesn't seem fair to me, but who am I to question the ways of nature?"

Maddie didn't trust herself to answer. How *could* she answer such questions?

"Thank you for finishing the chute," she said instead. "I can see it will be very useful."

His gaze met hers across the mare's back. "Does this mean I get invited to supper again?"

"If you don't expect much, you can stay today," she surprised herself by offering. "Mary's not here, so it will be simple fare."

"Fine by me. I'm not picky. Right now, I'm hungry enough to eat whatever's set in front of me—a plateful of fried snails, a bucket of worms. Whatever you've got, Miss McCrory."

Maddie bit back a smile. "I will endeavor to make my humble offerings plentiful and satisfying."

"Anything you care to provide should be satisfying—*most* satisfying."

Maddie gave no indication she had caught any deeper meaning; every word Chase spoke, every glance he gave her, held a hint of innuendo. He put a sexual spin on everything—or so it suddenly seemed to her.

"Excuse me while I get supper started then."

"Will your pa be joining us tonight?" Chase carefully backed the mare out of the chute.

"I don't know. He wasn't feeling well this morning when I left for town. Why do you ask?"

"No particular reason. I just wanted to tell him about the chute—maybe show him how it works."

"I doubt he'll be interested, but you can always try—assuming he joins us."

"Maybe *you* should try, Maddie. Maybe you should insist he get off his butt and walk out here to see it."

"I will, if he's feeling better. And I would have done so without the crude reminder."

Annoyed, Maddie turned to leave. In addition to the effect he had on her senses, Chase Cumberland was capable of annoying her profoundly.

"Wait, Maddie. . . . I don't mean to goad you, but I always end up doing it somehow, don't I? Let's call a truce. At least for tonight. I promise I won't say or do anything to ruffle your feathers. I'll try anyway."

Maddie hesitated, but his apology sounded sincere. "All right. But what shall I promise? If this is to be a bargain between us, I have to agree to something, too."

The mischievous light returned to his eyes. "Why, you

promise to let me kiss you again. If I can last through supper without making you frown at me or assume that hostile look in your pretty blue eyes, then I win a good-night kiss. I swear I won't tell you how to handle your father again—or your brother and sisters, though I might give you a few good tips on training horses."

"You presume to teach a McCrory about training horses?"

Irritation flared anew—until she realized he was teasing her again. He could not, it seemed, resist teasing her, just as she could not resist taking offense at every little criticism or suggestion. It should be easy to avoid being kissed . . . if that's what she wanted.

"I can teach you a few training tricks, but I can also learn from you. It works both ways," he assured her. "Or it does when I remember not to be a conceited jackass—excuse me, donkey."

Once again, Maddie inadvertently smiled. How charming and agreeable he could be when he tried! But he would have to work hard to win a good-night kiss; she still hadn't forgotten the last one and the unhappy way it had ended. If *any* woman would do for a kiss, there were plenty in town to oblige him. Hopewell couldn't compare to Abilene or Dodge City for licentiousness, but the ladies at the Ruby Garter were said to be quite free with their kisses and not *only* with kisses.

She imagined that Lily Tolliver would be more than happy to welcome a virile man like Chase into her establishment—and probably into her bed. Yet Chase was here bantering with *her* as if he actually preferred the company of a plain, aging spinster to a beautiful, silk-clad "calico queen."

"You're very lucky," she said. "You almost lost this bargain before I agreed to it. Fortunately, you managed to redeem yourself in the nick of time. But it's a long way 'til supper, Mr. Cumberland, and frankly, I don't think you can guard your tongue sufficiently well to win this wager."

"Then you hardly know me, Miss McCrory. I never make a wager expecting to lose."

"I've already witnessed that character trait, and I'm not sure it's an admirable one."

"How else would you prefer a man to behave? Have you a taste for weak, indecisive men? You prefer someone you can manipulate? Some women do."

He had her there—and he knew it. Whiskey had turned her father, the strongest man she had ever known, into a bumbling, shaky, irresponsible old coot, interested in little except where his next drink was coming from.

"No, I much prefer strong men over weak ones, but I also want a man who goes out of his way to be fair and to try to understand another person's point of view. It takes a *really* confident man to admit he might be wrong occasionally. I know you find it hard to believe, but my father was like that prior to my mother's death. It's too bad you didn't know him then; you might have learned something from him."

Chase's gaze didn't waver. "I'm sorry I didn't know him then—but as I've told you before, I do know a thing or two about men who drink too much. My brother could have gone the way of your father—*still* could, I imagine. Except he knows I won't stand for it. Call it cruel if you will, but I've made that clear to him. He's got a choice—me or whiskey."

"I can't say that to my father. He's not my brother. He's the man who gave me life and raised me. And now it's his turn to be . . . needy."

Fearing she had said too much, *revealed* too much, Maddie fell silent. Why did their conversations so often revolve around Pa? Or come back to him. It was almost as if Pa stood between them—a disagreement that could never be resolved. Even if they managed to work out everything else, they would never see eye to eye about her father.

Chase still held the mare, and now, he idly stroked her neck. "I understand your concern for your father, Maddie, only you have needs, too. Why won't you admit it? Your whole family has needs. You're allowing *his* need to consume all of you. Maybe you can't see it, but I can—as an outsider. You're worrying right now about how your pa is gonna behave tonight and whether or not he'll embarrass you. You deserve better than that."

Maddie lowered her gaze. To avoid looking at Chase, she studied the mare's front legs and discovered that the animal was slightly knock-kneed. If worked at high speed, she'd likely cut herself on her own hooves. She wouldn't be good for racing and could possibly pass this defect onto her foals. Should she point this out to the owner? Would the man appreciate hearing about it any more than she appreciated Chase's comments about her father?

"Pa probably won't behave very well tonight," she conceded. "But I'm willing to take a chance if you are. He ran out of whiskey three days ago. When that happens, until he figures out a way to get more, he's sick, miserable, desperate, and liable to try anything. I hated to leave him this morning, but I had to go into town. He was too sick to complain, but I suspect we'll all be hearing plenty of complaints when he discovers I didn't bring back any liquor, as he begged me to do."

"You did the right thing, Maddie. Just remember that. You did the right thing."

She had an absurd urge to throw herself into Chase's arms and succumb to another fit of weeping. But she had a meal to prepare, supplies to put away if the twins hadn't already done so, the house to straighten before Chase set foot in it—and her father to face. A thousand details of daily living screamed for her attention. She didn't have the luxury of succumbing to wild, inappropriate impulses. Responsibility beckoned, as it always did, as it always would. There would likely never come a time when she could put her own needs, desires, and impulses first, ahead of the needs of others.

"Come up to the house when you're finished here. I'll have supper ready as soon as possible."

Chase started toward the stable with the mare. "No need to rush," he told her over his shoulder. "I thought while I was here I'd give your brother a hand fixing that shed door that's about to fall off. The door's too heavy for him to manage alone."

"No, don't. I don't want to be . . ." She quit midsentence, before the word "beholden" slipped out of her mouth.

Who was she kidding? She was already beholden to Chase.

Fortunately, he didn't appear to hear; he was busy leading the mare away.

"So you built a special chute t' make the breedin' go easier, huh?" With a trembling hand, Pa set down his spoon and peered at Chase.

Maddie smeared honey on a hunk of corn bread and thanked whatever heavenly being was responsible for her father's decision to join them at the supper table tonight. Somehow she had managed to persuade him that the noodle soup she had hastily thrown together was just what he needed to calm his tremors and make him feel better.

He hadn't even gone on a rampage about her failure to bring back some "medicine." He had merely asked: "Don't suppose ya brought me anything from town, did ya?"

"Flour," she had answered brightly. "And sugar and beans. A little bacon, too. I thought I'd make corn bread and noodle soup for supper. I'll add vegetables to the soup and cook up some greens to serve alongside . . ."

It was the best she could do in a hurry. She had hoped Chase and Little Mike wouldn't be too disappointed at the lack of meat. Thus far, no one had mentioned it. They had attacked the food like a horde of starving grasshoppers.

Chase lowered his coffee cup and eyed her father with interest. His hair was still wet from the slicking up he had done in the horse trough, and the shadow of a beard darkened his jaw. The first time Maddie had sat across from him during a meal, she had experienced a quiet thrill and satisfaction watching him eat and imagining what it would be like to have him sitting across from her at every meal.

That same feeling assaulted her now. His presence seemed to fill the room, infusing the entire house with a magic quality. She watched his hands—so masculine, sun-browned, and capable—rest on the table as he took his time forming an answer. He had long, agile fingers, endowed with a curious sort of grace she had never before associated with a man's hands. His hands can be gentle, as well as strong, she thought. She pictured them touching her body, and the blood simmered in her veins, heating her flesh and making her long for . . .

"I was hoping you'd come out and have a look at it," Chase said. ". . . and give me your opinion. Every time I build a breeding chute—and I've built four so far, counting this one—I refine it a little. Make it narrower or higher or sturdier, whatever I think it still needs."

"Ain't never used one. Ain't never heard of anybody who did."

Pa reached for his spoon again, fumbled, and dropped it into his soup. The soup splashed onto the wood tabletop, puddling there, and Maddie quickly rose to wipe it up. Since this was an informal affair, she hadn't taken out any of Ma's good linens. The tablecloth she had used the last time Chase came to dinner had been laundered but not yet ironed. Carrie and Zoe hated ironing with the heavy old flatiron known as a sadiron, and Maddie had been too busy to do it herself or bully one of them into it.

"Don't know why you'd want my opinion anyhow," her father continued. "I'm too old to change the way I always done things. If Little Mike hankers t' use it, that's fine. He's welcome to try anything he likes."

Chase leaned back in his chair. "I want your opinion because you've bred more horses than I have—or ever will. I normally leave my mares at the stallion's farm and come back and get them when it's all over. Only once did I actually own a stud and try to stand him myself. I found it to be a dangerous, unpredictable process. The old rogue kept breaking out of whatever pen I put him in. If he could see mares, he wanted to be with them."

"Sounds natural t' me," Pa said with a chuckle. He moved his elbow as Maddie swiped a towel across the table. She offered to get more soup for him, but he shook his head. "Can't eat no more, Maddie. It tasted good though. Would have tasted even better with the right accompaniment."

He winked at Chase—a man-to-man sort of wink, testing to see if Chase shared his desire for a drink of whiskey. Chase ignored it and doggedly continued his transparent efforts to draw her father into conversation and taking an interest in the family activities.

"You ever hobble your mares for breeding?" he now asked. "You know, loop a rope around each of her hind legs and then tie the ropes around the mare's neck so she's working against her own strength if she tries to kick or buck."

"Naw." Pa shook his head. "Never went in for nothin' fancy like that. Too easy for the mare to hurt herself, but I was always real particular about teasin' her. I never brought a stallion up to a mare unless I knew she was ready. Didn't usually have much trouble with the stud misbehavin' either. What I always did was hold a short, thick hickory stick, and if the stud got unmannerly, I whacked him with it. He learned soon enough that whenever I carried that stick it was time t' mount a mare, an' if I didn't have it, he wasn't doin' no breedin' that day. Got to be that as soon as he saw that old stick, he'd start snortin' and drop his . . ."

"Pa!" Maddie remonstrated, guessing what he was going to say next. "That isn't fit table talk. Especially not in front of the girls."

Chase and her father both grinned. The girls sighed and shook their heads. "It isn't as if we've been blind all our lives, Maddie. We know what part of his body a stallion drops when he wants a mare," Zoe cheekily informed her.

"I'm the one Little Mike tried to make hold a mare, remember?" Carrie added.

"Yes, you're the reason Mr. Cumberland decided we needed a breeding chute. But I still don't think this is fit conversation for a supper table."

"Whatever happened to that hickory stick?" Chase turned to Little Mike, who as usual, wasn't saying much and indeed seemed curiously sullen and withdrawn. "You don't use it now, do you, Mike?"

"The stick's still hangin' by a thong in the barn. I remember Pa holdin' it, but I didn't know *why* he held it. He never told me, an' I never thought t' ask. When I took over the breedin,' I thought it was too much t' hang onto—Gold Deck *and* the stick. Besides, I never saw Pa whack a horse. He always said whackin' 'em makes 'em mean."

"There's whackin' t' teach a lesson, and whackin' jus' fer the hell of it. Ya gotta know the difference." Pa shoved back his chair. "All this jawin' is tirin' me out. Guess I'll go back t' bed now."

"I didn't know about the stick either." Maddie hurried around the table to help her father rise. "If we had only recognized the stick's purpose, we could have been using it all this time to help control Gold Deck. Pa, you should have told us."

"Should have done a lot of things, I guess. But it's too late now." Pa rose shakily. Leaning on her arm, he stood there a moment, swaying. "I'm too old t' breed horses anymore," he muttered. "Too old t' be of much use t' anyone."

"That's not true, Pa. The hickory stick is a perfect example of how you could have helped us. I remember how you used to whip-train our horses to race, too, but I never knew how you did it. You would just hold up the whip, and the horse would know it was time to race. When you lowered it, he would take off running. You never did use a whip to beat or punish a horse, but only to whip-train him."

"That was a long time ago, Maddie, girl . . . a long, long time ago."

"But I still remember! You could teach us how you did it—couldn't he, Little Mike?"

"He don't want to. He don't give a damn about us." Little Mike jumped up. "We don't need the old sot anyway."

Her brother crossed the room in two long strides and slammed out of the house.

"Mike!" Maddie was aghast, yet she couldn't run after her brother and either reprimand or comfort him because of her father.

"Leave him be," Pa croaked in a hoarse whisper. "He's right. I'm an old drunk, and you all don't need me anymore. I shoulda left when your ma did. Shoulda gone along with her. Don't know why in hell I didn't. Lacked the courage, I guess. She's the one who gave me gumption t' do the things I did all my life. But she up and left me finally—and then what could I do? What the hell could I do?"

His blue eyes sought Maddie's, and nothing she could say seemed adequate. There was no way to ease his pain, not if he truly believed that without his wife, life was no longer worth living.

"Bed," he mumbled. "Put me t' bed, Maddie. Maybe I can lose myself in sleep. If God were truly merciful, I wouldn't have t' wake up. That's what I pray fer every night—that when dawn comes I'll be gone."

"Pa, you don't mean that."

Her father didn't answer, and no one else said a word either. Unable to work miracles, Maddie could only assist him in shuffling from the room.

Twelve

When Maddie returned to the front room after settling her father for the night, she found the twins quietly clearing up the supper mess and no sign of Chase or Little Mike.

"Where did Mr. Cumberland go?"

Carrie nodded toward the front porch. "He said to tell you he'd be outside. I think he went looking for Little Mike."

Maddie exited through the front door, descended the porch steps, and went around to the side of the house where she finally spotted Little Mike and Chase standing together talking near the poultry yard. The setting sun had stained the sky crimson, and against the ruddy hues of scarlet and gold, the man and the youth were starkly silhouetted. Maddie couldn't see their faces clearly, but as she drew nearer, Little Mike glanced her way, then set off for the stable, clearly avoiding her.

Maddie would have gone after him, but Chase waylaid her. "Give him some time alone, Maddie. He'll be all right. I just talked to him. He was angry about the hickory stick; that's all. He thinks if your pa had ever bothered to teach him how to use it to train Gold Deck, the breeding chute wouldn't be necessary."

"He's probably right. However, I can remember when Little Mike spent all his time resisting Pa's efforts to teach him anything. That was before Ma died. By the time Little Mike was anxious to learn, Pa wasn't up to teaching him. . . . And anyway, the chute is *still* a good idea, since it protects the stallion from an aggressive mare. The hickory stick doesn't do that."

"Little Mike knows that. He won't admit it, but I suspect that what's happened to your father is what's really bothering him. He's blaming it on the hickory stick, but your Pa's helplessness is the thing he resents the most. Lashing out doesn't help matters, of course, but your brother's feelings are bound to erupt one way or another."

Maddie sighed. "I'm sure you're right, Chase. Little Mike never has been as vocal as the rest of us, but lately, he's grown so moody. Sometimes, he scares me. He's brooding over Pa almost the same way Pa's been brooding over my mother. The only difference is that Little Mike hasn't taken up drinking. At least, not yet. I can only pray he doesn't as he gets older."

"Treat him like a man, Maddie, not like a little boy, or worse yet, a baby brother, and he'll come out of it. Above all, don't nag him. Young men hate to be nagged."

Maddie straightened her shoulders and tossed back a long skein of her too-red hair. "Watch it, Mr. Cumberland. You are about to lose your bet. No woman enjoys being told she ought not to nag. Some women might actually take offense at the suggestion that they don't know when to keep their mouths shut."

"Sorry. . . . Thanks for the warning. Guess that's all the advice I've got for now . . . Come walk with me a bit, Maddie. It's a fine evening. We can watch the sun go down and the stars come out before I have to leave."

"All right."

Maddie took the arm he offered and let her fingers rest lightly on the worn fabric of his sleeve. Chase had donned his shirt for supper, but she could still feel the warmth of his sun-kissed flesh beneath it. A tremor raced through her. It would have to be dark before she'd allow him to kiss her—and he would have to avoid lecturing her in order to claim that kiss.

They strolled in the direction of the creek, which cut through the field Chase wanted to buy. The heat of the day had faded, but the faint gurgle of water drew them with its promise of coolness and refreshment. For awhile, neither spoke, and Maddie simply took pleasure in Chase's company and the fading beauty of the day.

She expected Chase to avoid the controversial topic of her

father, but he suddenly surprised her. "About your Pa, Maddie. I apologize for thinking he should have been able to conquer his grief by now. After watching him tonight, I have a better understanding of why he drinks."

His admission startled her. "You do?"

Chase nodded. "I realized tonight that your father isn't pretending to be miserable, and he isn't just using his misery as an excuse to drink. It makes no difference how long it's been since your mother died, he still misses her and can't imagine living without her. For a moment tonight, he looked so . . . so lost. About as lost as I've ever seen a man."

"So you saw it, too—his terrible despair. When he's sober, it's much more apparent."

"I've witnessed despair, but never that bad. I almost offered to go into town to buy him some whiskey. Or volunteered to shoot him in the head the way I would a suffering horse or dog."

Maddie clutched his arm. "Then you understand how hard it is to say no to him!"

Chase turned to her. "I do now, Maddie. I didn't before, but I do now."

"Oh, Chase!" Abandoning all pretense of propriety, she flung her arms around him and hugged him. "You don't know how glad I am to find someone who understands. The worst—the absolute worst—times are when he swears to me that he doesn't have a problem. He can quit drinking any time he wants. But why should he quit? he always asks. If he quits, there will be nothing to dull the pain. He talks about his pain as if it's *physical.* And maybe it is. All I know is that he's suffering the tortures of the damned, and drinking helps him escape, if only for a little while."

"No matter how wrong he is, he starts making sense, doesn't he?" Chase held her and patted her back, imparting a comfort she sorely needed. "That's the frightening part; he starts to make a weird kind of sense."

"Exactly. I know I shouldn't listen to him. Yet sometimes . . . when I see how unhappy he is . . . how lost . . . how alone and afraid . . ."

"You want to give in and do whatever it takes to make his life more tolerable." Leaning back from her, Chase cupped her face in his hands and gazed down into her eyes. "That's how insidious despair is, Maddie. It doesn't just swallow its victim; it poisons everyone else around him. It makes us start to lose hope. It saps our energies. Soon, we can't argue anymore. We can't fight. Can't prove how wrong the other person is. Despair sucks us under, the same as quicksand. Before we know it, we no longer think life is worth living either."

"You've had to live with despair, too, haven't you?" Maddie couldn't tear her gaze from Chase. For the first time since she'd met him, she felt as if they were truly communicating—and not just on a physical level. "You describe it so well. Did you learn all this from your brother?"

Chase's hands fell to her shoulders. His warm breath stirred her hair as he pressed his lips to her temple. "Yes, it was Buck who taught me about despair. He's battled it for years. There were times when I doubted he'd ever make his way back to the living. He got as bad as your Pa once, but somehow . . . he made up his mind not to let it lick him. These days, he's as happy as I've ever seen him."

"Then perhaps there's hope for my father. I cling to that hope. Sometimes, I think it's all I've got."

"Maddie . . ." Chase's lips moved down the side of her face and along her cheek. He rubbed his jaw against hers, and the faint stubble of new beard abraded her skin, sensitizing it. "Maddie, how about that kiss? It seems as if I've been waiting for it forever."

A little moan of surrender escaped her throat. She didn't even consider refusing; she, too, had been waiting forever. She had been waiting all her life for Chase Cumberland, a man who not only heated her blood but soothed her pain. Angling her head to meet him halfway, she eagerly offered him her mouth. He kissed her as if it were his right—as if he owned her, and a kiss was the least he intended to claim. His arms stole around her waist, his hands captured her hips, pulling her closer, and their bodies merged together in a whirl of dizzying sensation.

Eagerly, she rediscovered the feel of him—his taste and textures, the hardness that complemented her softness. His embrace was wonderfully familiar, yet the man himself remained a revelation. A glorious surprise. She hadn't expected this kiss to be more wonderful and exhilarating than it had been the first time, but it was.

He didn't give her a chance to breathe, think, or protest. One kiss flowed into another . . . and yet another . . . until she was clinging to him in breathless wonder. And still, he kissed her, caressed her, and moved against her in a growing frenzy that echoed her own rising desire.

Long moments passed, as she joyfully submitted to the madness his kiss engendered. When he reached between them and covered her breast with his hand, her heart seemed to leap into his palm. His touch wildly excited her. He brushed a thumb over her distended nipple, and she couldn't stop herself from crying out. He drank the sound from her mouth and held her tightly, his big body suddenly motionless, his hand over her breast, giving her time to adjust to the startling new intimacy.

At the same time, the hard bulge of his sex taunted and teased her; if she were a mare, she surely would have "winked" at him in invitation. As it was, she leaned toward him and spread her legs a bit to accommodate him. Then she realized what she was doing and drew back in shock.

"Chase . . . you . . . we . . . must stop this," she finally managed to whisper.

"Why must we?" he growled, his voice roughened by passion. "If you want it, and I want it, it can only be right, Maddie. The rules of others needn't apply to us."

"But . . . someone could see us."

"No, they can't. It's getting dark."

"My sisters might come looking for me at any moment."

"Your sisters are old enough to be discreet. They have enough sense to leave you alone when you're with me."

"But I'm not providing a very good example. I *shouldn't* be alone out here with you—much less doing what we're doing. Where is all this leading?"

He sighed heavily, as if the question gave him pause. A moment later, his hand left her breast, and his warm body abandoned hers. "You *would* have to ask that, wouldn't you?"

He sounded rueful. Regretful. It was dark enough now that she couldn't read his expression easily. He seemed reluctant to look her in the eye. "I didn't ask the question in order to make you feel uncomfortable," she said. "Don't worry, Chase. I'm not demanding anything merely because you kissed and . . . and fondled me. After all, I encouraged you. I wanted it. But I do think we should stop now and consider whether we mean to . . . to continue with this, in view of where it might possibly lead."

"Do you want it to lead somewhere, Maddie?" His tone had a hard edge to it.

Yes, oh, yes! her inner voice cried.

"I . . . I . . . don't know," she evaded. "We both have so much to think about. Neither of us is quite free to . . . to become involved. There are so many other considerations."

"I can't argue with that." Now, she suspected he was angry. A definite chill had come into his voice. "I, for example . . . well, you're going to find out about this sooner or later. . . . One of my considerations is that race between you and Lazarus Gratiot."

Startled at his mention of the race, Maddie wondered how Chase knew her opponent's name. She hadn't mentioned it in front of him, had she? As she recalled, she'd done everything possible to avoid discussing the subject after her sister had let it slip about the race.

"What about the race?"

Chase drew a deep breath, then blurted: "It's no longer just between you and Gratiot. I've entered Bonnie Lass to run against you both."

Maddie's heart shuddered to a standstill.

"What? . . . You went behind my back to Mr. Gratiot and talked him into letting you enter?"

"The race was still open, Maddie. Gratiot said you had agreed to another entry. You just didn't want it to be me, did you?"

"No!" she cried, suddenly furious. "You *know* I don't want

to race you again, yet you deliberately did this sneaky, underhanded thing to spite me. Do you even have five thousand dollars to wager?"

"Do you?" he countered. "I had to enter it, Maddie. This is business. It's what I do. Call it sneaky and underhanded, if you will, but then what do you call your own failure to tell me that the race was open to another entry?"

"Self-preservation," she snapped, growing angrier by the minute. "I just never expected you to bully your way into my deal. No wonder you wouldn't agree not to race me again; you were intending all along to lure me into another competition, no doubt hoping you could once again walk away a winner."

"I intended no such thing. But when I heard about the race, naturally I had to check it out. If you didn't want a three-horse race, you should have insisted it be limited to two at the very beginning."

"I tried, but Gratiot wouldn't agree! And the chance to win that much money was too good to let pass."

"Funny, that's exactly the way I felt. I couldn't let the opportunity pass either."

"So that's why you showed up to build the chute today; you're trying to salve your guilty conscience!"

"I've done nothing to feel guilty about. It was my right to enter that race, and I did. What's more, I've just told you about it. You've no cause to be spiteful. You're being unreasonable about this, Maddie."

"I'm being unreasonable? You show up unexpectedly, build us a breeding chute, befriend my brother and sisters, give me unwanted advice about my problems, try and . . . and *seduce* me, and all the while you're secretly plotting to take away my family's farm. When I protest your evil little plan, you call me unreasonable. Should I have *invited* you to enter that race? Is that what you would call reasonable?"

"That would have been the sporting thing to do. Something I might expect from a man. I should have known you'd react like a woman—and accuse me of secretly plotting to take away your farm and worse yet, of trying to seduce you. Believe me,

Maddie, when I decide to seduce you, you'll know it. I won't stop with a few innocent kisses and caresses."

Maddie suddenly realized how very foolish she had been. How incredibly naïve. She had walked into this with her eyes wide open. Chase Cumberland had made it clear from the start what he wanted: her land and to breed his mares to her stallion. All along he'd been pursuing his goals single-mindedly, only she had chosen to believe that he wasn't quite as ruthless and predatory as she had at first suspected.

She had thought she had discovered a kindness in him and a bounty of shared experiences. She had imagined they had so much in common. In a little forbidden corner of her heart, she had begun to hope that here was a man she could care for—a man with rough edges—but one she could trust and respect. One who might share her hopes and dreams for the future. One who was beginning to care for her, as she was beginning to care for him.

Until this moment, she hadn't admitted her feelings to anyone, least of all to herself, but now, seeing it all slip away, she became acutely conscious of what she was losing. Chase Cumberland was exactly what she had suspected him of being in the beginning: a cunning wolf of a man entirely devoted to obtaining his own selfish ends. As long as he got what he wanted, he didn't care who got hurt in the process.

"You . . . you conniving bastard." She despised the tremor in her own voice, but was helpless to stop it. "Thank God, I discovered what you are now, instead of later."

"What's that supposed to mean?"

"It means I'm glad we didn't go any further tonight, before I learned what sort of man you really are."

"I'm the same man now as I was five minutes ago. I've never misrepresented myself or tried to pretend I'm something I'm not. If you're so scared of losing, why don't you go to Gratiot and withdraw from the race? He might let you out of it. You're exceptionally good at arousing male sympathy. Try weeping on his chest to soften him up. Or fixing him supper. Or batting your lashes at him. You know all the tricks."

"How dare you!" Maddie raised her hand to slap him, but he caught her wrist and held it suspended between them.

"I'm wise to you now, Maddie, but Lazarus Gratiot has only just met you. He'll be no competition at all for your feminine wiles. I'll bet you can maneuver him any way you please. But if he asks me what *I* think, I'll have to tell him the truth: Little girls who butt into men's games shouldn't be granted any favors. They deserve what they get."

"Let go of me!" Maddie wrenched free of him.

She didn't want to hear another word. Couldn't bear to endure his mockery another second. "Go home, Chase!" she spat. "And don't come back here. I never want to see you again!"

"You'll see me on race day whether you want to or not. Unless you decide to pull out."

"I'll never pull out. I can't, and you know it. It's the same as forfeiting. You knew that when you entered the race. And you knew I could win it, so long as you *didn't* enter. Well, you made your choice, didn't you? I just hope you can live with it."

Picking up her skirts, she turned and ran. She thought she heard him say, "Damn!" but she didn't stop to look back and confirm it. She ran as if a pack of wolves had been let loose to chase and destroy her. But there was really only *one* wolf, and he had already mortally wounded her.

Chase watched Maddie flee toward the house, her hair streaming out behind her, her skirts flying, and he cursed himself for having told her about the race . . . but *not* for having entered it. Maddie was dead wrong. He was more certain of it now than ever. She expected him to sacrifice everything he wanted, just because he was interfering with her personal plans.

He had only told her he had entered the race because he realized how angry she would be if he didn't—and she'd been angry anyway. He'd tried to do right by her, and it had blown up in his face. He ought never to have mentioned the race, at least not tonight. He should have taken time to think of a gentler way of telling her, instead of just blurting it out. But how else could he have said it?

She wouldn't have been any happier about it if he'd begged her pardon for daring to challenge her. Her typically feminine reaction was a powerful example of why women shouldn't be permitted in match racing. There was no room for sentiment in the sport. It was pure masculine competition. Why hadn't the participation of women been outlawed? Probably because so few women *did* participate. They had enough sense to know better.

Following at a discreet distance, Chase waited to retrieve his horse until Maddie disappeared inside the house. Hoping to avoid another confrontation, Chase quickly and silently saddled Bonnie Lass and rode away. He took his time going home and let the mare choose her own pace. Bonnie Lass wasn't in a hurry, which left him lots of time for thinking . . . and the more he thought, the worse he felt.

He assured himself he had done nothing wrong; Maddie's expectations were completely unrealistic. But he couldn't seem to convince his heart that he hadn't behaved in a shameful manner. The McCrorys needed that money as much as he did. Hell, they probably needed it more—but then they should have let him buy the field he wanted.

The reason he felt guilty, he finally decided, was because he had kissed and held Maddie whenever the opportunity presented itself. By treating her as a woman instead of a competitor, he had changed the nature of their relationship. It had shifted from adversarial to . . . to what? Maddie herself hadn't been willing to define it.

And *that's* why he had blurted out the truth about the race. She'd been so damned indecisive, hemming and hawing, refusing to say how she felt about him, that he'd gotten annoyed—and suddenly remembered the race. Which was just as well, because if he hadn't mentioned it tonight, she'd have been doubly hurt and angry when she did find out.

By the time he arrived home, Chase had half convinced himself that he owed Maddie an apology—for hurting her feelings, if nothing else. The one thing he hadn't meant to do was hurt her feelings. She had been angry, yes, but she had also been hurt . . . and he had done it. He wasn't about to forfeit the race to make it up to her, but he could at least apologize and try to explain his point of view. They could still be friends—couldn't they?

Hell, no, they couldn't.

Chase glumly dismounted, and by the light of the moon which had recently risen, unsaddled Bonnie Lass and put her away for the night. He was walking toward the house when a faint sound reached his ears. He halted mid-stride and listened. The night wind blew softly from the direction of the river, and he strained to decipher the messages it carried.

Yes! He heard it again—a light sound, like a woman's distant laughter. The Solomon River lay beyond his boundaries, but Chase had found little reason to visit it. The work at the ranch consumed all his time. Now, he was curious. What would a woman be doing down by the river at this time of night?

There were no homes nearby—nothing but an old abandoned soddy house. He had discovered the house on the day he had ridden out to take a look at the farm. He hadn't gone inside, but from all outward appearances, no one else had set foot on the property in years. A tangle of old berry vines had almost swallowed the small structure.

Chase wondered what Buck was doing. The soft glow of lamplight bathed the window overlooking the yard, but the front door was closed. He ought to let his brother know he was home before he set out to investigate that laugh—if indeed, he had heard one.

Quickening his stride, Chase hurried up the front steps and entered the house. Buck wasn't inside. He hadn't been in the barn either, and Chase suddenly realized where he might find his brother. It was time to unravel the mystery of where Buck had been going alone at night. The distant laughter undoubtedly had something to do with his disappearances.

Chase searched for three quarters of an hour without finding what he was seeking. Prowling along the river bank, he spotted the soddy house but no people. Not until he explored the bank further downriver did he again hear a woman's laughter, and her softly murmured invitation.

"Come join me, Silver Hair. Water not cold. See? It feel warm."

Chase dropped to his hands and knees, and crawled through the underbrush to where the river lapped the bank. Crouched behind a screen of wild plum bushes, he saw an amazing sight. There in the moon-dappled shallows of the river, his tall, naked brother played with an equally naked woman. As Chase watched, the woman splashed Buck, tossed back her long glistening hair, laughed, and retreated deeper into the water, daring Buck to follow her.

Grinning widely, Buck waded after her. A splashing match ensued—with both Buck and the woman furiously flinging water at each other. In the moonlight, the drops sparkled like diamonds, partially obscuring them. Then the woman dove underwater and resurfaced closer to Chase. She stood up, and water sheeted off the curves of her full breasts and generous hips. She tilted back her head, still laughing, and silver light poured down on her upturned face.

In that instant, Chase recognized her. His brother was sporting in the river with Pawnee Mary!

As Chase watched, completely dumbfounded, Buck chased after Mary, catching her by the hair. Playfully, he pulled her to him, and Chase glimpsed his brother's expression. Buck looked enraptured, as did Mary. Oblivious to everything around them, the two stared into each other's eyes. Slowly, with a gentleness Buck normally displayed only with animals, he wrapped his arms around Mary's gleaming body. He bent toward her, and their lips met in a long, passionate kiss.

As quietly as possible, Chase retreated from the river and made his way back to the house. He had never seen Buck so happy and carefree. Couldn't recall him playing like that since they were children. Tall and statuesque, Mary was the perfect partner for his brother—except she was Indian. What the hell! They were *both* outcasts. Why shouldn't they find whatever joy they could together? Chase decided he heartily approved of their secret liaison. At the same time, he couldn't help feeling a twinge of jealousy.

He tried to imagine himself sporting in the river with a woman, but the only female he could picture doing it with was Maddie McCrory. He'd love to see her red hair dripping diamonds in the moonlight, and her slender naked body awash with silver light. Sadly, he'd never see such a thing, because she now hated the sight of him.

But it was too late to change things now. His best recourse was to win the race as he had planned and pay the McCrorys an outrageous price for their field. Actually, it was his only recourse.

When he reached home, Chase crawled into bed without bothering to remove his boots. Hands behind his head, he lay sleepless for a long time, thinking about Buck and Mary . . . and wishing it had been him and Maddie in the river instead. His brother tiptoed into the house about an hour before dawn, but Chase pretended to be sleeping. Until Buck mustered the courage to tell him about Mary, Chase vowed not to breathe a word about the relationship.

Buck must decide what the future held for him and the Indian woman. As pleased as Chase was that his brother had found someone, he couldn't see Buck and Mary formalizing their union by getting married. If society couldn't accept a man like Buck—or a woman like Mary—how would it ever accept the two of them together? A few torrid moments in the river might be all they would ever have.

When his room brightened with the first rays of the rising sun, Chase finally gave up trying to solve either his brother's problems or his own. He rolled off the bed and headed for the barn to saddle Bonnie Lass. From now until the race, he meant to work the mare every morning before it got hot. He'd take her over to the flat stretch of terrain near the McCrory's field and let her gallop to build up her wind, muscles, and stamina. She probably didn't need such a rigorous conditioning program, but he was taking no chances. He was going to win that race.

A half hour later, Chase noticed that he wasn't alone exercising his horse in the dewy morning. Gold Deck was out, too, but the slender figure on the stallion's back was Maddie, not Little Mike. Her face red from exertion, she reined the big red horse around as soon as she saw Chase, and galloped off in the opposite direction.

Realizing that she didn't intend to speak to him or acknowledge him in any way, Chase took a perverse pleasure in deliberately crossing the invisible line separating his property from hers. He was sure that would gain her attention, and it did. She turned at the end of the field and came racing back.

Chase pretended he didn't see her until she skidded to a stop ten feet away. Bonnie Lass needed to keep moving to cool down from her work out, and Chase kept her at a steady walk, though she took an immediate interest in the new arrival, pricking her ears and nickering softly.

"What do you think you're doing?" Maddie demanded, falling in step beside him.

Gold Deck took one look at Bonnie Lass and started arching his neck and prancing, until Maddie firmly reminded him that he was under saddle—and therefore expected to ignore the opposite sex.

Biding his time before answering, Chase looked Maddie over from head to foot, secretly delighting in the telltale red stain that spread across her cheeks. She was no more immune to him than the two horses were to each other. As usual, she wasn't dressed for seduction. As usual, he longed to seduce her anyway.

Today, she wore a pair of Little Mike's trousers, held up by a length of twine tied around her waist, an old shirt big enough to be her father's, a pair of ugly, oversize, brown boots, and a black felt hat with the brim turned up in front. Red curls spilled around her shoulders, and a streak of dirt smudged her nose.

Except for her scowl, Chase thought she looked breathtakingly beautiful and utterly charming, rather like an untidy Kansas sunflower, which he much preferred over carefully cultivated garden roses. Somehow the sight of her always gladdened his heart.

"I'm doing exactly what you're doing," he finally answered. "Exercising my horse so she'll be ready to race next month."

"I mean what are you doing on our land?" Anger crackled in Maddie's bright blue eyes—eyes he wanted to make glow with passion. "Don't deny you don't know this is our land; it's the very field you want to buy."

"And a nice field it is," he drawled. "Even has a tree on it. And a creek running through one corner of it. However, I thought I was riding along the edge of it—a good flat place for galloping a horse. Bonnie Lass enjoyed her run."

"Get off our land," Maddie muttered through her teeth.

"Don't snarl at me that way. Makes you look like a weasel."

"I don't care what I look like! I don't want you on our land! You don't belong here. I insist you leave."

"There's plenty of room for both of us," he pointed out. "Besides, I'm not doing anything but cooling out my horse. Looks to me like you must be almost finished yourself. Gold Deck's sweating hard. Better not overwork him."

"Stop giving me unwanted advice! I thought I told you last night that I never want to see you again—so why are you here?"

"I was hoping I could change your mind. Guess not. Do you really hate me, Maddie? Tell me you don't."

"You haven't the slightest idea how much I loathe you, Chase Cumberland. But the next time you trespass on our land, you'll find out, because from now on, I'll be toting a six shooter."

"Threats, Maddie?"

"No, promises. I'll shoot you if you trespass again."

Chase thought it best to ignore her venomous outburst. "How's your father this morning? And Little Mike and the girls?"

"We *all* loathe you. We can't stand the sight of you. Now, will you *please* get off our land?"

"Well, since you finally asked me politely." Chase pressed his calf into Bonnie Lass's side, and she obediently side-passed several steps. "Is this far enough?"

"Hell wouldn't be far enough. Good day, Mr. Cumberland."

"Come on, Maddie, wait. At least, talk to me . . ."

But she wouldn't wait. She signaled for a lope and veered away, almost running down Little Mike, who was coming across the field toward them and not looking at all happy.

"Damn it, Maddie, watch out!" the youth cried, jumping to one side.

Maddie set the stallion down on his haunches. "What do you want, Mike? Why are you following me and cussing like that?"

"Because conditioning Gold Deck is *my* job. What are *you* doing up on him? Even Pa says you should get down and leave Gold Deck's training to me."

Maddie promptly slid off Gold Deck and handed the stallion's reins to her brother without a word of explanation or apology. Then she stomped off in a huff.

Chase didn't need to be told why she'd been riding Gold Deck this morning. She was worried. Possibly even terrified. Most of all, she was determined to have the stallion in the best possible shape to beat Bonnie Lass.

Feeling guiltier than ever, Chase headed for home.

Thirteen

Three days passed. On each of those days, Chase exercised Bonnie Lass by the field. He didn't see Maddie, Little Mike, or Gold Deck. On the fourth day, it rained. The rain came as a shock because it had been dry for so long. It rained all day, and Chase stayed in the house with Buck and watched his brother display all the signs of boredom and restlessness he himself was feeling.

On the fifth day, the sunshine returned, and by midafternoon, Buck had already disappeared. Chase couldn't find him anywhere, and he knew he *wouldn't* find him unless he went down to the soddy house by the river. He contemplated the chores his brother had left undone, but couldn't convince himself to be angry. He understood his brother's desperation to see Mary, because he was growing increasingly desperate to see Maddie.

When it wasn't raining, Buck was a different man these days—positively exuding good spirits—while Chase had assumed the role of the taciturn, morose brother, dissatisfied with everything. Knowing where Buck had gone and what he was likely doing didn't help Chase's mood. He was suddenly so lonely and depressed he couldn't bear to stay around the empty house another minute.

Succumbing to impulse, he decided to ride over to the McCrorys and again try to make amends with Maddie. She might shoot him on sight, but at the moment, he'd welcome a bullet in his hide if it meant he could see her. On the way over, he lined up his arguments.

Being rivals in another horse race was no reason for them to be enemies. If Maddie were a man, she wouldn't take things so personally. Men were able to compete in contests of skill, strength, or speed and still remain friends. Of course, if Maddie were a man, he wouldn't be running over to see her. He wouldn't even care that they were no longer friends . . . and he certainly wouldn't be spending any time imagining her in his arms or better yet, in his bed.

Arriving at her house, he noted the horse and buggy in the front yard and wondered who had come to visit. He saw no one outside, so he tied Bonnie Lass to the porch rail and sprinted up the steps to knock on the door. Zoe answered.

"Oh, Mr. Cumberland!" She looked surprised to see him and darted a quick glance over her shoulder, presumably at whoever was inside the house.

"I'd like to speak with your sister," Chase told her. "Could you tell her I'm here?"

"Carrie or Maddie?" As if she didn't already know who he meant, Zoe not-so-innocently batted her lashes at Chase.

"Go get Maddie, or I'll get her myself," Chase threatened.

"I can't. Maddie's busy."

"Doing what? I need to talk to her."

"Sorry, but she already has a gentleman caller. That's his horse and buggy right there out front."

The girl looked disgustingly smug as she imparted that startling information, and Chase had all he could do not to wring her neck.

"I still want to see her."

"I doubt she wants to see you."

Chase jammed his boot in the doorway, so she couldn't close the door on him. "Either tell her I'm here, or I'm coming inside. Right now."

"For heaven sake, Zoe. Who's there?"

Recognizing Maddie's voice, Chase glared at Zoe, warning her to tell the truth.

"It's Mr. Snake-In-The-Grass himself, Maddie," Zoe sang out. "I already told him you don't wish to see him."

Maddie suddenly appeared behind her sister. "I'll handle this, Zoe. Please pour another cup of coffee for our guest. Entertain him for a moment, while I get rid of this unwelcome intruder."

"Evening, Maddie."

Chase removed his hat, as he almost never did, but Maddie failed to look impressed. Aside from her annoyance, what she looked was downright lovely—and feminine. Surprisingly, *blatantly* feminine. She wore something white and frilly, with big, puffed sleeves over a dark-colored skirt that emphasized the narrowness of her waist and the pert swell of her hips. Her hair was piled on top of her head and secured there with a tortoise shell comb. Chase's fingers itched to pull it out and let the glorious red curtain tumble down around her shoulders, the way he liked to see it. His hands trembled with the need to span her narrow waist and haul her to him for a kiss that would mark her as his forever.

Sad to say, she did not appear equally affected by *his* appearance.

"I won't say good-evening to you, sir. Unfortunately . . ." she lifted her head in the air as if she smelled a noxious odor. ". . . the evening has just turned sour."

Chase strove to win a smile. "Is that because I arrived—or dare I hope it's because of your other caller?"

"It's because *you* arrived, and you know it." Maddie stepped out on the porch and pulled the door shut behind her, so Chase couldn't see inside the house.

"I want you to go home and stop bothering me," she began.

"Hey," he said, holding up his hat to block any blows that might be forthcoming. "I only stopped by to ask you to come out for a walk with me. I'd like to talk to you. I *need* to talk to you, Maddie."

"I can't. I'm entertaining a guest."

"Who is he?"

"It's none of your business."

"I'm making it my business. Who is he, Maddie?"

"Please keep your voice down. I don't wish to have an unpleasant scene enacted on my front porch."

He lowered his voice. "Then tell me who it is."

"Horace Brownley, the bank president and illustrious mayor of Hopewell. However, it's no concern of yours whom I wish to entertain this evening."

Chase concealed his shock behind a sneer. "A bank president, huh? And the mayor, too. Fancy that. What do you like most about him—his kisses or his cash? Or is it his ability to draw votes?"

"What I like most about him is that he isn't you. Please leave now, Chase. Don't make this any more awkward than it is already."

"I don't barge in where I'm not wanted, Maddie. Unlike some stallions I could name, I'm very well behaved around fillies, especially one in whom I'm interested."

"That's good to know. But this particular filly is not interested in *you.* If necessary, I'll fetch the hickory stick from the barn and show you I mean business when I say leave me alone."

"No need for violence. I only have one more question. Answer it, and I'll leave immediately."

Maddie tapped her foot impatiently. "What is it?"

"Does Mr. Horace Money-Bags-and-Power Brownley make you melt in his arms when he kisses you? *Have* you kissed him?"

"That's two questions, and I refuse to answer either one of them."

"But *I* make you melt in *my* arms, don't I, Maddie? And that's why I'm here tonight. Because the way we feel when we're together—and when we kiss—is far more important than any horse race."

She suddenly looked hopeful. "Does that mean you've withdrawn from the race?"

"No," he admitted, and her face fell.

"Then we have nothing more to say to each other. Goodnight, Mr. Cumberland."

"Maddie . . ." He was determined to make her see reason. Regardless of the outcome of the race, the feelings he had for her—and he hoped she had for him—weren't going to go away. The sooner she realized that, the better.

"Maddie?" said a male voice that didn't belong to either Maddie's father or her brother. "My dear, who's out there?"

My dear? Chase didn't like the sound of that at all.

"No one, Horace. No one important, that is," Maddie responded. "Just a neighbor looking for a . . . a lost pig. He's leaving now. I'll be there in a moment."

"A lost pig? . . . No one important?" Chase leaned toward her, but she placed her palm flat on his chest and shoved him—hard.

"Get out of here, Chase! I mean it. I'll fetch Pa's Colt if I have to."

"And how *is* your father tonight? What does Horace think of him? More importantly, what does your pa think of Horace?"

"Get off this porch!"

"All right. I'm going. But I won't be back to apologize again. Next time, you'll have to come to me."

"I'll never come to you. What we had—whatever we *might* have had—is over, Chase. Don't come here again."

Turning on her heel, Maddie yanked open the door and disappeared inside the house. Chase stood still a minute—seething—then jumped down from the porch steps. He stalked to his horse, stuck his foot in the stirrup, and leapt into the saddle. Halfway across the yard, he changed his mind about leaving. He wasn't going anywhere until he'd gotten a good look at his rival.

Dismounting again, he led Bonnie Lass back to the barn and put her in an empty stall. Then he went to the chicken house, kicked out a large fat hen intent on pecking at his boot, and stepped inside. From the front doorway, he was hidden from the house but had an excellent view of the horse and buggy tied up out front at the porch rail.

He didn't have to wait long. Less than a half hour later, Maddie and an overdressed, citified gentleman departed the house. The man was short and squat, with a belly that bespoke years of sitting in a chair instead of in a saddle. No competition, Chase thought to himself. Maddie couldn't possibly be interested in this dandified man from town, even if he was the mayor and the town banker. Not his feisty Maddie—the fearless tamer of stallions who rode horses astride and dared to compete against men.

Nonetheless, she followed the dandy around to the side of the buggy and didn't object to the man's pudgy white hand on her waist. There, Horace Brownley stopped and turned to her. With one finger, he shoved his spectacles up on his nose, then encircled Maddie's narrow waist with *both* hands.

Chase heard Maddie say, "Horace, we're in full view of the house."

To which Horace replied: "Well, if your sisters are spying on us, they had better grow accustomed to the sight of me expressing my affections for you, my dear. Haven't you told them about us yet?"

"Well, no . . . um . . . that is, they certainly know of your interest, but . . ."

"But nothing, my dear! You must tell your family of our intentions. Your father especially. If you can catch him in a sober moment, that is."

"Now, Horace, about my father . . ."

"But I don't wish to spend this private moment with you discussing your father, my dear. What I wish is . . . *this.*"

He ducked his head and bussed Maddie on the cheek. He had been aiming for her mouth, but at the last moment, Maddie turned her head.

"Horace, please . . ."

"Nonsense, my dear. I want a kiss before I leave. I've been missing you so much lately I can scarcely stand it. You simply *must* make more time for me. I know how busy you are this time of year, but surely, you can attend the Fourth of July picnic with me. Why, I don't even know what you've been up to lately or how you've been spending your time, which you *should* be spending with me . . ."

A faint roaring sound filled Chase's head. Rage such as he had never known before coursed through him. He was about to leap from concealment and attack Horace Brownley when Maddie herself stepped back from the man. His hands on her waist prevented her from going very far, but at least she was making the effort to put some space between them.

"There's just so much to do, Horace, what with breeding season still in progress and preparing for our next race. Besides, I really need to be here to keep an eye on my father. I've already told the girls and Little Mike that we won't be going into town for the festivities, because the Fourth of July is a perfect excuse for Pa to . . ."

"And when *is* your next race, my dear?" Horace rudely interrupted.

"Mid-July. Saturday, the fourteenth, actually," Maddie said. "Don't worry about it. It's . . . it's just a . . . a small one."

A small one? Chase wondered why she was lying—and why she permitted this fat slug of a man to even touch her. To what extent was Maddie involved with Horace Brownley? What right did the man have to insist that Maddie make time for him or attend the Fourth of July picnic in his company?

Chase had enough doubts about the situation, enough questions that needed answering, that he couldn't decide what to do. His instincts told him to go out there and throttle Horace Brownley, but as long as Maddie herself willingly endured the man's presence, as long as she appeared comfortable with his familiarity, Chase couldn't seem to act on his instincts. He had to stand there watching and slowly dying inside.

"The breeding season—and the racing season, too, for that matter—can't come to an end soon enough to suit me," Horace said. "Maddie, my darling, I am growing increasingly desirous of spending every waking moment in your company. You can't know how I'm suffering. Lately, all I can think about is . . . is . . . Oh, Maddie, I *must* have you!"

With that, Horace grabbed Maddie, and his mouth crashed down upon hers. She struggled, but he held on tight and thrust his pelvis at her like a lust-crazed stallion.

Chase sprang from the hen house. He had no plan of action save to destroy Horace Brownley and hurl him from the face of the earth. Within seconds, he was upon him. Hooking his fingers in Horace's shirt collar, he dragged him away from Maddie, drew back his fist and let fly with all the power he could muster. Horace sailed into the air and slammed into the buggy. The horse reared and broke free of the porch railing. Maddie screamed.

It ended quickly. Horace lay on the ground gasping like a fish out of water and fumbling for his broken spectacles, which lay shattered on the ground beside him. Maddie somehow managed to grab the horse by the bridle, and Chase found himself standing over the prostrate figure on the ground with his fists balled and his teeth bared. He wanted nothing so much as to kill the man where he lay.

"Get up, you bastard, so I can knock you down again. I'm a long way from finished with you."

"Chase! Please don't hurt him anymore. Oh, Horace are you all right?" Shoving one of the horse's lines at Chase, Maddie bent over Horace. "Heavens, he broke your spectacles!"

"Broke my nose is more like it!" Huffing and puffing, holding one hand to his nose, Horace climbed to his feet. He searched his pockets for a handkerchief, found one, and wiped blood from a split lip. Then he cast a malevolent eye on Chase.

"You madman! You damn near killed me! Who *are* you and where did you come from? Why did you assault me for no good reason?"

Still caught in the grip of jealousy, Chase didn't mince words. "You lay hands on Miss McCrory again, and next time, I'll break your neck, not just your nose or your spectacles."

Eyes widening at the threat, Horace rounded on Maddie. "Who *is* this madman? He's threatening to *kill* me, but I'm quite certain I've never seen him before."

"Ch-Chase Cumberland," Maddie said. "He's the man whose horse beat Gold Deck. Didn't you meet him when he collected the two thousand dollars from the bank?"

Chase answered for him. "The fat toad never came out of his office. He had his clerk give me the money—*after* he kept me waiting for half an hour."

"He had to count it out, obviously!" Horace defended. "But what, sir, is your precise relationship to Miss McCrory, if I may be so bold to ask?"

"Horace, I have no relationship to Mr. Cumberland," Maddie quickly denied. "I can't imagine what Chase thinks he's doing—attacking you in front of my house!"

"I'm defending your virtue," Chase bit out. "Unless you appreciate being mauled by this . . . this . . . slug."

"What do you mean—*slug?* And what possible concern is it of yours what Maddie and I feel for each other?" Horace waved his bloody handkerchief in the air between them. "Come now, sir. I demand an explanation for this outrage. You've broken my spectacles and made my nose bleed."

"Your lip," Chase corrected. "All I did—more's the pity—was split your lip. I should have cracked your head open."

"You are truly mad, sir—and this is outrageous! I shall inform Sheriff Smith about this incident at the earliest opportunity. I shall press charges, and then you'll be sorry."

"No! Oh, no, Horace . . . please," Maddie begged. "This is all an unfortunate misunderstanding. Mr. Cumberland obviously thought you were . . . ah . . . . compromising my virtue. He didn't mean to actually *hurt* you."

"The hell I didn't," Chase muttered, somewhat chastened by the mention of a sheriff. Did Hopewell also have a town marshall? Some towns had both. "He's lucky I didn't do worse. If he touches you again, I will."

"Be quiet!" Maddie shot Chase a look of steely blue fire. "You aren't helping matters any." She swung back to Horace Brownley and touched his sleeve in a placating manner. "Really, Horace. There's no need to involve Sheriff Smith. I'll be most embarrassed if this matter goes any further."

"Well, all right, my dear. I suppose you're right. But I demand an apology."

"An apology!" Chase exploded. "You'll get an apology when it starts raining gold nuggets from the sky."

"Why, you . . . you bloodthirsty assassin! You common riffraff! If you don't apologize this instant, I'll have my friend, Moses, the *sheriff,* who got elected to office on my recommendation, on your . . ."

"Stop it!" Maddie suddenly screamed, stamping her foot.

"You will *both* apologize. If you refuse, I will never speak to either one of you ever again. I will refuse to even look at you. This entire situation is ridiculous."

"Maddie, I will ask you one more time," Horace said, his jowls quivering. "What is this gentleman to you?"

"He is *nothing*. He is less than nothing." With another fiery look, Maddie dared Chase to deny it.

He couldn't—not when she was looking at him with daggers in her eyes.

"And what is this . . . *gentleman,* to you?" Chase inquired with a calmness that belied his true feelings.

"Horace is . . . a friend," she said. "You had no right to attack him."

"Friends don't force themselves on defenseless females," Chase pointed out. "But if you truly welcome his bull-moose advances, then of course, I apologize."

"All right, I apologize, too!" Horace said. "Though Lord only knows why *I* am apologizing, when he is the one behaving like a criminal who should be locked up in the county jail."

"I accept your apologies." Maddie's face was stiff as a whalebone corset. Only her eyes betrayed any emotion. "Now, I suggest you both depart."

"I'm not leaving until after *he* does," Chase informed her. "Let him go first, and I'll be only too happy to hightail it out of here."

"The man is clearly mad," Horace said. "He shouldn't be allowed to wander loose around the countryside. Like a dog foaming at the mouth, he should be confined—or shot."

"If that's a threat, we can draw guns right now," Chase growled, knowing his tormentor would take the cowardly way out and back down.

He did. "No, no. . . . I'm leaving. To spare you any more distress, my dear, I shall depart at once. It's obvious that unless I do, this madman will continue to inflict his dangerous, violent presence on us both."

"Thank you, Horace. You are most considerate. I hope your nose isn't broken, and that you can see well enough to find your way back to town." Maddie gave him a brittle smile—but it was still a smile, and whenever she glanced at Chase, her smile froze into a grimace.

Chase stood and waited while Horace collected his broken spectacles and climbed into the buggy. Only after he had saluted Maddie with his whip, scowled at Chase, clucked to his horse, and driven out of sight, did Chase move a muscle.

Stepping in front of Maddie, he said: "Next time you want to be treated like a calico queen, let me know ahead of time, and I won't lift a finger to save you."

"What you did was despicable. How dare you spy on me! And how dare you leap from nowhere and attack a guest in my own front yard!"

"You actually *wanted* that man to touch you? I can't believe it, Maddie. If you're that desperate for a man, surely you can do better. Not that I'm volunteering."

Out of his hurt, Chase sought to inflict hurt. He simply couldn't believe Maddie would actually prefer Horace Brownley to him. Yet she wasn't denying it. She had encouraged Horace to think he stood a chance with her—and *dis*couraged him. Her rejection sorely wounded him. He wished now that he hadn't reacted with jealousy; it was unlike him to attack a man who couldn't defend himself. Unable to settle things in a man-to-man fist fight, all Brownley could do was threaten to call out the sheriff.

Maddie blinked at Chase. His sarcasm had produced a suspicious sheen in her eyes, but she seemed determined to keep her distance from him, and that hurt him even more.

"I don't care what you think of me," she said. "Or of Mr. Brownley. I *need* Horace's friendship. Already, he's been a friend to me far more than you ever have. I have problems about which you know nothing, and Horace has willingly offered to help me, which is more than I can say for you or anyone else . . ."

"You mean monetary problems. You need money. Is *he* the one putting up your five thousand dollars for the race? Or should I say—the one you're hoping to convince to put up that money?"

"That's none of your business, Chase, and I'll thank you to keep your nose out of . . ."

Just then, the front door opened, and surprisingly, Big Mike McCrory shuffled out of the house. "What's all the shoutin' out here? You're loud enough t' wake the dead, Maddie. Your sisters and brother are in there tryin' t' figure out what t' do about it, but I thought I'd jus' come out and tell ya' t' either solve yer problems or go someplace else t' conduct your arguin'."

"How are you this evening, Mr. McCrory?" Chase called out. "You seem to be doing much better than the last few times I've seen you."

"What?" Big Mike squinted at him. "Do I know you, young feller? You look kinda familiar, but . . ."

"Chase Cumberland. You remember me, don't you? I'm a friend—*former* friend—of Maddie's."

"Oh, . . . well, I'm doin' all right, I guess. 'Cept I'm thirsty all the time an' Maddie don't like it when I go around her t' satisfy my thirst. But I go around her anyway." He waved his hand in the air and chuckled. "Yes, siree . . . I know how to go around her. Can't let females rule your life, son. Only one I ever let rule me was Maddie's ma . . . but she was special. Yes, sir, she was real special. Now she's gone, I don't have t' answer t' nobody no more."

Muttering to himself, he shuffled back into the house again, leaving Maddie and Chase alone.

"You want me to go, don't you?" Chase asked after an awkward moment of silence.

Maddie nodded. She refused to look at him and seemed reluctant to speak.

"Then I'm going. But I meant what I said earlier, Maddie. Next time, you'll have to come to me. . . . Only don't come until you're ready to admit that what's between us is more important than a horse race. It's far more important than whatever's between you and Horace."

"I'll never come. You'll never see me, Chase."

Still, she wouldn't look at him. She kept her head down and mumbled the words in the direction of her feet.

Seething with frustration, Chase almost snatched the shell comb out of her hair. Almost seized her and kissed her, just to show her the difference between his kiss and Horace Brownley's. Almost volunteered to drop out of the race if that's what she wanted. Almost offered to *give* her five thousand dollars if money meant that much to her.

But in the end, he did nothing.

"If that's the way you want it, Maddie."

"It's the way *you* want it," she disputed.

"Yeah, it must be all my fault," he agreed. "See you at the race."

Leaving her, he went to get his horse. And he managed to ride away without once looking back to see if she was bothering to watch his departure.

The Fourth of July passed quietly. All of the McCrorys stayed home, though the girls complained bitterly, and even Little Mike allowed as how he *should* go into town to watch the small-stakes match races being held before the fireworks. Maddie agreed they ought to be racing some of their young stock in these minor races, but she held firm that the Fourth of July wasn't a good day to go into town with Pa. Once her father realized that a special holiday was in progress—always celebrated in the past by having a few drinks after the races—it would be hard to hold him back. He'd find a jug, or maybe even a barrel, somewhere; his old drinking buddies wouldn't deny him on the Fourth of July. Pa hadn't been any happier lately, but at least, he'd been sober, and Maddie wasn't about to place him in the way of temptation.

However, a week after the disastrous encounter between Chase and Horace Brownley, Maddie *had* to return to town to buy coffee, one of the items she had forgotten to purchase in her eagerness to depart Hopewell the last time she was there. She dreaded going, because this time, she knew she'd have to stop and see Horace—let him know she was in town—but first, she lingered in the mercantile looking at a batch of beautiful bolts of fabric that had just arrived.

She couldn't afford to buy any, but just looking at them gave her pleasure. Since the girls hadn't accompanied her this time, she could look to her heart's content and not have to worry about their reaction. She was examining a blue fabric, the same shade as her new bonnet, when Mrs. Grover sidled over to her and lowered her normally strident voice.

"Maddie, dear, how *are* you?" Mrs. Grover was a little mouse of a woman with a great penchant for gossip. Knowing that if she said anything interesting, it would be all over town within a matter of hours, Maddie immediately raised her guard.

"I'm fine, Mrs. Grover. Just stopped in to do some shopping, that's all. I hope you don't mind my looking at your lovely new shipment of cloth."

"Oh, you can look, dear, but be careful not to finger it if you're not buying. Customers don't care for fingered goods; I've discovered that through painful experience."

Maddie removed her hand from the lovely blue fabric. "Guess I shouldn't be touching it at all then."

"Perhaps that would be for the best. . . . Want a cup of tea before you go, dear?"

Maddie froze. Mrs. Grover never offered her tea; indeed, she hadn't been particularly friendly since the family had fallen on hard times.

"Tea, Mrs. Grover?"

"Dear, you positively *must* sit down with me and tell me all about your new neighbor. I understand that the man is *mad.* I mean, quite unpredictable and likely to perpetrate violence. How ever is your poor family managing—way out there alone in the same vicinity as a madman?"

Maddie was at a loss. Had someone seen Buck Cumberland—Chase's brother? If someone had spotted him, was the gossip that Chase so feared beginning to spread in Hopewell?

"What do you mean about a madman, Mrs. Grover? We have no mad neighbors that I'm aware of."

"Why, Chase Cumberland, of course. The fellow who bought

the old Parker place. Mayor Brownley is telling everyone how Mr. Cumberland attacked him for no good reason—broke his glasses, almost broke his nose, and threatened to *kill* him. Horace even told the sheriff about the attack."

"He told Sheriff Smith?"

"That's right. But he also said he wouldn't press charges—*this time.* If it should happen again, of course, he'll have him thrown in jail. He just wanted the sheriff to know what kind of riffraff is settling in the area. Why, before you know it, Hopewell will be as bad as Abilene or Dodge City. Can't let folks like that into our town, now can we, Maddie? . . . Has Mr. Cumberland bothered you or your family? Mr. Brownley said Mr. Cumberland was skulking around your property when it happened. You'd better watch out, Maddie. You've got two pretty young sisters to think of, and a man like that is capable of anything. What was he doing skulking around your place anyhow? If the man's actually *mad,* he's bound to be dangerous. Probably spying, he was. Trying to get a peek up your sisters' petticoats, I'll bet. . . . Where are you going, Maddie? I thought you wanted to buy something."

"Not now, Mrs. Grover. I've a pressing matter to take up with Mayor Brownley."

"But my dear. Don't forget your parasol. It looks like rain." Mrs. Grover came after Maddie with the parasol she had brought in case of damp weather. The day had started out cloudy, suggesting a shower might be on the way.

Maddie snatched the parasol and sailed out the front door of the mercantile. Once outside, she practically ran all the way to the bank.

Fourteen

Maddie marched into Hopewell Savings and Trust, bypassed the surprised clerk waiting on people in the front lobby and headed straight for Horace Brownley's private office. She didn't bother knocking, but opened the door and swept into the room. Frowning in annoyance at the intrusion, Horace never looked up from the stack of papers on his desk.

"Elwood, I thought I told you I did not wish to be disturbed for any reas- . . ."

"I am *not* Elwood."

Horace's head jerked up. When he saw Maddie, he jumped to his feet, came around the side of the desk, and extended his arms to her. "Maddie, dearest!"

Suspecting he was about to grab her and kiss her again, Maddie acted on impulse; lifting her parasol, she gave him a resounding *whack!* on his balding head. He fell backward—looking stunned and aggrieved, but she felt perfectly wonderful. Whacking Horace Brownley with her parasol suddenly seemed like one of the most satisfying things she had ever done.

"Why did you strike me? What's wrong? Surely, I've done nothing to deserve having a parasol broken over my head."

Maddie glanced down at her parasol; it was indeed broken, or at least severely bent. Too bad. It had belonged to her mother, and she regretted ruining it. But she didn't regret striking Horace Brownley.

"How dare you spread ugly rumors about my neighbor, Chase Cumberland? You even went to the sheriff, when you promised you would not. I had hoped to keep that embarrassing incident private, but now I find you've told the entire town, bandied my family's name about, sullied a man's reputation, and made me an object of ridicule . . ."

"I never mentioned I was *kissing* you when he attacked me!" Horace protested. "All I did was warn folks that we have a madman in our midst—and why shouldn't I warn them? I'm the mayor, I'll thank you to remember, and Chase Cumberland is exactly the sort of violent, unstable troublemaker that decent, law-abiding communities like Hopewell can do without. We don't want our town turning into a wild, lawless place like Abilene or Dodge City, where folks have to be afraid to even walk down the streets in broad daylight."

"Oh, for goodness sake. All he did was punch you in the nose."

"In the mouth," Horace corrected. ". . . and he broke my spectacles."

"He thought he had good reason, but you neglected to tell anyone *why* he did it. Besides, his threats were harmless, made in the heat of anger."

"He had no right to touch me! I certainly wasn't doing anything wrong by kissing my intended. If Mr. Cumberland ever dares attack another citizen of Hopewell, he'll be arrested and run out of town. Sheriff Smith has promised to keep an eye on the man and do his duty if the occasion warrants. If Chase Cumberland dares approach another person in a violent manner, Moses will apprehend him at once. Why, I'm a leading citizen of this town, Maddie—a pillar of the community, if I do say so myself. As such, I must do all I can to prevent Hopewell from going the way of so many other Kansas cow towns. And the way to do that is to expel all the troublemakers before they gain the upper hand here."

"I know all that, Horace. I appreciate your . . . your determination and civic pride. But I cannot condone your making a minor incident into a major one, and dragging a man's good name through the mud while you are at it. The plain truth is that Chase Cumberland was defending my honor. That doesn't mean he's a criminal or undesirable element. You have gravely wronged him."

"Because he gravely wronged me." Fingering his upper lip as if it was still puffy and swollen, which it wasn't, Horace returned to the chair behind his desk and sank down on it, sighing as though from weakness brought on by his many injuries. "He could have killed me. As it is, I'm half blind until the new glasses I ordered from the East arrive. And this enlarged lip is a blot on my appearance and a detriment to my position. The pain and discomfort Mr. Cumberland inflicted upon me is a constant reminder of the vigilance we must all exercise if we are to keep our town a safe place to live."

Maddie leaned over the desk. "You've gone too far, Horace, and I am severely disappointed in you. Forgive me for striking you with the parasol, but I myself was momentarily touched with a bit of madness. Come to think of it, I still am."

"Well, when such a mood possesses you, I should think you would stop and recall all you owe me. Were it not for my generosity, the bank would have foreclosed on your family's farm long ago. I've kept you afloat, Maddie; it's not the bank itself that's done it. It's *me,* Horace Brownley. You were too poor of a risk to meet the bank's requirements for a loan, so I lent you that two thousand dollars from my own personal funds. Even now, it's *my* money keeping a roof over your head. Our policy is to foreclose immediately on any properties with outstanding debts. To get around the policy, which I myself instituted, I've had to make your mortgage payments—and again, I'm using my own funds, not the bank's."

"I . . . I didn't realize that."

Straightening, Maddie swallowed to keep from gagging on the bile rising up her throat. She felt suddenly ill. She had never dreamed she was so beholden to Horace *personally.* All this time, she had thought she owed her survival to the Hopewell Savings and Trust. Horace had supposedly only used his influence with the bank to help her, but the bank itself was her rescuer. Discovering otherwise was an unpleasant shock.

Sitting there in his big chair, Horace reminded her of some

fat hairy spider lurking in the center of a web—and slowly drawing her toward him. Even if she won the race and could pay back every single cent she owed him, she would still feel obligated, and the only way she could dispense that obligation was to marry him.

The familiar weight of worry and discouragement settled heavily on Maddie's shoulders. "I . . . I am most grateful for all you've done for me and my family. I was simply embarrassed to hear Mrs. Grover discussing my affairs in the mercantile. You know what a gossip she is. If she hasn't already done so, she'll spread the story to everyone."

"Yes, yes, my dear. She's a terrible gossip," Horace agreed. Once again, he rose and came around the side of the desk, took hold of Maddie's hands, and held them tightly. The bent parasol poked him in the belly, but he seemed not to notice. "And you are right to worry about gossip. My future wife's reputation must be above reproach. We can't have even a breath of scandal attached to your name, Maddie, for when we marry, you, too, will become a leading citizen. You'll be expected to take part in the city's political and social functions. I must attend them all, and you will have to be at my side. Had you realized that?"

"Not . . . entirely. And I'm not certain I'm up to it. Perhaps you had better reconsider your proposal of marriage, Horace. I'm not at all sure I'm the right girl—woman—for you. You need someone who possesses far more social graces than I do. When it comes to politics and entertaining, I'm hopelessly inexperienced and dull-witted. I . . ."

"Nonsense. I am committed, dearest Maddie. Haven't I made that clear to you by now? I can imagine no one else for me but you. Besides," he added with a chuckle. "Our financial affairs are now so hopelessly entwined, we'll have to marry just to keep everything straight. How would you ever manage without me?"

How, indeed? If she lost the big race in Abilene, would Horace be willing to cover *that* debt? She suspected he'd be furious, but he'd probably just take over the farm—and sell it or auction it off to settle her obligations. He'd insist on getting rid of the horses, too, for how could they maintain them without the farm?

Lord only knew what he'd do about her family. She didn't even want to *think* about it.

Giving him a small, reluctant smile, playing a role she abhorred, Maddie managed to escape Horace's presence without having to endure another one of his sloppy, enthusiastic kisses. In this, she was aided by the intrusion of Elwood, the clerk, who had come to fetch Horace to take care of a pressing business matter.

Leaving the bank, Maddie set out across the dusty, unpaved street and there encountered the very man whose reputation she had just been defending.

"Chase!" As she recognized the tall figure coming toward her with his head down, in a rush and not watching where he was going, Maddie stopped dead center in the street.

Glancing up, he narrowly avoided a collision with her. "Maddie . . . what a surprise. But I'm sure you're not here in town to see *me.*" His gaze fastened on the building she had just left. "Have a nice visit with your old friend, Horace?"

From his tone of voice, he might have been discussing a particularly disgusting sort of vermin to which Maddie had become inexplicably attached.

"I had a terrible visit. We discussed the vicious gossip Horace has been spreading about you. You're going to have to be very careful from now on, Chase. Because of what happened between you and Horace, the whole town will be watching your behavior. If you so much as raise your voice at anyone . . ."

"Cumberland!" a man suddenly yelled, and Maddie saw Sheriff Smith approaching from the direction of the town jail.

Her heart plummeted. Big, blustery Moses Smith, his sheriff's badge shining brightly on his leather vest, swaggered toward them like a huge, menacing bear. Whenever he engaged in sheriff-type duties, he made it a point to swagger, for he had an absurdly puffed-up opinion of his own importance.

Beside her, Chase insolently studied the man from beneath the brim of his black Stetson. "The sheriff, I take it."

Maddie nodded. "Oh, Chase, do watch your tongue! If you don't, Moses is liable to lock you up while he's thinking of a crime for which he can hang you. Our sheriff takes his position seriously. He's always been jealous of his competition in Abilene and Dodge City, you see. They have hangings or shootings or some kind of trouble every week in those towns, and the lawmen there have gained fierce reputations. Here in Hopewell, however, we don't get much excitement, and Moses is therefore a nobody."

"Thanks for the warning." More loudly, Chase said: "Afternoon, Sheriff. Nice day, isn't it?"

"Humph," Moses grunted. "Looks like rain t' me. Don't try sweet-talkin' the law, Cumberland. 'Cuz I know what kind of feller you are. I've heard all about you. Too bad you ain't totin' a six-shooter, or I could run you inta jail in a minute."

"I saw the sign banning weapons in Hopewell the first day I rode in here, Sheriff," Chase responded. "Even if I hadn't seen it, you would never catch me with a pistol or rifle because I don't believe a man should carry one unless he plans on using it."

"Just what sort of man do you think he is, Sheriff Smith?" Maddie planted herself in front of the sheriff and eyed him with a mixture of false sweetness and genuine contempt.

"Why . . . uh . . . I ain't sayin' he's a gunfighter, but I heard what he done over t' your place, Miss McCrory . . . uh . . . ma'am."

Sheriff Smith always got a little tongue-tied around women, Maddie had noticed. He could be a bully with men, but he didn't stand up to females nearly as well. Perhaps it was because he wasn't married, though he'd been doggedly courting Alice Neff, a sweet little old widow lady—thus far without much success.

Maddie could well understand Alice's hesitation; marrying the heavy-handed, ambitious sheriff would be akin to rushing headlong into a bear's den and hoping the bear wouldn't take a swat at you.

"Oh, you heard that Mr. Cumberland stopped by to help build a breeding chute for us?" she inquired of the sheriff with a bat of her lashes. "And he fixed our broken shed door while he was at it? The gossips informed you he's been the *perfect* neighbor ever since he moved in?"

"Waal . . . no, I didn't hear that, Miss McCrory. Horace, over t' the bank, told me this here feller beat him up and broke his glasses. And that ain't somethin' I'm about to put up with. Now that we've rid the area of upstart Injuns—fer the most part, anyway—I ain't gonna let white trash spoil the neighborhood."

"The incident to which you refer was an unfortunate misunderstanding, Sheriff Smith," Maddie explained. "Mr. Cumberland thought Mr. Brownley was up to some nefarious purpose."

"Ne-far-i-ous purpose?" Moses repeated. "What's that supposed t' mean?"

"It means wicked. That's why Mr. Cumberland attacked Mr. Brownley. He thought he was up to no good."

"That's right. I did," Chase added, taking his cue from Maddie. "Sometimes the best-dressed men have the worst motives of anyone. Haven't you ever noticed that? You can't trust a man just because he wears a suit."

"Sure. I knew that," Moses blustered. "But he's the mayor an' also the town banker; he's supposed t' dress like . . . like."

"Like an undertaker," Chase supplied with a twinkle in his eye, and Maddie sucked in her cheeks to keep from laughing.

"Humph. We don't have no undertakers in Hopewell. We ain't big enough yet. But if we ever get a railway spur through here like everyone wants, we will be someday."

"Undoubtedly. As a new resident of the area, I'm pleased to meet you, Sheriff Smith." Smooth as butter, Chase extended his hand for a handshake, and the sheriff could hardly avoid reciprocating, though he still didn't look convinced of Chase's innocence.

"Why don't you allow me to buy you a drink over at the Ruby Garter, and we can become better acquainted?" Chase suggested.

"Waal . . . I don't know." Sheriff Smith scratched the back of his neck in indecision. "I don't usually drink while on duty—and I'm on duty most of the time. Town can't afford a marshall. Which means as soon as I turn my back, all hell is like to break loose."

"Folks will understand you've got to take time off once in a while," Chase urged, surprising Maddie with his cordiality toward a man he could have no good reason to like. "I was just on my way over to the saloon to have a whiskey before I head for home, and I'd appreciate the company."

"They say that whiskey is the devil's own brew, gentlemen, and I can personally verify the claim." Maddie glared at Chase. His behavior around the sheriff had suddenly reminded her of his astounding ability to be two-faced and opportunistic. This was just one more example of how he could entice people into friendship, even when they had nothing to gain by it and might, in fact, have a great deal to lose.

Obviously, he didn't need *her* assistance in convincing the sheriff that he wasn't some mad man prone to violence; he seemed to be doing quite well charming Moses Smith all on his own. He had his brother to protect, of course, but nonetheless he was a shade too smooth and manipulative to suit Maddie. She was sorry she had rushed to his aid, especially after she had vowed to have nothing more to do with him. She hoped Chase didn't take her warnings as a sign that she had reversed her position in regards to him. She *still* wanted nothing to do with him.

She had better things to do with her time—such as preparing for the race. Chase Cumberland, it was perfectly clear, could take care of himself.

"Since you two are now headed for the saloon, I'll bid you good-day," she said.

"G'day, Miss McCrory." Sheriff Smith tipped his hat to her, but Chase merely nodded.

"Good day, Maddie. Hope you don't get caught in the rain going home. Your parasol doesn't look as if it can provide much protection." He indicated the bent parasol with a skeptically raised eyebrow.

"You'd be surprised how much protection a parasol can provide," she retorted. "Rain or no rain."

Leaving the two men staring after her in perplexity, Maddie marched off, convinced more than ever that Chase Cumberland simply could not be trusted.

Chase had not one but two shots of whiskey with the sheriff, and the more time he spent with Moses Smith, the less he liked him. The man was a big, dumb ox—and inordinately proud of the fact that in his youth, he had helped round up all the Indians in the region and hustle them onto reservations. As a result of his zealousness in "cleaning out the riffraff," he had won his position as sheriff and now saw it as his sworn duty to "keep the town decent."

By this he meant that anyone who didn't meet his particular standards should be thrown out of Hopewell and its surroundings. That included all Indians, anyone with even a drop of Indian or "tainted blood, if'n you know what I mean," anyone who looked or acted suspicious, preached or professed a strange religion, had an accent or "funny way of jawin' ," or raised sheep instead of cattle, horses, pigs, or poultry for a living, plus anyone whom Mayor Horace Brownley didn't like.

"You got off on the wrong foot punchin' him like you did, Cumberland," he told Chase over his fourth whiskey, while Chase was still nursing his second. "You want t' live long in these parts, you better mend your fences with Horace Brownley, 'cuz sooner or later, you're gonna be needin' him. Not only is he the mayor, but the Hopewell Savings and Trust is the only bank in the whole county. Why, even Dodge City ain't got a bank yet. There's nobody else for miles around to lend money t' folks."

That's why Maddie allowed him such liberties, Chase realized with a grimace. His suspicions were confirmed; she *must* owe him money. Brownley probably had put up the two thousand dollars Maddie had lost to Chase—and he was likely putting up the five thousand for this next race. She had indeed sold herself to the highest bidder. Of course, she was just doing what she had to do to take care of her family. He understood that; what she failed to understand was that he was just doing what *he* had to do to take care of Buck.

He didn't enjoy sitting here drinking with Moses Smith any more than Maddie probably enjoyed kissing Horace Brownley. Unfortunately, they both had to protect the ones depending upon them.

It's all for the best, he consoled himself. Maddie didn't need him; Buck did. At this very moment, a wanted poster with Buck's description and a crude drawing of his likeness might be hanging in Moses Smith's office at the town jail. To keep the sheriff from snooping around his farm, he'd have to convince him he had nothing to hide.

He mustn't arouse the man's suspicions in any way. He'd been so careful to hide Buck's tracks; if he could just befriend this big buffoon, Buck should remain safe.

"Thanks for the good advice, Moses. . . . Now, how about another drink?" Chase caught the eye of Lily Tolliver who'd been watching them like a hawk from the minute they'd set foot inside her establishment. He raised his hand to signal to her. "I'll get us a whole bottle, instead of one drink at a time."

"Naw. . . . Four's my limit, Cumberland. Wouldn't do for the sheriff t' go staggerin' down the street like . . . like Big Mike McCrory. If word gets back t' Alice Neff that I even stopped by this place, she won't speak t' me for a week."

Chase lowered his hand, and Lily looked disappointed. "You and this Mrs. Neff have a relationship?"

Moses nodded. "I popped the big question to her weeks ago, but so far, she's lettin' me dangle. Claims it's too soon after she buried her last husband for her to think about marryin' again. But I think two years is a long enough time t' mourn, don't you?"

"Seems like it to me, but then I've never been married or even sweet on a woman . . ." *Except for Maddie,* " . . . so I can't really say. Big Mike McCrory is still mourning *his* wife, so who's to decide Alice Neff can't still mourn her husband?"

"Waal . . . she don't get drunk over it, like Big Mike. Fact is, she don't like drinkin' a'tall. I shouldn't even be settin' here."

"Now, now. . . . You can't allow a woman to dictate to you, Moses. If you let 'em, they'll soon be telling you everything you can and can't do."

"Right. You're damn right, Cumberland." Moses clunked his glass down on the table. "All right, I will have another. And maybe another after that one."

Chase nodded to Lily, the buxom proprietress, who was still watching with an eagle eye. She flashed him a toothy smile and held up a bottle. He nodded. A moment later, she sashayed over to the table, arriving in a cloud of floral scent that made Chase feel like gagging.

"You boys are mighty thirsty today, ain't you?" she purred in a deep, throaty voice. She set the bottle down on the table. "Anything else I can get for you?"

"Don't git any notions, Lily," Moses hastened to warn her. "I ain't interested in no saloon whore. My sights are set a mite higher than a soiled dove."

"Why, Moses, you hurt my feelin's." Lily pouted, her red lips curving downward.

"You're just lucky I don't put you outa business. But as everyone says, a cow town's gotta have a saloon. Cowpokes won't bring their beeves here t' sell if they can't cut up afterward. Hell, Abilene and Dodge City have saloons up and down both sides of their main streets."

"There. You see? I'm good for Hopewell, and don't you forget it, Moses." Lily Tolliver stuck out a hip and rested one hand on it. "If it weren't for me, this town would be plumb dead, and you know it."

"Quiet, you mean. Not dead," Moses disputed. "It would be calm, quiet, and law abidin' with only the occasional horse race t' stir things up a bit."

"Speakin' of horse races," Lily said, her painted face brightening. "I hear there's gonna be a real big one in Abilene, and you're gonna be in it. That right, Mr. Cumberland?"

"I'm not just gonna be in it, I'm gonna win it," Chase corrected her. "So if you've got a few dollars to spare, you might as well put them on my mare, Bonnie Lass."

"Oh, I'm thinkin' about it. I was also thinkin' of takin' a wagonload of folks over t' Abilene t' watch the race. From what I hear, half of Hopewell is plannin' on bein' there—at least, the folks who know about the race already. There won't be no business in town that afternoon anyway, so I might as well go."

"Seems like I heard about that race, too," Moses said, pouring himself a full glass of whiskey. "Yep, I saw a man puttin' up a handbill about it jus' this mornin'."

"A handbill?" Chase questioned, frowning.

He didn't much care for handbills or posters of any sort; in his experience, if they had anything to do with him or his brother, such things always meant trouble.

"Can't rightly recollect exactly what all it said." Moses downed half a glass of whiskey in one long gulp, then smacked his lips before continuing.

"Well, try," Chase muttered.

"Oh, yeah. Now I remember. It said somethin' about the great Kansas champion Gold Deck goin' up against horses belongin' to one Lazarus Gratiot of Abilene and the Madman of Hopewell."

"The Madman of Hopewell? It didn't mention my name or the name of my mare?"

Moses Smith shook his head. "Not that I recollect. It jus' referred to you as the Madman of Hopewell."

"I been hearin' about the Madman of Hopewell, too," said Lily. "That's what everybody's callin' you, Cumberland, ever since you took a poke at that prig, Horace Brownley."

"Don't you be sayin' nothin' bad about our Horace." The sheriff was beginning to slur his words, and his eyes were unfocused, but he managed to focus them for a moment on Lily.

"Horace Brownley is a prig, if you ask me," Lily insisted. "And a hard-nosed little tyrant to boot. Oh, he can grin and shake hands with the best of politicians, but if a body is even so much as *one* day late on a mortgage or loan payment, Horace

Brownley starts circlin' around them like a big old turkey buzzard scenting spoiled meat."

"Waal, hell, that's his *real* job. He's a banker," defended Moses.

"He's the one who started this Madman business." Chase shoved back his chair. "But it beats me how it spread fast enough to get on a poster."

"Ha!" Lily barked with laughter. "Ain't you realized it yet, Cumberland? This town's so small that if a man farts in the east end, everybody in the west end knows about it almost immediately. Why, a truly juicy bit of gossip spreads faster'n fleas in a whore's mattress."

"You sure got a mouth on you, woman," Sheriff Moses mumbled.

"If my speech is too colorful for you, Sheriff, you better run on back to the widow woman, Neff. I only talk this way 'cause I've spent too many years listenin' t' men guzzlin' whiskey."

Chase had to grin at the woman—though he still wasn't happy about being branded as the Madman of Hopewell. Still, better him than his brother. Suddenly, he wanted to get back home with the beans and bacon he'd come to town to get. The talk of posters had made him uneasy—or maybe spending an hour with the sheriff had done it. Whatever the cause, he wanted to leave. He had accomplished all he could today anyway; if he left the bottle for Moses Smith, the man would surely remember his generosity and be less inclined to hostility the next time they met. And hopefully, he'd stay away from the farm.

Rising to his feet, he dug in his pocket for money to pay for the whiskey, but Lily Tolliver held up her hand. "Nope, it's on the house, Cumberland. 'Course, I'm considerin' that the next time you win a race, you might be willin' t' celebrate here in my saloon. That's what Big Mike McCrory always done after he won—stand everybody in town t' a free round of drinks at the Ruby Garter."

"And that's why you've been slippin' him whiskey all this

time?" Chase asked. "You're the one who's been supplying his stash?"

Her chin rose, and her brown eyes flashed. "Yes, but no more. I'm done givin' him credit, and I told his daughter that, too. She ain't got the fastest horse around here no more, so there's no chance she can pay the bill her pa's run up with me. I've had to throw him out a coupla times now, 'cause he didn't have no cash on him. However, if *you* should want credit, all you gotta do is ask, Mr. Madman of Hopewell."

"Thanks, but no thanks." Chase pressed several coins on her. "I don't hold much with credit—or with celebrating my victories in saloons either."

Lily took the coins and slid them down the front of her low-cut red gown, which revealed an unseemly expanse of snow white skin. "Have it your own way, then."

"Hope to see you both at the race." Chase started for the swinging doors of the saloon.

"Cumberland!" the sheriff bellowed. "Wait a minute."

Chase paused to look back at the man hunched over the bottle he had just paid for. "Sheriff?"

"Don't think jus' 'cause you bought me some whiskey that I'm givin' up keepin' my eye on you. Could be you *are* a madman."

"Could be I am, Moses. There's always that possibility." Chase tipped his hat to the sheriff and sauntered out of the saloon.

"Humph!" he heard Moses grunt, and Lily Tolliver laughed. "If Cumberland *is* a madman, he's a damn good-lookin' one," she said. "Seems to me, madmen usually look wild an' scary."

Like Buck.

Chase started down the street toward the livery where he'd left the horse and spring wagon he'd brought to town, in case he decided to get a roll of barbed wire to fence off the back end of his property from any chance intruders. Suddenly, he noticed a man tacking up posters farther down the street. White handbills now hung from nearly every available pole lining both sides of the town's main thoroughfare. They had gone up in the brief time since he'd been in the saloon.

With the race only a week away, Chase supposed it was only natural that the advertising should begin in earnest. Still, his gut reaction was to tear down every one—on the off chance that they *might* refer to Buck, instead of the race. Drawing a deep breath to calm his racing heart, he took the time to read one of them first. The poster indeed advertised the race, and it said exactly what Moses Smith had told him it said.

His real name wasn't even mentioned, nor was Bonnie Lass's. He was referred to only as the Madman of Hopewell, spelled out in large block letters. The McCrory name was also in big print, but Lazarus Gratiot merited only small print, as if the race were primarily a rematch between Bonnie Lass and Gold Deck. Actually, that's what it was. One-Eyed Jack didn't stand a chance against two such superior horses, but Lazarus Gratiot seemed to be the only one around not to realize it.

Chase tore down the poster so he could take it home to show Buck. He figured his brother would get a good laugh out of him being called the Madman, for a change. . . . One week. He had one week to go before the race, and he shouldn't even be spending any time in town so close to such an important event. He was surprised Maddie had come all the way into Hopewell; the fact that she had done so—had apparently found it necessary to visit Horace Brownley—told him more than he wanted to know. Just how far would Maddie go to save her family from destitution?

He thought of the love and loyalty that shone in her eyes whenever she looked at the members of her family—or even spoke of them . . . and Chase knew without a doubt that she would go as far as she needed to. She'd do whatever it took. She would sacrifice herself entirely, caring not at all what it cost her personally.

He understood her single-mindedness, for he himself would give anything—*almost* anything—to have her look at him like that, to have her love him even half as much, to possess even a small portion of her loyalty. Horace Brownley didn't deserve

Maddie McCrory, but if Maddie intended to waste herself on the man to save her family, there was nothing he could do about it. He didn't have Horace's money or influence, and besides, *his* loyalty belonged to Buck.

Fifteen

The following day, after a night of soft, gentle rain, Chase again saw Maddie, but this time, she made it a point not to speak to him. He was exercising Bonnie Lass by the McCrorys' field, and Little Mike was working Gold Deck, while Maddie rode a nice-looking youngster bearing the stamp of his illustrious sire. Ignoring Chase completely, Maddie put the sorrel colt through his paces, her expression so intent that she might have been a hundred miles away for all the notice she gave Chase or her surroundings.

By now, the grass had grown long, and some of it had already been cut to make hay. The night of rain had left the footing soft and uncertain in places, and the best stretch to work the horses was along Chase's side of the field. Maddie doggedly kept to the fringe on the opposite side, and when the colt began to tire, she took him home, leaving Chase, his nerves stretched as taut as barbed wire, alone with Little Mike.

"Nice youngster your sister was riding," Chase called out to the young man. Just because Maddie sorely aggravated him didn't mean he disliked her brother. Actually, he liked Little Mike a great deal.

Not in the least unfriendly, Little Mike nodded. "We call him Red, 'cause he's redder than his daddy. Don't know if he'll be as fast though, because his mama wasn't the best sprinter."

"Gold Deck's sure looking fine these days." Chase urged Bonnie Lass closer and dropped to a walk beside the stallion.

The mare nickered her interest, as she had the last time she'd seen Gold Deck, and Gold Deck nickered back. Bonnie Lass's breeding time had come and gone already, and Gold Deck appeared to know it. This time, he didn't bother to arch his neck and prance beside her, but settled into a companionable walk.

"He's gettin' real fit," Little Mike said, slanting Chase a long glance. "I've been workin' him hard, and I don't think you'll find it so easy to beat us this time. We're ready for you now."

Chase didn't mention that he'd been working Bonnie Lass hard, too. Instead, he took advantage of the opportunity to have a close look at his rival. Gold Deck had lost weight, and his muscular haunches were more clearly defined. He'd been galloping in the field when Chase arrived, yet he had barely raised a sweat. His reddish-colored coat gleamed with golden highlights and the kind of shine only good health and contentment could produce. Here was a racing animal in his prime—a wondrous assemblage of body parts all designed to work together to achieve a specific goal: short bursts of dazzling speed. Chase had confidence in his mare, but he had to admit that Gold Deck had "winner" written all over him.

"You might be right, Mike. Your stallion won't be easy to beat. However, Bonnie Lass and I aren't ready to concede defeat yet."

"My sister's real upset with you for enterin' that race against us."

"And what about you? How do you feel about it?"

Little Mike shrugged. "Isn't that why we raise Quarter horses—to race 'em every chance we get? Of course, we expect a lot more of them than just racin', but I wouldn't back away from a race because some female didn't want me in it. Maddie may be my sister, but we don't agree on everything. A man shouldn't let a female influence his decisions anyway; he should just do what he wants."

Recalling the boy's father saying very nearly the same thing, Chase grinned. He also remembered the sheriff's dilemma—and his own. "Wait a couple of years, and you might change your mind. Especially if the female doing the influencing is one who appeals to you. Somehow, women always see things differently, and men have to decide whether or not to humor them."

Little Mike shook his head as if women thoroughly baffled him. "Maddie sure was riled about that race. Still is. But I figure if you want to throw away five thousand dollars, that's your business, not hers. You got a right."

"Thanks. I knew you'd be more reasonable about it than she is. Though I didn't figure you'd be quite as confident of beating me as you are."

"I'm confident because I know I've got the best horse," Little Mike said quietly, giving Chase a glimpse of the determined man the youth was fast becoming. "Maddie thinks she's the only one who ever worries about this family or dreams of a better future for 'em. But she's not. I've got my own dreams, and next Saturday, when we race, I'm gonna do everything I can to start makin' 'em come true."

Chase gathered his reins in one hand and offered Little Mike the other. "Whatever happens, I hope we remain friends when it's over, Mike."

Little Mike offered a man's handshake—firm and strong. "We will. . . . Guess I better be getting back now, before Maddie throws one of her fits."

"Guess you better." Chase suddenly discovered a suspicious lump in his throat. If he had a younger brother, as well as an older one, he'd like him to be someone like Little Mike. The boy had gumption and more maturity than Maddie realized.

Chase kept busy all that day, and so did Buck. By early evening, both men were sweaty, exhausted, and starved. However, Buck ate almost no supper, and afterward, started heating water in a big kettle.

"Why are you doing that?" Chase demanded, annoyed by his brother's unflagging industry.

Buck signaled that he intended to shave and clean up.

"Going somewhere tonight, Buck?"

Buck merely grinned, and Chase decided it was time he had a talk with his brother. It made no sense for two grown men to keep pretending nothing out of the ordinary was happening.

Buck usually did his share of the work, but there had been times lately when projects had been left for Chase to finish because Buck was in such a rush to get over to see Mary.

"I know where you're going, big brother, and who you're gonna see. Tell me. Are you planning on having Pawnee Mary move in with us—or are you moving in with her? I'm only asking because this sneaking around at night has got to stop. It leaves you too tired to get all your work done, and I'm starting to resent picking up where you leave off."

Buck's jaw had dropped at Chase's mention of Mary, but as soon as Chase finished speaking, he signaled: *I do my share and more around here.*

"I'm not saying you don't. But you could use more sleep than you've been getting. Some days, you look plumb wore out, big brother—a bit like a stud who's been servicing mares too often to recover his strength between times. Come on; admit it. Your nights have grown real interesting, haven't they?"

Buck nodded, and his grin returned. *You really wouldn't mind if I moved in with Mary?* He carefully formed each word so that Chase could read his lips as well as his hand signals.

"No," Chase said. "But wouldn't you rather have her move in with us?"

Buck shook his head emphatically. *Too crowded. Mary wouldn't like living here with both of us. I'd rather go there.*

"Is that old soddy house even fit to live in?" Judging from the way the house looked on the outside, Chase couldn't believe it wasn't a complete wreck inside.

It's nicer than you'd expect. Only thing wrong with it is the roof leaks. But I'm going to fix that problem as soon as I find the time.

"I'd be glad to help," Chase volunteered. "Why didn't you tell me all this sooner? How long did you intend to wait before you let me know you had found a lady friend? I've known about it for some time, you know. One night, I spotted the two of you playing naked in the river."

Buck looked chagrined. *I didn't want to make you feel bad. Didn't want you to think I don't appreciate . . . all this.* Buck spread his arms wide to encompass the house. *I don't want to give up what we have here; I just want Mary, too. In case you haven't noticed, we could both use some female companionship.*

"Hell, I agree." Chase smiled at his brother. "But I guess you're the one with all the luck in this family. You know, for years I've worried I might want to get married some day, but wouldn't feel right about deserting you. Now *you're* worrying about hurting *my* feelings. Strange how things work out, isn't it? I'm real happy for you, Buck, but I have to admit when I saw you playing in the river that night with Mary, I was so damned jealous I could hardly stand it. Just how did you get so lucky all of a sudden?"

Damned if I know. From the moment I first saw Mary, I just knew she would become my woman; she was made for me. With her, I don't have to speak; she seems to know what I'm thinking before I do. Sounds crazy, but it's true.

Chase wondered how Buck did communicate with Mary; there were limitations to Indian sign language, and Mary could not have learned so quickly the additional signs Chase and his brother had developed, nor mastered the art of reading lips which had taken Chase years to learn. His present methods of communication with his brother had evolved over a long period of time, through much trial and error.

"It's downright amazing you two can communicate at all," he said. "You really are lucky, Buck. I wish I could get along half as well with the woman I'd like to claim."

You're sweet on Maddie McCrory, aren't you?

The question rattled Chase. He had never said it, never let himself *think* it, never dared admit that what he felt for Maddie was . . . love. But the truth now hit him squarely between the eyes. He wasn't just sweet on her; he loved her. Loved her courage, bravery, and feisty spirit. Loved the patience and tenderness with which she cared for her father, even though Big Mike didn't deserve it. Loved her matter-of-fact willingness to cook, clean, counsel, scold, and perform all the tasks involved with raising her brother and sisters.

Loved her unruly red hair and impudent freckles, her snapping blue eyes and sweet, vulnerable mouth. Loved and lusted after her slender, feminine body.

Yes, damn it, he loved her. But she apparently didn't love him. . . . So why bother discussing it?

He simply shrugged. "I don't know what to call what we have—or don't have—between us. It sure can't be love, because she wants nothing to do with me. What I mostly feel when I see her these days is miserable."

I'm sorry, Buck said. *I thought since she already knows about me and is good friends with Mary—and because you get a certain look in your eyes whenever she's mentioned—she might be the right woman for you. Then we could* both *be happy.*

"Well, she isn't the right woman for me. Truth is she can't tolerate me. Even if she cared for me, her family would still stand in the way. They mean everything to her, and they still need her, at least until her brother gets a little older, and her sisters are ready to leave home and marry. I don't know what'll happen to her father; the way he's going, he'll probably be dead by then. If she loved me and was willing to marry, we'd still have a long wait ahead of us. I can't imagine Maddie leaving home while her family has so many problems."

Too bad. Buck issued a sympathetic sigh.

"Hell, don't feel sorry for me. Go ahead and be happy, Buck. After all the misery of these last few years, you deserve it. I wish you and Mary well."

Buck stepped closer and clapped Chase on the back. *Now that I have your blessing, I'll tell Mary tonight she can plan our wedding.*

"Your wedding? How are you gonna pull off a wedding without involving a preacher?"

Mary says we can marry without one. We'll make our own ceremony. We'll honor some white customs and some Indian ones. I want to give her a horse as a wedding gift. I thought perhaps that young filly I've been training. Let me have her, and I'll make it up to you somehow.

"The horses aren't *mine;* they're *ours.* Take whichever one you want. As long as it's not Bonnie Lass, I don't care. Of course,

I'm assuming that after a few days off for the wedding and honeymoon, you'll be back to work as usual."

Buck nodded, his face suddenly serious. *More than ever, I want to make a success of this place, Chase. Mary and I might have children. If we do, I'll need your help when it's time to send them to school. That all right with you?*

Chase gave a long low whistle. "You *have* been making plans, haven't you? Naturally, if the need arises, I'll help all I can. Don't know how we'll pull it off though. Maybe we can pretend they're orphans who show up on my doorstep unexpectedly. I can be their long lost uncle or something; after all, I'll *be* their uncle. . . . Wait a minute. You don't already have a kid on the way, do you?"

Buck's grin illuminated his entire face. *Not that I know of. But it's not because we haven't tried. Mary's no calico queen, mind you, but she thinks I'm on the same level as . . . as a god. I've told her I'm no god, but she refuses to believe it.*

"I can see how rough you've got it, brother. Want me to go over and tell her? She might be more inclined to listen to an objective opinion."

She won't believe you either.

"Then just tell her I said hello, and I'll be proud to call her my sister-in-law."

Buck suddenly seized Chase in a bear hug, then clapped him on the back again, this time hard enough to bruise him. *Thanks, little brother,* he said, stepping back. His wild eyes were gentle as a newborn foal's, and his face radiated a joy Chase had never seen there before, not even *before* Buck had been struck by lightning.

Chase could only nod in answer. He begrudged his brother nothing—yet, it was still hard not to be envious. If Buck—who was so different from most men—could find a good woman to love and cherish, why couldn't Chase accomplish the same relatively simple task? Why for him was it so damn difficult?

For years, he'd been telling himself he didn't want or need love in his own life; finding a home—a safe haven—for his brother would be enough. Now that he had finally gained far more than he had ever dared hope for, all he felt was great sadness and deep loss. He desperately wanted what his brother had found: the deepest sort of communion and unity with a woman. The sense of being one with her, mind, body, and soul.

Maddie was the woman he wanted; but it was clear she didn't want him. He had ruined any chance he might have had with her when he entered that damn race. Worse yet, he still didn't think it was wrong to have entered it.

What in hell was he to do?

Anticipating Silver Hair's appearance within the next hour or so, Pawnee Mary set down the axe she'd been using to split firewood in the waning light beside her house. For a moment, she rested her hands on her flat womb; surely a new life had taken root there and was now growing. Imagining the joy of telling Silver Hair her secret, she closed her eyes and smiled to herself.

Her time of female bleeding usually arrived promptly at the same time during each cycle of the moon, but this time, it had not arrived at all. She was nine days late. That and the tender fullness of her breasts, as well as the nausea that had plagued her that very morning had finally convinced her she had conceived a child—and tonight, she would tell Silver Hair.

With sudden haste, Mary abandoned her chopping and made her way to a shallow spot in the river a short distance downstream from her little house. Before Silver Hair arrived, she wanted to bathe and cleanse the day's sweat from her body. Sometimes, her passion for Silver Hair—and his for her—flared so hotly that they couldn't take time to eat or to wash before they fell into each other's arms. Already, she had cooked supper so it would be ready and waiting for later, but she didn't want to be caught smelling like some of the people in town who regarded bathing as a once-a-year chore.

Quickly, Mary shed her clothing, left it in a pile on the bank, and waded into the cool water. She submerged herself, undid her long braid, shook out her black hair, and leisurely combed her fingers through it. The water felt so good on her overheated flesh that she debated staying in the river and forcing Silver Hair to come looking for her. He might appreciate a swim on this hot summer night, and she had greatly enjoyed their water games the last time they had played together in the river.

Paddling further away from the bank, she flipped over and floated on her back. Lazily, she gazed up at the stars and contemplated how wonderful her life had become since Silver Hair had entered it. Before they had found each other, she had believed herself doomed to loneliness. She had never imagined such happiness could be hers. Never dreamed that a white man would become her friend and lover . . . the very core of her existence.

She knew Silver Hair would be thrilled to learn that their love had produced new life. His eagerness to have children—and to wed—had surprised her; it seemed to bother him not at all that she was Indian, but then, considering how much he himself had suffered from the sting of rejection and loneliness, perhaps it was not so surprising, after all. He had learned to judge people by what was in their hearts, and in her heart, he had found only love and acceptance.

Perhaps she should wait to tell him about the baby until they were wed; the news would be a wonderful gift she could give him to celebrate the occasion. She so wanted to give him something special! What could be more special than a son or daughter?

As she floated in the water and thought about the future, which now looked so bright and promising, an alien sound suddenly intruded—destroying her serenity and anticipation of Silver Hair's arrival. Alerted to the possibility of danger, Mary regained her footing and crouched low in the water. Quickly, she arranged her black hair to hide the gleam of her face and shoulders. She strained to listen and again heard a noise—the snort of a horse where no horse should be. The sound was much closer this time, and accompanied by the muffled thud of hooves and a low murmur of voices. Men were riding along the river bank.

A moment later, two black shapes emerged from the screen of brush and wild plum bushes dotting the bank. The men dismounted and allowed their horses to drink from the river very near the spot where Mary had left her clothing. Hoping they wouldn't notice her things, she cringed when a startled cry reached her ears.

"Hey! Lookit *this.*"

"Lookit what?"

"A woman's dress. My horse almost stepped on it. You don't suppose it belongs to that whore we rode all the way out here to see, do ya? Hell, it *must.* There's a pair of moccasins here, too."

"That means she must be around here somewhere. That feller in the saloon in Hopewell wasn't wrong, after all. He claimed there was an Injun squaw livin' out here in an old soddy house, and this proves it."

The first man's voice was high-pitched and thin. The second sounded older, his voice deep and guttural. Remaining motionless in the water, Mary anxiously studied their silhouettes. To her dismay, she realized that both men were big—the first tall and well proportioned, the second short but built like a bull moose.

"Charlie, you got that bottle of whiskey we brought? Get it out pronto. I say we should tie up our horses and have a little drink while we're waitin' fer the whore t' come back and claim her clothes. If she stripped and went swimmin' in the river, she'll see us soon enough and come out t' earn herself a few coins."

"Not if she ain't in the mood, she won't. Injuns can be mighty touchy. Maybe we should hide the horses away from the river, then come back here and keep quiet 'til she comes out an' we can surprise her."

"Naw, all we gotta do is show her our money. Hell, Injuns in this part of the country are starvin'; they'll do damn near anything fer a few coins. Anyway, squaws ain't got the same morals as white women. Could be the bitch is in heat and won't even insist on us payin' her. Why, by the time we're done, I'll bet she'll be beggin' us t' come by fer a visit the next time we're in the neighborhood."

High-pitched laughter followed this pronouncement, telling Mary the man was likely drunk.

"Seems to me you don't hardly need that bottle of whiskey, Daniel. You had enough before we left town t' start talkin' like a damn fool. We don't even know fer sure she's a whore. The fellah who claimed she was, admitted he hadn't never tried her himself. Could be we'll have t' force her."

"Only one way t' find out: ask her. . . . Hey, squaw-woman! You hidin' out there in the river? Don't be skeered. We're jus' two lonesome cowpokes who wanna little fun t'night. That's why we rode out from town t' see you, an' we ain't gonna leave 'til you talk t' us. You might as well show yourself, darlin'. If you're willin'—and pretty—we'll make it worth your while t' be friendly. *Real* friendly."

"You fool. She ain't gonna just walk outa the river, greet you with a big wet kiss, and fall down on the bank with you."

"Well, hell, why not? Like I said, I'll show her my money first. Wait a minute, an' I'll get it out."

"Maybe we should go on back t' that soddy house and wait for her. She's gotta come home sometime; when she does, we'll be waitin'. We can be comfortable there—an' if she never shows up, we'll just drink our whiskey, eat that nice stew she had asettin' on the stove, and get a good night's shut-eye."

"You know somethin,' Charlie? You got the imagination of a stump. But I 'spose you're right. It'd be a lot more comfortable back at her house than waitin' here on the river bank. B'sides, I'm hungry, an' that stew settin' on the stove sure smelled good."

"I knew I could count on one of your appetites t' cancel out the other."

"Don't mean I'm givin' up; I'm jus' postponin' my pleasure. . . . Hey, darlin'! We're goin' on back t' the house t' wait fer you, and we'll leave your clothes right here where we found 'em. But you needn't bother puttin' 'em on again, 'cause we'll jus' hafta take 'em off when you get there."

"Oh, that should reassure her jus' fine, Daniel. Now, she'll never come out of the damn river."

"Sure she will. Squaw women like it rough. The rougher, the better."

"How do you know? You ever had a squaw before?"

"Naw, but I heard stories. I'll tell ya all about 'em back at the house."

The men remounted their horses, and the black shapes retreated from the riverbank. Mary waited several moments to be sure they were gone, then hurried toward the riverbank and her clothes. She had to waylay Silver Hair and keep him from going to the house—assuming he hadn't already arrived there. She sent a silent plea to Tirawa to delay him somehow and prevent him from encountering these men. The men were surely armed, while Buck always arrived on foot, without rifle or pistol.

She suddenly realized how careless and complacent she and Silver Hair had become—believing they need have no fear in this isolated spot. Normally, she carried at least her skinning knife everywhere she went. But tonight, she hadn't been thinking of danger; she'd been thinking only of telling Silver Hair about her pregnancy. She'd used her skinning knife to cut up meat for the stew and left it lying on the table. And the axe was sticking out of a log in the wood pile. . . . Oh, how she wished she had one or the other now!

Tossing her wet hair over one shoulder, Mary shoved her feet into her moccasins. As she bent down to pick up her dress, a man's arms slid around her waist and lifted her off her feet.

"Charlie, come quick, I got her! I knew she'd come out of the water soon as she thought we'd gone. . . . Damn, she's a lively one!"

Kicking and squirming, Mary struggled to break free of her captor. Panic engulfed her, but she kept her wits about her and resisted the urge to scream. If she screamed and Silver Hair heard her, he'd come running to the rescue, and that was the last thing she wanted, for she had finally come to accept how much he feared discovery.

She managed to elbow her captor in the stomach, and he let

go of her, but before she could take advantage of his moment of weakness, the other man—the strong one—loomed in front of her. Grabbing her wrists, he held them so tightly she feared her bones would snap.

Recovering almost immediately, the first man—Daniel—again grabbed her around the waist. "Charlie! Did you get a look at—or a feel of *this?"*

His hard rough hands groped Mary's body, touching her intimately. Trembling, she had no choice but to endure it with gritted teeth. She refused to cry out and call Silver Hair to her aid. Somehow, some way, she must escape on her own.

"This Injun's pure female, Charlie. Let's get her back t' the house, where we can shut the door, and nobody'll hear her screams."

"Why ain't she screamin' now? Hell, she ain't said a word. If you ask me, that's a mite strange."

"She ain't screamin' 'cause she knows there's nobody out here to help her. . . . Ain't that right, darlin'?"

Daniel squeezed her left breast—hard. Ignoring the sudden, excruciating agony, Mary bit her lower lip. Oh, where was Silver Hair? She didn't want him to come. She dreaded exposing him to danger. At the same time, she longed for the comfort of his presence. She was no match for these men. They would shame her, hurt her—not just her body, but her soul. Already, she felt violated. Before they finished with her, she knew she would feel much worse.

A new terror rose to taunt her: Would they cause her to lose her child this night?

When Mary thought of losing the child, she couldn't subdue the sudden hysteria that gripped her. For the child's sake, she had to fight. It mattered not that fighting might harm them both; she couldn't remain still any longer.

Throwing back her head, she released a keening wail, the Pawnee war cry she herself had never heard—but only heard about. It erupted from the depths of her soul, along with the shadowy, ancient memory of battles fought and won, scalps taken, horses stolen, captives seized, and victory dances before leaping flames.

The time of her ancestors had come and gone, but this was *her* time. As her ancestors had fought to protect their families and children, she must fight to protect her unborn child.

A hand clapped over her mouth with enough force to split her upper lip.

"What in hell kind of scream is *that,* Charlie? Hold her! Hold onto her or she'll get away—or kill us if she can. Looks like she means to fight."

A fist drove into Mary's stomach, and she doubled over, gasping from the impact of the blow. Grabbing hold of her hands and feet, the men dragged her toward the cabin. Mary summoned all her strength and will power to fight them every step of the way. She fought like a wild animal, driven mad by the scent of her enemies. The men stank of sweat, whiskey, and rising lust. Their odor nauseated her—or perhaps the blow to her stomach caused her distress—and halfway to the cabin, she succumbed to a fit of vomiting.

The men laughed, seized her by the hair, and continued toward the shack. Mary managed to claw a forearm and earned a second punch in the stomach. This one sent waves of shock and pain throughout her entire body. She screamed, and the men laughed even harder.

They wrestled her into the house and threw her onto the raised pallet she had lined with animal furs to make a comfortable bed for herself and Silver Hair. One of them held her down while the other lit the lamp on the table.

"I wanna see the bitch," he said. "Hold her a minute, Charlie, so's I can see her."

"Hurry up, damn it!" Charlie cried and punched her again to keep her still. "Don't see why I hafta wait fer you."

He straddled Mary, so she lay between his knees, and he began to knead her breasts. Mary writhed in agony. A terrible pain racked her lower abdomen, causing her to arch her back and moan. Charlie laughed and fell upon her, then drew back a moment later to free himself from his trousers.

As Charlie raised himself above her, Daniel, already naked, joined them on the bed and held her hands to keep her in place. Disabled by pain and weak from struggling, Mary almost gave up. But then she gazed past her tormentors and saw Silver Hair standing in the doorway. His eyes blazed with a wild blue light, and a muscle twitched in his lower jaw. In his upraised hands, he held the axe from the woodpile.

Another pain sliced through her, and Mary cried out in anguish. Even as Silver Hair attacked, something hot and wet gushed from between her thighs.

Sixteen

Chase had never before had such a wonderful dream. Somewhere in the middle of it, just as he was reaching the best part, he realized it was only a fantasy. This couldn't be happening. Maddie wasn't snuggled up to him, holding him tightly, and begging him to never let her go.

Nor was she saying: "I want you so much, Chase. I need you. I'll go anywhere you want—do anything you ask. Only hold me. Love me. Make me yours, my darling."

It's a trick, Chase told his bemused self. *Someone's playing a trick on me.*

But as he took Maddie in his arms and smiled down into her shining blue eyes, he prayed he wasn't dreaming and no one was deliberately fooling him. He hoped Maddie was truly there in his bed, in his arms, and all he had to do to make love to her was lean over and start kissing her.

Just as their lips met, the sound of pounding intruded, destroying the blissful moment. Even in his dreams he couldn't escape her damn family! It was probably one of her sisters, or her brother, or her drunken father. Hell, even Gold Deck claimed more of Maddie's attention than he did, and she never lost her temper with the stallion as she did with him. . . . He decided to ignore the pounding in the hope it would go away.

It didn't. Grudgingly opening his eyes, Chase realized the pounding was real; he wasn't dreaming it. Someone was banging on his door, and from the sound of things, they didn't intend to go away.

Muttering to himself, he sat up, reached for the clothes he had dumped on the floor beside his bed, struggled into them in the dark, stubbed his toe, banged his elbow, and finally decided to light a lamp before he killed himself.

Blinking against the lamplight, he made his way to the front door, started to unlatch it, then thought better of the idea. "Who's out there? Identify yourself before I open this damn door."

"Open up. It's the sheriff, Cumberland. An' you better hurry or me an' the boys'll break the door down."

The man sounded serious. What was all this nonsense about "the boys?" People didn't break down doors in the middle of the night unless they had a good reason, but he couldn't imagine what that reason might be.

Opening the door, he stepped out onto the porch and held up the lamp so he could see his visitors. He need not have bothered with the lamp. Light flooded his front yard, for his visitors had brought torches. He peered at the half-dozen men on horseback, most of whom he knew from town. They all looked grim as death and as self-important as judges. Moses Smith was smirking at him as if he'd just found a cache of pure gold.

The sheriff held up a white handbill and pointed to it. At first, Chase thought it was one of the posters advertising the race. Then he saw it contained a drawing of a man's face; *Buck's* face, and over it, in bold black print were the words, WANTED: DEAD OR ALIVE.

"This you, Cumberland?" Moses demanded.

Chase squinted at the likeness of his brother. "Nope. Doesn't look like me. I've never seen this man before, Sheriff, and I look in a mirror every morning when I shave, so I imagine I'd know if it was me or not."

"Humph! To me, he looks a lot like you. And if you read the poster, he sure sounds like you."

"What does it say? I just woke up, and I'm not much in the mood for reading."

"It says you—or whoever this feller is—is wanted for murder down in Texas."

"Never been to Texas. I was born in Missouri."

"Then how's come you sound like a Texan?"

"Damned if I know. Coincidence? Where'd you get this thing anyway?"

"A couple of bounty hunters showed up in town t'day and brought a bunch of 'em. They been looking fer you—"

"Not me. Whoever's on this poster, you mean."

Jowls quivering, Moses glared at Chase. "All right, they been lookin' fer this feller for years. They been all over. And every town they go to, they ask if anybody's seen a white-haired feller name of Buck Courtland."

"Well, Sheriff, that should convince you it isn't me. I haven't got white hair, and my name's Chase Cumberland, not Buck Courtland."

"You coulda colored your hair. . . . Aw, forget the hair; there's a few other coincidences that make me awful suspicious."

"Such as?"

"Such as this Buck Courtland has a brother named Chase. And the brothers used to breed and race Quarter Running horses down in Texas. They was especially partial t' mares, and they had some good ones, includin' a few from the Bonnie Scotland line."

"Lots of men breed and race Quarter horses, and the Bonnie Scotland line is popular. My mare, Bonnie Lass, comes from that line, but that's not enough evidence to convict me of murder. . . . If you think my hair's really white, you're welcome to examine it closely. Better yet, why don't you come inside and see for yourself that no one's here except me?"

"I might just do that. On second thought, I'll let the boys check the house and the property while I keep my eye on you."

"Go to it, boys." Chase motioned to them with his free hand.

Three of the men dismounted, tied up their horses at the hitching rail, and spread out to investigate the farm. One of them bounded up the steps and handed his torch to Chase before entering the house. Chase had seen the man in town on the day of his race with Maddie, but he couldn't recall the fellow's name. Apparently, he'd been made a deputy, for a silver star—smaller than the one Moses wore—winked on his chest.

Near the doorway, the deputy paused and eyed Chase malevolently. "I lost two months' wages bettin' on the McCrory's stallion when you beat him, Cumberland," he growled. "Serve you right if we find enough evidence t' take you t' jail t'night. I wouldn't mind at all if you was t' stand trial for murder, be found guilty, and get sentenced t' have your neck stretched. Hell, I'd be willin' t' supply the rope."

The sheriff coughed and cleared his throat. "Get goin', Buford, an' check the house before somebody climbs out a back window. The rest of you fellers ride around t' the other side an' secure it, so nobody has a chance t' escape."

Chase almost sighed out loud in disgust. If Buck *had* been hiding in the house tonight, he'd have had plenty of time to escape by now; that's how inept the sheriff was at his business. Chase rejoiced in the man's ineptness—but he also felt contempt for him and worried about his laziness. If Moses did apprehend Buck, he wouldn't bother checking out the accusations against him. He'd simply assume Buck was guilty and hang him.

"Wipe your feet before you enter my house, Buford," Chase drawled in an insulting tone. "I don't like dirt on my floors."

His reward for venting his contempt was a muttered cuss word as Buford stomped past him. Chase knew he shouldn't go out of his way to make enemies, but he thoroughly resented having his house searched by a sore loser in a horse race. Now that he thought about it, every man there looked like he held a grudge; it was suddenly clear to Chase that these men regarded him as an outsider who had come to town, beaten one of their own, and taken their money—money that had helped buy this farm.

If the posters had been circulated this afternoon, it was a wonder the sheriff had waited until tonight to come get him.

Buford returned in a matter of moments, bristling with authority. "There's no one else here, Sheriff," he announced. "But he's got two rooms fer sleepin', an' he only needs one. Seems mighty strange t' me he was bedded down in the smaller room in the smaller bed. Why would a man who lives alone put hisself out like that?"

"I'll tell you why," Chase answered, thinking fast. "I've got the big room all fixed up for when I bring home a bride, and I don't want t' mess it up. I even have a nice quilt on the bed; didn't you notice the quilt, Buford? My clothes and my gear are spread out between both rooms, but I plan t' clean up everything nice and tidy before my new wife moves in."

The sheriff's upper lip lifted in a sneer. "I didn't hear nothin' in town about you gettin' married, Cumberland. Who's your bride? Is she from around here?"

Chase forced himself to concentrate and come up with something creative. He'd thought his explanation for the evidence of Buck's presence was downright inspired—but now he wasn't so certain. He had a feeling no matter what he said, it wouldn't be the right answer.

"Um . . . well, I haven't asked her yet, Sheriff, but I'm planning to do it soon, and I'm sure she'll say yes."

"So who is it?" Moses prodded Chase in the stomach with the barrel of his Colt pistol—which Chase had only just noticed he was carrying.

"Maddie McCrory," he burst out. "I'm planning on proposing to Miss Maddie McCrory."

"Hah! You don't stand a chance with her, Cumberland. She'll never say yes to you."

"Why not? I've got a nice little place here to offer her."

"Yeah, but she's already promised t' someone else. That's why. And he can offer her ten times what you can."

"Are you saying Maddie's engaged to Horace Brownley?"

Moses rocked back on his heels, his little eyes alight with triumph. "Horace tells me she is. All they gotta do is set the date fer the weddin' an' make up the invitations."

"I . . . didn't know that." Chase recalled his suspicions, but the truth still came as a painful blow, especially since Maddie hadn't had the decency to inform him of her intentions. The night he'd punched Horace, she'd denied anything more than friendship between herself and the fat banker.

"Miss McCrory may have defended you as a neighbor, but it's the mayor of our town she's chosen fer a husband," Moses gloated. "Horace is one of us. At least, he's lived in these parts a lot longer than you, and he ain't never taken our money in a horse race."

So it *was* his victory over Gold Deck that had set the sheriff and these men against him.

"Maybe Horace hasn't taken your money, but Maddie's pa sure as hell has—and so will Maddie herself if she possibly can. None of us who race Quarter horses go into it hoping to lose, Sheriff. We all want to win, and we'll collect whatever we can—as much as we can—from people foolish enough to bet against us."

"You think you're gonna beat her again in Abilene?" Moses laughed. "Could be you will, Cumberland—if you live that long. And could be that's why she won't ever say yes to a proposal comin' from you. She don't like the taste of defeat. Besides, a gal like Maddie's got too much pride t' marry a drifter from nowhere, even if he does have a fast horse."

"Looks like you might as well move into the biggest room and stow your boots under the biggest bed," Buford sneered. "No sense savin' it fer a gal who's already made her choice an' decided it ain't gonna be you."

Chase's patience ended abruptly. "Get off my land. And don't show your faces here and try to arrest me unless you've got a hell of a lot more evidence than a few nasty suspicions."

"Come on, boys—mount up," the sheriff called. "Y'all didn't find nothin' in the barn, did ya?"

"Not a thing, Moses," a man answered. "Maybe we oughta go back t' town, look up them bounty hunters, and see what else they kin tell us about this murderer, Buck Courtland."

"Maybe we oughta," Moses agreed. "Only problem is the last time I saw 'em, they was ridin' out of town—headed this direction, which was why I thought I might find 'em here. By the time I'd rounded up you boys t' help me, they was long gone. . . . You ain't seen 'em, have you, Cumberland?"

"No, but if I do, if they dare trespass on my property, I may have to shoot 'em. I consider bounty hunters as a species of life even lower than a snake. Or a banker. Or a politician. Or, for that matter, a sheriff."

By now, Chase no longer cared if he was insulting his enemies. His world had suddenly crumbled; everything he had tried to build here was fast slipping away. All he had dreamed of and hoped for had once again come to naught. Maddie was engaged to marry Horace Brownley, and bounty hunters were hot on Buck's trail. He and Buck had to pick up and leave; if they didn't, eventually the bounty hunters would find them . . . *Dear God, why now?* Just when Buck had finally found a little happiness, the whole nightmare was beginning anew.

"You do any shootin'—trespassers or not—an' we'll string you up fer sure, Cumberland. Don't know as we'll even hold a trial. The circuit judge don't come this way too often, which leaves all the responsibility for upholdin' the law t' me an' Horace. He's got authority t' act as magistrate when we need one, and we'd both rather hang a troublemaker and be done with it than have him takin' up space in our jail."

"Now, why doesn't that surprise me?" Chase drawled. "I know what you want, Moses—to build your reputation until you're as famous as Wild Bill Hickok or Wyatt Earp."

Moses Smith nodded. "Now you got it, Cumberland. And they ain't my only competition; there's also young Bat Masterson comin' along over in Dodge City. But even if I never do get t' be famous, I got this town's support. Ain't that right, boys?"

"You tell him, Moses," agreed a thin man with hard eyes and a handle bar mustache. "We're all standin' behind you t' make Hopewell the safest town in Kansas."

"I'll try and remember that." Chase bit down so hard his jaw ached.

The world held no place, it seemed, where he and Buck could be safe from petty, small-minded, ambitious men—and women—protecting their interests against feared and despised outsiders. Damn all of them! Including Maddie McCrory. *Especially* Maddie McCrory.

Chase stood on the porch and watched the men ride off. He waited until the house and yard were once more silent, save for the night creatures and the Kansas wind that never stopped blowing. Then he put the lamp back inside the house and began collecting items he thought he might need. Or more accurately, that Buck and Mary might need.

A new and daring idea had taken hold of him: Why not have Buck and Mary flee, while he stayed here in Kansas to confuse and mislead the bounty hunters? . . . Buck had to get the hell out of here, but he was sick of running. This time, he wanted to stand and fight. Staying here would also give him the opportunity to win the race now less than a week away.

He'd give his brother and Mary a couple of fast horses, as much food as they could carry with them, and every cent he had, and he'd urge them to go further west to Indian Territory and there try to make a new life for themselves. Wild, unsettled places still existed where Indians and what was left of the buffalo roamed. He and Buck hadn't had any luck trying to settle down together, so maybe Buck and Mary should just travel with the wind and go wherever fate took them.

As for himself, Chase wanted to stay in Kansas. He'd set down roots here, and he'd be damned if he'd let the bounty hunters or the greedy townspeople—or even Maddie McCrory—force him out. This time, he refused to abandon his land or be robbed of his future.

Buck had Mary now; he didn't need Chase anymore. And Mary had no reason to stay in a region where Indians were despised. It only made sense for the two of them to go away together and seek their destiny in the West—or even up north.

The more Chase thought about it, the more excited he became. Working quickly, he assembled supplies, bedrolls, a change of clothing for Buck, money, and a rifle. Then he saddled and loaded a couple of their best mares and set out for Mary's house.

By the time he arrived at the soddy house, it was practically dawn, but still too dark to see without a lantern. Chase had brought one, and he lit it then held it up high as he rapped on the closed door of the cabin. No one answered his summons, but he was reluctant to make any more noise. With bounty hunters lurking in the area, he didn't feel comfortable even holding a lantern.

Fortunately, he had met no one on his way over; if Buck and

Mary rode hard and fast, they could be gone from the area before the sun rose very high in the sky.

"Buck!" Chase rattled the door latch. To his surprise, the door swung open. Raising the lantern to light his way, he stepped inside.

A terrible sight greeted him. The bodies of two naked men—one on the earthen floor at his feet, one on the pallet in the corner—lay sprawled unmoving. Their eyes were wide open and their lips drawn back in the rictus of violent death. Blood was everywhere; Chase stood in a puddle of it. Gouts of deep crimson and splashes of bright red dotted the walls, furnishings, floor, table, dishes . . . everything inside the little shack.

Chase didn't have to ask himself how the men had been killed; an axe stuck straight out from the exposed belly of the biggest man.

He had to fight the impulse to run screaming and retching from the dwelling. He couldn't leave without searching for Buck and Mary. Drawing several deep gagging breaths, he quickly determined that the two dead men were the only occupants of the house. There was no sign of his brother or Pawnee Mary.

Heart thumping, stomach roiling, Chase set down the lantern on the blood-spattered table. He hated to do it, but he had to examine the bodies, or at least the clothing of the dead men. He didn't recognize them but assumed they must be the bounty hunters the sheriff had mentioned. Before he left here, he had to know for certain.

Trying not to look at the corpses, Chase rummaged through the pockets of the victims' discarded, blood-soaked trousers. His search yielded the proof he dreaded: wanted posters for Buck. The men's pockets were stuffed with them. Unfolding one, Chase gazed upon his brother's face and read the horrible message. WANTED: DEAD OR ALIVE.

The men had probably come from Texas. The most determined bounty hunters—the ones who had chased him and Buck back and forth across several states—always came from Texas, which meant Luke Madison hadn't given up yet. Reading further, Chase discovered that Luke had increased the amount of the reward money, and the price on Buck's head was now a whopping ten thousand dollars. That was more than enough incentive to entice violent, useless, lazy men—the dregs of the earth—to set off on a manhunt.

Chase crumpled the "wanted" poster in his hand. *Buck was no murderer,* he told himself. But if he wasn't, who had killed these men? Who had hacked them up, chopped them to pieces, and reduced them to bloody carnage? One man had even been . . . *gelded,* he noticed with a sick feeling.

Looking down at the fellow on the floor, Chase saw he was holding a Bowie knife in one hand and an ivory-handled pistol in the other. He had apparently fought back with everything he had. Blood smeared the long silver blade of the knife. Chase gingerly pried the weapon from the stiffly curled fingers and held the knife up to the light.

Buck owned a similar knife with a carved handle made of wood. The handle of this knife was either bone or horn, which proved it wasn't Buck's . . . but was it his brother's blood on the blade? Or was it Mary's?

Chase shuddered. Looking down, he saw that his hands, trousers—even his shirt and boots—were drenched with blood. Searching the dead men's clothing had been a messy business; a person could hardly move in the shack without becoming contaminated. Buck and Mary must have been here—or someone had been. A trail of red footprints led out of the house and across the front porch.

Studying the prints, Chase discerned the mark of a pair of boots and the unmistakable mark of bare feet. The prints made by the bare feet were smaller and daintier than those made by the boots

"When it gets light, I'll have to see where they go," he said aloud, startling himself with the sound of his own voice.

Just then he heard more voices. *Male* voices and the sound of horses. Dousing the lamp, he listened intently.

"Hey, Horace! Looks like we found our bounty hunters. See? Their horses are tied up right in front of Pawnee Mary's shack. Guess we know how they spent the night, huh?"

Laughter sounded. Chase identified the voice of the speaker as belonging to Buford, the new deputy. Chase wished he had closed the door to the soddy house when he had entered it. He wished he could remember if there was a window big enough for him to climb out of. He wished he hadn't left the horses in plain sight out front. He wished he hadn't come—or had left before the arrival of the sheriff and his men. He wished he were anywhere on earth but where he was.

In the darkness of the house, lit only by the eerie glare of the torches outside, Chase stumbled about, searching for a hiding place. He couldn't run out the front door; they'd see him in an instant. And the soddy house had no other exit. Bumping into things, slipping and sliding on the blood-slick floor, he found a tall wooden cupboard along one wall.

Frantically, he removed objects and clothing from it, tossed them on the floor, and stuffed himself inside. He had barely gotten the door closed and not tightly, when light flared, illuminating the shack.

"Holy hell! Moses, come look at this!" It was Buford again. The man was snoopy as a cat.

Ponderous footsteps creaked the wood on the porch step, and a moment later, the gruff tones of the sheriff raised the hairs on the back of Chase's neck.

"It's them bounty hunters—butchered worse'n hogs at harvest time. . . . But where's that Injun whore, Pawnee Mary? You think *she* coulda done all this? . . . Damn it, I knew I shoulda come out here, checked out the rumors, and run her out long ago."

"No female coulda done this, Moses," Buford argued. "Even an Injun. Hell, she about cut off this one feller's arm, and he's missin' his . . . uh . . . private parts."

He's right, Chase thought dismally. No female could have fought off two men and done all this by herself. What had happened was clear; Buck must have arrived at the shack, surprised the men in the act of raping or hurting Mary, and gone after them with the axe.

"What a mess," the sheriff grumbled. "Tell the others t' get in here. We'll have t' take the bodies back t' town and search this whole damn place, lookin' fer clues t' who done it."

Chase listened to the thud of Buford's boots going past the cupboard. "Damn! We shoulda worn our slickers for this job. I sure ain't lookin' forward to it."

Chase made a sudden decision. Now was the time. Before they found him cringing in the cupboard, he'd better make a run for it. He waited until he heard Buford outside, then exploded from the cupboard and dashed for the door while Moses was looking the other way. He got only as far as the front porch, where he slammed into Buford himself, returning to join the sheriff.

Thrown off balance, he lost his footing on the slippery surface and went down, striking his head against the doorpost as he fell. Buford promptly jumped on top of him, Moses stumbled from the house waving his six-shooter, and within moments, Chase was surrounded by men aiming their guns at him.

"Waal, now. Looks like we found our murderer, boys, tryin' t' escape the scene of the crime." Moses nudged Chase's leg with his boot. "Yer all covered with blood, Cumberland. What happened? Did ya' walk in on them bounty hunters havin' some fun with yer squaw woman?"

Chase said nothing. He couldn't. He sat up, and his head spun. Lights danced before his eyes, and he feared he might pass out. He couldn't think clearly, but he knew enough not to open his mouth and say anything to incriminate himself or his brother. Let the sheriff draw his own conclusions.

"I wouldn't think a squaw would be worth fightin' over, Cumberland. So maybe you jus' killed them bounty hunters t' get rid of 'em. Did ya' have t' make such a bloody mess of it? The wanted poster said you're a violent, dangerous man, but this goes t' the extreme. Choppin' up men with an axe and violatin' the one like you did is the work of a madman. Horace Brownley was right. You got a wild streak in you that makes you a menace to society, an' the sooner we hang you, the better fer all the good folks in Hopewell."

The men muttered agreement, but Chase maintained his silence. He refused to even look at them and instead stared out across the river, where dawn was now brightening the horizon. They dragged him to his feet, tied his hands behind his back, and all but threw him down the front porch steps.

Chase landed on his knees. He knelt there, disoriented, while one man tossed a rope tied with a slip knot over his head and drew it tight. For one startling moment of panic, Chase thought they meant to hang him then and there.

His thoughts flew to Maddie and Buck, the only two people for whom he truly cared in all the world. The sheriff assumed he was Buck, so if he died this morning, Buck would go free. The bounty hunters would stop looking for him. As for Maddie . . . she'd marry the damn banker and have all the money and power she could ever want or need.

But oh, he regretted never having told her he loved her! Never having held her and *made* love to her with all his body's passion and his heart's longing. He so regretted all the things he'd missed in life—things he'd never known he wanted until he met Maddie. A woman's love and loyalty. Her tenderness and laughter. The warmth of family and mutual commitment. Having children. Watching them grow and mature. Teaching them. Wondering what they would become. Growing old beside the woman he loved.

Closing his eyes, Chase set his jaw and waited for the end. Someone jerked on the rope.

"Get up, Cumberland," Moses growled. "It'll be slow goin,' but you can walk back t' town. Scum like you ain't fit t' ride. Hell, you ain't even fit t' hang. I wish we could jus' carve you up like you did them poor bastards in the shack. . . . But I guess we gotta do this proper—take you back t' town first, hold a trial, and then hang you from the big bur oak where everybody in the county can witness the price of wickedness."

"I'm all for hangin' him now," Buford said, and several of the men murmured their agreement.

"Waal, you ain't in charge here, an' I am," Moses snapped. "First, we try him, *then* we hang him, an' that's the way it's gonna be."

Seventeen

Everyone had eaten breakfast but Pa, and Maddie was clearing dishes and hoping Pawnee Mary would show up today to help with the preparations for their impending departure for Abilene. Suddenly, she heard voices on the front porch and glancing out the window, saw Nathan Wheeler, Zoe's beau, talking to Zoe and gesturing excitedly.

Smiling at the youth's enthusiasm, Maddie decided to leave the two young people alone for a few minutes to visit. Nathan had probably come to fetch his family's mare, who'd been bred to Gold Deck. With the mare's departure, the young man would no longer have an excuse to spend so much time at the McCrory farm. Opportunities to visit with Zoe would evaporate like mist on a sunny morning.

The Wheelers raised corn and kept cattle, pigs, and horses. If Zoe did marry Nathan one day, she'd lead a busy but comfortable life—and her children would probably be little brown-eyed towheads just like their father, and they'd use their hands to make a point when they spoke.

Turning her attention to the work awaiting her, Maddie hurried to finish her chores, so she could get out to the barn. She left covered dishes on the table for her father, peeked into his room to see if he was awake, and closed his door again when she saw he wasn't.

Yesterday, she'd caught him trying to sneak into town with a yearling filly—one of their best racing prospects. He denied it, but he'd obviously been intending to sell the filly to get money for whiskey. Other than that, he had behaved fairly well lately. He hadn't been drunk, which greatly pleased her, though she still worried about his general deterioration.

He spent hours sleeping during the day, went to bed early, rose late in the mornings—and still refused to participate in the family's daily activities. Mostly, he just sat, staring into space and sometimes talking nonsense. Often, he couldn't remember the simplest things, like where he'd left his hat or what he'd eaten at his most recent meal.

Maddie had taken to assigning one of the girls to keep him company whenever she had to leave the house. Zoe and Carrie chafed at this restriction, as it hampered their own activities, but Maddie didn't trust her father to be alone for long periods of time. His helplessness appeared to be worsening, and he reminded her more of a withdrawn cantankerous child than a grown man.

"Mary, Mary, what have you been up to lately? I really need you today if we're going to get out of here on time tomorrow," Maddie muttered, as she gathered soiled bed linen and wondered how she would get everything done.

Pawnee Mary had appeared only once in the last several weeks. Something had been different about her—so different that Maddie lacked the nerve to question her friend about the changes she sensed in her. Mary's step was much lighter—her face more radiant, but she spoke little and offered no explanations for her long absences.

Maddie didn't know what to make of her behavior; she hated to pry and simply hoped that Mary would see fit to enlighten her soon, for she was indeed curious. With her arms full of sheets, Maddie headed for the front door and the washtub she had already set outside in the yard.

Just as she got there, the door flew open, and Zoe rushed into the house. "Oh, Maddie! I have to tell you what Nathan just told me. You won't believe it; Chase—I mean Mr. Cumberland—was arrested this morning and locked up in jail for murdering two men. Maddie, the men were bounty hunters! Mr. Cumberland killed somebody in Texas, and the men came to get him, because he's wanted down there for murder. Now that he's murdered two men here in Kansas—hacked them to death with an axe—they're going to hang him here, instead of taking him back there!"

Maddie's armload of sheets slowly slid to the floor; for a moment, all she could do was gape at her sister. "Hang him? They're going to hang Chase Cumberland for murder?"

Nathan Wheeler appeared in the doorway behind Zoe. "It's true, Miss McCrory. Sheriff Smith came and got my pa to ride in his posse last night when he went out to question Mr. Cumberland. Seems the sheriff didn't want t' go all by himself—facin' a possible killer and all. Mr. Cumberland claimed he didn't kill the man down in Texas, and Sheriff Smith had to let him go for lack of evidence. All the sheriff had was this wanted poster the bounty hunters brought to town yesterday. So then he went lookin' for the bounty hunters t' ask for more proof. Why, the posse was ridin' around almost the whole night—but they finally found 'em."

"F-found who?" Maddie questioned. "The bounty hunters?"

Nathan nodded, and a lock of his light, flaxen hair fell across his eyes. "Yes, ma'am. They was chopped up something horrible. The whole house ran red with blood."

"What house?" Maddie gasped, fearing the worst.

"Pawnee Mary's." Nathan glanced at Zoe. "I always told Zoe it was a big mistake lettin' an Injun become your friend. Trouble seems t' follow 'em. Mary lives in a soddy house down by the river, an' . . ."

"I *know* the house, Nathan," Maddie interrupted, though she hadn't known that Mary was living there. "And Mary *is* my friend, so you had better not say bad things about her."

"But Miss McCrory, they say in town she's a . . . a . . ." Again, he glanced at Zoe and then whispered the word. ". . . a soiled dove, and she . . . entertains . . . men in her house, which was where they found the bodies."

"If they found the bodies in Mary's house, why are they accusing Mr. Cumberland of the murders?"

"Well, because . . . because . . ." Nathan seemed reluctant to say it, so Zoe said it for him.

"Maddie, he was all covered with blood and hiding in the cupboard!"

Maddie had never fainted in her life, but she feared doing so now. The whole room began to sway, and darkness hovered at the edges of her consciousness. She felt hot, then cold. Her heart slammed against the walls of her chest, and she could scarcely breathe.

Zoe grasped her arm. "Maddie, you don't look so good. Maybe you'd better sit down."

"Maybe I'd better." Maddie made her way to the rocking chair and sank into it. She leaned her head back against the headboard, closed her eyes, and tried to make some sense of all she had just heard.

Chase. A murderer.

It didn't seem possible. It *wasn't* possible. He would never do a thing like that. She was sure of it.

"They found him hiding in the cupboard?" Her voice came out hoarse and strained, as if she were about to cry, but tears were beyond her.

"And . . . and covered with blood," Zoe repeated. "Oh, Maddie, I'm so sorry."

The girl sank to her knees beside Maddie and took her hand. "I know you liked Mr. Cumberland. So did I. So did Carrie. I'm as upset as you are. I thought he was so handsome and nice—and here, he turned out to be a murderer! It's hard to believe, isn't it?"

Maddie shook her head. "I don't care what anyone says; I don't believe it."

"It can't have been anyone else, Miss McCrory," Nathan insisted. "He—Mr. Cumberland—didn't even deny it, and Pa said he looked guilty as hell. They almost strung him up on the spot. But the sheriff said he's gotta stand trial first. It wouldn't be right to string him up without a trial."

"When . . . when will the trial be held?"

"I don't know, but soon. Everybody's sayin' it should be before the big race this weekend in Abilene. You know, the one between your stallion and Mr. Cumberland's mare and that horse named One-Eyed Jack. Some folks have already made their bets, and some were planning to do it soon, but now, no one knows what's gonna happen. Doesn't look like Mr. Cumberland's gonna make it to the race."

"The hell with the race." Maddie rose in agitation. "Is that all people can think about—a horse race? A man's about to stand trial for his life, and all anyone cares about is whether or not he'll be able to race his horse this weekend."

"If he has to forfeit, he'll lose twenty-five hundred dollars," Zoe pointed out with blunt practicality. "Of course, if he's dead by then, it won't matter. Will they take the money from his farm, do you think? Or sell his horses to cover the debt?"

"Zoe, stop it!" Maddie rose and began pacing the floor. "The important thing to remember is that Chase didn't commit those murders—or the one down in Texas either."

"How do you know, Miss McCrory?" Nathan looked troubled. "Pa says he did it. Pa says there ain't any doubt."

"I just know it. That's all. He *couldn't.*" Maddie paused in her pacing. She recalled Chase carrying her drunken father into the house . . . and building the breeding chute . . . and laughing, talking, and teasing . . . and kissing her. Cold-blooded murderers didn't show such tenderness or concern for others.

She remembered the gentle look in Chase's eyes when he talked about his brother—*Buck!* Buck might have committed these murders, but not Chase. When she had discovered Buck in the barn that day, she'd been absolutely terrified. Buck exuded danger and violence, and even Chase admitted that his brother didn't get along with people.

She was suddenly sure Chase was protecting Buck, keeping even his existence a secret.

"Nathan, what exactly did that poster say happened in Texas—where Mr. Cumberland is supposedly wanted for murder?"

"Wait a minute." Nathan fumbled in his back pocket. "I got one right here. Pa brought a couple of 'em home yesterday afternoon from town t' show Ma. He don't—doesn't—like it when Ma goes to town by herself. Says it's too dangerous, and he brought the posters home to prove it to her."

Nathan produced a tattered, folded handbill similar to the ones Maddie used to advertise Gold Deck's availability to race, except this one was printed on sturdier paper. The soiled handbill was the common type of announcement tacked up on posts and buildings everywhere to let people know what was happening.

With shaking hands, Maddie took it, unfolded it, and quickly scanned its contents. She was right! The bounty hunters had come in search of Buck. The poster clearly stated the man had white hair, though it failed to mention his inability to speak. It also described Chase and gave the men's last names as Courtland, not Cumberland.

Several of the words were misspelled, Maddie noticed, as though whoever had printed the poster had been careless or uneducated. But then, many men didn't read or write well. Cowboys, especially, thought it a waste of time to learn reading and writing, as such pursuits didn't help a man ride a horse or punch cattle any better.

Studying the drawing, Maddie had to concede it resembled Chase. If she hadn't seen Buck for herself, she would assume it *was* Chase. She didn't blame Sheriff Smith or Nathan's father for jumping to conclusions; they didn't know about the real Buck, so naturally they concluded that Chase was the criminal.

"Zoe, I'm going to town. Take care of Pa until I get back. Little Mike's exercising Gold Deck, and I don't know where Carrie is, but explain the situation to both of them."

"What are you going to do, Maddie?"

"I'm going to see the sheriff and explain about Mr. Cumberland's brother. He's the one wanted down in Texas, not Chase. And I think he's the one who might have killed the bounty hunters."

"But what happened to Mary? Nathan's Pa said they never found her. She wasn't in the soddy house where the bodies were discovered."

"I have no idea, Zoe, and I'm afraid to hazard a guess. That's another thing I wish to discuss with the sheriff. A search must be mounted for Mary. She . . . she could be lying hurt or wounded somewhere. For that matter, so could Mr. Cumberland's brother. I don't imagine those bounty hunters surrendered their lives so easily. They must have fought back. Didn't the sheriff wonder why Mr. Cumberland wasn't wounded? . . . He wasn't, was he?"

Nathan flushed. "Not that I know of, Miss McCrory. All I know is what Pa told us: Mr. Cumberland surprised them bounty hunters while they was . . . was . . . doin' something bad to Pawnee Mary. Since she's only a Injun, he probably killed the men t' keep them from takin' him back to Texas to hang for murder. If Mr. Cumberland has a brother like you say, Pa don't know about him—and neither does the sheriff."

"Precisely. Furthermore, if you think about the situation, Nathan, you'll grant it's quite odd. How can a single man hack *two* men to death with an axe and survive the incident without a scratch?"

"But he was covered with blood, Miss McCrory! And hidin' in the cupboard. Sure makes him sound guilty of *this* crime, even if he ain't the one who killed the man down in Texas."

"Enough. I've got to go. . . . Oh, did your pa say when the circuit judge would be coming to town? Mr. Cumberland can't be tried until he appears."

"He didn't say, ma'am. Fact is, he never mentioned the circuit judge. But I heard him tell Ma that Mr. Brownley has authority to act as magistrate whenever the need arises. Him bein' mayor an' all, *he* can try Mr. Cumberland."

"Surely not in a murder case! Horace can handle smaller crimes, of course—when someone's drunk or disorderly or if they refuse to check their weapons at the jail while they're in town. But murder? I think not, Nathan. *Certainly* not when I can attest to the fact that Mr. Brownley already detests Mr. Cumberland and couldn't possibly judge him fairly."

"Oh, Maddie! It doesn't sound very good for Mr. Cumberland. By the time you get to town, they may already have hung him!"

"Calm down, Zoe. Nothing happens that fast in Hopewell. Fetch my blue bonnet, will you? This situation calls for whatever feminine influence I can muster."

Maddie wore her blue bonnet to town, but she also rode Gold Deck astride, because he was the fastest way of getting there. By the time she left the house, Little Mike had returned from exercising the stallion, but he was still saddled, and Maddie simply hiked up her skirts and climbed aboard over Little Mike's protest.

"Zoe will explain everything," she told her brother and galloped for town.

Upon her arrival, she headed for the county jail, which was located just around the corner from Main Street. A crowd of people stood out front, so Maddie dismounted further down the street, wrapped her reins once around the rail of the boardwalk, and started toward them. Halfway there, she encountered Horace Brownley.

He grabbed her arm and steered her to one side, out of earshot from the townsmen—and a handful of women—who were milling about and talking in angry voices in front of the small clapboard building.

"Where are you headed, Maddie? Have you heard the news? That madman you're always defending was caught red-handed last night—or I should say, this morning. Must say I'm not a bit surprised to learn he's a hardened killer. Killed one man in Texas and two right here in Kansas."

Maddie wished she'd brought along her parasol to give Horace another whack. Abruptly, she decided to confront the sheriff first and deal with Horace later. "Things are not always what they seem, Horace. Out of my way, please. I have important information for Moses."

"You might as well tell me why you're here, Maddie." Horace puffed up his chest and gave her a look meant to impress her with his importance. "I'll probably be conducting the trial—and soon. Possibly tomorrow or the next day. We'd like to hang Chase Cumberland before Saturday, so everyone can still go to the race in Abilene. . . . About that race, Maddie. When were you going to tell me the details? You said it was a small one, but I read on a handbill that you've agreed to put up five thousand dollars. . . . Maddie, that's a fortune! If you don't win, you'll lose everything. I can't cover a loss like that—well, perhaps, I can, but I won't. You have no right to expect that of me."

"Horace, right now, I don't give a damn about the race. I came here to save the life of an innocent man, and you are delaying me. You shouldn't even be conducting Chase's trial. You should disqualify yourself for already being prejudiced against him."

"Me—prejudiced? Maddie, the man is *mad.* He's a danger to society. Surely, even you can now see his true nature."

"Has Pawnee Mary been found? Has anyone gone out to look for her? Before a trial takes place and people talk of hanging, everyone involved should be heard. We need to hear Mary's side of the story. After all, the men died in her house."

"For God's sake, Maddie! The woman's only an Indian. Who cares what she has to say or what's happened to her? We don't need her testimony to convict Chase Cumberland of murder. The evidence is overwhelming. At this very moment, Elwood is preparing the opening arguments for the prosecution."

"Elwood, your clerk?"

"Have you forgotten? He's also the City Attorney. He will present the case against Mr. Cumberland."

"And what about an attorney to represent Mr. Cumberland? Is there another one in town?"

"Hopewell's too small to have more than one attorney, Maddie. We're fortunate to have a bank, a mayor, and a town council—as well as the office of the county sheriff and the jail located right here."

"You aren't going to provide an attorney for Mr. Cumberland?"

"Naturally, he can have one if he insists upon it. Though we'll probably have to send to Abilene to obtain one. Fellow may not be able to get here in time anyway."

"I don't believe this!" Maddie exploded. "In your haste to hang Chase, you're making a complete travesty of justice!"

Horace's fingers tightened around Maddie's arm. "Were I you, my dear, I wouldn't waste my time worrying about Chase Cumberland. The facts in this case are clear; he's a murderer. His fate is sealed, and I shall personally see to it that he hangs as soon as possible. I suggest you save your worrying for the race coming up in Abilene."

"If Chase's mare can't run in that race, I myself might decide to forfeit," Maddie declared, goaded past caution.

"That would be most unwise," Horace warned. "If you lose—or forfeit—that race, don't count on my continuing financial support. Considering how reckless you are with money, I'm not sure I'm still willing to marry you."

"Marriage is no longer even a distant possibility, Horace. Guilty of murder or not, the Madman of Hopewell holds far more appeal for me than you do. I'd rather give myself to him than to you any day of the week."

Horace's face seemed to swell like a toad's. He turned a dark red color and began to breathe heavily. "You will pay dearly for that insult, Maddie—you and your whole family. You'll rue the day you chose Chase Cumberland over me."

"The only thing I rue is that I didn't realize sooner what kind of man you are—and what kind of man he is. He didn't kill those bounty hunters, but I know why he's allowing everyone to think he did. And I am going to save him from the gallows tree."

"You can try, but you won't succeed. People in Hopewell listen to their banker and their mayor, Maddie, not to a headstrong spinster whose father is a drunkard and whose only claim to respectability is a horse she rides like a man. You need me; I don't need you. As I said, you'll live to regret this day."

"Do your worst, Horace. I don't care anymore." With a flounce of her skirts, Maddie turned away from the odious man.

Underneath, she *did* care. She cared very much. Despite her brave words, she dreaded what might happen to her family as a result of her rebellion. But she wouldn't let Horace Brownley see how much she feared him . . . and she wouldn't let an innocent man die, not even to save her father, sisters, brother, or herself.

Chase Cumberland had his faults, but he wasn't a murderer. If anything, he was the most loving, loyal, self-sacrificing man she had ever met. Apparently, he was willing to die to save his brother; only she wasn't willing to let him. If Buck had indeed committed those murders, *he* must be the one to pay for his sins, not Chase. However, before she allowed either man to hang, she intended to discover what had really happened in that soddy house last night.

Chase lay on the single solitary bunk in a darkened cell with one barred window which let in a small square of daylight. The cell was hardly bigger than the breeding chute he'd built for the McCrorys, and it lacked every amenity save the bunk and an empty pail, presumably so he could relieve himself if he felt the necessity.

He was thirsty, bored, dirty, and miserable. Blood had dried on his hands, boots, and clothing. He was sure he looked as bad as he felt, but Moses Smith had thus far refused to honor even his most simple requests—a glass of water to drink and a basin of water in which to wash himself. Other than that, he hadn't said much; he was waiting for the opportunity to fully state his case.

From time to time, Moses or other men came down the narrow hallway, at the end of which stood Chase's cell. They gave him sly, unsettling looks, shook their heads at his appearance, and without saying a word to him, retreated again. Occasionally, Chase could hear voices raised in anger and accusation; sometimes, they came from the sheriff's one-room office at the front of the jail, and sometimes, they came from outside.

Chase couldn't see out the window because it was too high off the floor, but there was frequent mention of "swift justice" and mere hanging being too good for a wretch like him. At least, he hadn't had to lie about his brother, because no one had asked for his version of what had occurred in the soddy house. They had just assumed he was guilty of murder.

He meant to make a case for himself citing self-defense as his reason for killing the bounty hunters. After all, one had been clutching both a knife and a pistol. But since he had no wounds on him, he might not be able to convince people that he had killed the men to save either Mary's life or his own. Folks would believe what they wanted to believe anyway; he knew this from years of running and hiding with Buck.

He just hoped Buck and Mary would stay hidden and/or keep running, if that's what they were doing. As long as neither of them showed up to dispute his story, he intended to refuse the services of any lawyers that were offered, and make his own arguments for self-defense. It was the best he could do. If he wound up hanging, so be it. He didn't want to die yet, but neither did he want to keep living as he had been doing. This was his chance to clear his name, once and for all, so he could finally lead a normal life—or it was the end of everything.

Assuming he was acquitted of murder in Kansas, he'd be sent back to Texas to stand trial for Clint's death, on the assumption that he was Buck. If that happened, he planned to tell Luke Madison and everybody else in Texas that Buck was dead. As soon as they saw he *wasn't* Buck, they'd have to let him go, he reasoned, in which case, he would try once more to start fresh somewhere else. If he did get another chance, he'd settle as far away from Kansas as he could get.

Once he left the state, he'd stay away for good; watching Maddie and Horace together didn't offer the prospect of much happiness or peace of mind.

Lying on the bunk and listening to the angry voices, Chase heard a woman's voice cut through the general babble coming from the inner office.

"I demand that you let Chase Cumberland go, Sheriff. Because he isn't the man you think he is—the man wanted for murder down in Texas."

No, not Maddie. What was she doing here? God, no. Please don't let her tell them about Buck.

Chase rolled off the bunk. Hoping to hear better, he went to the corner of the cell nearest the front room.

"Don't make no difference whether he is or not, Miss McCrory. He's guilty of murder here in Kansas, so here's where he'll swing."

"You don't understand, Sheriff. I believe Chase is trying to protect his brother, Buck Cumberland—Courtland, rather—the man who might actually have killed those two bounty hunters. When I tell you about Buck, you'll understand why I think as I do."

Chase slipped off one of his blood-encrusted boots and banged on the bars with it. "Sheriff! Don't listen to her. I accept full responsibility for the murder of those two men. Sheriff! Get in here, will you?"

But it was Buford who appeared. "Finally find your tongue, Cumberland? Up 'til now, you been mighty quiet."

"Get me the sheriff."

"Can't. Sheriff's busy."

"If he wants my confession, he'd better show his face. I'm willing to confess right now, but if he waits until later, I'm liable to change my mind."

"I'll tell him that. . . . Wait. Looks like he's comin' this very minute—an' he's got Miss McCrory with him."

"Maddie McCrory doesn't know what in hell she's talking about. Ignore her, and listen to me. I was there, so I know what happened."

"Right this way, Miss McCrory," Chase heard the sheriff grumble. "Seems to me you better repeat what you just said in front of the prisoner. I want t' see his reaction."

As Maddie and Sheriff Smith emerged from the gloom, Chase had eyes only for Maddie. He drank in the sight of her. She refreshed him like a drink from a clear, running brook in the high heat of summer. He'd never seen her eyes so blue, her mouth so vulnerable, or the slant of her chin so determined. Maddie had come to do battle on his behalf.

The thought that she cared enough to want to save him warmed Chase like a flood of sunlight into the dark and cold reaches of his heart. But all the while he was rejoicing at her appearance, he was busily planning his rebuttal of her claims and deciding how he might make her look foolish. For his sake, she meant to expose Buck, but for Buck's sake, he must convince Sheriff Smith that she was mistaken in what she thought she knew and had come here to say.

Eighteen

Maddie's first glimpse of Chase wrung her heart. He looked even worse than she expected. What Nathan had told her was true: Chase was covered with blood. He had dried blood on his hands, clothing, boots, even in his hair!

Her resolve momentarily faltered—until she looked into his eyes. They were the eyes of a cornered wolf: trapped but still proud and defiant. Ready to fight back if the opportunity presented itself. Chase would never cringe before his enemies. He'd go bravely to his death . . . unless, of course, she saved him by revealing the truth about his brother.

"Cumberland!" the sheriff bellowed as he stopped in front of Chase's cell. "Miss McCrory tells me you got a brother livin' out there on your farm. A fella with white hair and wild-lookin' eyes who got struck dumb when he was hit by lightnin' some years back. She says he's the feller on the wanted poster, not you, like I suspected. That true?"

Chase's eyes never left Maddie's face as he slowly, emphatically shook his head "No, Sheriff. It's not true. There's no such person as Buck. I invented him to keep the law in Texas from catching up with me. Buck is a story I made up to protect myself—and to discourage Miss McCrory from snooping around my place. It galls me to admit it, but your suspicions were right, after all."

"Nonsense. I *saw* your brother," Maddie insisted. "In your barn."

"What you saw was me." As usual, Chase looked convincing; he never so much as blinked at the falsehood. "It was dark in the barn, and you were scared anyway, so I let you think I had a half-crazy brother. It's a tale that's served me well in the last few years whenever people got a little too friendly or suspicious."

"Then how do you explain the silver-white hair? The man I saw in the barn had the hair of a much older man—and his eyes were different, too."

Chase's tone remained perfectly reasonable. "I had a mare with a silver-white tail once. When she died, I found a new use for her tail. As for the eyes, you must have been imagining things. I'd be hard put to change the color of my eyes."

"I know what I saw, Chase, and the man wasn't *you*. You're just trying to protect Buck. Sheriff, the 'wanted' posters mention *two* Courtland brothers, Chase and Buck. Surely, the authorities in Texas aren't mistaken about the existence of both of them."

"I been wonderin' about that," the sheriff said. "You got any explanations for that peculiarity, Cumberland?"

Chase glanced toward the ceiling; he seemed to be thinking. Releasing a long sigh, he said: "All right, I admit it. Buck *was* my brother. But he's dead now. Been dead for two years. I merely resurrected him to keep Maddie away."

Maddie could have screamed in frustration at his stubbornness. "Sheriff, Chase's wild-looking brother is still very much alive, and I saw him. Buck is strange—different from most folks—and possibly dangerous. He has silver-white hair, like the posters say, light-colored eyes, and he can't or won't speak. Chase told me that everywhere Buck goes, he causes comment and gets into trouble. When the Cumberland—Courtland—brothers moved here, they decided to keep his existence a secret, and now Chase is trying to protect him. He'll do anything for his brother, even accept responsibility for crimes he didn't commit."

"Oh, he committed this one, all right," the sheriff retorted. "Look at him. He's got the blood of his victims all over him."

"If the men were hacked up as bad as everyone's saying, no one could walk through that house without getting blood on them," Maddie argued. "Maybe Chase just went there looking for his brother at the same time you happened to show up. Maybe he hid in the cupboard, hoping you'd never find him. Sheriff, if you hang Chase Cumberland for killing the bounty hunters, his brother will go free, and who knows? Buck may kill again, but you won't realize you hung the wrong man until it's too late."

Chase gripped the bars of the cell, his lips drawn back in a savage snarl. "Sheriff, don't listen to her! She doesn't know what she's talking about. Buck's dead, I tell you. When you brought that wanted poster out to show me, thinking the man was me, I denied knowing him and claimed I'd never seen him before. *That's* when I lied. The man on the poster *was* my brother, but I couldn't see any advantage to admitting it. He's gone now anyway. Died of a fever. I had to bury him in an unmarked grave somewhere out on the prairie."

"Sheriff, he's lying *now.*" Maddie crossed her arms over her bosom and glared at Chase. "You can see by his eyes that he's spinning a tall tale for us."

Moses Smith looked from Maddie to Chase and back to Maddie again. His brow furrowed in apparent indecision. "Could be you're right, Miss McCrory. Could be he didn't kill them two bounty hunters, and his brother did. Or could be he killed 'em to *protect* his brother and keep the bounty hunters from takin' Buck Courtland back t' Texas t' hang for murder. This may be a case of us havin' *two* murderers in our midst."

"One. You've only got one, and I'm it!" Chase shouted.

Moses Smith stepped closer to the bars of the cell. "You got any proof your brother is dead?"

"I told you. I had to bury him out on the prairie somewhere west of here. You know how big the prairie is; I could search for his grave for years and never find it again."

"So we only got your word to go by. Is that what you're sayin', Cumberland?"

"That's what I'm saying, Sheriff. I killed the two bounty hunters, and I confess to it. However, I did it to keep them from killing me and Pawnee Mary. If I hadn't killed them first, you'd have found Mary's body and mine, instead of theirs."

"So that's your story—self-defense." Moses sneered. "I might've guessed it."

"That's another thing, Sheriff," Maddie burst out. "Has anyone gone looking for Mary? She can probably shed light on this tragedy, since it happened in her house."

"I ain't about t' accept the testimony of no Injun whore as to what happened t' two white men," the sheriff said. "And I don't think anybody else around here will accept it either."

"Pawnee Mary is not a whore. I know her well, Sheriff. She works for my family, and I can vouch for her character."

"Beggin' your pardon for bein' blunt, Miss McCrory, but them two bounty hunters was gettin' ready t' have sex with someone. . . . Hell, they was buck naked. If it wasn't Mary they was after, who was it?"

"They were getting ready to rape her, Sheriff," Chase cut in. "I heard her screams and ran to the rescue. I was unarmed, so I grabbed the axe from the woodpile. I didn't intend to kill the men, but when I burst into the shack, one of them drew a knife and a six-shooter. I had to fight for my life—and Mary's."

"Humph! A likely story, Cumberland. Them two men wound up dead, while you ain't got a scratch on you. I bet you planted them weapons, just so you could claim self-defense. The trick might fool some men, but not me. You made your biggest mistake when you hid in that cupboard. Only a guilty man would hide from the law."

"I hid because I didn't know who was coming. It could have been friend or foe. It might have been two more men bent on raping a defenseless woman."

"Not a defenseless woman—a whore. Your slick arguments don't convince me none, and they won't convince a judge or jury neither. We caught you red-handed, Cumberland, and I'm bound and determined to see you pay the full price."

"Sheriff," Maddie interrupted. "We must stop this senseless arguing; it's helping no one. Could I possibly have a few moments alone with Mr. Cumberland? And could you fetch some water and clean clothing? It's barbaric to leave a prisoner covered with blood like this."

"It's barbaric what he done to them men, Miss McCrory. Why would you want to be alone with such a violent feller? You bein' a lady and all, it ain't proper."

"I wish to discuss his defense with him. He *is* entitled to a defense, isn't he?"

"I'll act as my own defense," Chase said. "I'll present my own case."

"Chase, you can't! You won't stand a chance. . . . Really, I insist, Sheriff Smith. Someone must talk some sense into this man, and since you've already made up your mind about his guilt, I don't think it should be you. Give me a few moments alone with him. It will be perfectly safe, I assure you."

"I don't like leavin' you alone with him," the sheriff stubbornly insisted.

"Sheriff, you're right down the hallway, and he's behind bars, so what can be the harm in it? Besides, you must have a great deal to do to prepare for this trial. Shouldn't you be contacting the circuit judge? A case this important should be heard by an impartial observer, not by anyone local—and especially not by Horace Brownley."

"Brownley?" Something flickered in Chase's eyes. "Brownley's going to conduct this trial?"

For the first time since Maddie had arrived at the jail, he looked concerned. His brows lifted in disbelief, and she glimpsed a hint of fear in his expression.

Moses nodded with satisfaction. "We ain't fixin' t' wait a whole 'nother month—maybe even two—for the circuit judge t' show up. He was just here last week, but I didn't have no cases for him. Since he's so busy in other towns, he said he might skip next month. . . . Hell, I ain't even gonna try t' contact him. That in itself would take too much time, 'cause I ain't sure where he is right now. No way are you gonna take up space in my jail and hafta t' be waited on hand and foot 'til I can locate him or he passes through town again."

"Sheriff, if Mr. Cumberland is to have a fair trial, you *must* contact the circuit judge or wait for his arrival."

"Can't do it. Won't do it." The sheriff's jowls set determinedly.

"Folks won't stand for it. Already, there's talk of stringin' up Cumberland without a trial. The longer he sits in this jail, the worse the talk'll get. If we don't have this thing settled and done with by Saturday, at the latest, folks far and wide will hear of it, and things could get downright nasty and dangerous."

"You mean because of the race," Maddie clarified.

Moses again nodded. "We don't need all of Abilene as well as Hopewell gettin' riled up because of it."

"Why would folks in Abilene be riled up?" Maddie asked. "Because you hung one of the participants before he could ride in the race?

"No, because of the violent nature of the crime. I ain't gonna risk havin' a mob lynchin' on my hands. If it's gonna be done, it's gonna be done proper. All nice and legal. When I conduct a hangin', folks can be sure it'll be done right."

"They just can't be sure you're hanging the guilty party," Maddie scoffed. "What a brave man you are, Sheriff Smith. You don't care at all about getting to the truth of the matter; your main concern is looking after your own best interests."

"The best interests of the town, ma'am; that's all I'm worried about."

"Let it go, Maddie." Chase's eyes burned in his sweat-streaked, beard-stubbled face.

"I will *not* let it go. Sheriff Smith, if you don't give me your cooperation in assuring a fair trial for Chase, I will personally post handbills all over Hopewell, Salina, and Abilene telling everyone about this miscarriage of justice. When people gather for the race on Saturday, expecting to see a contest between three contestants and discovering that one has been hanged, I'll blister their ears with my opinion of your ineptness in handling this case. I'll accuse you of malfeasance. I'll . . ."

"Hell, Miss McCrory, I don't even know what mal-feasance means! I'm just tryin' t' do my duty. I found this man hidin' in a cupboard in a shack full of blood and dead bodies; he can argue self-defense until it hails in July, but the truth is he's still alive, and they're dead, and nobody else coulda done it. Nobody else had reason t' do it. In my book, that makes Cumberland guilty, unless of course, you can produce this mysterious brother and *he* admits t' the crime."

"Sheriff, in Kansas, sometimes it *does* hail in July," Maddie tartly reminded him. "At least, let me talk to Chase alone. Fetch him some water and clean clothes. And a hot meal. Has anyone brought him food or drink while he's been here?'

Chase refused to answer; he only glared at Maddie as if he wished she would go away and stop bothering him. But the sheriff—grudgingly—shook his head.

"Who usually provides these basic necessities for your prisoners?" Maddie persisted.

"Alice Neff," the sheriff answered.

When Maddie arched her brows in surprise, Moses hastened to explain. "Since her husband died, she ain't had no way of makin' a livin'. Lookin' after the prisoners don't bring in much, since I don't usually *have* prisoners. But it's better'n nothing."

"I imagine it is." Maddie had thought Alice Neff survived by letting out a spare room in her tiny house in town—the one she had moved into after she lost her husband's farm. The poor woman was probably lucky she had someone to look out for her, even if it was only Moses. "Will you go and ask her to prepare a meal for Mr. Cumberland and to provide for his other needs, as well?"

Sheriff Smith's jowls worked furiously. At first, Maddie thought he was going to refuse, but then, quite abruptly, he relented. "All right, Miss McCrory. You win—but only on issues pertainin' to the prisoner's comfort. Don't think I'm gonna delay the trial 'cause you say so, 'cause I ain't."

"Thank you, Sheriff. Knowing Alice, I'm sure she will agree that *all* prisoners, regardless of their alleged crimes, deserve fair and humane treatment."

"Humph! She won't think we oughta wait for the circuit judge t' try a man we already know is guilty of murder."

"Excuse me, Sheriff, but we *don't* already know he's guilty of murder. That still remains to be proved."

"Self-defense," Chase muttered. "It was self-defense, not cold-blooded murder."

"So you say, Cumberland, but I got my doubts. . . . I'll be back shortly." Moses pointed a pudgy finger at Maddie. "If the prisoner gives you any trouble, you just holler for Buford. I made him my deputy 'til this is over, and he's right in the front room."

Maddie longed to ask him what trouble a man behind bars could possibly be, but having gained this much, she decided not to goad him further. As the sheriff retreated down the hallway, Maddie mentally prepared herself to do battle with Chase. He would not be as easy to manipulate as the sheriff, but she didn't intend to leave the jail without persuading him to admit to his brother's existence and possible involvement in the murders of the two bounty hunters.

Turning to him, she was disheartened by his chilling expression and the mask of indifference he now wore.

"You shouldn't have come, Maddie," were the first words out of his mouth. "I don't need you to fight my battles for me."

"If you aren't willing to fight them yourself, you certainly do need me—or someone."

"I killed those men in self-defense," he repeated, as if he could make the words true simply by saying them over and over.

"I don't believe it, Chase. I'll never believe it." Maddie pressed closer to the bars and gripped them the way Chase had been doing. "I won't allow you to take the blame for what your brother might have done."

Chase quickly stepped back, as if he didn't trust himself to get that close to her. "My brother's dead."

"Don't lie to me, Chase. You can lie to the sheriff; you can lie to the town; you can lie to the judge—whoever he turns out to be. But don't lie to me."

"Why not?" he hurled at her. "You chose Horace over me. I don't owe you anything. I don't want or need your help, and I wish you'd back off and leave me to my fate, whatever it is."

His words stung like barbs, but Maddie refused to let them wound her. "Chase, you once said that 'next time,' I'd have to come to you, and I shouldn't come until I was ready to admit that what's between us is more important than a horse race—and more important than what's between me and Horace. . . . Well, here I am. A little late, perhaps, but then it took me awhile to figure out exactly what *is* between us."

"Nothing," Chase ground out. "Nothing at all. We shared a few kisses. We laughed together a couple of times. We competed against each other. We argued. We parted. That's it."

Maddie clung to the bars, willing herself to find the right words. Revealing herself to Chase—apologizing—trying to reach him—was the hardest thing she had ever done.

"That isn't *it,* and you know it," she whispered. "There's far, far more. When I'm with you, I . . . I feel things I've never felt before. I dream dreams I never dared to dream. I . . . I want to touch you, kiss you, and be touched and kissed by you."

"Well, when I'm with you, I want to let down your hair and rip off your clothes," Chase said harshly. "What does that prove? Only that we're male and female, and we desire each other."

Maddie's cheeks burned at his crude way of describing the wondrous feelings he engendered in her. Yet she sensed that he was only trying to deflect her from her goal—and she wouldn't turn tail and run so easily.

"It isn't only desire between us," she gently disputed. "I . . . I admire you. You can be gentle, as well as strong. Your loyalty to your brother is . . . is touching and praiseworthy. I've come to see we share much in common: love of family. Love of horses. Love of the land. You pretend to be so independent, even cruel, but your actions speak differently, Chase. You're not the wolf you appear to be."

"I'm not some puppy dog either. Don't make me more than I am." Raising his arm against the bars, Chase leaned his head against it, hiding his face from her. "Don't say these things to me now, Maddie," he groaned. "Don't make the sacrifice harder than it already is."

"Chase, I *have* to say them. I understand now what I've been feeling, why I'm so happy when I'm with you and so miserable when we're apart. You mean more to me than any horse race ever could. This thing that's been growing between us—it's called *love,* Chase. I love you. And I think—I hope—you love me."

"Maddie . . ." He lifted his face to her, and she was amazed—and deeply moved—to see tears sparkling in his eyes. "It's the wrong time for us now. We had our chance, and somehow we lost it."

He slipped a hand though the bars to caress her cheek. "I wish it weren't so . . . but don't you see? Nothing's changed for us. In fact, everything's gotten worse. You still have your responsibilities; I still have mine. There's no hope for us—no future. Life is one big card game, and we have no choice but to play the hand we've been dealt."

"Chase, I told Horace I'd never marry him, and I won't. No matter what happens. I've done the best I can to take care of my family and to hold onto the farm—but I won't marry a man I can't love, not after I've discovered what love really is . . . Oh, Chase! For you, I'll do anything—*anything*. I'll give it all up—the race, the horses, the farm, my family, whatever you want. Whatever you need. I'll be here for you, Chase . . ."

Tears streamed down Maddie's cheeks. She wept now, too, engulfed by emotions she could no longer resist. She had always thought of herself as a strong person, committed to her own ideals. Suddenly, she realized just how weak and needy she really was. She craved love as a parched cornfield craved rain after an endless drought. She craved *Chase's* love and felt she would die without it. What did anything else matter?

"Maddie, I couldn't—wouldn't—ask you to abandon your family." Chase's thumb stroked her tears away. "Part of why I love you so much is because you're so fiercely protective of the people you care for—including me, apparently."

"So are you!" she said fervently. "Chase, do you mean it? You actually love me?"

Again, he bowed his head against the bars. "God help me, I do."

The admission seemed wrung from the depths of his soul, as if he never intended to make it.

"Then for my sake, tell the truth, Chase! I'm not asking you to accuse your brother; I'm only begging you to tell the truth!"

He raised his head to gaze into her eyes. "Maddie, you just

said you love me. If you do, don't beg me to betray my brother. Don't try and find a way around me. If I can, I'll try to save myself. I'm not all that anxious to hang, you know."

"They'll never believe it was self-defense!"

"Then I'll have to hang. But I won't let them hang Buck."

"Chase, please . . ."

"No! He's suffered enough because of me, Maddie. I won't let him suffer any more. What happened down in Texas was an accident; Buck never meant to kill anybody. But because the family of the man who died was rich, they've been hiring bounty hunters and pursuing Buck relentlessly for years. We thought we had finally found a safe place here in Kansas. Turns out we were wrong. I can only hope Buck and Mary are long gone from here."

"Buck and Mary?"

"You don't know about them yet, do you? Buck intended to wed Mary. Somehow they met and fell in love. In each other, they found the perfect match, and last night, he was going to her house to plan a small, private ceremony where they would pledge their lives to one another's keeping. I think Buck must have surprised the bounty hunters in the act of raping Mary. That would be enough to . . . to enable him to do what I'm afraid he did. But if you repeat any of this to the sheriff, I'll deny every word."

"Oh, Chase, I'm so sorry for both of them! Yet I still can't allow you to sacrifice yourself to protect Buck."

"Maddie, you can't stop me."

Maddie banged on the bars in her frustration. "But you can't let them hang you, Chase! I won't *let* you."

Chase reached through the bars and grabbed her wrists. "I can, and I will, Maddie. Buck can't speak to defend himself and tell a jury what happened. They'll take one look at him and get out the rope. He's the kind of man people love to hate. Trust me. I've lived with this for years. I myself stand a better chance than he does of convincing a jury of my innocence."

"Not with Horace Brownley as your judge. Not with these townspeople as your jury. Some might be willing to listen, but most will refuse. They don't trust outsiders, and quite a few lost money betting on Gold Deck to beat Bonnie Lass in our first match race. They hold that against you, too."

"I'm aware of how they feel about the race," Chase grimly informed her. "And I'm afraid the whole town's in a hanging mood. I can't help it. It's out of my hands. Out of your hands, too, Maddie."

"But . . ."

"Let go of her, Cumberland! Damn, I knew I shouldn't have left you alone with him, Miss McCrory." Sheriff Smith lumbered down the hallway toward them. "Let go, I say."

As he fumbled to draw his six-shooter from its holster, Chase released Maddie, and she turned to face the sheriff.

"He wasn't hurting me, Sheriff. We were just talking."

"The hell you say; I know what I saw. I shoulda followed my first instincts about you, Cumberland, and run you outa town after Horace warned me about you. You're sly and dangerous. You can't be trusted. Don't try and protect him, Miss McCrory; he grabbed you when you wasn't lookin', didn't he? And he was holdin' you against your will."

"Sheriff, that's ridiculous. Nothing of the sort happened."

"Buford! Get them leg irons in here. We're gonna have t' restrain the prisoner so's he can't reach through the bars no more. Keep Alice out there in the front room until we do it."

"Sheriff Smith, you aren't listening. . . . Once again, you're making foolish assumptions."

"Sorry, Miss McCrory, you gotta leave now. That's all the time with him I can give you."

"I'm not finished yet. I . . ."

"Come along now, ma'am." Moses grabbed her by the elbow and all but dragged her down the long corridor.

Maddie didn't even have time to say good-bye to Chase. She hung back, but Moses kept a firm grip on her. Short of making a silly scene, she couldn't resist. She caught a last glimpse of Chase, who looked like he wanted to kill Sheriff Smith for touching her. Knowing she had only a moment, she used it to mouth the words: *I love you.*

Then she was whisked out into the front room where she nearly tripped over little Alice Neff, standing there with a basin of steaming water in her hands and some towels over one arm. While Buford rushed past them holding the leg irons and a heavy chain, Alice Neff pursed her lips and shook her head.

"Maddie, honey, are you all right? That killer didn't hurt you, did he?"

A tiny woman in a blue-checked calico gown, Alice wore a straw bonnet over her wispy, grayish-blond hair and had a direct, lively manner that normally charmed and delighted Maddie. But today, Maddie could barely be civil to her. Moses had apparently already turned Alice against Chase, or perhaps Horace had done it—spreading his lies and innuendoes.

"Chase Cumberland is no killer, nor is he a madman, Alice. You shouldn't believe everything Moses tells you."

"Oh, I don't, dear . . . Moses has a good heart, but he's a bit of a blusterer, so I usually only believe about half of what he tells me."

Lowering her voice, Alice leaned forward, reminding Maddie of an inquisitive little sparrow. "Is Mr. Cumberland as ferocious as they say? If he is, why did Moses leave you alone with him? Mercy me, I shudder to think of having an actual murderer here in Hopewell. If this keeps up, before long we'll be as bad off as Dodge City."

"Weren't you listening, Alice? I said, Mr. Cumberland is no madman or murderer."

"Oh, it's not me you have to convince, dear. I heard you perfectly well, though in light of the evidence, I do wonder how you can be so certain. I myself believe every man has a right to be considered innocent until he's proven guilty. Unfortunately, there's a whole crowd of people outside all claiming he's a bloodthirsty villain."

"How dare they judge him before the trial? They haven't heard his side of the story yet—or Pawnee Mary's."

"But Pawnee Mary's a soiled dove, dear. Or so I've heard. If that's true, those men were just buying what she sells all the time. They didn't deserve to be killed because of it."

"They were bounty hunters, Alice. Hardly innocent men themselves."

"Perhaps not, but I still don't think they should have been hacked to death with an axe. Why, they're sayin' the killer mangled 'em something horrible. Anybody who'd do such a thing must certainly be punished."

"Alice, I can't explain the whole story right now, but I assure you: Chase Cumberland is innocent. Right now, to prove it, I have to see if I can find a witness to the murders."

"Dear me! A witness, you say?"

"Yes. Don't let them hang him before I get back, Alice. Stand up to Moses and insist that Chase Cumberland receive a fair trial."

"Oh, I will, dear. I was hoping they might try him this afternoon yet, but Moses said it will probably be tomorrow afternoon or even the following morning, with the sentence to be carried out immediately after. The longer they wait, the more upset folks'll become. You should hear the crowd out there; it's getting bigger and louder by the moment. They didn't want to let me pass with this basin of water so he could wash his face and hands. They think the blood should stay on him as proof of what he's done."

Maddie thought of the damning stains on Chase's clothing and boots. Anything said at his trial would have far less impact than that gory evidence.

"He needs clean clothes if he's to have a fair hearing, Alice. But I don't have time to find some for him. Do you think you could undertake that chore?"

"Why, I expect I could. I still have a trunk full of my husband's garments—things I couldn't bear to part with. I can't guarantee the fit, of course . . ."

"The fit doesn't matter. If you would just make certain Mr. Cumberland presents a decent appearance, I think it would help immensely."

"I'm always glad to be of use, Maddie, but I'm afraid Moses won't be pleased by my interference."

"Surely, it's more important to protect an innocent man than to please Moses."

"Why, yes, dear, you're right. Besides, I'm still making up my mind about Moses. Not many men would be inclined to propose to an old widow woman like me, so I'm somewhat disposed to . . . to overlook his shortcomings, so long as he doesn't get too bossy or uppity, of course."

"I wish you every happiness in the future, Alice—with or without Moses. Only please help me now. There's no one else I can ask."

"Then you run along, dear. Do whatever you must. I'll take care of things here. Guess I better hurry and get this water into the prisoner—your Mr. Cumberland—before it gets cold again."

"Thank you Alice. Thank you so much." Maddie hurried out the front door of the jail, her spirits soaring at the mention of *her* Mr. Cumberland. He was indeed hers, and she would do everything in her power to save him.

At sight of the angry faces outside, Maddie abruptly lost any sense of optimism she might have had. These were her friends and neighbors, but they looked anything but friendly.

"What were you doin' in there, Maddie?" Mrs. Grover waspishly demanded.

"Didja see how Cumberland was drenched in blood?" Jake Bussel growled. "Proof he killed 'em, if you ask me. Too bad, I say, 'cause I liked the feller."

Amos Pardy, Silas Grover, and Jefferson Potts formed a wall in front of her, and Mr. Potts puffed out his chest and hooked his thumbs in his suspenders as if he had important news to impart. "That rascal won't be beatin' you in any more races when we get done with him, Miss McCrory. Fact is, he won't be racin' you come Saturday. Me an' the boys'll see to that."

"Please don't do anything rash and foolish, Mr. Potts," Maddie pleaded. "I'm asking all of you: Go home now, and leave the prisoner—Mr. Cumberland—alone. The whole story about these gruesome murders hasn't been told. Don't assume the man is guilty until you've heard it all."

"What're you talkin' about, Miss McCrory?" Hiram Garret

stuck his face close to hers, his breath almost knocking her over. "What more do we need t' know? The man was found at the scene, his hands red with blood. Why, Horace Brownley says he's guilty. Why, Horace knew what he was long b'fore the rest of us caught on to him."

"Let me pass, please." Maddie pushed her way through the onlookers.

"Ain't you gonna stay for the trial and the hangin'?" It was Mrs. Grover again, but Maddie didn't stop.

"There isn't going to be a hanging," she shouted and continued briskly on her way.

Nineteen

On the way home, Maddie made her plans. She had to find Mary and Buck. Without one or both of them to tell her exactly what had happened in the soddy house, she could never prove Chase's innocence. She desperately needed a witness to testify at the trial itself, and despite her reputation, Mary was the logical choice. Because of Buck's inability to speak—as well as the fact that he was wanted for murder in Texas, Buck must stay well hidden. He might even have to flee the area.

If neither one could be found, Chase stood little chance of remaining alive. Maddie didn't doubt for a minute that the townspeople would prefer to believe he was guilty than to accept her story about his brother—and as long as Chase himself kept insisting he had done it, the only decision to be made was whether or not he had acted in self-defense. Maddie feared that the sheriff's skepticism on that issue would be shared by her neighbors. The local people *wanted* to believe the worst of this stranger in their midst—this so-called madman.

A lynch mob might break down the jail and hang Chase before Maddie could even help him. Plucky little Alice Neff was her only hope to prevent that from happening. Because Moses was courting Alice, he might listen to what she had to say—if indeed, she stood up to him as Maddie prayed she would, and if Horace Brownley didn't persuade Moses to allow the hotheads in town to have their way.

By the time Maddie arrived home, her head was spinning with frightening possibilities. The sun had sunk low on the horizon; in an hour, it would be dark, making it difficult, if not impossible, to start searching for Buck and Mary. Maddie hated to delay, but she realized she'd *have* to wait until morning.

The first person she saw as she dismounted by the barn was Little Mike. One glance at his face told Maddie her brother was furious. "Where've you been, Maddie? Gold Deck looks wore out. How's he supposed to travel all the way to Abilene tomorrow and still be rested up for the race on Saturday? After I rode him hard this morning, he shoulda been allowed t' take it easy the rest of the day."

"Mike, stop complaining. Didn't Zoe tell you the news?" Maddie led the stallion into the barn, and Little Mike stamped after her.

"What news? I was so mad at you for takin' Gold Deck and gallopin' off like you did, I lit out of here and went huntin' for the rest of the day. I just got back and haven't seen hide nor hair of anybody yet—Zoe, Carrie, or Pa."

As Maddie untacked and rubbed down the tired horse, she told Mike about the murders. His reaction—thank God—echoed hers. "Chase couldn't have done it, Maddie. I can't imagine him doing something like that—especially the worst stuff, like cuttin' off a man's . . . you know."

"I know," Maddie sighed, giving the stallion his dinner. "I agree with you. But unless I can find Mary to go back to town with me for the trial, I'm afraid they may hang him, Mike."

"Hell, Maddie, you can't let that happen."

"I don't intend to let it happen, not if I can stop it. I'm leaving first thing in the morning to search for Mary and Buck. You'll have to take care of everything here."

They finished in the barn and started walking back to the house. Darkness had fallen, but Maddie could still see Little Mike's face, now creased with worry. "But . . . but what about the race? It don't—doesn't—seem important at a time like this, but what should we do about it?"

"I'm too tired to think about the race tonight, Mike, but I'm considering forfeiting."

"Maddie, we can't! We'd have to pay that guy . . . what's his name . . ."

"Lazarus Gratiot."

"Lazarus Gratiot half the stakes money. We don't *have* that much cash, do we?"

Maddie released another sigh. "No, we don't. Which means we'll lose everything—the farm, the horses, the house . . . everything. They'll take it all to satisfy our debts, and we'll be left with nearly nothing."

She paused at the bottom of the porch steps. "I don't want such a disaster to befall us. I've fought long and hard to prevent it. But I have to help Chase now. His life is at stake, so I have to put his needs first, ahead of ours."

"I could take the wagon, the girls, Pa, and Gold Deck to Abilene. We could do it without you, Maddie."

"Mike, you're only fourteen years old. I know you consider yourself a man—and you practically are—but it's a long way to Abilene. The trip is hard, and there's so much to take care of; it's such a great responsibility."

"I can do it. I can handle everything as well as you and Pa ever did. Besides, I'm almost fifteen."

"But you won't get any help from Pa and not much from the girls. If you have trouble with the wagon or horses, the girls will be no use at all. They usually just go along for the ride anyway. . . . Oh, Mike, are you sure? Have you done any of the things we normally do the day before we leave for a race?"

Guiltily, Mike shook his head. "No, but I'll stay up all night if I have to and get them all done. I'll grease the wagon axles, oil the saddle, groom Gold Deck until he shines . . ."

Knowing it was the only solution available, Maddie capitulated. "I suppose the girls can prepare food, at least, enough to last for several days. If they were waiting for me to do it when I got home, they, too, will have to stay up half the night."

"Don't worry, Maddie. You won't have to help with anything. Leave it all to me, Carrie, and Zoe."

Little Mike looked so earnest that Maddie didn't have the heart to remind him that in the past, he, Carrie, and Zoe hadn't always been reliable. Just to get the everyday chores done, she usually had to ride herd on them, and this was far from ordinary.

"I have no choice but to leave it all to you three; you're our only hope for winning that five thousand dollars."

She and Little Mike went into the house, where the girls pounced upon Maddie, begging her to tell them what was happening in town. She explained the entire situation, including what she must do in the morning, and the girls agreed to share the responsibility of attending the match race with Little Mike. As Maddie had feared, nothing had yet been done to prepare for the journey; her whole family, with the exception of Pa, had been waiting for direction.

Pa had already gone to bed, and Maddie knew he didn't remember they even had a match race in Abilene—nor did he care. Would her siblings be able to stop him from visiting the saloons in that wild, lawless town? If he seized the opportunity to indulge in a drinking spree, they would just have to deal with it the best they could.

As it happened, only Maddie's father got much sleep that night. About three hours before daybreak, Maddie considered abandoning the effort and telling her brother and sisters to go to bed. Delaying their departure another day would mean Gold Deck would have no time whatever to recover from the journey before he had to race, but the delay couldn't be helped. They needed another day to get ready.

"Are you finished out there in the barn yet?" Maddie asked Mike when he came inside the house to get something.

"Almost," he proudly answered. "We should be all set to go about an hour after sunup."

Maddie exhaled in relief; so far so good, she thought.

"I'm glad we're almost done in here," Carrie grumbled. "If I don't get to bed soon, I'm gonna fall off the wagon on the way to Abilene, because I won't be able to keep my eyes open."

"We all need sleep," Maddie agreed as a disturbing thought entered her mind: Who would look after the rest of the horses, the milk cow, the chickens, and the cat, with all of them gone? At the match races they had attended away from home since

Ma's death, Pawnee Mary had volunteered for the job—but Mary wouldn't be doing it this time.

Maddie pondered the matter and finally came up with the only possible solution. "Carrie and Zoe, I've changed my mind about this whole endeavor. One of you is going to have to stay here to manage things while Little Mike goes to the match race with the other. Pa should remain here, too; he'll just get into trouble in Abilene anyway."

"Oh, Maddie!" both girls chorused.

"I want to go to the race," wailed Zoe.

"So do I," Carrie added with a pout. She thought about it for a moment, then added: "Well, actually I wouldn't mind staying here if I can go to town to watch Mr. Cumberland's trial."

"That's not fair," Zoe immediately objected. "I want to see the trial, too. Why can't we both stay and Mike can go to Abilene by himself?"

"None of you will attend that gruesome trial," Maddie sternly informed them. "I will represent the family most adequately. Girls, get the broom. You'll have to draw straws to see who stays here and who goes with Little Mike. He needs someone to go along and help him."

Grudgingly, the girls obeyed . . . and it was Carrie who won the trip to Abilene. Even so, Maddie didn't like the idea of the two young people being on the road by themselves all that distance. She recalled several incidents when Pa had tangled with nasty characters and the unexpected hazard—a rain-swollen river to cross, an unexpected hail storm, once even a twister, and a surprise encounter with a herd of buffalo. The buffalo were mostly gone now, but the threat of cattle drives had replaced it. If they found themselves in the middle of a cattle drive, the cattle could stampede, injure the horses, and overturn the wagon. At this time of year, it was entirely likely they might encounter a big drive involving a couple thousand head or more.

How could she allow a fourteen-year-old boy and a thirteen-year-old girl to undertake such a perilous journey alone?

As if guessing her thoughts, Little Mike said: "Quit thinkin' the worst, Maddie. Zoe and I will be fine. If we leave at sunup, we'll be in Abilene by sunset. If we have a problem, we'll just make camp and go on the next morning."

"If you don't suffer some disaster."

"There won't be any disasters," her brother proclaimed with all the arrogant cockiness of youth.

"I hope not." Maddie turned away to hide her anxiety. "Hurry up, and let's finish, so we can all sleep for a couple hours. I myself have to leave as soon as it's light."

"Where are you gonna look for Mary and Mr. Cumberland's brother?" Zoe asked.

The question was a good one; Maddie as yet had no idea.

"I'm waiting to be inspired," she admitted. "I've been thinking all night where I should start. So far, the only thing I've come up with is to start at Mary's house."

"You gonna go there *alone?*"

Carrie spoke, but Little Mike and Zoe looked equally horrified.

"I imagine the dead bodies have been cleared away by now," she drily commented.

"But Maddie!" Zoe exclaimed. "It'll be so spooky."

Maddie shrugged. "I can't help that. I don't know where else to start looking, so I'll have to search the area for clues as to where Mary and Buck might have gone."

"You're awfully brave," Carrie murmured. "I wouldn't go near a place where two murders were recently committed."

"Funny, I don't feel brave. I only feel desperate. Now, let's finish our work."

They finished shortly thereafter and sought their beds for a few hours. It seemed to Maddie she had barely fallen asleep when Little Mike began shaking her shoulder.

"Maddie! Maddie, wake up! There's something wrong with Gold Deck. I went out to the barn to feed him his breakfast, and I found him sweatin', pawin' the ground, and twistin' his head around to look at his flanks."

Maddie snapped upright in bed. For a moment, she couldn't think, much less focus on the problem. "What time is it?"

"Almost dawn. It's getting light out."

"Damn. I'll be right out, soon as I dress."

As she struggled into the clothing she had laid out the night before, Maddie searched her memory for a list of possible ailments that could afflict a horse without any warning. Little Mike returned to the barn, but was back moments later.

"Maddie, he's down in the straw and rolling! I can't get him to stay on his feet."

Now, she recognized the problem. "It sounds like he's got the colic."

She threw open the door and joined her brother in the front room. His eyes held a glint of pure terror.

"What'll we do, Maddie? I ain't never handled a colicky horse before, and I can't remember what Pa used to do."

They hadn't had a horse down with colic in a long time, and Maddie herself wasn't certain what to do. Dimly, she recalled her father preparing a special mash for a mare who'd been in foal at the time. She remembered him walking the horse for hours on end, massaging her belly, preventing her from lying down and rolling. . . . It hadn't been enough. The mare had gone into labor prematurely, delivered a foal who died within minutes, and herself had lain writhing in agony for a good portion of the night.

When it became apparent that the mare wouldn't make it, Pa had sent Maddie away from the barn. Cowering in Ma's arms, she had heard the single shot which had ended the horse's suffering. She had wept and been inconsolable for days afterward. The mare's name had been Daisy, and Maddie had insisted on calling the tiny, perfect foal, Daisy's Darling. They were buried in the same grave, marked with a small wooden marker, about a hundred yards from the barn.

Maddie shivered as she recalled the tragic outcome of the mare's bout with colic and considered its implications for Gold Deck. Was this the end for the wonderful stallion? Had he run his last race?

She hurried out to the barn with Little Mike and found Gold Deck on his feet again. But his head was hanging down to his knees, and he looked miserable. Pain clouded his warm brown eyes, normally so lively, alert, and proud, as if he knew his own value and relished it. He hadn't touched his breakfast, which he always consumed with great enthusiasm. Maddie stepped into his stall and ran her fingers across his damp, shining side. Little Mike had indeed groomed the horse to gleaming perfection. It seemed ludicrous that such a healthy-looking animal could be so sick. Bending over, she placed her ear against the stallion's belly and listened for the faint rumbling sounds that normally accompanied a horse's digestive processes.

Pa had taught her that such sounds indicated a well-functioning gut, and if they were absent, the horse was sick. Gold Deck's belly proved ominously silent.

"Mike, did you feed him anything unusual, either last night or this morning?"

Mike shook his head. "Of course not. I know better than that, Maddie. If I was going to change something, I especially wouldn't do it now—just before a big race."

Maddie checked the dried-grass hay at the stallion's feet. It had come from the field Chase wanted to buy. She saw nothing wrong with it—nor with the corn kernels in his feed bucket. Pa had often lectured her about the importance of making certain there was no mold on any of the feed they fed the horses. "Moldy feed can sicken a horse quicker'n anything," he had told her many times.

She couldn't guess what might have gone wrong—until she spotted a piece of broken corncob in the straw. "What's that corncob doing in here?"

"Corncob?" Spotting it, Mike bent and picked it up. As he looked at it, comprehension slowly dawned in his eyes. "I was rubbing him with dried corncobs to bring out the shine in his coat. You don't s'pose . . ."

He glanced over the side of the stall where an empty pail stood atop an old crate. "Oh, no!"

"What?" Maddie demanded.

"I had a bucket of old, stripped corncobs right here. Now, they're all gone. Gold Deck must've leaned over the side of the stall and eaten 'em during the night."

Maddie fought the urge to scream at her brother, to berate him for his carelessness and stupidity. The look in Little Mike's eyes helped keep her silent. He knew what he had done, and he loathed himself enough for both of them.

"I've as good as killed him, Maddie! He's gonna die, ain't he?"

"I don't know, Mike. Put his halter on, get him out of here, and start walking him. Whatever you do, keep him moving. Don't let him get down and roll any more, not if you can stop it."

"Where are you going? Don't leave me alone with him, Maddie. I . . . I'm a damn fool! I can't be trusted."

"Yes, you can! You made a mistake, that's all. I'm going to get Pa. He's the only one who can save Gold Deck now. I'll get Pa, and then I'm leaving. I have to find Pawnee Mary and Chase's brother."

Tears glimmered in her brother's eyes, but he nodded and reached for Gold Deck's halter hanging on a nearby nail.

Maddie ran from the barn, sprinted up the porch steps, and dashed into the house. She didn't waste time knocking on her father's door, but barged into his room, and began shaking him to awaken him. He opened one eye and gazed up at her in surprise.

"Maddie? What's wrong? You look like you jus' swallered a grasshopper."

"Nothing's wrong with me, Pa. It's Gold Deck. He's got the colic. At least, I think that's what it is. He ate a bucketful of old corncobs. . . . Pa, I need your help to save him."

"Corncobs, huh? Why'd you feed him that? A bit of corn won't hurt him none, but the cobs . . ."

"We didn't do it on purpose, Pa. It was an accident. But he's sick because of it, and I have to leave, and Little Mike doesn't know what to do. . . . Get up, Pa. You have to help us."

Her father sat up and lifted a hand to his head. "I . . . I don't know as I can, Maddie. I feel a mite . . . dizzy. Don't know as I can remember what t' do anyway . . ."

"You've *got* to remember. Come on, Pa. I'll help you get dressed."

Halfway through dressing, her father sat down on the edge of the bed. "Maddie, quit rushin' me. These old bones can only move so fast. An' I can't think at all yet. 'Course, if I had me a little . . . you know . . . wee nip, I could do better. I could maybe recall what t' do fer colic."

Maddie clamped her hands on his shoulders and spoke slowly and distinctly. "There's no whiskey in this house, Pa. There's none for miles around. Forget about having a drink and think about your family for once. We need you, Pa. Gold Deck needs you. He'll die if you don't help him. And if he dies—if you don't pull yourself together and try to keep him from dying—I'll never forgive you. I'll walk out of this house, and I won't look back. You'll never see me again."

"Maddie, honey. . . . What are you sayin'? Why are you makin' threats an' talkin' this way t' your old Pa who loves you?"

For the first time in many days—in many weeks, perhaps even months—Maddie had her father's complete attention. He was listening at long last.

"Pa, you've become a weak, dependent, needy old man. A helpless old drunk. Since Ma died, you've stopped living—fighting—loving—helping. I can't stand by anymore and watch you fade away. I have a life to live, too, and that's what life is all about—struggling to *do* the best and *be* the best you can possibly be and to live each day you're allotted. You're not allowed to . . . to just give up. You have to keep trying, every day, for as long as you live . . ."

"I try, Maddie." Hurt and bewilderment shone in her father's eyes, and for a moment, Maddie felt shame for berating him. Then she realized he was doing it *again*—making *her* feel guilty for *his* shortcomings.

"No, Pa," she gently corrected. "You don't *try.* What you do is try to *escape.* By drinking, sleeping, brooding. . . . But we still need you. We need you here and now. Little Mike's outside waiting for you. He's walking Gold Deck, and he doesn't know what more to do for him. You have to go out and help him. Teach him. Be his father. I can't do it, Pa. It's *your* responsibility, not mine. I've got my own responsibilities."

Leaning forward, Maddie kissed her father's beard-stubbled cheek. "I love you, Pa, but I've got to go now. Whatever happens, it's all up to you."

"Maddie . . ." he started to say, but she whirled on her heel and left the room.

"Maddie!" she heard him holler, but she ignored the plea.

Chase needed her now. She might be wrong in what she was doing, but she had made her choice. Her family would have to learn to survive without her.

Zoe met her in the front room as she was ready to rush out the door. Clad in her long nightdress, the girl held the tin coffeepot. "Maddie? I thought I'd make coffee before you go. I'll make it good and strong, so it'll keep you awake."

"Thanks, Zoe, but I don't have time for it. Make some for the others. Pa can sure use it."

"Pa? Isn't he still sleeping?"

"No, he's getting dressed. Gold Deck's got the colic, and Pa's going to help him get better."

"Pa?" Disbelief echoed in her sister's question.

"Yes, Pa. You're in charge of the house, Zoe. I'll be back when I can."

Twenty

By the time Maddie arrived at Pawnee Mary's house, a strong wind was blowing, flattening the wild plum bushes growing along the river. Despite the bent-over greenery and bramble vines, the place still looked familiar. Years ago, as a child, Maddie had occasionally visited the family who had first built the soddy house. The Coys had had a daughter named Emily, about the same age as Maddie, and the two girls had picked plums and berries together, while their mothers made jam and jellies. Since the departure of the Coys, Maddie had avoided the property, because the abandoned shack represented a family's failed hopes and dreams. Plagued by a series of misfortunes, including the death of a child from cholera, the Coys had given up and gone elsewhere—back East, Maddie believed.

So this is where Pawnee Mary has been living all this time, she now thought, sliding down from her horse.

The whistling wind made an eerie sound, and Maddie suddenly dreaded snooping around the shack. Tying the horse to a plum bush some distance away, she reluctantly approached the old structure. Dark stains splattered the porch and the steps, and someone had boarded up the front door with several planks, making entry impossible. That left only the outside to explore, which eased her fears somewhat.

Maddie searched with care, noting where the grass was trampled and the soft earth held the prints of many horses. Not far from the house, she found more bloodstains; if the men had died inside the house, as everyone said, why was there so much blood outside? . . . Why did a trail of blood seem to be leading *away* from the house?

Following the trail, Maddie discovered that it led along the river. Beneath a plum bush, she found a large reddish-brown spot, as if someone had lain there bleeding before mustering the strength to rise and continue walking. On the riverbank, she encountered several sets of footprints, some going toward the house and some away from it . . . and then she spotted a lone moccasin.

Picking it up, she recognized the distinctive beaded design on the footwear; the moccasin definitely belonged to Mary. The ground in the area was trampled and further on, she stumbled across some items of female clothing. Apparently, Mary had come to the river to bathe and been surprised by the . . . bounty hunters?

Maddie sought to reconstruct what might have happened, then realized she was wasting time. Neither Mary nor Buck were here, and she was no closer to finding them than she had been when she arrived. Turning back toward the house, walking slowly as she tried to make sense of things, she continued studying the bloodstained grass; whoever had killed the men must have been severely wounded. In their escape, they had marked their route clearly; if she wanted to know what had become of them, she had only to follow the trail.

This she did for about ten minutes, but then the trail disappeared. Growing discouraged, Maddie asked herself where Buck and Mary would go, especially if one of them were hurt. The answer came to her immediately; they'd run to Chase! Knowing they needed food, money, and fast horses to escape, they would undoubtedly seek Chase's help. Maddie retrieved her horse, mounted, and rode toward Chase's farm, which proved to be closer to the soddy house and the river than she had realized.

She was nearing the house when she spied another large stain on the ground, where someone had obviously stopped to rest a moment. As she rode closer, her sense of dread returned. With a macabre interest, she eyed her surroundings. A group of horses grazed peacefully in a corral, and in a separate enclosure, Bonnie

Lass was busily cleaning up a windblown pile of hay someone had set out for her. The water troughs were full to the brim.

Maddie scolded herself for not once thinking of Chase's stock and arranging to care for his animals—yet someone had thought of them. She dismounted and tied her horse to the hitching rail in front of the house, then ascended the front steps. She knocked on the door. When no one answered, she opened it and calling softly, entered the house.

"Mary? Are you here?"

In a matter of moments, Maddie discovered that the house was empty. Her attention turned to the outbuildings. She recalled the day she had encountered Buck in the stable, and moving quickly, lest she change her mind, she strode toward the barn and stepped inside. Darkness enveloped her. The wind shook the old building and moaned through the rafters.

Holding her breath, she walked slowly and silently down the center aisle. Something creaked behind her, and she spun around, expecting to once again come face to face with Chase's wild-eyed brother. But it was Pawnee Mary who stood watching her. Only this wasn't the serene, gentle woman Maddie knew. Holding a pitchfork, ready to attack with it, Mary faced her, her expression so proud and fierce that Maddie wondered if she had taken leave of her senses.

"Mary?" she said tentatively. "It's only me—and I've come alone."

Pawnee Mary slowly lowered the pitchfork. She sighed and seemed to sway a bit. Maddie reached out a hand to steady her, noticing as she did so the woman's soiled, bloodstained garments and sweat-streaked face. Mary wore a skirt with a torn hem and a fringed leather top that had seen better days. She was barefoot, and her normally neatly braided hair hung in a wild tangle on her neck and shoulders. She looked as if she'd survived a war—and not without serious injury.

A strange thought crossed Maddie's mind; could it have been Mary herself who killed the bounty hunters? "Mary, what happened? I've been looking all over for you and Buck. Is he here?"

Maddie half turned to peer into the gloom, but the Indian

woman quickly stepped in front of her, as if to prevent her from searching the building. Maddie again touched her friend's buckskin sleeve.

"Mary, I've come to help. Won't you tell me what's happened? I truly need to know."

"Two men," Mary finally said. "Come looking for me. Find me swimming in river. Drag me to house. Throw on bed. Then Silver Hair come."

"Silver Hair? Do you mean Buck?"

Mary nodded, and tears suddenly welled in her dark eyes. "Men hit me in stomach. Make me lose baby." Her hand came up to rest protectively on her belly. "Silver Hair not even know yet I have baby growing inside me. But he have big anger to see white men hurting me. He brave warrior. Fight with axe from woodpile. Men fight back. Draw knife and six-shooter. Shoot Silver Hair."

"Oh, no! Is he badly hurt? Did they kill him?"

"Not dead yet, but shot bad in stomach. When I see him shot, I *think* he dead, and I go—how you say—loco . . ." Mary pointed to her head. "Like cattle who eat bad weed and charge people. I grab axe. Grab knife. Punish for bad thing they do. I kill men for killing baby and Silver Hair. I almost scalp them. But then I find out Silver Hair still lives. That stop me."

Picturing the terrible scene, Maddie expelled a sigh. "What happened next?"

"Silver Hair bleed much. I bleed much. Floor slick with blood. I try stop bleeding and get Silver Hair away from house before whites come. We hide near river, then come looking for Son of Wolf. We wait. Silver Hair suffer much, but Son of Wolf not come. . . . I want take Silver Hair far away from here, but he too weak travel. Must rest. Must heal. Grow strong again. Then I take him. Go find my people. If he live, I give him new, better life."

"Oh, Mary! Let me see him. I must tell both of you all that has happened." Maddie started to push past the woman, but Pawnee Mary stopped her.

"No. Better you not see. Then no have to lie when whites ask about Silver Hair." Mary frowned, her mouth a grim line. "You good woman. Always speak truth. They know if you lie."

"Mary, listen to me. Those men you killed; they were bounty hunters. They came to Kansas to find Buck—Silver Hair—and take him back to Texas to hang for murder. The sheriff rode out here to question Chase about the wanted posters they brought with them. Chase went to your shack to warn his brother. He found the bounty hunters dead, and while he was there, the sheriff arrived with a posse. Chase hid in a cupboard, but they captured him when he tried to escape. Everyone thinks *he's* the murderer, and they plan to hold a trial and hang him, just as soon as they can. You'll have to come back to town with me and tell them what really happened."

Mary's face hardened. Her eyes lost all semblance of warmth. "Can't. They hang me and Silver Hair, too. I kill white men. Silver Hair help. He look different. Act different. No can speak or explain. That why they hate him. He not kill white man in Texas on purpose; it was accident. But no one listen. No one care. If we surrender, they hang both of us and laugh while they do it."

"But they'll hang Chase if you don't tell the truth! I'll be right there with you, Mary. I'll *make* them understand what happened. Some might discount your story, but most of the people in Hopewell are fair-minded and just. They won't condemn you for fighting back; all you did was defend yourself and Buck. . . . Listen, Buck needn't go with us. He can stay here. We'll refuse to tell where he is. But if you don't agree to testify, Chase will surely hang."

Still frowning, Mary glanced away. She seemed undecided.

"There's really no choice," Maddie added. "What kind of life will you and Buck have if Chase *does* hang for a crime he never committed? How will both of you feel about allowing him to take the blame? . . . By the way, I think you should know that Chase has admitted to killing the two men. He's doing his best to protect Buck. He's claiming self-defense as his reason for doing it, but no one believes him. Unlike you and Buck, he has no injuries or wounds to show that the men attacked him. Right now, the good citizens of Hopewell don't even want to wait for the circuit judge to conduct his trial; Horace Brownley is going to act as judge, and Horace already has reason to hate Chase. You can't say no, Mary . . . You *can't.* It wouldn't be right, and you'd never forgive yourself."

Mary's head lifted. An inner fire lit her dark eyes. "Can whites forgive themselves for what they do to Indians or Silver Hair?"

"Considering what whites have done to Indians *and* to Chase's brother, that's a fair question, but one I can't answer. Please, Mary. . . . Come to Hopewell with me; you're Chase's only chance."

Still, Mary hesitated, her face stoic, her inner battle reflected in her expressive eyes. At last, she sighed. "All right, I come. First, I tell Silver Hair. For him, I do this. I know him well. He not want brother to die."

Mary turned and calmly walked toward the far corner of the stable, and Maddie followed. In the dark shadows of an empty stall, on a pile of straw, lay Chase's brother. He stirred as they approached and lifted a trembling hand. The tall Indian woman sank to her knees beside him, took his hand, and wordlessly clasped his fingers to her cheek. The couple gazed into each other's eyes. In the silence of the tender moment, Maddie had a chance to study Buck. What she saw made her cringe inside.

His haggard face was very nearly the color of his hair, and every line of his features revealed suffering and exhaustion. He wore no shirt, and his midsection, below his rib cage, was heavily bandaged. Blood had seeped through the bandage, but it did not appear fresh, and that gave Maddie at least a slight hope that he might eventually recover. Newly stitched cuts crisscrossed his arms and upper body, and a pungent smell emanated from the poultice covering one shoulder. These other wounds appeared minor and no immediate threat to his life; it was the stomach wound that worried Maddie.

"Silver Hair," Pawnee Mary whispered. "I must leave you for short time. Until my return, sleep and grow strong again."

Buck jerked his head in denial. Using hand signals, he communicated with Mary, and Maddie waited more or less patiently for an explanation.

"Silver Hair, no!" Mary exclaimed. "You too weak. Better you stay here."

More hand signals followed.

"What is he saying?" Maddie asked.

"He hear us talking. Know what happen. Want go town, too."

"Mary, he can't. I wish he could, but now that I've seen him, I doubt he's strong enough to survive the trip. Besides, if he goes, he's liable to be arrested and put in jail for that murder in Texas."

"Stay here, Silver Hair. Rest," Mary pleaded, but Buck struggled to rise to a sitting position, gritting his teeth against the agony the movement caused him.

Pushing him back down, Mary lifted her gaze to meet Maddie's. "He refuse stay. Say he go. No let brother hang in his place."

"But . . ." Maddie started to protest, only to have Mary insist: "No use argue. Silver Hair expect to die anyway. But he wrong. Stay or go, *I no let him die.*"

"At least, if we take him to town, we can send to Salina or Lincoln for a doctor," Maddie pointed out, reconsidering her own position.

To her surprise, Mary responded with anger. "No! Must keep white medicine man from touching Silver Hair, or he die for certain. *I* only one who can keep him alive. Use old Indian remedies."

"Surely, you'll allow him to have some laudanum for the pain," Maddie protested.

Pawnee Mary narrowed her eyes. "This laud-anum. I have heard of it. Maybe I let him have few drops—but nothing else. Indian remedies better. I not trust white medicine."

Maddie's thoughts turned to the method of transportation. There was no way Buck could ride a horse. "We'll have to take him to town in Chase's buckboard. We can fetch blankets, quilts, and pillows from the house to make him more comfortable."

"Is good idea," Pawnee Mary agreed.

They set to work on the preparations, and the only problem they encountered was in choosing a horse to hitch to the buckboard. Maddie put her own horse in a stall with hay and water, for it wasn't trained to drive. But the first one she took from the corral refused to stand still to be harnessed. The second kicked when it felt the breaching strap encircle its hindquarters.

"Mary, ask Buck which of his horses is broken to drive. At this rate, we'll be here all day and might even get hurt in the process of hitching one."

Mary left the stable yard, returned to Buck, and came back several moments later. "He say take little bay mare with white stocking. She pull anything."

Maddie fetched the proper horse from the corral, hitched it without incident, and helped Mary carry Buck to the buckboard and load him in the back. Mary climbed in beside Buck to pillow his head in her lap, while Maddie took the front seat, gathered the lines, and clucked to the little mare. The bay mare surged forward obediently, and they headed for town.

The sun poured down on them, but the persistent wind—hot and dry as the dust on the worn track—kept them fairly comfortable. Maddie did her best to avoid the ruts and rough spots, for whenever she hit one, Buck gritted his teeth and clutched the sides of the buckboard with whitened knuckles. His bravery in the face of excruciating pain made Maddie want to weep, but she managed to avoid shedding any tears in front of Mary, who guarded her own feelings as zealously as Buck fought to subdue his.

Halfway into town, Maddie spotted a distant figure driving toward them in a small, partially enclosed buggy of the sort that could be rented for brief outings at the livery stable in town. The young man handling the lines looked faintly familiar, but not until the buckboard was almost even with the buggy did Maddie recognize him. It was Peter Johnson, the messenger boy from the bank. He was another of Horace's employees, in addition to Elwood, the clerk, but Peter usually only swept floors and ran errands.

As soon as he saw Maddie, young Peter hauled back on the

lines, as though the placid, ribby, old horse pulling the buggy was some fiery, runaway steed. "Miss McCrory!" he shouted. "I was just coming out to your place. I have some important papers to deliver."

"Papers?" Maddie couldn't imagine what he was talking about. "I don't have time to look at any papers. What's happening in town? Do you know?"

"In town?" Peter peered at her from beneath the brim of his hat, which he wore low over his forehead to shield him from the sun.

"Have they started the trial for Mr. Cumberland yet?"

At that moment, Peter noticed Pawnee Mary sitting in the bed of the buckboard. His eyes widened, and he looked as if he expected her to jump up and attack him right then and there.

"His t-trial will be held this afternoon. I . . . I was hoping to get to your place and b-back in time for the hanging."

"There isn't going to *be* a hanging," Maddie stonily informed him. "I'm sorry, Peter, but I can't delay any longer. I really must be going."

"But Miss McCrory—wait! Mr. Brownley ordered me to deliver these documents to you. He—Mr. Brownley—is demanding immediate repayment of the p-personal loan he gave you, and the bank is calling for all your overdue m-mortgage payments, plus interest. You have three d-days to settle your debts in full, or the bank will foreclose and assume p-possession of your entire estate, including land, horses, f-furnishings, and . . . and . . ."

The youth's stuttering indicated how much he feared Mary, but also revealed how much he disliked delivering such unsettling news. Too bad he had to be the one to do Horace's dirty work. Normally, Horace gave that job to Elwood, his mousy little clerk, but Elwood, obviously, had better things to do with his time today.

"Thank you for the message, Peter." She picked up the whip lying at her feet and flicked it over the back of the little bay mare, sending her into a brisk trot. She didn't need to hear any more; she already knew what Horace Brownley would do if she couldn't provide the money she owed him within three days' time. Her family would be destitute, turned out to fend for themselves on the prairie.

Since she couldn't turn around and head for home, Maddie refused to worry about it. Gold Deck's condition—and whether or not he'd be able to get to Abilene in time for the race—were out of her hands. God willing, her father had rallied, successfully treated Gold Deck for colic, and somehow, they would all make it to the race and win it. She simply prayed that she herself would make it to Hopewell in time to save Chase from being hanged. That was all that really mattered.

Maddie drove the rest of the way into town at a breakneck pace. As she turned down Main Street, it became obvious the trial was already in progress. Not a single soul was on the boardwalk or in any of the little shops and business establishments fronting the main thoroughfare, but a crowd spilled out of the saloon, and people were standing on crates looking over the shoulders of others as they tried to see into the building itself. Horses, wagons, and buggies lined both sides of the street. It might have been a race day; apparently people had come from miles around to witness this exciting event.

Maddie should have guessed the trial would be held in the Ruby Garter; Hopewell as yet had no courthouse, and the saloon was the largest structure in town. Not far away stood the big bur oak, the town's most prominent natural feature. As Maddie's gaze swept the leafy landmark, her blood suddenly chilled in her veins. A thick rope had already been tossed over one of the heaviest branches, and from the end of the rope dangled a noose. The good people of Hopewell and its environs were so certain of the trial's outcome they had already made arrangements for the execution to follow.

Maddie could recall only one previous hanging in Hopewell. It had taken place when she was only a child and Little Mike was a babe in arms. Pa had taken the whole family to town to watch it, for he considered it his civic duty to uphold the enforcement of the law in the area. Plagued by visions of a body twitching and jumping at the end of a rope, Maddie had suffered nightmares about the incident for weeks afterward—which was why she was so determined to prevent her younger siblings from witnessing such a violent event.

Now, as she thought of the man the townspeople intended to hang, her heart raced madly, and her palms grew damp. A roaring sounded in her ears, and her knees quivered. She imagined how Chase must be feeling—surrounded on every side by people who wanted to watch him swing—and she regained her courage and something else: an explosion of love and admiration so deep, so all-encompassing, and so sweetly piercing as to rob her of breath.

Hopewell had only the occasional traveling preacher to tend to the religious needs of the small, scattered community, but Maddie suddenly remembered a stirring revival sermon she had been privileged to hear one summer. It had centered around the theme: *Greater love hath no man than he be willing to lay down his life for his brother.*

Chase was willing to die for Buck, and that fact coalesced all of Maddie's feelings for the man into one driving certainty: How could she *not* love Chase?

None of his past failings mattered a whit when balanced against the basic core of the man. Maddie knew she loved him totally, desperately, and quite beyond anything she could have imagined possible. If she had to get a six-shooter and fight off the whole damn town, she would not let him die.

She drove down the alley next to the saloon, turned to Mary, and said: "Wait here. I'm going inside. Don't be afraid; we're going to win this battle."

Mary gave her a long, doubtful look, and the weight of responsibility for all of them settled heavily onto Maddie's shoulders. This time, she welcomed it. Her entire life up to this moment had been preparation for what lay before her now. She had never shrunk from responsibility, and now she knew *why* she had embraced it so zealously. She had been practicing for the very hour when all she held dear, all she cherished, depended upon her ability to carry the load and carry it well.

Squaring her shoulders and lifting her chin, Maddie climbed down from the buckboard and marched toward the entrance of the saloon. She had to push her way through the crowd, stepping on a few toes in the process, but she finally gained entrance into the building itself. Once inside, she examined the scene with a single glance, then walked straight down the center aisle, which had been cleared of tables and set only with chairs on either side to provide seating for the onlookers.

The crowd murmured at her boldness, but Maddie ignored the whispered comments. Her goal was a row of tables set together near the bar. Horace Brownley sat behind one, flanked on either side by several of the town's other leading citizens—Mr. Grover of the mercantile, Jake Bussel, the blacksmith, Bartholomew Parks, the largest local landowner, several of the Town Councilmen, and surprisingly, Lily Tolliver, who looked quite smug to be presiding over the proceedings being held on her premises.

Moses Smith occupied a chair near the prisoner, and then there was Chase himself, bound hand and foot and shackled to the chair on which he sat. Maddie's anger flared at these indignities, but she kept her mind on her objective and refused to be sidetracked by lesser distractions.

Head down, unaware of her presence, Horace pounded his gavel to still the onlookers. He was looking at a sheaf of papers lying on the table before him. As usual, he was dressed for a role of authority, in marked contrast to everyone else around him. Only Elwood, who stood off to one side, sported a suit like that of his employer.

"Mayor Brownley," she called out, stopping only when she had reached him. "How dare you presume to conduct a trial with yourself as magistrate when you hold a personal grudge against the accused? As I told you before, this case should be referred to the circuit judge, and if you refuse to do it, the matter should go to the Town Council for a vote."

Horace's eyes bulged behind his spectacles as he raised his

head and stared at Maddie. "How dare *you* interrupt these legal proceedings, Miss McCrory? The Town Council has already voted to hold the trial with *me* as magistrate. If you doubt it, ask them. They're all present."

"Ah, but did you tell them of your enmity toward the accused?"

"It doesn't signify. They all know I'm a fair man," Horace shamelessly boasted. "Have you nothing better to do than come here and attempt to impugn my integrity? Surely, with a race scheduled for the day after tomorrow, you ought to be on your way to Abilene."

"Nothing could be more important than saving the life of an innocent man," Maddie declared.

"Innocent, hah! The accused has already admitted his guilt before the whole town. We've naught to decide now but whether or not he acted in self-defense. If you will take a seat, the City Attorney will continue presenting his case against that notion."

Someone shoved a chair in Maddie's direction, but she ignored it. "Mayor Brownley . . ." she couldn't bring herself to call Horace "Your Honor," because she didn't think he possessed any honor. "This trial is a travesty of justice, and I insist on being heard before you continue any further with it."

Again, the crowd murmured, their voices rising like a sweep of wind at Maddie's back. Horace pounded his gavel and grew red-faced from the effort. "Sheriff, remove this bothersome woman. She's disrupting these proceedings and making a nuisance of herself."

Moses Smith rose heavily to his feet, but Jake Bussel held up his hand. "Wait jus' a gol-danged minute. I know Miss McCrory an' her family real well. So do most of the folks in this here saloon. If she wants t' say somethin', I think she's gotta right t' say it."

To Maddie's intense gratification, several of the onlookers called out their agreement. "Let her speak. We wanna hear what she's got t' say."

Horace's face swelled with anger, but he nodded curtly.

"Make it brief, Miss McCrory. You are wasting the court's valuable time."

Maddie wasn't sure who the jury was supposed to be, but she automatically turned to face the townspeople, for without their support, she knew she would achieve little. Before she opened her mouth, however, Chase suddenly spoke.

"Maddie . . ." he said in a low voice that was like a hand reaching out and squeezing her heart.

Maddie darted him a glance; it was nearly her undoing. She had the odd notion that she and Chase were the only two people in the room. No one and nothing else mattered. His dark, weary face and vivid amber eyes conveyed more than mere words ever could. She read pleading and love in them, combined with a determination to equal hers. In a single brief look, he managed to tell her that he loved her, understood her motivations, but didn't want her to do this.

"Maddie, don't," was all he said.

"I must," she answered and looked away.

Turning back to the waiting crowd, she began stating her case. "There is much you don't know about Chase Cumberland, the accused. . . . For one thing, he has a brother."

It didn't take long to explain the entire situation, starting with Buck's tragedy and the alleged murder in Texas. Maddie spoke into a well of silence, commanding everyone's attention so completely that it seemed no one breathed, let alone moved.

"So you see, Chase and Buck Courtland came to Hopewell to escape prejudice and pursue a dream—that of breeding and racing prime Quarter horses. As all of you know who witnessed the race in which his mare beat our stallion, his horses possess the finest bloodlines; in years to come, have no doubt, Chase and Buck will become successful, outstanding citizens of the area—worthy of our pride and esteem."

"Except that one or both of 'em has committed murder," sneered Horace.

"That's a distortion of the facts, Mayor Brownley," Maddie protested. "As I've already said, Chase is assuming the blame for these deaths because he wishes to protect his brother . . . his *disabled* brother. What happened in that soddy house can best be explained by one who was there, the woman we all know as Pawnee Mary. Having come of their own free will, Mary and Buck are both outside in a wagon, waiting to tell their side of the story."

A collective gasp erupted from the audience. Voices rose in exclamation, and a number of people raced outside, Horace again pounded his gavel. When he achieved quiet, he pointed his finger at Maddie. "You expect this court to accept the testimony of a half-breed Indian whore?"

"She is indeed Indian, but it has yet to be proven that she's a whore. Whatever she is, she's a human being, Horace, the same as you or me. She's a woman who was dragged by the hair to her bed, where her two brawny assailants attempted to rape her. Because of their rough treatment, she lost the babe she was carrying. Buck arrived on the scene in time to stop the attack, and they carved him up with a knife and shot him in the stomach. Mary rose from her bed to continue the battle, which she, fortunately, won—or else the two dead bodies in the shack would have been Mary's and Buck's. . . . But why am I telling the tale, when Mary can relate it just as easily?"

"We got her!" A man cried from the doorway. "We got the Injun, and a couple fellers have gone t' get a pallet t' bring in the white-haired feller."

"Take your hands off her!" Maddie cried, as several men propelled Mary into the saloon.

Reluctantly, they did so, but the fleeting expression on Mary's face cut Maddie to the quick. It was an "I told you so," look that flashed like lightning and then disappeared, leaving a stone-faced mask in its place.

"Brownley!" Chase struggled helplessly against his bonds. "If my brother is indeed lying gut-shot in a wagon, I demand that a wire be sent to the nearest town and a doctor be summoned to tend him."

"We'll decide what's to be done, Cumberland," Horace growled. "Right now, I'm not at all happy about these disturbances in my court. . . . Come here, gal, and let's hear your story."

With all the dignity of a foreign princess, Mary walked slowly and regally down the center aisle, coming to a halt only when she reached the table and Maddie's side. Maddie seized Mary's hand and squeezed it to give her friend confidence.

"I've already told them what happened, Mary," she said softly. "All you have to do is confirm my testimony."

"Someone get her a chair," Horace directed. "Elwood can question her, same as he would any other witness. Miss McCrory, step back now; you've had your say. It's *her* turn now."

Maddie moved to one side, and a backless stool was brought for Mary and set beside Chase. Mary never so much as looked at anyone directly. Seating herself on the stool, she kept her eyes fastened on the empty space in front of her and didn't acknowledge anyone in the room.

Elwood adjusted the spectacles on his thin nose, nervously straightened his scrawny shoulders, and thrust a book in front of Mary. "She better be sworn in, Mr. Brownley, so we can be sure she's tellin' the truth."

"You fool! Indians don't hold the Good Book as sacred; there's no way to make sure she's telling the truth except perhaps to hold her feet to a fire."

Maddie's head swung around at the remark. She glared at Horace, but he didn't appear in the least embarrassed. "I didn't mean we should actually harm her; however, everyone knows the word of an Indian cannot be trusted. Unless they're being tortured, they won't speak a word of truth—and sometimes not even then."

"And how would you *know* that about Indians, Horace?" Maddie shot off.

"Wouldn't surprise me if he once took part in such atrocities," Chase muttered under his breath.

"Silence in this courtroom!" Horace bellowed, pounding his gavel. "Now then, Elwood, you may begin your questioning."

Twenty-one

"Did you kill them two bounty hunters, ma'am?" was Elwood's first question, to which Mary briefly bowed her head in answer.

"Did you then . . . um . . . cut off one of the victim's . . . uh . . . manly parts?"

Another nod.

"Ma'am, why'd you do that? If the feller was already dead, what reason did you have t' mutilate him?"

Maddie could see that the question vitally interested the crowd—particularly the men in it, who made up the majority of the onlookers. All of them were scowling, as if by doing this, Mary had proven herself guilty of cold-blooded murder.

"Man I cut force me mate with him." Light flared in Mary's eyes, and her hand clasped her lower abdomen. "When I fight, he punch me here. Kill baby growing inside. Also try kill Silver Hair."

"Who's Silver Hair?" Elwood asked, bewildered.

Maddie couldn't keep still. "That's the name she's given to Buck Cumberland, I mean, Courtland, Chase's brother."

Horace banged his gavel. "Let the witness answer the questions, if you please."

"Silver Hair lie bleeding on floor. I think he dead," Mary explained in a flat unemotional tone. "Is right killer be dishonored. So I cut him. I think of taking scalps, too."

At this, the crowd murmured angrily, but Horace didn't reprimand them, and Mary had to raise her voice to be heard. "I no take scalps because Silver Hair move, and I see he live. So I forget bad men and try keep him alive."

"I see." Elwood paused significantly. "Then you don't deny you hacked those two men to death."

"I *glad* I kill them," Mary answered. "If I do not, they kill me. I never manage it except they think I weak woman, and therefore they not expecting attack. Anger give me strength."

"Appears to me we're trying the wrong person here, Judge," Elwood gleefully announced. "We *ought* to be tryin' this here Injun instead of this white man."

He nodded toward Chase, and the crowd hollered their agreement. "Free Cumberland. The Injun *did* it. Hell, she admits to it."

Maddie's spirits sank as all the old hatred the people still felt toward the Indians boiled to the surface. In fighting for their lands, the Indians had killed many relatives of the area's families, and folks hadn't forgotten it. Just as she had feared, Pawnee Mary was now in danger of being hung for her "crime."

"Wait a minute!" Maddie shouted. "Just wait a minute."

"Order!" Horace bellowed. "I demand order."

Failing to get the crowd's attention, but determined to be heard, Maddie climbed on top of the chair that had earlier been set out for her. "Please!" she cried. "Listen to me. I have something more to say."

But order was not restored until Moses drew his six-shooter and fired a shot into the ceiling. Debris rained down on his and Chase's head, but he achieved his objective, and the onlookers quieted.

"Let Miss McCrory speak," little Alice Neff demanded, pushing her way to the front of the crowd. "She brought the squaw here, as well as that poor man out in the buckboard—the one they're carrying in now. If anyone knows what's going on, it's Maddie. Moses, Mayor Brownley, you best let her speak now, or I, for one, will be mighty upset. Frankly, if a couple of men ever tried to force themselves on me and made me lose a child in the process, I'd be right happy to cut off their male parts for them, and I reckon a lot of other females feel the same way about it."

"That's tellin' 'em, Alice," echoed a second female voice. "Let Maddie speak. I wanna hear what she's got t' say."

"Well!" Horace harrumphed. "Seems you've loaded this crowd with your supporters, Miss McCrory. So go ahead and speak. But this will be the last time I allow anyone to interrupt these proceedings. . . . Moses, I authorize you to shoot anybody who gets out of line from here on out."

Moses blew the smoke away from his Colt and laid it in plain view on the table. Maddie saw that everyone was watching her expectantly, but she waited while four men carried Buck into the saloon. They had loaded him onto a wooden pallet, and they set the pallet down right beside her. Buck opened his eyes, blinked a couple of times, as if trying to focus, then gave up and closed them again. Pawnee Mary immediately rose from her chair and knelt down next to him. Leaning over him, she gently stroked his forehead and murmured soothingly in her own language, which roused not a few whispered comments.

A wave of nervousness flowed over Maddie; so much depended on her ability to sway the crowd. She sought courage by glancing at Chase. He nodded, and a small smile turned up the corners of his mouth. She could almost hear him saying, "Don't quit now. You're doing fine. Give 'em hell, Maddie."

Strength replaced nervousness, welling up in her like a gushing fountain. Fearlessly, she faced her friends and neighbors. "Ladies and gentlemen, good citizens of Hopewell. As many of you know, my mother passed away last year, and my family has had some . . . difficulties. One person has shown up regularly to lend a hand, and that person is Pawnee Mary. I have come to know her very well, and no one can tell me she's a heartless murderer; she had good reason for killing those men. Pain, grief, and agony drove her to it. Had they done to me what they did to her and Buck, I would have fought back, too. I might not have been as successful as she was, but I'd have tried to do my best to stop them."

"She's just a squaw-woman and a whore besides," Horace

muttered. "She killed and mutilated two white men. To me, that's just cause for hanging."

"To you!" Maddie cried, incensed. "And just who are *you,* Horace? You think yourself better than anyone else in this town, but you're not. You're as greedy, demanding, and manipulative as those two bounty hunters. Using their superior physical strength, they sought to take what they wanted by force, while you resort to position and power to achieve your objectives. Frankly, I see little difference between you and them."

"That's not true!" Horace sputtered, his jowls quivering with shock and outrage.

"It *is* true, and you know it!" Maddie again addressed the crowd. "If Mary's a . . . a soiled dove, then many men here must have paid for her services, and there's an easy way to prove what she is. Gentlemen, if you yourself—or any man you personally know—has paid Mary for the use of her body, raise your hands and admit to it. Now's your chance to brand her as a whore forever."

"Listen here, Miss McCrory," Lily Tolliver suddenly spoke up. "Just because a gal has to *work* for a living, don't mean she's a murderer. I am personally acquainted with a number of soiled doves, and none of them ever kilt a man. Though I can't say they wouldn't have done so if a feller had tried to leave without payin' for their services."

That brought a raucous laugh from the crowd, so again Maddie challenged. "Is no one willing to admit he paid Pawnee Mary for the use of her body?"

Not a single man volunteered, but several looked sheepish, as if this particular line of questioning struck a raw nerve. Maddie wondered what would happen if she had included Lily herself or some of the "girls" who worked in the saloon in her inquiry.

"Then I guess it's safe to say she *isn't* a whore, is she? However, she *is* an Indian and can't do anything about her heritage. Still, should she be punished for the sins of her people? If so, then it logically follows that we should also be punished for the bad things whites have done to Indians."

A number of people looked thoughtful and nodded their

heads, and Horace rose to his feet. "You're twisting things all around, Maddie McCrory. Such bleeding-heart sentimentalism has no place in a court of law. This . . . this *female* probably enticed those bounty hunters into attacking her, and when she only got what she deserved, she turned around and behaved like an animal, a typical savage. Our little community can hardly be considered safe when creatures like her are residing in or near it."

"You hypocrite!" Maddie hissed. "You hold yourself up as a pillar of this community, but . . ."

"I *am* a pillar of this community."

"What you are is a blood-sucking parasite, growing fat on the sustenance provided by *us,* the inhabitants."

"Just because you cannot make your mortgage payments and *personally* owe me a huge sum of money . . ."

"Oh, stop it, Horace! Just because I refuse to marry you, you've called due all my notes and threatened to cast my entire family out on the prairie. You proved what you are this morning when you sent your messenger boy to tell me I have three days' time to repay what I owe you . . . *three days.* Even if our stallion wins the race in Abilene, I'd be hard put to collect my winnings and give you the money in only three days."

"*I* will pay what she owes you," Chase interrupted. "As soon as someone releases me, I'll make sure you get your damn money, Brownley, every last cent of it. If I can't come up with the money, you can take my place instead."

"Why, what he's doing to Maddie, he did to *me!*" Alice Neff exclaimed, stepping forward and facing the crowd. "My late husband wasn't cold in the ground before Horace Brownley appeared on my doorstep and gave me *two* days to settle my debts. I asked for a bit more time, 'cause I couldn't raise the money that fast, and he turned around and foreclosed on me and took my farm right out from under me!"

"Alice! You never told me that," Moses growled like a slumbering bear suddenly stirred to life. "It was 'cause of Horace that you lost your farm and had t' move inta town and take in boarders?"

Alice Neff shot her suitor a disgusted look. "You never asked me what happened, Moses, but now, you know. Truth be told, I always wondered 'bout the company you choose t' keep and why Horace, of all people, is such a good friend of yours."

"Mr. Brownley did the same thing to me," another woman hollered from the back of the crowd. "Only he let on that if I'd jus' be a little *nicer* to him when he came around, the bank would carry me a while longer."

"So what did you do, Maud?" someone asked.

"Why, I got out my shotgun an' told him that if he insisted on usin' his influence t' get under my skirts, I'd be happy to blow his balls away fer his trouble."

"That's quite enough!" Horace thumped the table, growing redder by the minute. "None of this has any bearing on this particular case."

"Oh, yes, it does!" Maddie disputed. "I believe you've just demonstrated that a person isn't always as he or she *appears* to be. Indeed, appearances can be most deceiving. For years, folks around here have thought the worst of Pawnee Mary and the best of you, when it seems they should have done just the opposite. Buck Courtland, Chase's brother, has had to suffer from the same bias and unwarranted suspicions as Mary. If a person happens to *look* or act differently, or is perhaps temporarily down on his or her luck, they become vulnerable, and people like you take advantage. I guess rich folks tend to think they own the world and can do whatever they please to the rest of us. But we can prove them wrong, can't we?"

Maddie scanned the faces of the onlookers and could tell they were growing more supportive. "I say those bounty hunters came here looking for blood-money and that was their right. But when they went after Mary and used violence against her, they got what they had coming to them. Release both Chase *and* Mary, for neither are guilty of wrongdoing."

Cheers erupted, and people shouted: "She's right! Let the two of 'em go."

In the ensuing pandemonium, Moses got to his feet, hitched up his pants, and reached for his six-shooter. As he raised the gun, the crowd fell silent. Clearing his throat first, he glanced around the room. "I agree we can't hold Cumberland or this here Injun. Still, if we're gonna be legal, we gotta vote on it. When the circuit judge rides inta town, I hafta be able t' explain what happened in this case. I don't want him askin' questions I can't answer—like what was the jury's vote?"

"You're plumb right, Moses." Alice moved closer to him. "So let's vote and lay the matter to rest here and now."

Moses beamed at her praise. "All right, we'll make it simple. All those who think Cumberland and the Injun should be let go, raise yore hands."

A forest of hands sprang up in the saloon. Only Horace, Lily Tolliver, and Buck refrained from joining the rest. Then Mary helped Buck to raise his hand and Lily, with a flutter of long lashes and a heaving sigh, placed one hand on her ample bosom, and slowly raised the other.

With a shriek of delight, Maddie jumped down from the chair and hugged first Chase and then Mary, while the crowd applauded, hooted, and whistled. Intoxicated by her success, Maddie felt like laughing and crying all at the same time.

"This is intolerable!" Horace protested when the din had died down a little. "Only the jury should be allowed to vote on this issue. Not only that, but the rules of the court haven't been followed. *I* should be running these proceedings, not you, Moses. You've overstepped your bounds and made a mockery of the entire trial."

With a furtive glance at Alice, Moses drew a deep breath and puffed out his chest. "In Hopewell, what the town says goes, Horace. It ain't all up t' you, y' know. You helped me get this job, but it ain't you who's gonna help me keep it. This is as legal a trial as I've ever seen, and I aim t' swear to it."

"You'll be sorry," Horace threatened.

"No, I won't. I ain't got no farm you can take away, so save your threats for helpless females. . . . And if he *does* threaten any of you ladies, y'all let me know, and I'll put a stop to it."

"That's tellin' him, Moses!" Alice gazed up at her burly

suitor in wonder. "Land sakes, I never realized you could be so forceful."

"Sheriff, will you please release Mr. Cumberland now?" Maddie begged the preening lawman.

Moses nodded, and while he was busy with Chase's shackles, she dropped to her knees beside Mary who had suddenly bent over Buck in an attitude of great concern.

"Look," Mary whispered. "Silver Hair bleeding again. Bleeding bad."

Alarm clanged through Maddie. Fresh blood stained the bandage across Buck's midsection, and his face had gone even grayer, if that was possible.

Chase pushed his way between the two women. "My God, he's dying right in front of us. . . . Buck! Buck, can you hear me?"

Buck's eyes fluttered open. He seemed dazed and disoriented; obviously, he had no idea where he was or even that they were all bending over him.

"Must get him out of here," Mary snapped. "He need tending. I try again stop bleeding."

"But where can we take him?" Maddie clutched Chase's arm. "The journey into town in the buckboard did this; we didn't want to bring him, but he insisted."

Alice tapped Maddie on the shoulder. "My house ain't far from here. I'll turn the place over to the lot of you for as long as you need it. Take him there. I got everything you'll likely need, and I can go stay with friends."

"Must find medicine roots," Mary murmured. "Plants to heal him."

"Well, I can't say as I've got what you're lookin' for, but I planted a little herb garden out back last year. Thought a few herbs might come in handy in a town that ain't got its own doctor or pharmacy yet. You're welcome t' use whatever you think will do him some good."

"Someone help me lift this man," Chase beseeched. "Maddie, Mary, stand back."

Jake Bussel and a couple of others hurried to lend a hand, but before they lifted Buck, Moses suddenly intervened. "Where you takin' him?"

"To my house, Moses," Alice told him. "I said they could. . . . Can't you see? The man's bleedin' t' death before our very eyes."

"He should be taken t' jail. If he lives, he's gonna have t' go back t' Texas t' stand trial for that other murder—the one on them wanted posters."

"He didn't commit murder," Chase said. "Miss McCrory already explained what happened in Texas. Clint Madison's death was an accident; Buck didn't intend to kill him."

"That ain't for me or you t' say, Cumberland. It's the job of the folks in Texas t' decide what really happened."

"You just want to collect the reward money," Maddie accused. "*Look* at this man; he's suffered enough for whatever he's done. He's suffering now. He can't even speak to defend himself. Let the past go, Sheriff. Other than the reward money, there's no reason for you to take him back to Texas. It won't help anyone here. Please. Have some compassion."

"Maddie's right," Alice agreed. "Moses, you best let the poor man live—or die—in peace."

Surprisingly, Moses only grew more adamant. "No, Alice, honey, I can't look the other way on this. It ain't clear-cut. I'm not doin' this t' get the reward money. I'm doin' it 'cause it's my duty. What kind of lawman would I be if'n I didn't return an accused killer t' Texas?"

"But you understood about Mary and the bounty hunters," Maddie pointed out in exasperation. "Why can't you understand about Buck?"

" 'Cause this is different. It ain't my job t' decide on this case; it's only my job t' see he goes back t' Texas, and I'm bound and determined he will. Assumin' he lives, of course."

"Well, he's in no condition to escape, so you might as well let us take him to Alice's, instead of to jail," Maddie argued. "If we don't tend to him soon, he'll die while we stand here discussing it."

"Moses?" Alice touched the sheriff's sleeve. "At least, let him stay at my place for t'night—until this crisis is past."

"Oh, all right," he caved in. "He can go t' your house, Alice. But soon as he's lookin' better, he's gettin' locked up in jail. And soon as he can sit a horse, he's goin' back t' Texas. I'll come by t'morrow mornin' t' see how he's doin' and if he's still alive, we'll move him then."

"You're a hard, stubborn man, Moses," Alice complained. "Too bad I discovered it jus' when I was beginnin' t' like you. Now I'll have to think some more on what you been askin' me."

Distress crossed the sheriff's thick features, but he set his mouth firmly. "I can be pushed only so far, woman, and then I gotta do what I think is right."

Maddie almost mentioned the reward money again, but a look from Chase stopped her. Besides, she sensed that perhaps Moses Smith really was trying to guard his integrity. Beneath all his bluster, Moses might actually be the stuff from which honorable lawmen were made. If so, she didn't want to disturb a legend in the making.

By early evening, Buck was settled in Alice Neff's spare bedchamber, and Pawnee Mary, having done all she could to stop the bleeding, was seated beside the bed, a cup of tea in hand, keeping vigil. The cup held a strong-smelling concoction of plants and herbs that Mary intended to get down Buck, one sip at a time. Beside her on a small table was a simple meal of bread, ham, coffee, and a bowl of corn mush that Alice had provided before she departed.

Helpless to know what else they could do, Maddie and Chase hovered over Buck's still figure. Buck's coloring had improved, and the bleeding had stopped, but Maddie knew he wasn't safe yet. She could almost sense the presence of death in the room, waiting to claim Buck as soon as no one was looking.

"Oh, Mary," Maddie sighed into the silence. "Will he live, do you think?"

Mary's nursing skills had much impressed Maddie; she didn't understand the how or why of much of what the Indian woman had done, but it was plain Mary knew what she was doing. Of the herbs growing in Alice's garden, Mary had recognized all but two, which Alice claimed weren't natural to the area anyway. Even then, Mary had carefully questioned Alice as to their uses and inquired whether or not she might have a cutting from each to plant later for her own use. Alice had assured her she could.

Now, Mary seemed to be thinking hard before she responded to Maddie. At last, she simply shrugged her shoulders. "Is up to Tirawa."

"Tirawa? Do you mean God?" Maddie asked.

"Sky-Dweller," Mary confirmed. "Same one you call God. If Silver Hair live to see dawn tomorrow, I think he recover. Tonight, he fight for life."

"Then he should live, because Buck's a fighter." Chase rested a hand on his brother's foot where it tented the bed coverings. "Always was, even before his accident. Whenever we had some tough old range stallion to break, I took my time getting out the saddle, but Buck would rush to get his. He'd not only manage to saddle the animal, but he'd keep working with it until the rogue became the most quiet, willing horse on earth. He just wouldn't quit until he won the battle."

Pawnee Mary smiled, her eyes warm. "When he wake up, I tell Silver Hair he must saddle dawn this time. This fight no different. He must not quit."

Saddle the dawn, Maddie thought. What a quaint way of describing Buck's struggle!

Tears stung her eyes, and she turned away before Mary could see them. She prayed Buck would live, but even if he did, his battles weren't over. Moses would take him back to Texas and there, his enemies would try and hang him. . . . Poor Buck! And poor Mary. Surely, these two misfits deserved to enjoy the happiness they had so obviously found in each other, but the world would never allow it. Swept with sadness and dragging with weariness, Maddie quietly retreated.

"Call me, if you need me, Mary," she said, pausing in the doorway. "I . . . I suddenly feel the need to sit down."

Chase followed Maddie out of the bedroom, closed the door

on Buck and Mary, and caught Maddie by the elbow. "Maddie? Are you all right? You look a little pale."

Maddie dashed away a tear. "Oh, Chase, I just hope everything turns out all right for them! They've endured so much—and still have so much ahead of them. It isn't fair."

Chase drew her into his arms. She burrowed into him, wanting to be held, to be safe, and to assure herself that *he* was finally safe. He was here with her and not on his way to the noose hanging down from the big bur oak. She should be satisfied with that, yet her emotions were all topsy-turvy. Now that there was no longer a need for strength, she had none to spare. Her knees had grown weak and shaky, and she desperately needed comfort.

Holding her tightly to his warm hard body, Chase nuzzled her neck. "If anyone can save him, it will be Pawnee Mary," he whispered. "After that . . . I don't know. The Madisons are a powerful family. If Buck goes back to Texas, I'm afraid he'll hang—but I'll be damned if I know how to prevent that from happening. I'd risk an escape tonight, but Buck's far too weak. If we attempted it, he'd die for certain. . . . Besides, we'd just be on the run again. The bounty hunters will keep coming; as long as there's a reward on his head, men will keep hounding him."

"Is dying the only way he can escape?" Maddie wailed.

"I'm afraid so, sweetheart. . . . Damn! But I wish I could think of some way out of this mess for him and Mary."

Locked in each other's arms, they wept together. Maddie could feel Chase shuddering with silent sobs, while she at least had the female luxury of letting the tears flow unheeded. Once again, she wet his shoulder and shirt front, yet even in the midst of her sorrow, she reveled in the knowledge that she and Chase were together and could share this burden. Buck and Mary, on the other hand, faced being separated for all time.

Somewhere in the swirl of thoughts that assaulted her, Maddie found herself considering alternatives—possibilities for preventing Buck's return to Texas in the event he survived the coming night. She stopped weeping and started thinking, and a few moments later, gently pushed back from Chase.

Using his thumbs, Chase wiped the tears from her cheeks, his own face so emotion-ravaged that Maddie almost began weeping anew. She touched his jaw, her love for him so overwhelming it defied being put into words.

Yet she dare not think of love now—not while so much remained to be decided. To be planned. Later—when this problem was resolved—she promised herself to think of *nothing* but her feelings for Chase.

"What is it, Maddie? I can see in your eyes that you have an idea for saving Buck."

She was amazed. How had he come to read her mind so easily? "It's . . . it's probably a foolish one. I . . . I can't imagine how it could possibly work."

"What is it?" The flare of hope on his handsome features only increased her misgivings. He was likely to seize upon anything she suggested as workable, even if it wasn't.

"Don't get excited, Chase. I told you: I doubt it can succeed."

"Woman, you'll be the death of me! Tell me or I'll . . . I'll kiss you senseless until you do."

She liked that threat so much, she briefly considered putting it to the test. "Well . . ."

He grabbed her and gently shook her. "Maddie McCrory, speak up. I'll tell you whether or not I think your idea's a good one."

"Well, what if . . . what if we pretend Buck has died, even if he lives? And we . . . and we bury an empty coffin, while Buck recuperates someplace safe? Then, when he's better, he and Mary can . . . can go away together and start a new life together someplace else."

Chase stared at her a moment, as if he thought she might have lost her senses. But then, he smiled—a slow smile that was like the sunrise after a night of thunder, lightning, and heavy rain. "It could work. We could *make* it work. The idea's brilliant—so brilliant *I* should have thought of it."

"Well, you didn't. *I* did. And if it does work, I expect you to be everlastingly grateful and humble."

"Where can we get a coffin made around here?" Chase's mind

had already leapt ahead to the details while Maddie was still savoring his acclaim.

"Jake. Jake Bussel. He made my mother's from a supply of pine he keeps on hand at his forge. Then he decorated the lid with a scrolled design worked in iron. No one had ever seen anything like it; Pa was so proud to have my mother laid to rest in a fancy box, as he called it. Unfortunately, it took months to pay for it."

"Will you go and ask him to start making another? Tell him we don't think Buck's gonna make it, and we just want to be prepared."

"Then I should have him round up some gravediggers, too. Do you want to plan for the burial at your farm? Or should we have it at the little cemetery right outside town?"

"It's not called Boot Hill, like the burial grounds in Dodge City, is it?" Chase asked, frowning. "Seems like half the small towns in Kansas have a place called Boot Hill."

"That's probably because so many cowpokes die with their boots on. However, you needn't worry that ours is called Boot Hill; Hopewell has no hills, so we call ours Boot Prairie."

Chase groaned. "Maybe I'll take him back to the farm."

"Better not," Maddie cautioned. "The burial should be here where everyone can witness it. I'll ask Jake to make a simple marker, too, so that if any bounty hunters show up in the future, they can be shown the grave, with Buck's name on it. BUCK COURTLAND, and the date, July 14, 1877."

"In addition to all his other talents, does Jake conduct services?"

"No," Maddie said. "He balks at that. We'll have to do the service ourselves—or else get Mr. Grover to read a passage from the Good Book. He's done it at other funerals."

"While you're making those arrangements, I'd better figure out where we're gonna hide Buck. We need someplace near here, where he can safely rest until we can fetch him after dark with the buckboard."

"Look out back, Chase. I went out there with Mary to examine the herbs Alice had growing, and I saw a nice large springhouse, as well as a shed for animals, and a . . . you know."

"I'm not hiding my brother in a smelly old 'you know,' or a horse shed. I'll take a look at the springhouse. If it's big enough for a pallet, we'll move him there before first light tomorrow morning, then come back and get him tomorrow night."

"It should be easy to bring a buckboard around the back of the house, except we'll have to tell Alice what we're doing, or she's bound to notice."

"Alice!" Chase exclaimed. "We can't tell her; she'll tell Moses."

Maddie shook her head. "I don't think so. Leave Alice to me. If we had her cooperation, this would be so much easier. I think I can talk to her and see which way the wind is blowing before I reveal our plan. We're just lucky Alice lives near the edge of town. I'd hate to have to sneak down Main Street with Buck lying in the back of the buckboard."

"Don't worry about that. We'll find something to cover him; no one will even know he's there. When I get him home, Mary can nurse him in the barn."

"Or at my place. No one will think to look for him at my place, Chase, while they might take it in their heads to search yours, if they grow suspicious."

"Better yet, they can camp out on the prairie near one of our farms."

"They can use our wagon! The one we take to match races. It will be perfect."

Chase kissed the tip of Maddie's nose. "You know something, Miss McCrory? We make a hell of a team when we pull together—just like your two big wagon horses; what're their names?"

"Shovel and Hoe. Oh, Chase, if your brother lasts the night, we'll save him! And we'll give him and Mary a chance for happiness. Come on, we'd better get busy."

"Wait a minute. Before you go, I want to say something."

Chase's expression suggested it was something momentous—something Maddie had waited all her life to hear. She grew suddenly breathless and could hardly contain her excitement. "What?" she demanded.

"I think we need to . . . saddle our own dawn, Maddie, while we still have the chance."

"What do you mean?" Maddie wanted him to say it; she needed to hear it, especially if it was what she thought it was.

"Maddie, I love you. I need you. Regardless of what happens tonight—or tomorrow, or the day after that—regardless of anything else that might yet come between us, will you marry me?"

"Yes!" Maddie burst out, flinging her arms around him and almost knocking him over.

"Maddie, are you sure? You won't think of ten good reasons why we should wait, you won't conjure a dozen excuses . . ."

"No!" she cried. "I know what's important now, Chase. It's acknowledging our deepest feelings and cherishing each day we have together before it's snatched away forever. I don't even want to wait to get married; I want to be yours as soon as possible!"

She could feel Chase freeze against her. "What?" he croaked in a thick voice. "What did you say?"

She leaned back from him to gaze into his startled, disbelieving face. "Chase, let's make all our arrangements for Buck. Let's do all that must be done and help Mary if she needs any help. But then, if we still have time, well . . ." She nodded toward the wide bed in the second bedchamber, where Alice Neff's boarders usually slept. "I don't intend to sleep alone tonight, Chase . . . and there's only one extra bed. I don't care what anyone thinks or says. From now on, I want to be with you—in every way a woman can be with a man."

"My God . . ." Chase murmured in a tone of awe. "When you finally make up your mind, you don't hold anything back, do you?"

Smiling, she shook her head. "No, my love. When I make up my mind to saddle the dawn, I . . . *saddle the dawn.*"

"My God," he muttered again. Then he lowered his mouth to hers, and Maddie knew she had indeed caught the rising sun, flung her saddle over it, and set out to tame it and make it hers forever.

Twenty-two

"I'm right sorry t' hear that the white-haired feller probably ain't gonna make it. But maybe it's fer the best, Maddie. His future didn't look too bright anyhow," Jake Bussel said.

"Pawnee Mary hasn't given up hope yet, Jake, but . . . you know how unlikely it is that a man who's been gut-shot will survive."

"I'm plumb surprised he's lasted this long—an' you're right t' start plannin' his funeral ahead of time. Considering this heat, if he croaks t'night, you'll wanna git 'im in the ground as soon as possible. Takes time t' make a coffin though, even if it is jus' a plain pine box."

Jake wiped his sweaty face with a square of damp, soiled linen and peered at Maddie in the dim light. The sun had already set, and the evening had cooled, but Jake's forge, where he'd been working when Maddie found him, resembled the outer chamber of hell. She wondered how he could stand it. Of course, Jake wore no shirt, and his huge, hair-covered chest and belly gleamed in the reddish light as if he had been drenched in oil.

Maddie had always wondered why Jake had never married or shown an interest in women, and now she thought she knew. His line of work kept him filthy; the man always reeked of horses and sweat. It would take a special sort of female to overlook these drawbacks and appreciate the gruff but kindhearted soul who spent almost his entire life next to a hot fire.

"Is Cumberland gonna want the box fancied up like I done yer ma's?" Jake asked.

Maddie pondered the question a moment. It would be an expense Chase wasn't expecting, but the fancier the box, the more likely it was that people would accept Buck's death as reality; nobody would spend good money on a *fake* coffin. Besides, if it turned out to be a real funeral, Chase might appreciate the little extras when he sent his brother to his eternal rest.

"Perhaps something simpler than you did for my mother," she suggested. "I think Chase would like that."

"Well, I wasn't thinkin' of flowers or nothin' too fem'nine," Jake muttered. "I thought maybe . . . a bird. With its wings spread out like it was flyin' away."

Maddie smiled. Jake Bussel's bent for whimsy always surprised her; considering his appearance and line of work, she just didn't expect it. "No, not a bird—but maybe . . . a horseshoe. Buck always had a special way with horses."

"A horseshoe?" Jake's disappointment was obvious. "Hell, Maddie, I make horseshoes everyday. I was hopin' fer somethin' t' challenge me."

Maddie pictured Jake laboring throughout the night to build the coffin and decided he deserved some challenge. "Then *you* decide, Jake. I trust you to do a good job. Hopefully, we won't even need the coffin, so you'd better make something that will appeal to your next customer, too."

Jake shrugged his massive shoulders. "You're right 'bout that. Coffins are always needed sometime. That's why I took up the business—t' give me somethin' t' do when hosses ain't waitin' t' be shod."

"Thank you, Jake. You've been such a good friend—acting as stakesholder for our match races, doing all our iron work, and keeping our horses' feet trimmed."

Jake colored as red as his fire. "What're friends for if not t' help each other out? I always liked your pa and ma, and I'll be here for yer brother when he takes over the family business—and I'll always be *yer* friend, Maddie, even after you marry that feller, Chase, who beat you in the race."

Maddie's face burned with embarrassment. "How . . . how did you know that Chase has asked me to marry him?"

Jake's lips twitched, then he let loose a big guffaw. "I knew you was fated t' hitch up with him the day I first seen you two t'gether at that race. Why, you was strikin' sparks off each other like a hammer hittin' an anvil."

"We were doing no such thing!" Maddie denied, but as Jake continued grinning at her, she reconsidered.

Yes, they had been. From the moment she had first gazed into Chase's wolfish eyes, she had known she was lost; but stubborn as she was, it had taken her a long time to admit it.

"Well, I'd better be going now, and let you get back to work," she said, plucking at her skirt.

"I'll line up some gravediggers, too," he offered. "What you gonna do about the big race? Has Gold Deck gone t' Abilene yet?"

The race. Maddie hadn't thought about the race all day. She hadn't given much thought to Gold Deck, her father, sisters, or Little Mike either. Her mind had been occupied totally with saving Chase and his brother. The hours she'd spent worrying about the race now seemed like a distant dream, and the person who'd so much concerned herself with its outcome was practically a stranger. It was only a race, after all, and if her family lost everything they owned, they would just have to start over. Whatever happened, she would help them the best she could, but she would no longer devote her entire existence to fulfilling their every need and expectation. Never again would she sacrifice all her own hopes and dreams in order to make someone else's come true.

The last few days had changed her—rearranging her priorities. She loved her family as much as ever, but she also loved Chase. The time had finally come to start sharing her responsibilities and living her own life. If everyone in her family pitched in and did a little bit more, she could do a whole lot less, and everyone would still get along just fine.

"Jake, I have no idea if Gold Deck and Little Mike made it to Abilene or not. When I left home this morning, Gold Deck had the colic. I told my father he would have to handle it. If the stallion recovers, Little Mike and Carrie will take him to Abilene and race him. If not . . ." Maddie shook her head. "Well, there's nothing I can do about it. I had to be here in town today."

"You'll have to pay the forfeit—half the stakes money, and if Brownley's demandin' everything you owe him . . . why, Maddie, honey, yer family could lose everythin'."

"That's right, Jake. We could and probably will."

"An' what about Cumberland? Even if he left town first thing t'morrow mornin', he'd barely get t' Abilene in time to race his mare, and she'd be plumb tuckered out from the journey. He's gonna lose a big chunk of cash fer certain."

"In light of the past several days, I don't think he cares, Jake. Didn't you hear him offer to make good on my family's debts? I won't allow him to do it, but he said he'd hand over *his* farm in place of ours, to satisfy Horace. After a day like today, possessions tend to lose their importance, I guess."

"He didn't offer t' do that 'cause a noose was waitin' fer him, Maddie. He did it 'cause he's sweet on *you.*"

Maddie's cheeks heated anew. "Yes, well . . . I'll let you know in the morning if we need the coffin, Jake."

"Good luck, Maddie. Appears t' me, you could use a dose of luck right about now."

Back at Alice Neff's house, Maddie joined Chase and Pawnee Mary at Buck's bedside. "Everything's arranged," she whispered to Chase. "How's Buck doing?"

Chase's brother appeared to be sleeping, but perhaps he had simply lost consciousness. Maddie couldn't tell. However, his color had definitely improved. The skin across his cheekbones was lightly flushed, and his lips had lost the bluish cast that had been so frightening. Chase motioned her out of the room, but paused before following and rested a hand on Mary's shoulder.

"Mary, if there's any change, just holler, and I'll come runnin'."

Mary's eyes never left Buck's face, but she nodded. "He need rest. I think he better. By morning, we know."

"I'll be back before then and give you a chance to rest."

"No, better you sleep and I watch whole night, in case he need more medicine. If he get worse, I come get you."

"Whatever you think best." Chase gently squeezed Mary's shoulder, then departed, closing the door behind him.

In the main room, Maddie walked into Chase's waiting arms. "He looks so much better; I have a feeling he's going to live, Chase."

"I don't know; I hope so." Chase clasped her tightly to him. "He woke up once, looked right at me, but didn't recognize me."

"Did he know Mary?"

"I'm not sure. I think so. At least, when he looked at her, something flickered in his eyes. Whatever she's giving him, he went right back to sleep again."

"I'm so glad. Alice offered Mary some laudanum to ease Buck's pain, but Mary insisted on trying her own remedies first."

"If he lives, it'll be a miracle—due entirely to Mary."

"And to Tirawa, the Sky-Dweller."

Chase tilted up Maddie's chin and gazed into her eyes. "For the moment, there's nothing more we can do, Maddie. Mary will call us if there's any change in Buck. Barring that, you and I have several hours to ourselves. How do you think we should fill them?"

Maddie couldn't help smiling. He was giving her a chance to back out on her earlier offer, yet the blaze in his eyes told her he was hoping she meant to go through with it. She glanced toward the darkened doorway containing the unoccupied bed. No one had voiced any objection to the fact that two unmarried females would be sharing a house with two unmarried males. They had probably figured that Buck's condition precluded any immoral activities, but hadn't taken into account her own eagerness to be alone with Chase.

"It might be months before a preacher comes to town," she said. "They're a lot like circuit judges. Until Hopewell is big enough and settled enough to support the building of a church and a courthouse, people will have to wait for justice and to get married. . . . But I don't think I can stand to delay sharing a bed for that long."

"Then let's say our vows and be done with it. When a preacher finally does show up, he can make it all legal—but as far as I'm concerned, my word alone is as binding as any preacher can make it."

"Mine, too," Maddie agreed. "All right, I'll go first."

She hesitated a moment, formulating the words in her head and attempting to regain control of her suddenly erratic breathing. The words had to be just right. They had to express everything that was in her heart. Once said, they could never—would never—be undone. This was a lifetime commitment.

Gazing confidently into Chase's eyes, Maddie finally said: "I, Madeline Elizabeth McCrory, take you, Chase Ezekial Cumberland—also known as Courtland—to be my most cherished husband, to love and to honor, to have and to hold, from this day forward, for better or for worse, in sickness and in health, until death do us part. . . . There. Did I do it right?"

Chase grinned. "You're asking me? It sounded great. . . . except you forgot the part about obeying."

"I didn't forget; I deliberately left it out—and it will remain out. Unless you'd like me to amend it with something like 'I promise to always take your wishes into account, just as you promise to always consider *my* wishes.' "

"You strike a hard bargain, lady. But I'll go along with that, providing you add another part you forgot."

"What part? I didn't forget anything else."

"Yes, you did. You left out the part about worshipping me with your body. I consider that *real* important."

Joy bubbled up in Maddie. She felt she might burst with it. "Now *that* I can safely promise. . . . With my body, I thee worship, until death do us part."

"The same for me," Chase said quickly and bent to kiss her.

"No!" she exclaimed, pushing him away. "You have to say the actual words."

Sighing exaggeratedly, he grinned and said them. "I, Chase Ezekial Cumberland—also known as Courtland—take you,

Madeline Elizabeth McCrory, also known as Sassy—to be my lawful wedded wife . . ."

"Cherished," she prompted.

". . . my lawful, wedded, *cherished* wife."

Somehow, Chase got through the rest of it, adding at the end, a most definite ". . . and with my body I thee worship and all my earthly goods bestow."

By then, Maddie's tears were flowing, dribbling down her cheeks to plop unheeded on her bosom.

"Oh, Chase," she whispered. "I love you so. I'll always be true to you and cherish you and worship you . . ."

"That's what I like to hear," he answered jauntily. Then he lowered his voice and gave her a long warm look that curled her toes. "And that's exactly how I feel about you, sweetheart."

He took her hand and led her toward the darkened room and waiting bed. Closing the door to the main room, he stood before her and lifted his hands to her hair. Maddie couldn't see him very well, but she could feel him pulling pins from her hair until it tumbled down around her shoulders. As her eyes adjusted, her vision improved.

Enough starlight spilled through the open window near the bed to illuminate Chase's face and form. She leaned into him, sighing with pleasure as he shook out her long tresses and tugged his fingers through the tangles.

"I love your red hair," he murmured. "It suits you perfectly, and I hope all our children inherit it."

"I shouldn't tone it down with buttermilk?" she asked dreamily as a strange lassitude flowed through her.

"You do, and I'll tan your backside. I love your freckles, too, and tonight I intend to kiss every single one of them."

"Oh, my!" she breathed softly, for she had freckles in the most unlikely places. "I doubt you'll be able to find them all."

"I'll find them. . . . Let's get you out of these clothes so I can start looking."

In a matter of moments, he had divested her of every last stitch of clothing she wore, and he made her stretch out on the bed while he took the opportunity of removing his own garments.

"Oh, my!" she repeated, studying his body in all its emerging glory.

She had never dreamed that a naked man could be so beautiful. Men always seemed to be such rough, hairy brutes—admirable for their size, strength, and impressive muscles. But she had never made the connection between *man* and *beauty.* Never until Chase, that is. He redefined the word for her as he stood in a shaft of moonlight, watching her lie on the bed and licking his lips with hungry interest.

"God, you're lovely," he said, stealing her thoughts before she could voice them. "Just the way I imagined you would be—all soft curves and inviting hollows."

He is almost too beautiful to be real, she thought breathlessly and reached for him.

He joined her on the bed, stretching out beside her and propping himself on one elbow to lean over her. "Maddie, you aren't afraid, are you? Now that you've seen me, I mean. You aren't having . . . doubts."

She assumed he was talking about the part of him that was meant to go inside her. Rather than being fearful—or even repulsed, as his tone suggested—she was wildly curious. Even fascinated. She wanted to explore the lower half of his body most of all. Reaching out her hand, she boldly wrapped her fingers around the part in question.

He almost leapt off the bed. Obviously, he hadn't been expecting her to touch him. Disappointed, she let go. "Shouldn't I do that?" she whispered. "I just wanted to know what you—it—felt like."

"Maddie . . ." he said, gulping air as if he couldn't get enough of it. "Don't worry about what's right or wrong; there isn't any right or wrong between people who love each other. Feel free to do anything you feel like doing."

He took her hand and guided it back to where it had been. "Go ahead. Touch me if you want. I'm ready for you now . . . I think."

Maddie again wrapped her fingers around him. Such strength! Such power! He was exactly like a stallion. This was *man,* the giver of new life, the sower of seed, who carried the future of the universe in his loins.

It thrilled her to touch him, and she explored him eagerly. He remained perfectly still and allowed her to do it, though his heavy breathing suggested a barely contained duress. She even cupped his testicles in her hand and marveled at the cool weight of them. Not until he groaned suddenly did she realize that what she was doing might not be pleasing to him.

"Does it hurt?" she asked solicitously, stroking the length of his arousal. "It's so hard and swollen."

"No," he managed in a strangled voice. "But Maddie, you've got to stop now; I can't take much more of this."

"Why?" she inquired. All Maddie knew of the mating act was what she had witnessed in horses. What happened between humans was still a mystery. Oh, she understood the essentials, but the details completely eluded her—and she desperately wanted to make this a memorable night for Chase, this night of their wedding.

Suddenly, savage as any stallion, he pushed her hand away and rolled over on top of her. "Maddie, quit! Don't tease me anymore. Woman, I burn for you. Don't you know that? In a minute, I'll be mounting you. I won't be able to wait. And you aren't even ready for me."

"But I am, Chase. I'm lying here naked. Of course, I'm ready for you. I *want* you to mount me and . . . and make me your own."

He expelled a heavy sigh. "Sweetheart, you haven't the least idea what I'm talking about, do you? First, I have to . . . to do certain things to you, to get you ready for me. To make your body ready."

"You mean so I'll . . . wink at you? Or whatever it is that women do to indicate their willingness to be bred?"

"Oh, God," he sighed. "Yes, something like that."

"But what shall I do?"

"Nothing. Just lie there, Maddie . . . and let yourself *feel.* That's all I want you to do."

"Certainly, Chase."

She lay still then and waited for him to do something—and after a long moment, he did. He began to kiss her. Slowly. Gently. Then with rising fervor. With his tongue, he coaxed her to open her mouth. She did, and he touched his tongue to hers. It gave her a curious—and wonderful—sensation in her lower abdomen.

His hand found her breasts and what he did there felt wonderful, too. . . . Oh, my, it was all wonderful! The kissing and touching and stroking. She opened to him like a flower unfolding its petals in the sun, her body responding in ways she could never have imagined. His mouth moved from her hands to her breasts, and she arched against him in a frenzy of sudden need and longing.

While his mouth plundered her breasts, his hand caressed her thighs. His fingers slipped between them. He touched her intimately, probing inside her, and she bucked in astonishment.

"Easy. Easy, sweetheart," he murmured.

"I'm all right," she assured him. "It's just . . . I feel so . . ."

"Tell me what you like," he whispered. "Tell me what feels good to you."

"That," she answered simply, as he slid a finger back and forth. "And that, too . . ."

Everything he did she liked!

"Sweetheart, I want to kiss you down there—to taste you."

"Chase . . . oh no!" she cried as he held her down and did it anyway.

Then she was lost. All sanity fled, and there was only feeling. Delicious sensations. Wondrous pleasure. Growing need. Spiraling excitement. She wanted . . . needed . . .

She was growing desperate.

Chase slid upward. His mouth descended on hers. She clawed at his back . . . wanting *something* . . . wanting . . . waiting. And then he gave it to her. With one fierce plunge he was inside her. Swift and sharp, the pain took her breath away. She cried out, and he soothed her with kisses. Blinking back tears, she clung to him. He filled her completely and then some. He was huge—enormous. He had torn her apart. . . . Good heavens, what would happen now?

"It's all right," he said. "Don't cry. It will never hurt like this again."

"No wonder mares kick," she wailed. "I'd kick too, if I could."

"Shhhh," he murmured.

She could feel him smiling, his lips curved upward against her temples. It wasn't fair. *He* wasn't hurting; *she* was.

"I'll make it feel better," he promised.

"How?"

"Trust me. I love you, Maddie. I'd never do anything to hurt you. You know that don't you?"

"You've already hurt me."

"Only this once. I swear it. From now on, you'll *love* what I do to you."

"Prove it. I'm still waiting."

He chuckled deep in his throat. "That's my feisty Maddie, the sweetest, sassiest, sexiest woman alive."

He began to move against her. *In* her. At first, it still hurt. Then, suddenly, it didn't. He rose above her, resting on his elbows, taking his weight off her, and thrust slowly and deeply. In and out. He set up a rhythm. It began to feel good again. It began to feel wonderful. She raised her hips off the bed and met his thrusts with little thrusts and wiggles of her own.

"That's it," he praised. "That's my good girl. Come on, Maddie. You can do it."

Do what? she wondered. And then she *knew.* It was starting again—that wondrous pressure. That exquisite need for relief. That building excitement. The sense of growing, expanding, reaching out, and becoming one with Chase. Oh, Lord! He pumped harder and faster. She pumped harder and faster. Together, they strained for the pinnacle . . . and together, they slipped over it.

Oh, it was too much! It was exquisite!

No wonder mares sometimes backed up to stallions, requesting to be serviced.

"Chase . . ." she murmured. "Oh, Chase . . ."

"What?" he answered, his tone hoarse, his breathing still ragged.

"Is this what heaven will be like, do you think?"

"If it isn't, it *should* be, sweetheart. Heaven could hold nothing finer."

"Was it like this when you did it with . . . other women?"

He stiffened above her, but she wouldn't allow him to pull away.

"Tell me, Chase. I need to know."

He leaned back, stroked her hair, and gazed down at her. "I swear to you, Maddie, what we just did was *nothing* like I've ever done with another woman. I won't lie and say I've never lain with a woman before now, but those women weren't you. And I didn't care about them, not like I care for you. So it's all different. All fresh and new and . . . healing."

"Then I forgive you for ever mounting another woman, Chase. I just couldn't bear it if I ever thought you had shared *this* with someone else."

"*This* doesn't happen with just anyone," he asserted. "*This* can only be experienced by two people who truly love each other and intend to spend the rest of their lives together."

"Chase," she whispered, her voice gone husky. "Let's do it again."

"Already? Maddie, honey, I don't know if I can. I need a little time to . . ."

"Yes, you can," she urged, moving against him, squeezing him eagerly.

A low groan escaped him. "Maddie, you're insatiable . . ."

"Yes," she agreed. "I've waited a long time for this, Chase, and I once thought I'd never have it."

"Well, you've got it now, sweetheart—all the lovin' you can ever handle."

He began to thrust again, and she could feel him swelling, growing larger inside her. Wrapping her arms and legs around him, she surrendered to the special magic only Chase could create—and the second time was even better than the first, because this time, she *knew* what she wanted, and she set out to achieve it for herself and most of all, to give it to *him.*

A long time later, Maddie lay sleeping—her dreams filled with a peace and contentment she had never known until now. Snuggled in a cocoon of warmth and happiness, she never wanted to wake up again. With Chase beside her, still *in* her, her dreams had all come true, and she desired nothing more of life but the chance to savor her new-found rapture.

But it was not to be. A tapping sound woke her, and she jerked upright, elbowing Chase in the side as she did so. Just as her befuddled mind registered that someone was knocking on the closed door to the room, Chase sprang from the bed.

"I'm coming, Mary!" he shouted. "I'll be right there."

In the darkness, he fumbled for his trousers, cursed when he couldn't find them fast enough, yanked the sheet off Maddie and wrapped it around his waist, then thought better of it and struggled into his trousers, after all.

"Buck," was all he said. "I told her to come get me if he took a turn for the worse."

Opening the door, he rushed out. Maddie dove for her own clothing. A terrible sense of guilt and foreboding filled her. While she had been dreaming pleasant dreams, Buck might have been breathing his last. Somehow, she managed to struggle into enough garments to be decently attired. She didn't bother with her hair. Barefoot, she fled the room.

It wasn't yet morning. Darkness still shrouded the house. The only light came from the room where Buck lay dying. Maddie was certain he was dying, if he hadn't already died. She entered the room with her heart thudding in her throat—only to find Chase and Mary, one on either side of the bed, smiling down at a wan-faced Buck, who was smiling back at them.

"I see you're still here, big brother," Chase was saying, looking mightily relieved. "And you know who I am, too."

Buck nodded, his gaze on Chase's face. Grimacing, he lifted his hand and pointed to his stomach.

"I know. Hurts like hell, doesn't it?" Chase sympathized.

Buck nodded again.

"But you're still looking much better. Mary's kept you alive."

Buck's hand moved on the bed, seeking Mary's. When he found it and laced his fingers through hers, he sighed and closed his eyes again. Mary bent down and kissed his knuckles, then gently extricated her hand and motioned Chase and Maddie from the room.

"He's going to live, isn't he?" Maddie burst out as soon as she could do so without disturbing Buck.

In the front room, Mary nodded and wearily sank down on a chair. "Tirawa smile on us. Silver Hair still live, and dawn come soon. He tell me he want see Son of Wolf. That why I wake you."

"I'm glad you did," Chase said. "It's time we put our plan into action."

"What plan?" Mary's head rose. Her nostrils flared. "Silver Hair weak. No can move him yet—or good chance he still die."

Chase exchanged glances with Maddie, who suddenly realized that perhaps they ought to have shared their plan with Mary before this. She didn't know why she hadn't thought to do so—except that last night, Buck's survival was highly in doubt, and all of Mary's energies were focused on that. Now that it appeared he might live, Mary would just have to refocus her energies.

"Mary," she began. "Hear me out before you make up your mind on this. We . . . we want to make it look as if Buck has died."

"What?" Mary frowned in confusion.

"So the two of you can go away together—and Buck will never be hunted down again."

Light flared in Mary's eyes, banishing the weariness, and a

radiant smile curved her lips. "Tell me what to do," she said. "I do anything."

Maddie nodded to Chase. "You explain while I find my shoes. Then you'd better see about fetching that coffin."

Twenty-three

The coffin took up half the main room of Alice Neff's little house. Resting on the seats of two wooden chairs in the center of the room, the long box filled the air with the scent of fresh-cut pine. Maddie watched anxiously as Chase thanked Jake Bussel for doing such a fine job on it and promised to pay him as soon as possible.

"Take all the time you need, Cumberland. I figure yer good fer the money. An' the truth is, I enjoyed makin' the runnin' horse t' go on top of the box."

"It's a beautiful coffin," Maddie assured the burly blacksmith. She was glad Buck was never going to occupy it but felt guilty about their deception, especially now that she had seen all the work Jake had put into the box. "You outdid yourself with the design of that horse, Jake."

On the lid of the coffin, which Jake had removed and propped in a corner soon after he, Chase, and two other men had carried the coffin into the house, was a lovely replica of a galloping horse. Done in a simple outline of iron, the running horse conveyed a sense of freedom—as if death represented escape. Maddie was much impressed.

"My brother would have appreciated your artistry," Chase commented, studying the coffin lid. "And I'm more grateful than I can say that you made the effort to do something special for him."

"My pleasure, Cumberland," Jake said gruffly. Turning to

Maddie, he asked: "You need any help gettin' the body inta the box?"

Maddie quickly shook her head. "No. We . . . we still have to wash and dress him, Jake. When we're finished the three of us can manage, I'm sure."

"Oh, I fergot. Pawnee Mary's still here, ain't she?" Jake nodded toward the closed bedroom door.

"Yes. Mary cared for Chase's brother a great deal. She thought she could save his life and is taking it hard that she couldn't. She . . . ah . . . wanted to be alone with him for a while; Indians have their own ways of mourning, you know."

"Tell 'er I'm real sorry he died," Jake muttered, self-consciously studying his feet. "For her sake, I mean. Seems t' me the man hisself has just up and gone t' a better place."

"I'll be sure and tell her, Jake. Thanks."

An awkward silence descended. As the three of them stood there looking at each other, Maddie hoped Jake wasn't getting suspicious. Then Jake cleared his throat, which sounded like a gun going off in the room and made Maddie jump.

"Uh. . . . What time you want me back here t' help carry out the coffin fer the burial? I got men already diggin' the grave. They didn't wanna start 'til it got light, but now that the sun's come up, they don't mind so much bein' out at Boot Prairie by theirselves."

"Give us a couple hours," Chase told him. "By then, we should be ready. If the sheriff doesn't get here first, I'll have to go over and tell him about Buck's death, and as soon as the mercantile opens, Maddie wants me to get Buck some new burial clothes. What he was wearing won't do, she says."

Maddie nodded. "Your brother should be dressed properly, in a new shirt, at least. That's the least we can do for him, Chase."

"I'm sure glad you're here to handle the details, Maddie," Chase sighed. "If it was up to me alone, Buck wouldn't have nearly such a nice burial. I would never think of all these things."

"Yep. Womenfolk know how t' do things up right and proper," Jake Bussel agreed. "You got a Good Book t' read from?"

"I found Alice's," Maddie said. "All I have to do now is select some readings."

"Then I guess everything's under control—except fer the food. If you need a hand puttin' on a spread fer the mourners, Maddie, I could maybe talk t' some of the other women and . . ."

Unaware they were anxious for him to leave, Jake couldn't seem to offer enough assistance.

Maddie waved a hand dismissively. "Oh, Mary and I will take care of everything. We don't anticipate many mourners, since no one around here really knew Buck, except for the three of us."

"Sad," Jake said, shaking his head. "Real sad. Well, I'll see y'all back here 'bout two hours from now."

He ambled toward the front door, and Maddie exhaled with relief to see him finally depart. Just before dawn, they had moved Buck into the springhouse, and ever since then, she had felt as if she might jump out of her skin at any moment. Duplicity went against her nature, especially when it came to friends like Jake Bussel, who had put himself out for her sake.

As soon as he was gone, she opened the door to the bedroom. "He's finally gone, Mary. Let's get to work before anyone else shows up."

They had decided to weight the coffin with large, heavy stones wrapped in squares of blanket, so they wouldn't rattle. Maddie had already cut up an old blanket, and they had found some big stones piled behind the springhouse and toted them inside while it was still dark. So far, their plan was working, but the real test would come when the sheriff appeared.

Hopefully, they still had at least an hour before that happened, and if they were lucky, Chase would be able to waylay Moses before he arrived. By the time Chase had made the rounds to the jail and the mercantile, the news would be all over town. But before people began arriving to extend their sympathies, they intended to have the coffin nailed shut, precluding the possibility of anyone actually viewing the body.

Maddie worried that Moses would insist on seeing it. She didn't trust the sheriff one bit; being the suspicious type, he could make things difficult. Chase had concocted a scheme to distract Moses, but Maddie wasn't sure it would work. Until the coffin was safely buried in Boot Prairie, she couldn't relax, as anything could happen to spoil Buck's chance of escape.

They worked quickly, loading the box with the blanket-wrapped stones and were nearly finished when a knock sounded at the front door.

"Damn!" Chase swore. "It's still too early for the sheriff to be here. Hell, the mercantile isn't even open yet. Jake must have gone over and told Moses. Hurry up, and let's set the lid in place before you answer the door, Maddie."

They had barely fitted the lid on the coffin when the door suddenly opened, and Alice Neff poked her head inside. "Anybody up yet? I brought some fresh-baked bread over for . . . land sakes!"

Carrying a large, cloth-draped basket, Alice stepped into the front room. "Didn't make it, did he? Too bad. I was afraid this would happen; gettin' shot in the stomach is almost always fatal."

Maddie hurried to take the basket from the older woman. "He died during the night, Alice. We . . . ah . . . just put him in the coffin that Jake brought over a while ago."

Chase rested both hands on the coffin lid, his head bowed in an attitude of grief, while Mary closed her eyes, tilted back her head, and released a high keening wail. Alice's eyes widened, and she stepped back, while Maddie carried the basket of fresh bread over to the table, which had been pushed to one side to make room for the coffin.

"Thanks so much for the bread," Maddie whispered, returning to Alice. "It was thoughtful of you to bring it by so early this morning."

"Goodness, that wailing makes the short hairs on the back of your neck prickle, don't it?" Alice confided, leaning closer. "What did you find to bury the poor feller in?"

The question stymied Maddie, who thought the answer was self-explanatory. "Bury him in? Why, this coffin, of course. Jake made it on the chance it might be needed."

"No, I mean what did you dress him up in? As I recall, he wasn't even wearin' a shirt."

"A. . . . no, you're right, he wasn't. As soon as the mercantile opens, Chase is going to buy something for him," Maddie responded, flustered.

"Oh, no need fer that," Alice protested. "Have you forgot about my late husband's clothes? Why, I got a brand new shirt in the chest in my bedroom. I sewed it up special fer him, but he died before I could give it to him, and it ain't big enough through the belly fer Moses. Jus' let me get it, and I'll help you put it on him."

She bustled past Maddie. "If the poor man ain't dressed properly fer his own burial, why did Chase already put the lid on the coffin? Tell him t' take it off while I fetch the shirt. You need clean trousers, too? I might still have a pair in that chest. I just hate t' throw out anything useful."

Maddie helplessly shrugged her shoulders and rolled her eyes at Chase, then followed Alice into the bedroom. She had to think of something fast, because Chase's expression told her he didn't know what to do either. Alice had surprised them before they were ready.

While Alice rummaged through the chest, Maddie gnawed her lower lip in indecision. She still hadn't made up her mind what to do when Alice gleefully held up a white shirt and crowed: "Here 'tis! And it's got some mighty fine stitchin' on it, too. I think you'll agree, Maddie. It oughta be a fair fit. If it ain't, we can make some quick adjustments. . . . Why, Maddie, honey, what's wrong?"

Maddie acted on sudden impulse. "Alice, I need to tell you something."

Quickly, she explained what they were doing and why. Alice listened open-mouthed, then snapped her mouth shut and shook her head when Maddie finished. Praying she had said all the right things, Maddie waited for her reaction.

"I guess I can understand why you're doin' this, Maddie McCrory, but don't you think the springhouse is a piss poor place t' hide a man as sick as Mr. Cumberland's brother?"

"You . . . you think we should hide him someplace else?"

"It'll be at least several days before you can risk movin' him in a buckboard, an' he can't lie out on a stone floor fer that long. T'night, we'll have t' sneak him back inta the house, where me and Mary can nurse him proper until he's fit enough t' travel. Then y'all can take him out on the prairie and let him recuperate in yer pa's race wagon like you plan."

Maddie was so relieved she almost burst into tears. "Oh, Alice, thank you! I was so afraid you wouldn't approve, and here you are, offering to help us."

"Land sakes, I thought I'd made it clear yesterday where my sympathies lie. That poor man has suffered enough fer whatever he did or didn't do down in Texas. Moses is stuck on doin' his duty, but that don't mean I hafta go along with it. I'm proud of him fer takin' a stand, but I got my own ideas of what's right, and I might be jus' the help you need t' carry this whole thing off."

"Oh, Alice, you're wonderful!" Maddie hugged the little woman, but Alice brushed her off as if her behavior were hardly remarkable. "Go tell that Injun t' quit that awful wailin'—or at least, t' save it 'til Moses shows up, and she's got someone t' impress."

An hour later, the sheriff *did* show up. Chase was about to leave the house before him, but no sooner did he open the front door when Moses Smith came huffing and puffing up the front steps, accompanied by—of all people!—Horace Brownley.

"We come t' get the prisoner," Moses pompously announced. "I already wired the authorities in Texas that I got Buck Courtland in custody, and they wired back that I better keep my eye on him 'cause he's about as slippery as a greased pig in a hog-catchin' contest."

Horace Brownley plucked at his collar and glared at Maddie who had stepped out on the porch right behind Chase. "As the mayor and acting magistrate, I've come along to make certain the prisoner goes to jail immediately. We can't have him loose in Hopewell. Indeed, I've told Moses that it's *my* job t' claim the reward money on behalf of the entire town. Moses is just doing his duty, after all. Therefore, it's not right he collect."

Chase's gaze flicked them up and down as if they were rotten eggs fouling the air he was breathing. "Sorry, but you're too late, gentlemen. My brother died during the night."

Horace and Moses exchanged stunned glances. "He up and died on us?" Moses demanded as if he didn't quite believe it.

"Can't you hear Pawnee Mary grieving?" Maddie nodded toward the open doorway. "The poor woman is beside herself with grief."

Right on cue, Mary's wail pierced the morning quiet; she sounded like a cat whose tail had been caught under a rocking chair, except the noise was more eerie. Moses' face flushed and so did Horace's. Horace turned to Moses and elbowed him in his beefy side.

"Better take a look at the body to make certain the man's really dead."

"Really, Horace . . ." Maddie began, but Moses was already attempting to shove his way past Chase.

"Let me in, Cumberland," the sheriff insisted. "I gotta examine the deceased and confirm his identity."

Chase stubbornly held his ground. "Sheriff, we've already nailed the coffin shut, and if I were you, I wouldn't open it."

"Jus' why in hell not? You ain't gonna try and convince me he died of some contagious disease, are ya? The man was gut-shot, so's I can understand why he might be dead—but I gotta see fer myself."

"No, Sheriff, I'm not trying to put something over on you." Chase eyed him steadily. "I had intended to wait to nail down the lid until you got here. Actually, I was just coming to fetch you. But Pawnee Mary was making such a fuss I had to nail the lid down tight to keep her from making off with my brother's body while I was on my way over to the jail. She wants to bury him Indian-style—wrapped in skins and hoisted up to lie on a platform out on the prairie."

"Is that so?" Moses warily inquired, and Maddie could see

he half-believed the story. "I always did hear that Injuns had strange burial customs. This just goes t' prove it, don't it?"

"How ridiculous!" Horace shook his finger at Chase and Maddie. "Do you take us for fools? We're not leaving here 'til we see the dead man's corpse."

"Then be my guests," Chase said smoothly, stepping aside. "I hope you brought a crowbar."

Just then a loud commotion occurred inside the house. "Stop it, Mary! Stop it, I say!" Alice screeched. "Mr. Cumberland! Maddie! Come quick! Mary's cut off half her hair, and now she's tryin' t' pry the lid off the top of the coffin!"

Everyone on the porch rushed into the front room where Mary was indeed playing her part with a wild abandon that shocked even Maddie. Wielding a large knife, Mary *had* cut off huge hunks of her hair which lay scattered about the room, and now she was frantically prying at the lid of the coffin, while Alice tried to stop her.

"Mary, honey, you can't *do* this! It ain't right. Buck's a white man, and he should be buried according to white customs, not some pagan Indian rites." Alice turned on Moses. "Moses, stop her! She's tryin' t' get in the coffin, and if she succeeds. . . . Why, the body was already startin' t' smell."

Moses grabbed hold of Pawnee Mary and wrestled her away from the coffin. "Somebody take away that knife!" he shouted, and Chase obligingly snatched it. "Now, you get a hold of yourself, woman! You hear me?"

Abruptly, Mary quit struggling, and Moses, gasping for breath, stepped back from her. "There. That's better. What'n hell's the matter with you? This ain't no Injun reservation; this is a white town, an' we got our own burial customs."

"Hah!" Pawnee Mary snorted. "Silver Hair my man. He should be buried *my* way. I want take him out on prairie. Build platform. Bury him where spirit can roam free."

"His brother wants him buried *his* way," Moses told her.

"In Boot Prairie," Chase added. "The grave's already been dug, and we plan to hold the burial later this morning. I already told you that, Mary. . . . Please cooperate. It will be a nice ceremony."

"Open box," Mary insisted. "Give me body. If not let me take out on prairie, I build platform in tree. Put him there."

"Tree? What tree?" Horace croaked. "There's no trees around here, except for our big bur oak."

"Then I put him there," Mary said stonily. "Is better burial place than dark hole in ground. When bones rot, I take away and hide."

"You can't leave a dead body up in a tree in the middle of town until its bones rot!" Horace was aghast at the notion. He turned to Alice. "Is it true? The body's already beginning to . . . to deteriorate?"

Alice nodded, her face grim, but Maddie detected a tiny twinkle in the woman's eye. Alice was thoroughly enjoying herself. She leaned closer to whisper in Horace's ear. "It's bad, Mayor Brownley. Real bad. I didn't want my house—you know—contaminated, so I urged Mr. Cumberland to hurry up and close the coffin permanent."

Alice whirled to confront Moses. "If you want t' verify there's a body in there, Moses, just ask me. I helped put Buck's shirt on. Had a time of it, too, 'cause he was all stiff and hard t' handle, and the stench was makin' me ill. Sorry, Chase, but that wound of his seemed to speed up the decay. If y'all are gonna open up this box, you're gonna have t' take it out on the porch first, 'cause I don't want any noxious fumes in my front room."

Chase glanced at Moses. "Sheriff? If you still insist on opening the coffin, you and Brownley and I can probably get it out onto the porch."

"Yes," Pawnee Mary said. "I help. You open box and give me body. Smell not bother me."

"No!" Horace burst out. "I forbid it. I absolutely forbid it. There will be no opening of this coffin. Furthermore, I think it should be buried as soon as possible. We'll have no heathen rituals either. Do you understand that, Pawnee Mary? If you make a fuss about the way Mr. Cumberland wishes to bury his brother, I'll have you thrown in jail."

"Wait a minute, Horace." Moses held up his hand. "It's not for you to say who goes t' jail or not. That's *my* job. I may have t' lock her up for interferin' in a funeral, but if I do, it'll be *my* decision, not yours."

"Well, of course. I just meant . . . that is . . ."

"You may be the mayor and banker, but *I'm* the sheriff," Moses added, and Alice Neff beamed her approval.

"No need put me in jail," Pawnee Mary said. "Since you refuse me, I go now. Shake dust of this town from my moccasins forever. No more you see my face."

"Oh, Mary, please try and understand," Maddie pleaded. "We don't want you to leave the area; we just want . . ."

"Yes, we do," Horace interrupted. "Your departure is for the best. You're an undesirable element in Hopewell."

"So are you, Horace!" Alice snapped, looking as if her patience had come to an end "Fact is, Hopewell don't need *you,* either. I been talkin' t' folks, and before I'm through, I aim to do some more talkin'. We're thinkin' of startin' our *own* bank and puttin' *you* out of business."

"You can't do that! I'm also the mayor. Have you forgotten?"

Alice shook her head. "Nope. Not hardly. But we're gonna do somethin' 'bout that, too, come next election. Jake Bussel might be persuaded t' run fer the office, an' if he won't do it, I got a few other good men in mind, includin' Mr. Cumberland here."

"Interesting as all this is, Alice," Chase cut in. "We have a funeral to conduct. Mary, I hope you'll stay for it, because my brother truly cared for you."

"All right, I stay," Mary reluctantly agreed. "But after burial, I leave this place. Go far away. . . . Give knife back now. I no try open box again."

Moses was immediately suspicious. "If you ain't gonna pry at the coffin again, why do you need that knife? Chase, don't give it to her."

"So I can cut off little finger," Mary responded. "Old Indian custom. Cut off finger to mourn dead loved one."

Everyone stared at her. Maddie silently applauded her friend's acting ability, but at the same time, she hoped that Indian cultural practices didn't include such barbaric rituals. Horace blinked like an owl: only Moses had the presence of mind to protest.

"Well, you ain't gettin' that knife 'til the burial's over, an' if I catch you cuttin' off yer little finger, I'll take the knife away fer good. Cumberland? Give *me* the knife."

Chase silently handed it over. Even he looked impressed by Mary's performance.

"You no catch me, white man," Mary softly scoffed. "When I do it, I be far, far away from here."

The promise sent a shiver down even Maddie's spine.

"Well!" Horace harrumphed. "Since matters have apparently been resolved here, I must get back to the bank now. But before I go, Miss McCrory, I must remind you that time is running out for you and your family. That money you owe me is due tomorrow."

"I must remind *you* that tomorrow is Sunday," Maddie retorted. "Is the bank now open on Sundays?"

Horace frowned and shook his head. "Seems I forgot about the weekend. Then it will be due on Monday. . . . No, wait. The bank will be closed Monday, Tuesday, and Wednesday for renovations. The roof leaks, and we're replacing it."

"Good, that gives me more time. Maybe by Thursday I'll *have* your money."

"You'll have it," Chase promised in a low growl that vibrated with anger. "I'll make sure you have it."

Now wasn't the time to argue with Chase, so Maddie didn't bother, and she was spared any further discussion of the matter by Alice Neff's intervention.

"Horace Brownley, your high-handedness is exactly why I'm gonna start a campaign t' get rid of you. It ain't just me you treated so shabbily, but everyone else, and we've all had about enough of it."

"This is *business,*" Horace said, red-faced. "And I've a perfect right to run my business in as prudent a manner as possible."

"And we have a perfect right to take *our* business elsewhere if 'n we don't like it. . . . But that battle can wait, I suppose. Moses, will you be here t' escort me t' the funeral?"

Moses broke into a wide grin. " 'Course I will, Alice, honey. I'd be right proud to escort you anywhere you'd like."

"To Boot Prairie will be fine for now."

"Then Boot Prairie it'll be."

"And afterwards, I'll go with you when you wire the authorities in Texas that Buck Courtland has gone to meet his Maker."

"What?" Moses frowned. "Oh, sure. Guess I gotta do that, too, don't I? They'll be sorry t' hear it, 'cause they sure wanted t' get their hands on him. Seems the Madison family is real influential down there."

Maddie watched the play of fleeting expressions on Chase's face. She wished she could hug him right then and there. Buck's nightmare of running was ending; all they had to do now was bury this empty coffin and make certain no one discovered that Buck still lived.

Horace and the sheriff departed, but Maddie, Chase, Pawnee Mary, and Alice didn't waste time savoring their moment of triumph. Too much still remained to be done. Mary and Alice headed for the springhouse to check on Buck, while Maddie gave her attention to food preparation, and Chase went to fetch the buckboard to carry the coffin to Boot Prairie.

An hour later, they held the funeral service. Amazingly, many of the townspeople turned out for it. Somewhere in the middle of a biblical reading conducted before they left the house, Maddie realized that everyone had come to show their support not only for her, but also for Chase and Alice, and maybe even for Pawnee Mary.

Weddings and funerals brought folks together as nothing else could, she mused, except perhaps for a match race or a good old Kansas barn-raising. She glanced around at the still, silent faces of the onlookers. The Grovers were there, and Jake, Jefferson Potts, Amos Pardy, Hiram Garret, Lily Tolliver and two of her saloon girls had also attended.

Moses stood next to Alice, who had taken his arm, but Horace Brownley and Elwood, his clerk, were conspicuously absent, and

Maddie heartily wished she never had to see either one of them again.

Closing her eyes, she listened to Chase's calm voice describing the Good Shepherd caring for his flock of sheep. Something about horses would have been more appropriate, but she hadn't been able to find any biblical passages mentioning ranching, horse racing, or breeding.

Closing the book, Chase said: "I suppose this is as good a time as any to mention my brother's good qualities. I haven't conducted too many burials, so I'm not really sure of the order of things. However, I *can* tell you about Buck—or the man Pawnee Mary calls Silver Hair."

He went on to describe several youthful incidents in which Buck had guided Chase on his journey to manhood, ending with the tragic incident that had left Buck impaired. "My brother didn't know when he rode out to help me bring in those cattle that his life was about to change—and not for the better." Chase caught Maddie's eye. "But if he *had* known, he still would have done it; he was that kind of man. And that kind of brother. But the most remarkable thing about him was that *after* it happened, he never once blamed me for being out in that storm in the first place. He never showed any regret or resentment. Never took out his anger or disappointment on *me.* I can only hope and pray that he's in a happier place now—and that his happiness will last forever."

Maddie's eyes filled with tears as she, too, prayed for Buck's—and Mary's—future happiness.

"A-men," Lily Tolliver announced in a loud voice, and everyone else echoed her.

When the time came to take the coffin to its final resting place, Jake Bussel handled the loading of it into the buckboard, then asked Chase and Maddie if they wanted to ride up on the seat with him or follow behind on foot. Chase chose walking, and he and Maddie held hands as they led the little procession of mourners down Main Street.

Mary walked beside them, her head held high, her emotions concealed behind her usual inscrutable expression. When they reached the newly dug grave site in the little patch of wooden crosses and other simple markers, Mary refused to join them beside the grave. Still playing her role, she stood off to one side and gazed out at the prairie shimmering in a haze of heat and sunlight.

Chase read another passage from the Good Book, this one about walking through the valley of darkness, and then he helped the gravediggers and Jake Bussel lower the coffin into the hole in the ground. Scattering dirt across the replica of the running horse, Chase nodded to Maddie that she should lead the others in doing the same.

The entire procedure lasted no more that three quarters of an hour, and soon, everyone was back at the house consuming the refreshments Maddie and Alice had managed to assemble. At some point, Maddie noticed that Pawnee Mary had slipped away unnoticed to the springhouse. One by one, people departed—but not before several had mentioned the match race scheduled for the next day.

Abilene was too far away for any of them to get there in time for it, and Maddie had long ago given up worrying about the whole thing. She had no idea—and indeed wouldn't know if her family had made it—until she returned home in the buckboard or borrowed a horse from the livery stable.

At last, everyone departed, and Alice picked up the remains of a ham she had asked the Grovers to fetch from the mercantile. "I'm gonna take this out to the springhouse so it won't spoil," she told Maddie with a smile and a wink.

Chase moved to waylay her. "Why not let me take it out for you?"

"Nope. Wouldn't be natural for you t' do it, now would it? Besides, I expect you two have lots t' talk about, so I'll be sure and find some chores t' keep me busy for a time while I'm out there. Any excuse you can find for visitin' my springhouse will hafta wait 'til after dark, when I'll need your help rearrangin' things, if you know what I mean."

Chase nodded. "You're right, Alice. . . . But let me know how things are going out there, won't you?"

"Quit worryin', Chase. Mary's with him, and there she'll stay 'til we can bring your brother back inside. He should be able t' travel in a couple of days, so whatever plans you need t' make before then had better be made now, doncha think?"

The little woman headed out the door, and Maddie, glad to be alone with Chase, waited only a moment before flinging herself into his arms.

Twenty-four

Chase buried his nose in Maddie's red hair and inhaled its sun-kissed fragrance. She smelled like summer, woman, and all things good and necessary to life, at least, to *his* life. He wondered if he would ever get enough of her—if he would ever feel sated. He'd spent half the night making love to her, but he wanted her again. *Right now.*

It was pure torture to know he couldn't have her, not with Alice, Mary, and Buck out in the springhouse. Not with plans to be made and the morning's happenings still to be digested. He couldn't believe they had gotten away with it, and Buck was *free.* However, if he was to remain free, they couldn't yet celebrate. They had to consider every possibility and figure out how to deal with it.

But surely for a few precious moments, he could concentrate on holding the woman he loved, reveling in her embrace, and pretending that all they had to worry about was their own personal future. Nothing else mattered. Not Buck. Not Horace's threats. Not the possibility that the entire McCrory family would soon be destitute—or else *he* would be, providing Maddie relented and permitted his help.

He had seen the look in her eyes each time he offered his assistance. To prevent his involvement in her family's financial affairs, she would fight him tooth and nail. That was something else they needed to discuss, for he had it all worked out—or nearly so. All he needed was her cooperation.

"It went well, don't you think?" he finally murmured into her hair. "There were times it almost seemed too real. I felt as if I were actually burying my brother."

She nodded against his shoulder, then lifted her head to give him a joyful look. "But we did it, Chase! We fooled everybody, and now Buck and Mary will have a chance for happiness."

"A chance is all it is, sweetheart. They still face many obstacles. Buck's recovery, for one thing. Granted, he's alive, but regaining his strength won't be easy—and that's just the first of his challenges."

"Oh, pooh! He's got Mary to help him; that's all he really needs."

"Is that all we really need—each other?" He kneaded her shoulders, so he could keep touching her. He wanted to touch far more than her shoulders but dared not risk it.

She nodded. "Does anything else matter?"

"Nope, but I was starting to doubt you felt the same. I'm glad you do, because then you won't mind if I cover your debts to Horace. I'll be left with precious little to support you, but somehow we'll manage."

Immediately, her blue eyes clouded, and her chin tilted stubbornly. "No, Chase. I won't let you cover my family's debts. This is *our* problem—I mean, the McCrory's problem. We either have to solve it ourselves or suffer the consequences."

"Nonsense. Your farm is better than mine. Hell, it's lots bigger, and the buildings are all limestone. It only makes sense for me to sign mine over to Horace and come live with you until we can make a new start for ourselves. Horace isn't getting the horses, and with what I can make matching races, and either selling or racing the foals produced by my mares, we should eventually be able to afford our own place. By the time Little Mike's ready to take over everything, we'll be out of there, settled someplace on our own, and . . ."

"Chase, I said no! It wouldn't be fair. It's too big a sacrifice on your part. Besides, I thought you were going to give your brother a stake. Money, supplies, horses. . . . That will deplete your resources even more. I *can't* let you do this. I'm sorry, but I just can't."

"Maddie . . ." Chase dug his fingers into her shoulders to make her listen. "Would you prefer that Horace take *your* farm, and you all have to move in with me? I'm not going to let your family camp out on the prairie or live in some old soddy house to survive."

"I . . . I don't know, Chase."

She lowered her eyes, and he could see the tug of her responsibilities. He wondered if she could resist the hold her family had over her and suspected she couldn't. The only answer was to let him help—and become a vital part of the family. If she refused, he risked losing her. She wouldn't—couldn't—allow her father, brother, and sisters to struggle along without her. As sure as he was of anything in this life, he was sure of *that.* It was why he adored her so much! She was a born lover; she existed to help those who needed her. The trouble was, *he* needed her most of all.

Now she had to learn that she didn't have to choose between them; she could have them both—if only she would let him help. He had to make her understand that by helping her, he was really only helping himself.

"I think we'd better talk some more about this—and think some more. We're both tired. I've got to stay in town to move Buck tonight and help look after him. Go home and get some sleep, Maddie. If you don't, people will wonder. I can find some excuse for staying here, but everyone will be expecting you to hurry home to see what's happening there."

"I do have to go," she admitted, still not looking at him. "If nothing else, I need to check on the horses. Yours, too. I'll stop at your place on my way home."

"Good idea. I'll come when I can. Tonight, I may pretend to leave town, but in reality I'll be hiding out at Alice's. It all depends on how quickly we can move Buck."

"As soon as possible, I'll prepare the wagon for Buck and Mary. We'll stock it well with supplies. . . . Oh, Chase! Do you think there's even the slightest possibility that Little Mike made it to Abilene, after all, and that he'll win that race tomorrow?"

"It's possible but a bit unlikely, sweetheart. I don't think we can count on it. So give my plan your most serious consideration. I *want* to help your family. They're my family, too, now—not just yours. By marrying you, I took on the whole damn lot of you. Hell, maybe I should change my name to McCrory, since I'm practically one of the tribe."

Maddie gave him a grudging smile and peeped at him through her long lashes. "You would actually do that?"

"Well, no," he admitted. "But it sounded so good I had to say it."

She burst out laughing and thumped her fists on his chest. "You'd better hope I don't hold you to your rash, impetuous promises, Mr. Cumberland!"

He caught her hands and raised them to his lips. "I wasn't making a rash, impetuous promise when I offered to cover your debts, Maddie. I said I'd do it, and I will. All I want in exchange is a lifetime of loving."

"Oh, Chase!" Once again, she hugged him "You don't have to do anything to get that! I'll love you forever and ever. We have our whole lives ahead of us to love each other."

But Chase wondered. He couldn't help wondering—and worrying. Maddie was just stubborn enough to decide she had to refuse his assistance and stand by her family through this crisis and beyond—to whatever other crises remained down the road. He could smell it coming. It might be *years* before he had her all to himself—and it was entirely possible he might never have her.

As she had promised, Maddie stopped at Chase's before going home, with the result that it was early evening by the time she finally turned her borrowed horse down the worn track leading to her front door. She found it odd and disheartening, but the closer she got to the McCrory homestead and all it represented, the harder she had to struggle with guilt and anxiety. Without Chase beside her to strengthen her resolve—and without some great threat hanging over *his* head—she could hardly believe she intended to leave her family and make a new life for herself apart from them. It amazed her that she had left her father and siblings to their own devices for this long.

She sternly reminded herself that she was a woman now, in every sense of the word, and everything was different. She deserved to have her *own* family. Why, she might already have a baby growing inside her! If that were true, she now owed her loyalty to that new little life and to any other children she might one day conceive.

No longer was she herself a child seeking her parents' approval and blaming herself for all that had gone wrong. Perhaps it was the peculiar burden of being the eldest, but somehow she had always been imbued with the need to try and "fix" everything for her family. Or perhaps it was only the devastating experience of watching her mother die that had solidified her sense of responsibility and all but forced her to assume the family burdens.

One night when Ma lay dying, she had turned to Maddie, touched her hand, and feebly urged: "Take care of your Pa for me, Maddie. Take care of Little Mike, Carrie, and Zoe, too. I've always been able to count on you; now I guess I need you more than ever."

Maddie hadn't realized the full scope of what she had been promising, but she had nodded eagerly, all too anxious to give her mother reassurance. She now realized that the dying woman had passed on to her a fearful legacy. This crushing sense of responsibility was something only one woman could do to another, something women had been doing to each other for centuries down through time. The bond of blood, family, and togetherness was primarily preserved by women. Maddie understood and accepted that she herself was a vital link in that chain. If she didn't maintain the McCrory family ties, the chain would be broken . . . but did that mean she couldn't have Chase?

She rebelled against such an alarming idea. Somehow, she must make him a part of that chain, strengthening and toughening it, not tearing it asunder. Yet she had no idea how to go about such a daunting task. She had no example. It wasn't fair to permit

Chase to sacrifice so much on their behalf. She resented the necessity of it—wished instead that she could present him a whole, healthy, supportive unit worthy of his admiration, rather than his pity. . . . If only he could have known the McCrorys in days gone by, when they were at the peak of their success and productivity!

She hated to admit it, but her family wasn't perfect. They had flaws. And they weren't strong enough, clever enough, or ruthless enough to survive without her. Her siblings would eventually achieve maturity and the ability to survive on their own one day, yet they might all remain needy in one way or another, and she'd probably *never* get over feeling responsible for them. She wondered if it was possible to reconcile her desire to put Chase first in her life with her need to fulfill her responsibilities. She couldn't live with herself if she didn't finish raising her siblings and caring for her father, even if Pa continued to decline and wound up wasting the remainder of his life. At the same time, she couldn't bear to saddle Chase with these burdens.

Wrestling with the dilemma, Maddie rode slowly toward the house. All was still and quiet. For once, even the wind had died down, leaving an almost eerie stillness. The house looked empty in the gathering twilight, betraying no sign of human occupancy. Growing uneasy, Maddie headed toward the stable. The chickens pecking in the poultry yard were the only evidence of life. Vainly she searched for the race wagon.

The wagon had been all ready to go. Little Mike had packed it with supplies and even greased the axles—but now it was gone. Maddie slid off the horse and quickly led it into the barn. Gold Deck's stall was empty, and so were Shovel and Hoe's. Presumably, they had left for Abilene! Quickly, she stripped the tack from her borrowed horse, put it in an empty stall, gave it a quick rubdown and some supper, and headed toward the house.

Racing up the steps, she hollered: "Zoe? Pa? Are you here? . . . Where is everybody?"

No one answered. In mounting panic, she tore through the quiet house and found no one. Thinking of the rest of the horses—the young stock and some of the visiting mares, she again raced out to the barn. Had everyone gone off and left the rest of the animals to fend for themselves? Since they weren't in the barn, they had to be out in the pastures. At this time of year, they had grass to eat, and of course, there was water. Still, Maddie would never have sanctioned the idea of leaving animals alone and unattended. The cow still had to be milked—and horses were known for getting into trouble when no one checked them at least a couple of times daily. Then, too, there was always the possibility of theft and injury.

Maddie was suddenly furious. This was a perfect example of how her family could not be trusted to manage on their own. Stalking past the barn, she spotted a distant figure coming toward her through the fading light—a young man leading a horse, but it wasn't Little Mike. Squinting, she tried to guess his identity but didn't recognize him until he was almost on top of her.

"Evenin', Miss McCrory."

Nathan Wheeler, Zoe's beau.

"Nathan! What are you doing here? Where's Zoe and my father?"

Nathan shuffled his feet and looked uncomfortable. "They . . . uh . . . ain't here. They went t' Abilene with Little Mike and Carrie. Zoe asked me t' look after things, and I was just bringin' in this mare t' doctor a cut on her pastern."

"Gold Deck recovered from his colic?"

"Sure did. Yer Pa fixed him up good, and when Little Mike said he was leavin' fer Abilene, yer Pa insisted on goin' along in case the colic came back before they got there—or some other problems popped up."

Pa was probably hitting the saloons in Abilene right this very minute.

"Why didn't Zoe stay here to look after the stock and the house?"

"She thought she better go along t' look after yer pa—so he wouldn't get into trouble in Abilene."

"And you just happened to show up, so she asked you to do *her* job."

But at least, they'd made some arrangements for caring for the animals.

Nathan grinned sheepishly. "I had stopped by t' see if she wanted t' go inta town with me t' watch the trial an' the hangin'. Did Mr. Cumberland get hanged?"

"No, I'm happy to say, he did not. It's a long story, Nathan. While we take care of that horse, I'll tell you what happened."

As Nathan washed and dressed the cut on the mare's pastern, Maddie brought him up to date on all the recent doings in town. The young man was extremely sorry to have missed everything and even sorrier to hear that Chase's brother had died of his injuries and been buried before Nathan himself had gotten a good look at him.

"Zoe told me he had white hair and strange eyes. Guess he must've looked like God on Judgement Day."

"Zoe never actually saw him. She only heard about him. Anyway, Buck is dead and buried now, and the whole thing is over. That's why I came home. . . . You can go home now, too, Nathan. Zoe won't be back for at least another two days, maybe three. I doubt they'll leave Abilene immediately after the race; it all depends on how Gold Deck is feeling and how tired he is."

"Can I stop by again in a couple days?" Nathan settled the mare in an empty stall next to the horse Maddie had borrowed. "Just t' hear who won the race and how it all went?"

"Of course. Stop by anytime. I'm grateful you were here to look after things. That cut could have festered and caused a serious problem."

"Oh, I'd do anything for Zoe! Anything at all. . . . That is, I mean . . ." Nathan swallowed hard, his Adam's apple bobbing, as if he'd revealed feelings he didn't want Maddie to know he possessed.

"Zoe will be fourteen soon, Nathan, but that's still very young. You yourself aren't that much older."

"I'm older'n Little Mike! I'll be sixteen next week."

"You and Zoe are still too young to be getting so serious about each other. Wait a couple of years. Grow up some. Zoe will still be here: Then you need not be embarrassed to admit what you feel for her—if you still feel something."

"Yes, ma'am!" Nathan beamed at Maddie. He seemed pathetically glad she hadn't ordered him off the property. "Guess I better be goin' then."

"Guess you'd better. It's getting dark."

After Nathan left, Maddie returned to the house, lit a lamp, fed the cat a saucer of milk, and wearily sought her bed. She was hungry but too tired to cook anything. All she wanted to do was sleep, preferably snuggled close to Chase. She missed him dreadfully. But he had his obligations, and she had hers. She didn't know *when* she'd get to share a bed with him again—or even *if.*

The thought depressed her. She wanted to spend hours alone with him—no, not just hours but days, weeks, months, and years. She wanted to lavish all her attention solely on him. Wanted desperately to have nothing coming between them or keeping them apart.

Feeling sorry for herself, she welcomed Cob's presence when he leapt onto the bed beside her, picked out a comfortable spot, and curled himself into a ball of soft, purring fur. She desired Chase in her bed, but was stuck with a cat—not a good forecast of things to come.

At last she slept, only to dream of Chase bending over her, kissing her, murmuring endearments, and touching her hip. Her body throbbed with sudden, fierce longing, and she reached for him and sighed his name.

"Yes, it's me," he whispered, slipping into bed beside her. "I couldn't stay away, Maddie. Buck is fine, Mary's with him, and Alice is there, too—so I thought, what the hell, I belong with my wife. I refuse to spend another night away from her side."

"No, you shouldn't," Maddie dreamily agreed. Her eyes flew open. She suddenly realized her arms encircled warm, living man—not an illusion and certainly not a dream. "Chase! What are you doing here? You're supposed to be in Hopewell with your brother."

He slid closer and kissed the tip of her nose. "I just told you.

Buck is at Alice's. He's got two women to look after him; he doesn't need me. He damn well better not die, and I told him so before I left. He said he wouldn't, so I got a horse from the livery and came straight here. I didn't expect to find you alone, but I've already checked the rest of the house, and nobody's here but you. Where are they?"

"Abilene. They all went to Abilene. There's no one here but us, Chase."

"Great. That means I've got you all to myself. I belong with you, Maddie. Wherever you are, whatever you're doing, that's where I want to be. That's where I'm *going* to be. Accept it, my love. From now on, I'm not letting you out of my sight, and I intend to tell your family that as soon as I see them."

"Oh, Chase!" Maddie promptly burst into tears mixed with laughter. Then she burrowed into him. Once again, he had managed to banish all her doubts, fears, and worries. How she would explain all this to her family and how they'd take *his* declarations, she didn't know, but if Chase intended to share her bed, her problems, and her life, she couldn't send him away. His presence gave her a strength, courage, and determination she was sorely lacking—up until now. "Oh, Chase!" she repeated, hugging him harder.

"You say that a lot, don't you? I like how it sounds—oh, Chase!" he mimicked. "Except I'd like to hear more passion in it. More . . . arousal. More surrender."

"Oh, Chase!" she breathed on a sigh as one of his hands captured her breast and the other slid between her thighs.

"That's more like it," he instructed. "Only say it more slowly . . . stretch it out. Wait a minute . . ."

He pushed the cat off the bed, and Cob yowled indignantly. "Nobody's allowed in bed with you except me." Returning to Maddie, he nuzzled her ear. "Now then, where were we?"

"You were teaching me how to say your name with a long, happy sigh," she prompted.

"Oh, yes . . . but first, I'd better give you something to sigh about, hadn't I?"

"I don't think you'll have any problem with that!"

His mouth descended and covered hers, and he kissed her with an urgency that left her incapable of breathing, let alone sighing. If she hadn't already been lying down, she would have collapsed into a mindless puddle at his feet. Lifting his head, he was the one who sighed. "Maddie, girl, I missed you so much! I *had* to come tonight. We belong together, and that's all there is to it. Promise me you haven't changed your mind about us; you won't let your family or their problems keep us apart."

"How did you know I was . . . worrying?"

"Because I know *you.* I know how you think. We can work it out, sweetheart. There's nothing we can't do if we just put our minds to it. But *we* come first—now and always. Everything else is secondary. Agreed?"

It was now or never, and Maddie knew it. She had already made her vows to this man—but then she had left him and gone home to worry herself half-sick about the future. She had permitted doubts and hesitations to creep in. She still didn't know what that future was going to hold, but Chase deserved more than a halfhearted commitment. He deserved everything she had to give.

"Maddie," he prompted. "I'm waiting."

"All right. Agreed," she whispered. "*We* come first."

"And if there's no other alternative, you'll let me help your family financially . . ."

"Oh, but I still can't . . ."

He stopped the argument with another kiss, this one so deep and drugging that Maddie had the sensation of plunging headfirst off a cliff into some dark, sensual void where the pleasures of the flesh were waiting to consume her totally.

"Yes, you can," he growled when the kiss ended.

Grasping his shoulders, shaking with her own wants and needs, she pulled him back down to her. "I'll do anything you say. Just don't stop loving me, Chase. . . . Never, never stop loving me."

As passion carried her away, Maddie had one last rational thought: Between a man and a woman, there were all kinds of surrender—of the mind, the body, and the emotions. Sometimes the best way to give oneself was one step at a time. And suddenly, it would happen, as it had happened to them. No longer were they separate entities, struggling alone to right the world's wrongs; they were a *new* entity, a single driving force, much stronger and better than either of them could ever be alone.

Lord, how she loved Chase Cumberland!

They enjoyed three days and three nights of uninterrupted privacy and glorious intimacy. Other than quick visits to town to check on Buck, with stops on the way home to care for his horses, Chase stayed with Maddie. When he had to leave her, Maddie rode along with him as far as the town limits and waited on the outskirts for his return. The mere hour or two they were apart seemed unbearable, and they fell upon each other with hungry kisses as soon as they were reunited.

Each day, Buck seemed a little better. With Mary's constant care, he made rapid progress. As soon as the wagon became available, Chase planned to move him out of Alice's. By the fourth day, Maddie was beginning to worry; where was her family? They should be home by now, but the day passed without any sign of them. Nathan Wheeler even stopped by, and Maddie had to send him away disappointed.

"Where can they be?" she fussed to Chase as they stood on the porch gazing out into the darkness and listening to the night music of the insects. "I expected them to be here by now."

"Maybe they got held up in Abilene—I don't mean robbed," he hastily amended. "But almost anything could have delayed them."

"Horace will expect his money tomorrow," she said. "Tomorrow's Thursday."

He slid his arms around her and nibbled her neck. "I'm not so lost in passion that I've forgotten what day it is, my love. Tomorrow, I'll go into town and take care of Horace."

"Don't go until late in the day," she pleaded, turning to him.

"At least, give them a chance to show up first—hopefully with the money they won at the race."

"They'll probably show up with Lazarus Gratiot in tow, looking for his forfeit money from me. I sent a wire telling him he'd have it soon, but he may not trust me."

"Oh, I forgot about *that.* That's even more money you've got to produce. Chase, you'll have nothing left!"

"Wrong. I'll have you," he countered. "All I need, remember?"

"But . . ."

"But nothing. Don't worry. The value of my farm should cover everything. We'll manage, sweetheart." He dropped a kiss on her nose. "Let's not spoil tonight by worrying about what may or may not happen tomorrow."

"You're right. You're always right. It's downright annoying." She stood on tiptoe to kiss him back. "You're alive. Buck's alive, and we've had this nearly perfect time together, so I shouldn't complain. Somehow, some way, we'll deal with whatever happens."

"That's what I want to hear. Come on. Let's go to bed." He took her hand and led her inside, but they got only as far as the front room before he took her in his arms, pressed his mouth to hers, and began to undress her.

They were both naked by the time they reached her bed, and there wasn't room in her head for worry. She could think of only Chase and what he did to her and she to him, and so their last night together passed in magnificent splendor.

Chase had gone out to the barn, and Maddie was peeling potatoes for supper when she heard the creak of wagon wheels and the snorting of horses. No sooner had the sounds registered in her mind, when she also heard a glad shout from one of the twins.

"Maddie! Maddie, where are you? Oh, I hope you're here. You're going to be so surprised. . . . Oh, my, *Mr. Cumberland!*

A squeal of laughter followed. "Oh, thank goodness! They didn't hang you, after all!"

Assorted voices chattered all at once—giving Maddie a moment to wipe her hands on her apron before she went out to hear the news—good or bad. From the sound of things, it had to be good, but she was afraid to hope for too much for fear she'd be disappointed.

Tucking a strand of hair back behind her ear, she walked calmly and slowly to the front door, opened it, and stepped out onto the porch. There was Pa, climbing down from the wagon then turning to offer his hand to help a strange woman climb down to stand beside him. What on earth . . . ?

Little Mike was grinning, Carrie and Zoe almost jumping up and down in excitement, and Pa . . . Pa looked surprisingly well. The woman—a small, plump, older woman with a pretty face and silver-streaked dark hair peeking out from beneath her bonnet—smiled shyly and looked around at everything, as if it vitally interested her.

Who *was* she? There was something naggingly familiar about her, but Maddie couldn't recall where she might have seen her before.

Little Mike sauntered up to the porch, head high, eyes shining. "Your worries are over, big Sister," he cockily announced. "We won that damn race easy as trottin' down Main Street."

"You did? You won it? Mike, that's wonderful! But what about Gold Deck's colic? How did you get him over it so quickly?"

"Oh, Pa taught me a few of his tricks—once he remembered 'em. I told him he'd better remember or I'd never forgive him. I had to shout and cuss up a storm, and for once, he listened. Somehow, I got through to him. Anyway, he remembered, and we had Gold Deck feelin' good again in no time. So we all went up t' Abilene and won that race without you."

"Why . . . that's just great, Mike. I'm so proud of you. Horace wants his money by today, so you got here just in time. But Mike . . ." Maddie lowered her voice. "Who's that woman with Pa?"

"Oh, you mean Agatha? Well . . . uh . . . maybe I better let Pa explain. She's the reason we're a little late gettin' home."

Just then, Carrie and Zoe rushed up to Maddie, and hugged and kissed her, both of them jabbering at once. "Maddie, isn't it wonderful? We won the race! And Mr. Cumberland's still alive and not locked up in jail. What happened to his brother? Oh, tell us the news. Come on, Maddie: *tell us."*

"In a minute, girls. Let me meet our guest first." Maddie gently extricated herself from their grip and walked toward her father and the strange woman. "Pa?"

Her father indeed looked well. The best he'd looked since her mother's death. The transformation was nothing short of amazing. Gone was the dazed, disoriented attitude. A new light shone in his eyes. His step had a new spring to it. He had helped the little woman down from the seat of the wagon, but he hadn't yet let go of her hand.

"Pa? Aren't you going to introduce me?" Maddie stepped closer, extending her hand in greeting.

"What? Oh, Maddie, honey, of course I am." Pa was positively beaming. "This here is Agatha," he proudly announced. "Agatha McCrory, my new wife, and yer new Ma."

Twenty-five

The world seemed to tilt. Maddie felt a rush of dizziness and swayed on her feet. Chase grabbed her arm and held her steady; without him, she would have swooned on the spot.

"Damn it all, Maddie, don't look so shocked," her father implored. "It ain't like she's a stranger or nothin'. You remember Aggie, doncha? You used t' play with her daughter, Emily. They lived in that old soddy house down by the river. Why, the Coys was good friends of ours. When they left here, they got as far as Abilene, where Tom found work in a dry goods store . . ."

"Tom died about the same time yer Ma did," Agatha continued. "And Emily's long since married and gone to Oregon with her husband. Forgive me, Maddie, I'm so sorry we surprised you like this. I told yer Pa we was rushin' things a bit, but he wouldn't hear of waitin'. Said at our age we couldn't afford it."

Maddie finally found her voice. "I . . . I'm sorry I didn't recognize you."

"Well, I don't blame you. I used to be thin as a stick, but I've filled out some since you last saw me."

"Hell, she's prettier'n ever, ain't she?" Pa declared. "I was walkin' down the street in Abilene when I spotted her, and it was jus' like a tree fell on me. I couldn't believe my eyes: Agatha Coy appearin' out of nowhere, after all these years! Why, I invited her out t' the wagon, and we stayed up all night talkin', sharin' our sorrows an' our mem'ries."

"There was never anything between us while my Tom and your ma were still alive, Maddie. Please believe that," Agatha begged. "But somehow, after only a day or two in each other's company, we knew it was fated we meet again and console each other in our losses."

"Couldn't see no reason t' put off marryin'. I didn't wanna bring her back here without makin' it all legal, and I couldn't stand t' leave her behind. Besides, there was a preacher in Abilene, and after the race, we had us a ceremony. It was some celebration, I can tell ya, Maddie, seein' as how we had *two* things t' celebrate."

"And just how did you celebrate, Pa?" Maddie studied him closely for some sign of drunkenness, but if he'd gotten intoxicated, he wasn't showing any ill effects now.

"Why, we had us a big feast. I wanted t' invite half of Abilene, 'cept Carrie and Zoe and Little Mike wouldn't let me. They said you needed our winnin's to pay off some debts. I did recall you mentionin' that."

"We need every cent of that money," Maddie confirmed. "About that celebration. Did you . . . um . . . behave yourself, Pa?"

"Behave himself?" Agatha echoed. "Why, whatever do you mean, Maddie? Your father was the soul of propriety. 'Course, I told him straight out he couldn't touch a drop of whiskey—not with me being the head of the Ladies' Temperance League of Abilene. Why, my friends and I have been working ceaselessly to close down the saloons and restore order and sobriety to that lawless town. I've no doubt we'll soon see prohibition throughout all of Kansas, and your dear Papa will be right there beside me, fighting for it. Won't you, Michael, honey?"

"He *will?*" Maddie couldn't conceal her shock. Beside her, Chase seemed to be strangling—or choking on suppressed laughter.

Her father looked affronted. "Damn right I will. I've seen the error of my ways, Maddie. I've ree-formed. Or maybe Aggie here done it for me. She's gonna start a Ladies' Temperance Movement in Hopewell, 'cept *I'm* gonna be the president."

"The chairman, dear. You're going to be the chairman and

encourage all the gentlemen in Hopewell to take a pledge of sobriety, right after you take one under the big bur oak."

"Jus' what do you think of that, Maddie, girl?" Pa eyed her triumphantly. "Yer old pa ain't such a wastrel, after all, is he? And me and Little Mike got big plans, too. We set up three more races for Gold Deck while we was in Abilene. But come next year, Gold Deck'll be too busy breedin' mares t' be racin'. Mike signed up a dozen mares, at least, fer next year. Didn'cha, Mike?"

Little Mike came up beside them. "Yep, I did. And Pa said I should pick the best of the two-year-olds to start training to race next year. I already know the one I think will be the fastest. Chase, I want you t' take a look at him first. I'd like your opinion along with Pa's before I decide."

"Whatever Little Mike picks is fine with me," Pa said. "That boy's got an eye fer horseflesh—and he can sure ride. You shoulda seen him ride that race, Maddie. He done the McCrory family proud."

"I'm sure he did," Maddie said. "I would have liked to have seen it. But there were important things happening here, too."

"Tell us about them, Maddie!" Zoe shrieked. "I'm just dying to hear. Did you see Nathan? He said he'd look after things while we were gone."

"He did," Maddie told her sister. "He's a fine young man, Zoe."

"Well, Zoe's not the only one with a beau," Carrie announced. "I met the handsomest young man in Abilene. His name is Andrew, and he promised to come visit me sometime real soon."

"Not too soon, I hope," Agatha interrupted. "You girls haven't reached marryin' age yet. I know your Ma's thoughts on that subject—and nearly every other subject, too—and I aim t' follow 'em, 'cause we shared a lot of the same opinions."

"We're almost fourteen," both girls protested. "That's old enough t' get engaged," Zoe pointed out. "Our birthdays are in August, a week after Little Mike's."

"Gotta be at least fifteen or sixteen before you marry," Agatha sniffed. "Ain't that right, Michael?"

Maddie's father, who had never in all his life answered to Michael, vigorously nodded. "Well, hell, Aggie, you know more about these things than I do. If you say fifteen or sixteen, then that's how long they'll hafta wait."

Amazed, Maddie just listened. She couldn't get over it. Chase squeezed her arm, and she glanced up to find him smiling at her. Then he winked. She had to smile back. And blink away tears. *Her family didn't need her anymore. They could get along fine without her. It was practically a miracle—one that played havoc with her emotions.*

"Let's go up to the house," she urged everyone. "I've started supper. I'm sure you must all be hungry. Maybe we should eat first before I tell you all my news."

"Maddie? What about Horace?" Chase reminded her.

Good heavens, she'd almost forgotten!

"Maddie, let *me* take the money into town to the bank," Little Mike said. "I earned it, with Pa's help, of course. So I think I should be the one t' pay off all our debts."

"Are you sure, Mike? You must be exhausted."

"I wanna do it," the youth insisted. "This farm is my future, so I think I should be the one t' pay the mortgage and the taxes from now on. I discussed it all with Pa and Aggie on the way home, and they both agree."

"He's right, Maddie," Pa said. "I'm glad t' turn the runnin' of the farm over t' Little Mike. He ain't so little anymore. I'll help him all I can, but he's gotta be the one responsible. Me and Aggie are both too old t' worry about things like that. Besides, we wanna enjoy what little time we might have t'gether."

He gave Agatha a fond look, and she stood on tiptoe to kiss his weathered cheek. "I still can't believe we found each other after all these years, Michael, honey. I can't believe we discovered love an' affection, at our age yet. I jus' hope yer family is as happy about it as we are."

"They damn well better be," Pa growled. " 'Cause I was headed down a bad road almost right up t' the minute I saw you, Aggie."

"Of course, we're happy." Maddie went to Agatha and

warmly embraced her. "How could you think otherwise? We're all delighted."

"See y'all later then," Little Mike said. "Save me some supper, 'cause I'm gonna be hungry enough t' eat a horse by the time I get back here. Old One-Eyed Jack better watch out or I'll be takin' a knife and fork to him."

"One-Eyed Jack?" Maddie questioned.

"I brought him home with me, Maddie. He's tied up behind the wagon with Gold Deck. Lazarus Gratiot was so mad he lost the race that he offered the horse to me for nothin'. I felt sorry for him, so I took him. Hope you don't mind."

"No," Maddie said, still reeling from the changes in everyone. "No, I don't mind at all."

Supper was over, but Maddie, Chase, Big Mike, and Agatha lingered at the table over coffee while the girls began clearing the table. Maddie had let Chase relate the tale of his brother, for she wasn't sure if he wanted her family to know that Buck was still alive and hiding out at Alice's with Mary or not. To her surprise and poignant satisfaction, he trusted them enough to tell the truth—but then he swore them to secrecy, particularly the girls.

Zoe wasn't too happy about that, because she wanted to tell Nathan, but Chase was adamant. "The fewer people who know the truth, the less chance there is of Sheriff Smith discovering that Buck is still alive. For Buck's sake, we can't take the risk, Zoe. Do I have your word you won't tell Nathan or anyone else?"

Zoe reluctantly agreed, and Pa moved onto the practicalities of assuring Buck's and Mary's escape. "If they need it, they're welcome t' take the wagon with 'em when they leave this area," he told Chase, and Maddie's heart swelled with pride at the offer.

Chase had been willing to sacrifice everything for her family; here was something the McCrorys could do for him, or at least for his brother. Chase looked thoughtful for a moment, then shook his head.

"No, the wagon would make them too conspicuous. Where they're going, they can travel better and faster by horseback anyway."

"Where will they go?" Aggie asked.

"They aren't really sure yet, but it'll be further west or maybe north. They hope to get as far away from civilization as possible. At this point, they don't even want to link up with Indians, since the future of any of the Indian tribes doesn't look especially bright."

"Wherever they go, I know they'll be happy," Maddie added.

Chase smiled at her and laced his fingers through hers where they lay on the tabletop. Aggie noticed the gesture, and so—amazingly—did Pa.

"What's this?" he said, nodding toward their hands. "Is there somethin' goin' on here I oughta know about?"

Maddie inwardly sighed. The changes in her father since he'd come back from Abilene were truly extraordinary. In Aggie, he'd found a new reason for living, and it had heightened all his perceptions, conquered all his weaknesses, and very nearly restored him to the man he had been. Not once had he mentioned a desire for a drink at dinner—but then, he was no longer seeking oblivion. For the first time in more than a year, he had eaten with relish and eagerly participated in the conversation. In many ways, he was like a man newly awakened from a long, troubled sleep.

"Pa," she said gently. "Chase and I . . . well, we love each other."

"And we're married," Chase added in a no-nonsense tone. "We tied the knot while you were gone."

"What?" the twins cried, descending upon Maddie like vultures scenting fresh blood. "When did you do it? Maddie, what did you wear? How could you have gone and gotten married without us?"

Maddie squirmed uncomfortably and shot Chase a quelling glance. This wasn't exactly the way she had envisioned telling her family about their relationship—and they weren't *legally* wed. Explaining their situation now seemed the height of awkwardness.

"Who was the preacher?" Pa set down his coffee cup with a thunk and a rattle that almost shattered the good china. "If I'd have known there was a preacher in town, Aggie and me would have waited t' marry until we got home, and you could've witnessed it."

Chase remained calm and matter-of-fact, while Maddie's stomach clenched with nervousness. "There *isn't* a preacher in town, so Maddie and I simply said our vows without one—and by the way, your daughter's going home with me tonight."

This time, a chorus of five, including Maddie, exclaimed: *"What?"*

Chase squeezed Maddie's hand, as if to infuse her with courage. "I said she's going home with me, tonight. She's my wife, and I'm her husband, and where I go, she goes."

Maddie gulped a deep breath and blurted: "That's right. I belong with Chase now. Besides, you all don't need me anymore. You can manage on your own now, especially with Aggie here, and it's time I lived my own life."

The silence was so profound Maddie could hear her own heartbeat. Chase glanced around the table and at the twins, daring anyone to dispute her claim—or so it seemed to Maddie. Then he grinned, as if to banish the seriousness of the moment.

"When a preacher finally does come to town, we'll make it legal, but as far as we're concerned, we're as married as any two people can be. In case you're all wondering, I've already taken Maddie to bed."

"Chase! You didn't have to tell them *that!"*

"Yes, I did, Maddie, because it's true. We're not *two* anymore; we're *one.* In every way a man and woman can be."

"Well!" said her father.

"Oh, Maddie!" cried her sisters.

"Maddie, honey, I think that's just wonderful," gushed Agatha. "Don't you, Michael? Why, they must've taken one good look at each other and fallen in love just like we did."

"Yes, but . . ." Pa began, but Aggie placed her hand on his and smiled brightly.

"You both have our blessings, don't they, Michael? But we'll have to start plannin' the actual weddin' right away, 'cause Preacher Smucker who married us, said he's plannin' on comin' t' Hopewell sometime in August t' hold a revival meetin'. Don't see why you can't be married all legal and proper then. . . . We can have such a wonderful celebration!"

"Fried chicken!" Zoe exclaimed.

"And cakes, pies, and watermelon," added Carrie.

"And corn on the cob," Aggie reminded them. "Corn should be perfect by then."

"Maddie, you'll get to wear a new gown, after all, if we get some fabric right away," Carrie continued.

"The wedding doesn't need to be fancy," Maddie protested, thinking of the cost. "As Chase said, we already consider ourselves married."

"Humph!" her father scoffed. "You're a McCrory, so it's gotta be done up right an' proper."

"I imagine all of Hopewell will want to attend," Aggie agreed. "And they should. Everyone knows the family, Maddie, so they ought to be invited."

"We'll have a fiddler and dancing," Zoe sighed. "I'll get to dance with Nathan."

"That's not fair," Carrie groused. "My beau lives in Abilene. If we really want to entertain folks, we oughta have a horse race, not a fiddler."

Another moment of stunned silence followed. Then Pa's eyes lit with excitement, and he gazed assessingly at Chase. "Looky here, son. You got any decent horseflesh over at your place?"

"Pa," Maddie said. "Don't you remember? He's got a mare out of Bonnie Scotland who beat Gold Deck the one and only time they raced."

Her father frowned in momentary confusion. "Seems I do recollect that—or maybe not. I ain't been myself fer a while, y' know, Maddie."

How well she knew.

"So your horse beat our horse already, huh, son?"

"Yes, sir," Chase told him. "But I've been wondering if she could do it again."

"What've you got to put up that says she can? I don't mean money; I don't bet money with members of the family."

"Pa . . ." Maddie began.

"How about the first foal she drops when she's bred to your stallion?"

"Hmmmm. That's an interestin' wager. But what've I got you might want—besides my daughter, I mean?"

"A field," Chase said. "You can put up that field that has a tree on it and a creek running through it—and as many free breedings as I want to your stallion."

"Chase!" Maddie cried.

"Hmmmm . . ." her father repeated. "Maddie, you've seen his mare; is he makin' us a fair offer?"

"Pa, listen to me. This is supposed to be a wedding, not a horse race—but yes, it's a fair offer. There's no finer mare in Kansas than Bonnie Lass, and she could probably beat any you'd find in Texas or in any other state within riding distance."

"Then it's done!" her father crowed. "We'll celebrate yer weddin' with a match race!"

Maddie knew she was licked. Both her father and Chase were grinning like beavers.

"There, there," Aggie soothed "We'll still make it nice, Maddie—a weddin' befittin' a McCrory."

One month later, on the very morning of their wedding, Maddie and Chase rode out at dawn to meet Pawnee Mary and Buck on the prairie. Today was not only their wedding day and the day of the match race, but also the day Buck and Mary were leaving to seek their destiny far from Kansas.

It was a beautiful, breezy morning, not yet hot, but Maddie had worn her blue sunbonnet to protect her skin when the sun rose higher in the sky. Chase teased her about the sunbonnet, saying she looked so pretty in it that she ought to wear it for the ceremony later that day.

"No," she told him. "The twins are making a garland of late-blooming flowers for me to wear on my head. But Aggie's sewn me a new gown in this same shade of blue—one to match the bonnet, so I've something to wear for special occasions from now on."

"I love you in blue," Chase said, his eyes dancing. "And also in brown, gray, green, orange, purple, and nothing at all."

She slanted him a wry look; he wasn't lying. He loved her best in nothing at all. Half the time, she walked around naked, because he was always removing her clothes, and she figured she might as well save him the trouble. They had been living together for the whole month, but no one but her family knew it. Everyone in town assumed she was still abiding in her father's house until the day of her wedding.

Buck and Mary eagerly awaited them beside the wagon, which they intended to take back to the ranch after the couple had left. As soon as they rode up, Maddie slipped down from her horse and hurried to embrace Mary. The tall, Indian woman hugged her hard.

"I miss you too much," she said, squeezing Maddie's waist. "Silver Hair miss you, also."

"I know." Maddie gulped back tears. "I wish we didn't have to say good-bye. I wish you could stay here forever."

"Better we go," Mary insisted. "Out there," she gestured toward the west, ". . . we find safety. Find place we can be happy always."

"I'm sure you will. Are you certain you have everything you need?"

Mary nodded and proceeded to show Maddie the loaded horses Chase had brought out the day before. They were taking a half dozen with them, two for riding, three pack mares who could later be bred, and a promising young filly. While Chase conferred with Buck, Maddie examined Mary's preparations for the long journey. One of the pack mares was also pulling a travois, loaded down with supplies.

"If Silver Hair get tired he can lie down and rest here," Mary whispered, indicating the travois. "He think he all better, but he still weaker than normal."

Maddie was amazed he was well enough to begin this adventure. Indeed, Buck looked wonderful—hale and hearty. Only when he moved could she sense a stiffness. A slight bulge beneath his shirt revealed the bandages Mary insisted he wear to provide support to his still-healing body. Somehow, his vital organs had remained intact, but he would have died had it not been for Mary.

As Chase enfolded his brother in a final bear hug, he had tears in his eyes. So did Buck, and Maddie was openly weeping. Only Mary managed to retain her usual dignity.

"We meet again," Mary assured everyone. "Someday. If not here, then Tirawa unite us in Happy Hunting Grounds."

"Oh, Mary, I pray that you and Buck have a long, joyful life together!"

"You and Son of Wolf also. Good-bye, my sister. I remember you always."

One last hug. One last farewell. Then Mary helped Buck to mount one of the riding horses. He grimaced as he swung into the saddle, but once there, Maddie could see he was quite comfortable. He had the look and ease of a man who'd spent half his life astride horses. The rising sun illuminated his face, eyes, and silver-white hair, and Maddie thought he resembled a wayward god come to earth for a brief visit.

Buck's gaze fell on Chase, and he lifted his hand to his brow and saluted him. Chase saluted back. Meanwhile, Mary had also mounted. Mary gathered the lead ropes of the other horses in one hand, smiled at Maddie, then turned her horse and quietly rode away with Buck beside her.

With Chase beside her, Maddie watched them until the prairie suddenly swallowed them, and they disappeared into the western horizon. Her tears had ceased flowing, but Maddie still felt an unaccountable sadness. They had long awaited this day—yet now that it had arrived, and Buck and Mary were actually gone, she couldn't help feeling sorrowful. She knew she'd never see them again. Chase had lost his brother, and she had lost a dear, kind friend.

Chase reached out unexpectedly and hauled her up close to him. "Well, Maddie, they're gone, but we're still here, and we're getting married today."

"And having a horse race," she tartly reminded him. "Which of the two excites you the most?"

"You have to ask? Damn it, Maddie, you surely should know."

"I *don't* know," she said, sidling away from him. "Tell me."

"Why, the horse race, of course!" he shouted, lunging for her and laughing.

She squealed and ran, and he chased her through the tall prairie grass, startling the remaining horses and a couple of prairie chickens. At last, she allowed him to catch her, whereupon he proceeded to provide uncontestable proof of his passion, devotion, and eagerness to wed—and that was how they wound up arriving late and almost missed their own wedding.

Maddie and Chase repeated their vows beneath the big bur oak in the middle of Hopewell, surrounded by family, friends, neighbors, and other assorted well-wishers. They had chosen the spot because of its proximity to the Hopewell Paths, where the race would be conducted a scant hour after the ceremony. It had one other positive feature—the patch of shade the tree provided. Even so, Maddie was damp from head to foot by the time the ceremony ended, and Chase looked equally as drenched on this hot August afternoon.

"You may now kiss the bride," Preacher Smucker intoned with a wink in Maddie's direction.

Chase enthusiastically bent her backward over his arm, which brought cheers from the onlookers. The crowd then moved to the long table, heavy-laden with food, set up a short distance away. Several men waylaid Chase, so Maddie went ahead and filled plates for both of them, then found a seat on a quilt spread out on the ground. As she hungrily sampled a chicken leg, she scanned the faces of those in attendance; there were many people she didn't recognize—strangers who had come for the race, not the wedding.

Both Chase and her father had placed many side bets and had already agreed that whoever won the race would pay for the wedding feast. All of Hopewell had shown up—with one notable exception: Horace Brownley. From where she sat, Maddie could see the "Closed" sign in the bank window, one of many such signs on the shops lining Main Street. Only the mercantile remained open, in case someone wanted to purchase something while they were in town for the race—but everyone else had shut down their businesses for the afternoon so that the shopkeepers themselves could attend.

Maddie wondered whether Horace was hiding inside his office, then forgot all about him as Alice Neff came to join her on the quilt.

"I see you've already been abandoned by your new husband," the little woman cheerfully announced, spreading her skirts and sitting down beside Maddie. "Mind if I join you? Moses is busy, too, makin' sure everyone minds their manners; when men start talkin' money and horses, you know how riled they can get."

"I'm so happy you came over, Alice." Maddie leaned closer to her friend and whispered: "Mary and Buck left just this morning. We bid them farewell out on the prairie, and that's why we were so late arriving in town for the ceremony."

That *wasn't* why, but Maddie wasn't about to reveal the *real* reason: their passionate interlude under the deep blue sky.

"So that's why, huh? Why, folks was startin' t' say you'd both changed your minds, but I set 'em straight, I did. I told 'em you'd be along shortly. Personally, I knew there had to be a good reason for you to be tardy; I'm just glad they've finally left the area. Now, I can rest easy that Moses will never find out."

"Thanks again for all your help, Alice. Without you, we never could have pulled it off."

"I was delighted t' do it. I just hope it's the last lie I ever have t' tell Moses—seein' as how he's gonna be my husband come October."

"October! Why, Alice, how wonderful!"

"That's as soon as Preacher Smucker can make it back t' town. B'sides, I need time t' make my weddin' dress. I aim t' have doin's as nice as your's, Maddie—only without the horse race."

Maddie laughed. "That should keep the crowd smaller and ensure you know all the guests. Some of these folks I've never seen before—and then there's one or two I was afraid I *might* see who thankfully didn't show up."

Alice's brows rose. "You mean Horace Brownley?"

"And Elwood, his clerk."

"Well, you might not see either one of 'em ever again. In case you ain't noticed, business at the bank has fallen down lately," Alice said smugly. "Why, I hear tell that Horace and Elwood are thinking of movin' t' Lincoln and openin' a bank there."

"But . . . we need a bank, Alice. I mean, I'd be happy to see Horace go, but losing the bank itself will be a big blow to the town."

"Oh, I've been workin' on that problem, too." Alice chuckled and plucked a piece of watermelon from her plate. "It's just amazin' what a body can do when she sets her mind to it. I still got family back East, you know, and I wrote and told 'em we sure could use a new banker in Hopewell. My nephew's gone inta bankin', and he's got a hankerin' t' explore this part of the country. I've already wrote and told him he oughta come fer my weddin' and see how he likes Hopewell. Could be jus' what he's lookin' for."

"Alice, you're a born schemer. Does Moses know what a manipulator you are?"

"Nope. And if I'm real careful, he won't ever find out." Alice bit into the watermelon, chewed, swallowed, and sighed blissfully. "Ain't this the sweetest melon you ever tasted?"

The horses were at the starting posts, facing backwards for the ask and answer. Chase sat relaxed and easy on Bonnie Lass, who was quivering with eagerness to race. Little Mike looked nervous, but Gold Deck had yet to break a sweat. The gleaming stallion showed no sign of tension. He gazed calmly at the crowd as if another race was all in a day's work.

Maddie wished she could achieve the same sense of calm as Chase or Gold Deck. Her loyalties were painfully split. In the past, she had always cheered for Gold Deck, but now, as Chase's wife, she wanted Bonnie Lass to win—or did she?

She didn't know what she wanted. She and Chase could sure use that field, and it would be a terrible sacrifice if they couldn't keep Bonnie Lass's first foal. However, the stakes weren't the most important thing; at the moment, deciding on whom to cheer for outweighed everything else.

"I can't watch," she muttered aloud. "I just can't stand to watch this."

She closed her eyes, only to have Carrie elbow her on one side and Zoe on the other.

"Maddie, who do you want to win?" Carrie asked.

"You'd better cheer for Bonnie Lass, or Chase is gonna be furious," Zoe sagely advised.

"But she can't cheer for the mare, or Pa and Little Mike won't speak to her for a month," Carrie pointed out.

Maddie turned her back, so she wouldn't be tempted to watch, after all. "I won't cheer for either one. I hope it's a tie."

"Ready!" cried Little Mike.

"Go!" shouted Chase.

The crowd roared. Pounding hooves thundered past Maddie. She could hear her father and Aggie screaming, along with the twins.

"Gold Deck's ahead by a nose!" Zoe shrieked. "Now they're neck and neck! Gold Deck's pulling ahead again. Oh, look, he's won!"

It was over that fast—but then quarter-mile races always were. If you blinked, you missed them. Maddie's legs wobbled beneath her. She had to concentrate to remain on her feet. Tears blurred her vision—poor Chase! Now she knew exactly where her loyalties lay: with her husband. She was devastated on his behalf. She never wanted him to lose at anything.

All around her, people were whooping and hollering. Carrie and Zoe were hugging and dancing a jig. Hoping to get to Chase—*needing* to be with him, Maddie pushed her way through the crowd. Down the paths they came, trotting side by side, her brother and her husband together, both of them grinning like two boys at play. Chase didn't look at all disappointed, as Maddie had expected. If anything, he looked exhilarated.

"What the hell!" He laughed heartily and clapped Little Mike on the back. "This time, you beat me! Good thing it's all in the family, or I wouldn't be nearly this happy!"

Spotting Maddie, he rode up to her, leaned down, and kissed her passionately on the mouth. When he drew back, he saw her tears. "Hey," he said. "Are those for me?"

She nodded. "This time, I wanted *you* to win."

"Sweetheart, when I married you, I won." He hooked an arm around her waist and lifted her up to sit in front of him on Bonnie Lass.

Pa suddenly loomed in front of them, with Aggie hanging on his arm. "Guess we know who has the best horse now!" her father whooped, and Maddie could have smacked him.

But then Pa reached up and handed them both a scroll of paper.

"What's this?" Chase asked.

"The deed to that field you wanted," Pa answered, proud as a rooster. "It's my weddin' gift t' you both. And as fer Bonnie Lass's first foal by Gold Deck, I insist we own it jointly—and never again compete against each other. My nerves can't take it."

"Mine neither," Aggie piped up. "I swear I was cheerin' fer *both* horses."

"They *are* the best horses anywhere," Pa declared. "I'm just glad as hell you're my son-in-law now, and we're a team instead of rivals."

"Suits me," Chase said. "I'd rather be partners than rivals any day. I've been telling Maddie that all along, but I had to go ahead and *marry* her before I could get her on my side."

"I never heard you say that." Maddie twisted around to see his face, and Chase promptly stole a kiss.

The crowd guffawed, then broke into applause.

"We need a little privacy," Chase murmured for her ears alone. He urged Bonnie Lass into a lope. "Good-bye, everyone! Time I take my wife home . . ."

Home, Maddie thought. Anywhere with Chase was home.

With his arms wrapped securely around her waist, they galloped through town and out onto the Kansas prairie. As Chase held her tightly and let his mare run, Maddie contemplated their future: The ride was just beginning—and what a joyful, winning ride it would be!

Afterword from the Author

Hopewell, Kansas can't be found on any map. It is a fictional town reminiscent of many small towns in Kansas during this era. I hope I have caught the flavor of the times, as well providing a glimpse into the history of the Quarter Horse breed. That history began with match racing, when people across this country bred their horses to obtain that near-perfect animal who could pull a plow or herd cattle during the week and still race on the weekend.

Some of the foundation sires of the breed, such as Bonnie Scotland, were actually Thoroughbreds. The Thoroughbred evolved in one direction, while the short horse or Quarter Horse went another, and the entire equine kingdom benefitted. Today, the American Quarter Horse is one of the largest, most versatile, and best-loved breeds to be found anywhere in the world. Ask anybody who owns one, and you will likely get a litany of praises—all well-deserved.

As any horse lover knows, horses provide inspiration, transportation, companionship, and unparalleled beauty, grace, and power, all of which serve mankind in a variety of wonderful ways. They are also a great source for stories. I hope you have enjoyed this one and will watch for more in the future. (Other Katharine Kincaid stories that feature horses include *Ride the Wind,* and *Windsong.)*